FIST OF THE
IMPERIUM

≡≡SPACE MARINE≡≡
CONQUESTS

More tales of the Space Marines from Black Library

FIST OF THE
IMPERIUM

ANDY CLARK

BLACK LIBRARY

A BLACK LIBRARY PUBLICATION

First published in Great Britain in 2020 by
Black Library,
Games Workshop Ltd.,
Willow Road,
Nottingham, NG7 2WS, UK.

10 9 8 7 6 5 4 3 2 1

Produced by Games Workshop in Nottingham.
Cover illustration by Neil Roberts.

See Black Library on the internet at

blacklibrary.com

Find out more about Games Workshop
and the world of Warhammer 40,000 at

games-workshop.com

Printed and bound by CPI Group (UK) Ltd, Croydon, CR0 4YY

*For Kate, my wonderful editor and friend, without whose expertise my
words would be on fire in a ditch, and my literary cats would remain
disastrously un-herded.*

It is the 41st millennium. For more than a hundred centuries the Emperor has sat immobile on the Golden Throne of Earth. He is the Master of Mankind by the will of the gods, and master of a million worlds by the might of His inexhaustible armies. He is a rotting carcass writhing invisibly with power from the Dark Age of Technology. He is the Carrion Lord of the Imperium for whom a thousand souls are sacrificed every day, so that He may never truly die.

Yet even in His deathless state, the Emperor continues His eternal vigilance. Mighty battlefleets cross the daemon-infested miasma of the warp, the only route between distant stars, their way lit by the Astronomican, the psychic manifestation of the Emperor's will. Vast armies give battle in His name on uncounted worlds. Greatest amongst His soldiers are the Adeptus Astartes, the Space Marines, bioengineered super-warriors. Their comrades in arms are legion: the Astra Militarum and countless planetary defence forces, the ever-vigilant Inquisition and the tech-priests of the Adeptus Mechanicus to name only a few. But for all their multitudes, they are barely enough to hold off the ever-present threat from aliens, heretics, mutants — and worse.

To be a man in such times is to be one amongst untold billions. It is to live in the cruellest and most bloody regime imaginable. These are the tales of those times. Forget the power of technology and science, for so much has been forgotten, never to be re-learned. Forget the promise of progress and understanding, for in the grim dark future there is only war. There is no peace amongst the stars, only an eternity of carnage and slaughter, and the laughter of thirsting gods.

PROLOGUE

Something moves in the empty darkness between the stars.

Monstrous shapes drift through the void like deep-sea predators winding sinuously along a lightless ocean trench. They are behemoths, huge and terrible, guided by an ineffable will that knows only insatiable *hunger*.

Miles-long tentacles trail behind them, barely limned by the pale rays of stars so distant they are already long dead. Chitinous plates shield fleshy innards from the killing cold. Limitless energies churn beneath that living armour, the potential for creation and destruction deific in its scope.

Yet these gods can create only to destroy. They can only want. They can only feed, and spawn, and feed again, on and on in an endless, eternal loop.

But now a storm rages. In every direction that their alien senses quest outwards, they taste it roiling and wrathful. Yet like those deep-sea predators in their fathomless trench, they are untouched by the maelstrom that spends its fury far away. They care nothing for it. It is other, insubstantial, irrelevant to them.

Their vast and singular attention fixes instead upon distant echoes that come to them through the storm, in some ways a light, in some ways a siren song, in some ways both and yet neither.

These they taste.

These they know.

These they seek.

Hidden from their prey by the incredible emptiness of the interstellar gulf, the shapes sweep onwards, relentless and impossibly swift. They will seek their prey and devour it. They will bring the end of days to another world, and another and yet more, and in doing so they will inhabit the mantle of godhead that terrified mortal beings ascribe to them. They will do this unknowing and uncaring, the thoughts and feelings and beliefs of their prey as ineffable to them as their will and nature is to those they devour.

They care only about their next feast.

It draws closer by the hour.

ACT ONE

I

The conclave chamber rose from atop the highest spire of Hive Angelicus. Circular in shape and with arched entrances at its four compass points, the chamber's lower level boasted klarwood panelling, brushed-copper flooring and artfully underlit armaglass cases in which were displayed symbolic relics of the planet's proud history. Here, an ancient pattern of mining laser hung in a suspensor field. There, rough-hewn chunks of enderrium ore orbited lazily around one another, their crimson sheen the only hint of their capacity to be refined into superior-quality las-cells. Cases contained hovering arrangements of human skulls, polished until they glinted and inscribed in flowing gothic script with the names of greater mining clans.

These last macabre relics were intended to remind all who passed them of the sacrifices made by the countless generations of miners who had lived and died on the planet of Ghyre. *By their noble sacrifice is our world made mighty*, read the High Gothic inscription around the base of each cabinet-reliquary. Imperial Fists Sergeant Torgan marched between the cabinets with Brother Unctor at his side. He snorted as he glanced at the words proudly etched into the brass.

'Always you do that, brother-sergeant,' said Unctor, keeping his voice low. 'Why?'

'Where in a life of ignorant menial labour is there nobility or sacrifice, Brother Unctor?' asked Torgan. 'Roofs over their heads, nutrient gruel to fill their bellies, labour to occupy their hours and entire decades of life shielded behind bastions and warriors whose existence they barely perceive. These people know little of sacrifice and less still of nobility.'

'As I understand it, the miners' lives are hard and short,' said Brother Unctor. 'Without their labours the munitions shrines of forge world Shallethrax would swiftly fall silent. These people bleed for their Imperium as we do. They do their part, in their own limited fashion.'

'Once, perhaps, but do they still?' asked Sergeant Torgan.

'That is the responsibility of those in the chamber above us,' said Unctor.

'On that we agree, brother. Let us see if they have stopped their banal bickering long enough to do their duty.' Torgan led the way to the foot of one of the two brass-and-armaglass ramps that rose in a helical spiral from the lower level, through the mezzanine floor and into the upper chamber where the ruling conclave of Ghyre convened. He marched up the ramp between the burning braziers flanking it. As he advanced, angry voices floated down to greet him. He shot a sour glance back at Unctor, whose graven features gave away nothing.

'...and I would remind the honoured high administrator once again that Ghyre supports eleven full regiments of airborne infantry, all of whom are trained and equipped to the highest standard that Prime Clan Kallistus can afford!' Torgan recognised the deep and cultured tones of High Marshal Anthonius Kallistus. 'That is to say nothing of the copious squadrons of dedicated fighter pilots who wait by their craft for the slightest sign of invasion or malfeasance, the teeming ranks of the hive militias and the exceptionally capable Enforcers under First Arbitrator Verol.' The high marshal paused, his attention drawn to Torgan and his brother. 'Ah! And here we see the crowning glory, our very own honour guard of Imperial Fists Adeptus Astartes!'

As Torgan emerged into the upper chamber, he saw Marshal Anthonius standing behind his podium and pointing triumphantly in his direction. He did not deign to respond to the man's words, though Anthonius' presumption caused him a familiar flare of irritation. The conclave of Ghyre stood in a circle around the room, each counsellor bathed by soft lumen that illuminated them, their gaggles of aides, scribes and hangers-on, and the carved stone podia that announced their titles. Torgan took in the great and good of Ghyre – the dashing High Marshal Kallistus, commander of the Ghyrish Airborne regiments, the spare and glowering High Administrator Jessamine Lunst, who the marshal had been haranguing, and the stocky, steely-haired First Arbitrator Mariah Verol, whose support the man was clearly hoping to win.

Lurking like a giant mechanical spider to Torgan's right was Magos Geologis Mendel Gathabosis, while to his left he noted Bishop Lotimer Renwyck standing humble and unassuming in a street preacher's hooded cassock.

He alone had not a single scribe or bodyguard at his side.

More figures stood further back and higher up the chamber's curving walls, between jutting sculptures of human skeletons that brandished mining tools and burning promethium torches. These were the lords and ladies of the greater clans Delve, Tectos and VanSappen, and the two haughty spire lords Agnathio Trost of Hive Klaratos and Yenshi Hal of Hive Mastracha.

Higher still, seated upon a huge throne of brass and stone and trunked wires that jutted from the chamber's upper wall, was Governor Osmyndri Ellisentris Kallistus III. Elegant and regal, she held the sceptre of office that marked her as the planetary governor of Ghyre and the ritual gilded pick that denoted her rulership of Angelicus Hive and all the mining clans who dwelt within and below it. She wore the crisply pressed and medal-laden uniform of the Supreme Air Marshal of Ghyre, which Torgan knew she had earned; the governor had been quite the ace pilot behind the controls of a Lightning fighter, skills that reputedly she had never allowed to atrophy. At her shoulder, lashed securely to a metal platform on the side of her throne, hunched the governor's ageing seneschal, a man called Gryft.

Above them all a half-finished mural of the Emperor glowered down in judgement. For thousands of years that ceiling had been a stained-armaglass dome that had looked out upon the stratospheric blue and star-studded black of Ghyre's skies. The night sky had been poisoned, now. Those who looked too long upon the tainted stars ran mad. A hurried edict had seen the armaglass slathered with layers of black paint to preserve the precious minds of Ghyre's ruling elite, and work had begun to paint a fresh fresco of the Emperor enthroned. It was only half done, but already Torgan's superior eyesight could pick out where the paint was blistering and peeling as though assaulted from without.

The skies, it seemed, resented being shut out. The Rift would not be ignored.

Torgan marched across the concave floor of the upper chamber, performed a smart about-face before the stanchions that held aloft the governor's throne and brought his boltgun up across his chest with a clang. Unctor fell in beside him, and the two Imperial Fists stood, eyes front, still as statues carved from granite.

'The conclave welcomes Brother-Sergeant Torgan and Brother Unctor of the Imperial Fists Fifth Company,' croaked Seneschal Gryft, his words amplified by his throat augmetics to echo around the chamber. Quill-fingered adepts clustered around High Administrator Lunst wrote in perfect synchronicity, the combined scritch of nib on parchment a harsh susurrus. Their mistress waited a moment longer to be sure that neither Torgan nor the first arbitrator was about to speak in support of Marshal Kallistus. Satisfied, she drew herself up to her full, considerable height, and her ocular implants flashed.

'We here assembled are all aware of the military strength of Ghyre's defensive regiments, high marshal,' she said. Her voice was clipped, her consonants hard, like the struck keys of a cogitator. 'However, what we have seen in the last two cycles has been unprecedented. Might I first remind you that those cycles themselves must now be estimated by digital choristry and astro-sidereal comparative augury, since the...' She paused, clearly searching for the most appropriate phrase. '*Malign phenomena* have rendered the traditional marking of the days impossible. Article the first...'

The high administrator held out a hand without looking.

A scroll thumped into it, proffered from behind by one of her many adepts. As it always did, the sound caused a muscle beneath Torgan's right eye to twitch with annoyance. He knew what came next.

Lunst unrolled the scroll in a puff of dust and read aloud.

'The conclave to be reminded of the epidemic of dark omens, dire portents, doomsayers, nightmares, mutational degeneracy and unsanctioned zealotry throughout Hives Angelicus, Klaratos and Mastracha and their dependent mining complexes that commenced on cycle eighty-eight thousand, nine hundred and sixty-four, sub-cycle eight-six-one, and has proceeded with no signs of abatement or remission.'

'I would remind the high administrator that my arbitrators have contained and quelled a record quotient of civil disturbances within the last cycle alone,' said First Arbitrator Verol, her voice stern and hard as iron.

'The conclave to record that neither offence nor criticism was intended by my utterances,' said the high administrator, sounding singularly unapologetic. Again, that muscle twitched beneath Torgan's eye.

'They believe themselves to be sparring within some gladiatorial ring,' he murmured so quietly only his brother would hear. Torgan briefly imagined how these preening fools would look caught amidst the gunfire and mayhem of a real battlefield, and the thought brought him some small comfort.

Lunst furled the scroll with a snap.

'Article two,' she proceeded, another scroll thumping into her hand and unfurling in front of her. 'The conclave to take note of the severe disruption to the planet's astropathic conclave and the plethora of confirmed and suppressed malefic manifestations across Ghyre in the sub-cycles since the astrological phenomena appeared in the night sky.

'Article three.'

Snap, thump.

'The conclave to consider the substantial disruption to intra- and inter-system shipping that we have seen in the last cycle, the reported faltering of the holy Astronomican and the prolonged period, only now beginning to abate, of astro-pathic silence from any planet or other Imperial void-borne installation beyond Ghyre's immediate stellar vicinity. The conclave to consider before passing judgement in this matter that we still do not possess the requisite corroborated data to fully comprehend what this period of sidereal and stellar disruption represents, or what it might presage.'

So much posturing, so much hemming and hawing, thought Torgan. *How the Chapter can call watching over this dusty flock of peacocks an honour, Dorn only knows.*

'Article four.'

Snap, thump.

'The conclave to note the, to date, twenty-three per cent net reduction in mining output and efficiency from the clan mining complexes that–'

'Amendment. The reduction in efficiency was last cogi-tated at twenty-two point eight seven two per cent,' came the grating voice of Magos Geologis Gathabosis, overriding by sheer volume the high administrator's report. 'Servitor mining units and all blessed geoexcavational machineries continue to operate within previously decreed tolerances. Fault lies with biological components. Exponential increase in predatory fauna growth of eighteen point four per cent since astrological phenomena manifestation. All appropri-ate measures and binharic prayers have been applied to the macro-purgation firethrowers to hold back hostile flora and fauna variables, but effectiveness has been reduced by a vari-able degree across the northern continental landmass.'

'So you're saying it's the jungle's fault for growing more quickly?' asked High Marshal Kallistus disparagingly.

'Correction. Needless oversimplification of a complex bio-logical variable intended to undermine and make ridiculous my logical conclusions. Comment discarded as irrelevant sociopolitical manoeuvring,' responded the magos. Torgan had to fight to keep the corner of his mouth from quirking up. 'Further and more substantial biological component failure observed amongst labour units of the mining clans. Moral dissolution, underperformance, extraneous social exchange and increased behavioural divergence from allocated duties noted as a detrimental variable throughout eighty-three per cent of clan labour forces,' finished Gathabosis, and Torgan's ghost of a smile was banished.

Whispers of the unrest amongst the miners had reached his ears through contacts he and the previous honour guard sergeants had cultivated over the years. What he had been unable to gauge was whether the increasing civil unrest amongst the planet's labouring class was due to the massive increase in warp storm activity and the concurrent malign disturbances of the planet's populace or whether some other moral rot was spreading. He felt that old, familiar itch in his trigger finger, and not for the first time wished he had an honest foe to turn his bolter upon.

Perhaps it had taken root before any of this began, before he and his squad even came to Ghyre – Torgan had seen the rise of Chaos cults before, had put them down himself with bolt and blade. He would suffer no such failure of the Imperial system while he stood watch.

It seemed that the representatives of the great clans had unpicked the criticisms implicit in the magos' rambling spiel. Lord Dostos Delve leaned forward over his podium, his jewelled rings clinking against the stone, his thick black brows drawn down beneath his heavy cowl.

'Clan Delve continues to labour as hard for the Imperium as we always have!' he barked. 'It can hardly be the fault of my people if the jungle is allowed to close off the mine trails and encroach upon the pit heads! What you call *behavioural divergence* is simply my folk forming militias so that they might protect themselves from coilthorn and the mist-beasts when your skitarii overseers vanish into their bunkers without a word. Let the conclave be aware that we have lost twenty-six miners in the last sub-cycle alone to being burned by the magos' macro-purgators while trying to fight back the jungle!'

Even the laxest of Astra Militarum regiments can lose that many soldiers in the space of a heartbeat, yet here you are bellowing and beating your chest as though you were some martyr to the Imperial cause, thought Torgan, wrestling down his contempt for Dostos Delve. Evidently his feelings were echoed by the magos' own, insofar as a servant of the Omnissiah could experience feelings at all, as he rebuffed Delve's posturing without pause.

'I make no apology for biological attrition in the application of optimal cleansing patterns,' said the magos. 'Were your labour units simply to–'

'They are not *labour units* – they are men and women of the Imperium!' barked Clan Lord Alamica Tectos, banging her augmetic fist down atop her podium.

'Repetition. Were your labour units simply to proceed along their allotted work patterns, they would not overlap with the purging cycle at any point,' said Gathabosis.

'You're asking our people to shuffle through danger like mindless servitors, to simply ignore the encroaching threats, to die without even fighting back,' shouted Clan Lord Torphin Lo VanSappen, his nasal voice shrill with outrage.

'I reiterate my observation to the conclave that upgrading all labour units to servitors would increase ore outputs by three hundred and fourteen per cent, while simultaneously eliminating all of the performance issues heretofore enumerated,' said Gathabosis.

This elicited fresh howls of outrage.

Torgan bit down on his temper as Agnathio of Klaratos spat accusations at the impassive magos geologis, while Yenshi of Mastracha querulously called into question the loyalties of the isolationist Clan Tectos for the third time that sub-cycle.

'Order in the conclave!' shouted Seneschal Gryft hoarsely, banging his electro-gavel against his resonator plate until the sound thundered through the chamber. 'There will be order in the conclave!'

'Thank you, seneschal,' said High Administrator Lunst into the resultant silence. 'There was, in fact, a *point* I was attempting to convey.'

'Point you were labouring to death, more like,' Torgan heard the high marshal mutter under his breath, and again he had to quash a slight grim smirk.

'In all of its history, Ghyre has never known such uncertainty and faced such potential for an as yet unspecified catastrophe,' Lunst finished.

'*As yet unspecified*? Is that what you want us to tell the wider Imperium, *if* we can even reach them through... whatever this is?' snapped Marshal Kallistus.

'If the rest of the Imperium is even still out there,' said the first arbitrator sotto voce.

Torgan stiffened at this and growled, preparing to remonstrate with the first arbitrator for the dishonour her remark cast upon his Chapter and his kind, protocol be damned. Yet before he could speak, another did so in his stead.

'My lady first arbitrator, do you doubt?' asked Bishop Renwyck, his soft voice carrying across the chamber like a cold breeze. 'Is there even the seed of doubt in your heart, in *any* of your hearts, that the wider Imperium has ceased to be? That we are, as some cry in the streets, the last loyal world? Messages begin to reach us once again, do they not? Is this not proof enough for you?'

Verol stiffened. 'No, of course not, bishop. I do not doubt. Let the conclave note that my comment was ill-considered pessimism brought on by irritation at these continued arguments. It was unbecoming, and I request it be struck from the records.'

Seneschal Gryft nodded and harrumphed.

Scritch, came the combined swipe of dozens of quill-fingers striking in unison.

Torgan eased back, though he kept his glowering gaze fixed upon the first arbitrator. From her hunched posture and the way she looked anywhere but at him, he was quite sure she felt its heat.

'The Emperor forgives you, of course,' said Renwyck, his firm, calm voice betraying nothing of his comparative youth. He sounded supremely confident, Torgan thought, utterly sure in his faith. 'We must, however, be wary of heresy at this testing time, however unintentional it might be, however innocent a wayward thought or bleak utterance might appear. Now is the hour in which we must show strength and conviction in the face of these trials, which have surely been sent by our glorious Emperor to test our mettle and prove our worth. Note, high administrator, that I say *we* must show strength, not the wider Imperium. If Emperor-sent trial this be, then it is not our place to appeal for aid from others who may even now be enduring their own tests of faith. Do you imply that Ghyre cannot stand alone, that our might or our faith is lacking?'

'I imply nothing of the sort,' snapped Lunst, visibly unfazed by Renwyck's questioning. 'The data all supports the supposition that there is a potentially violent upswell amongst the planetary labour population, and that deviant groups, mutant cults and terrorist cells are at work even now throughout the planet's infrastructure. You have all heard, by now, of the instances of violence instigated amongst Klaratos Hive's underslums and at several mining complexes by those claiming to fight for Imperial overthrow in the name of a being they call "Father"? You have heard of this being they call Shenn, also known as the three-armed gunman, seen the profane graffiti claiming that he offers the populace salvation? This *cannot* be allowed to continue. With all of the detrimental circumstances I have already listed, it surely becomes obvious that it is our duty as the ruling body of this planet to request military aid in rapidly rooting out and quelling any and all insurgency.'

Torgan's eyes narrowed as the delegates continued to argue in ever more vociferous terms. He thought carefully about all that he was hearing, about the whispers that had reached him from his informants. He appreciated that to cry for help because of unsubstantiated reports, to needlessly draw off reinforcements from openly prosecuted Imperial war fronts, would be an unforgivable error of judgement. His pride, too, rankled at the thought of Ghyre calling for aid. The miners were restless, the mutants were forming militias, and dissidents had sabotaged a few outlying Imperial holdings. Surely he and his four battle-brothers alone should be the equal of such a disparate and dissolute threat?

Yet Torgan had fought the Emperor's wars for over a century; his hard-won warrior's instinct was needling at him that there was more he could not see. The sergeant was becoming increasingly convinced that there was some greater pattern at work here, some greater threat, and that to delay in the face of such danger would prove dereliction of the worst sort.

Then again, he thought, *can we even call for help should we wish to? They say the darkness is fading, that the astronomican has been glimpsed again at last, but is that any guarantee that the surviving Ghyrish astropaths could force a message through the empyric distortion that still tortures the void? It has been long cycles since we were able to contact the Chapter, or they us.*

He realised Dostos Delve was even now belabouring that very point.

'...and what then, if we rupture the minds of our planet's astropaths trying to force out a message they cannot send? If they claim the empyrean is clearing, then I say let it clear, give it time! And, as the revered bishop and honoured high marshal suggest, give *us* time to set our own planetary affairs in order without resorting to wasteful and potentially costly hysteria.'

'Hysteria?' cried the high administrator. Before the delegates could begin another round of bickering, there came the sharp ring of metal striking metal from above. Torgan looked up, as did the delegates of the conclave. He saw Governor Osmyndri Kallistus striking her pick and stave against one another slowly and deliberately. She looked down upon them, her old soldier's features unreadable, the half-painted Emperor peering one-eyed over her shoulder.

'Let the conclave acknowledge that we have heard and considered their words,' she said. Her voice was stern and commanding, and even Torgan found his attention captured by the intensity of her gaze. 'We thank you all for your contributions to this session and remind you that your capacity is purely advisory in nature. It shall be our final decision whether or not the current situation merits an attempt to send word to the wider Imperium for aid.'

A direct rebuke, Torgan thought, but not uncalled for. Still, for the governor to openly give voice to her authority was out of character. In the year that Torgan had known her, he had never found Governor Kallistus to be anything other than entirely composed and self-assured in the quality and security of her rule. She must be deeply concerned, he thought, to wield her power so openly.

All waited on her word, faces turned up to regard their governor. Torgan wondered what was going on behind the carefully neutral expressions of the delegates. Did any harbour agendas of their own? Undoubtedly, most likely all of them; Torgan's experience with the Imperial ruling classes was unfortunately extensive and had never left him with much more than a general sense of abiding contempt that exceeded even that he felt for the sheep who formed their flocks. They all sought power and advancement. Few but the Adeptus Astartes had the clarity and selflessness to understand what was truly at stake and fight not for themselves but for the good of the Imperium. Yet these people did not see that, he thought grimly. The noble warriors of the Space Marine Chapters were little more than living weapons in their eyes – terrifying, certainly, even awe-inspiring, but no less biddable or limited than any other military force.

'There is one voice of experience that has not yet spoken, and whose thoughts we would hear before we make our decision,' said Governor Kallistus. 'Brother-Sergeant Torgan, what say you of this?'

Torgan blinked in surprise, the cynical bent of his thoughts thrown off by the unexpected enquiry. He could almost feel

Unctor's quiet amusement and made a mental note to chastise his battle-brother later.

'My lady governor, the duty of myself and my brothers is to serve as protectors,' he said. 'We are not politicians here to advise.' His distaste for their role was clear in his inflection.

'In the first instance, brother-sergeant, we would consider the provision of sound strategic advice in the matter of the planet's defence to be a natural and implicit extension of your remit,' said the governor. 'In the second, please do not insult the dignitaries here gathered by implying that one of the Emperor's own Angels of Death does not possess an informed and uniquely post-human opinion upon the wider strategic implications and potential causal links between the myriad troubles that now beset this world. We would hear that opinion, brother-sergeant, before making our decision.'

Torgan studied Governor Kallistus, his brow furrowed.

'Of course, my lady governor,' he said. 'It is my belief an astropathic message should be sent directly to my Chapter, requesting aid.'

Cries of outrage burst from around him, but Torgan simply spoke louder, his booming voice easily overriding those that sought to challenge him.

'The message should be sent without delay.'

Seneschal Gryft's gavel banged against its resonator plate again, forcing the dignitaries into resentful silence. Torgan could feel them straining at their leashes, ready to attack him or each other again the moment they got the chance. He felt the angry glares of the high marshal, of the first arbitrator and assembled clan lords. They impacted him no more than a laspistol might wound a Baneblade.

For some reason, it was not so easy to ignore the steady,

appraising gaze of Bishop Renwyck, whose expression was unreadable.

'It would please us if you could explain the reasoning behind your suggestion,' pressed Governor Kallistus. 'It is no small thing, to appeal directly to a Space Marine Chapter for aid. What if this turns out to be a situation that we can handle on our own? Would there not then be censure most severe for wasting the precious time of the Adeptus Astartes?'

'Do not question my understanding of the demands placed upon my Chapter, lady governor. Nor the authority I possess as regards communicating with them as I see fit,' barked Torgan. 'The threat is greater than currently visible – of that I am certain. There are insurgents reported in all three of Ghyre's hives. That suggests numbers. They have struck at Imperial holdings despite the efforts of the arbitrators and Ghyrish regiments to prevent them. That implies organisation and access to military-grade weaponry. Most disturbing, they all claim fealty to the same entity, "Father". That implies widespread organisation and a heretical faith. Couple that with the warp storm activity the assembled dignitaries are all too frightened to name, and I see the first stirrings of planet-wide insurrection. If we delay, it won't be disruptions to quotas, it will be war, perhaps disaster.'

'And if you are wrong, sir?' demanded Marshal Kallistus.

Torgan locked eyes with the marshal, fury roaring within him. The man quickly averted his gaze.

'Then the censure will be mine alone, human.'

Governor Kallistus struck her stave against her pick once, twice, thrice as ritual demanded, the symbolic echo of picks striking rockfaces all across Ghyre's single, vast continent.

'The people of Ghyre are loyal, faithful and true. We believe that they find satisfaction and value in their honest toil, and that they are as dedicated servants as the Emperor has ever known. Therefore, if corruption has spread through even such a loyal and worthy people as these, we believe that it must be a perilous and powerful heresy indeed. The esteemed high administrator and brother-sergeant are correct in their assessments. By the pronouncement of Governor Osmyndri Ellisentris Kallistus XXI, in the sight of the ruling conclave of Ghyre and by the authority of the Immortal God-Emperor of Mankind, we do this day approve the composition and despatch of an astropathic call for aid directly to the Imperial Fists Space Marine Chapter. Let there be contained within it the particulars of the threats that we face, and full and frank expression of the urgency that Brother-Sergeant Torgan of that same Chapter believes that it merits.'

Quill-fingers scritched on parchment. A flight of servo-skulls detached themselves from the workings of the governor's throne and whirred away on grav-impellers to transmit her commands directly to the necessary organs of governance.

She continued, 'In the interim, let the spirelords return to their hives and look to the neutralisation of these insurgent elements within our society. Let the high marshal and first arbitrator put their full forces at the disposal of the lords of clan and hive that we might do everything in our power to combat the spreading rot and withstand the darkness both within and without. Let the holy men of the Imperial faith pray for our salvation in this hour, and let the servants of the Omnissiah look to the maintenance of our quotas by whatever means they must. So have we spoken, and so shall it be done.'

Muttering spread through the conclave chamber, building rapidly through a rumble and into a roar of agitated conversation. Aides and scribes scurried off into the shadows, departing the chamber through heavy plasteel security bulk-heads to carry their masters' instructions hither and thither. Torgan watched them go, a frown creasing his brow.

'What of us, brother-sergeant?' asked Unctor, sub-vocalising so that only Torgan would hear him. 'Do we stand watch over the governor? If you are correct about how far the rot has spread on this world–'

'I am, and no, we do not,' replied Torgan. 'The governor has a great many bodyguards in her employ, but a bare handful of mortal warriors stand watch over the astropathic sanc-tum. If the enemy are organised enough to strike, they will strike there.'

He set off across the upper chamber, making for the ramps with Unctor at his shoulder. As he went, he felt the level gaze of Bishop Renwyck following him all the way out.

II

The *Dutiful* soared through Ghyre's cold blue skies. It was a sizeable shuttle, Heraldus class, and it was en route to the upper spires of Hive Angelicus to deliver medicae personnel to the astropathic sanctum. A message was to be sent off world, a cry for aid. It would be a trying endeavour. The lives of the planet's precious astropaths must be safeguarded at all costs.

The *Dutiful*'s capacious hold was packed, but not with the medicae personnel it should have contained. Those unfortunates, along with their assigned pilots, had met a swift and comparatively merciful fate before their craft could depart its landing pad. In their place was a force of nearly one hundred neophytes and acolytes of the Cult of the Wrything Wyrm. They wore miners' rubberised enviro-suits patched here and there with scavenged plates of flak armour and decorated with daubed cult sigils. Most cradled crudely machined autoguns or dangerous-looking mining tools. Many wore curved blades that dangled from their webbing, the coiled wyrm-form glyph industrially stamped into each one.

The more human amongst these men and women could have strode down any street in the hive's Laboritas district and raised no comment. Their more gifted brethren, however, would have sent the ignorant masses fleeing in panic at the first sight of their hairless and elongated heads, their fanged mouths, the segmented and chitinous bone that layered their limbs and the talons that tipped their fingers. This was to say nothing of the spare, three-armed figure of Shenn the gunman, who stood silent and inscrutable in their midst, his features echoing those of the purestrain Blessed. The Star Children gave generously, but the blinkered slaves of the Imperium saw only monstrosity where in truth beauty lay.

That was not their fault, of course.

They would all be educated in time.

In the midst of the gathering, staring with rapt fascination out of an armaglass porthole at the glowing fog banks below, stood their magus. She affected the same miner's garb as her brothers and sisters, though hers had never seen a day's labour at the ore-faces. A high collar, flowing skirts and layer upon layer of elaborate decoration had been worked into her outfit by the hands of devoted faithful. Tokens of their respect dangled from cords at her neck, wrists and waist, each small metal charm representing the faith and blessings of those whose hopes she carried with her. The magos' head was hairless, her skin a pale shade of mauve, while her eyes were two liquid umber orbs that glinted with the reflected cobalt blue of the planet's skies.

The magus' name was Phoenicia Jai.

'Hive Angelicus approaching, beloved magos,' came the voice of one of the shuttle's pilots, crackling through the craft's internal vox. 'Initial airspace interrogations forthcoming and codes proffered in response. Hive command have approved our *flight path and rune-designated* Dutiful *for priority passage. Five minutes to docking.'*

Phoenicia Jai turned from the porthole with a twinge of regret. Her life had been spent almost exclusively concealed in chambers and corridors far from prying eyes. The stark blue of the upper atmosphere enchanted her, and its contrast with the whirling mists below struck her as beautiful. She had been fascinated by the pulsing lights in that sea of vapour, hinting at the bioluminescent jungles down below. Yet she wasn't here to admire the view, Phoenicia admonished herself. Father had appointed this task to her, had given her a chance to strike back at the Imperial oppressors. She would not disappoint him.

'You all know me,' she said, her voice deep, mellifluous, resonant with the underlying psychic gifts that Father, and through him the Star Children, had given. All eyes turned towards her. Cultists' blast goggles reflected her image, haloed by the hard daylight at her back. 'I am a daughter of Clan Delve, born to the cult during the Season of Whirling Mists. I did not know my parents, could not now pick them out from amidst the labouring masses who work the ore-faces of this world. They knew that the gift they had been given by the Star Children was meant for all, and thus, selfless, they gave me up to Father's care. They sacrificed for their beliefs. Stars' blessings upon them.'

'Stars' blessings upon them,' murmured those of her brothers and sisters who could vocalise in the human fashion.

'Yet I never lacked for family, for the Cult of the Wrything Wyrm have given me all that I could ever want,' said Jai, and the warmth in her tone was not affected. She truly loved her people, loved all those who toiled and strove beneath the lash of the Imperial oppressors. That love gave her strength.

'All of Father's faithful offered me succour and devotion, for I am the magus of our cult, chosen by the Star Children to prophesy their coming, blessed with their gifts that I might aid Father in preparing all for the Day of Ascension. I do not take such a charge lightly. And the Day of Ascension is coming, my friends, when the Star Children will drift down through golden skies with their arms outstretched and welcome all into their light, that we might become one with the beauty and serenity of their eternal embrace. You all know this. You have all heard me preach Father's word to the devoted and the aspirant alike. So lucky, I am, to bring hope for something better to the toiling and the downtrodden, the sorrowful, the starving, the crippled and the oppressed.'

The murmuring around her grew in volume. A few cultists reached out with fingers of flesh or chitin to gently touch the hems of Jai's skirts. The gesture was rumoured to bring the Star Children's blessings, she knew, and so she let them. With her gifts, it was not difficult to sense the comfort and strength that the superstition brought them.

'I have enjoyed every day of my task, for who could not rejoice at the chance to bring hope and happiness? Even as Primus Lhor stockpiled armaments against the Day of Ascension, as Nexos Sharrow laboured to implant faithful amongst the upper Imperial strata and Shenn the gunman brought hope to the masses with his adventures, so my task was far easier, for what was I but the font of faith for those who desired it? But though I have enjoyed my task, now it must change. Now, like my parents before me, I must sacrifice. The Star Children expect more. The Imperial oppressors are at last waking up to their peril. Slow, lumbering, indolent and stupid though they are, at last these ineffectual fops that call themselves our leaders have realised that the populace they believed slaves are in fact their greatest foes. We have the strength to defeat them. We have the numbers, we have the weapons, and we have the faith!'

The cultists cried their agreement. They snarled and slathered. They beat their weapons against the shuttle's bulkheads.

'Yet in their fear the Imperial oppressors seek to cry out for aid,' spat Magus Jai, injecting her words with a psychic nudge of disgust at the fearful weakness of the foe. She saw her followers shudder with her transferred emotion and felt satisfaction that they truly understood. 'Father has charged me with the sacred duty of choking off that cry before it can escape into the void. I must silence them so that in this hour of darkness, sent to us by the Star Children as their blessing and their signal both, we can commence our Ascension without interruption by the heretics without. And in this task I need your aid, my faithful. *Will you aid me?*'

This time the outcry was louder, a roar of mingled aggression and fervent belief that sent a thrill through Jai's soul.

'They will fight us, faithful. Some of us will fall this day, and in dying so shall we hasten early to our Ascension, not in joy but in sorrow, shorn of our beloved brothers and sisters. And yet! And yet to sacrifice all that you have, all that you are so that Father's great undertaking might see completion, oh faithful, what greater reward can there be? As my blessed parents gave up that which was most precious to them, so must we be willing to do no less!'

Roaring. Cheering. Chanting. The hammer and bang of work boots beating the deck and weapons hammering the bulkheads.

'Then be ready, brothers and sisters, for we strike unveiled and unshrouded at last. Now let the Imperial oppressors see our true visage and know terror at its divinity! Stars' blessings upon you all! Let our Ascension begin here!'

Jai snatched her tall iron stave from the shuttle's equipment webbing and, clutching it firmly, strode through the throng of faithful to stand directly before the shuttle's rear ramp. The wyrmform icon atop the stave thrummed with invisible psychic power, focusing and amplifying her abilities exponentially. The stave had been a gift from Father.

It all had, really, she supposed.

Behind Jai, the faithful divided into warrior bands and ran through last checks upon their weapons. Magazines slammed into autoguns and pistols with solid clacks. Industrial saws screamed then wound down to stillness as they were revved and their machine-spirits appeased. Voices muttered low, fast prayers to Father and the Star Children, some tight with excitement, some quavering with fear.

Phoenicia Jai felt no fear, nor truly excitement either. Rather, she knew the absolute certainty of victory, felt her faith burn hot in her breast at the righteousness of her cause. She knew she was ready, and she met the perils of battle at last with a calm acceptance.

Father had appointed this task to her, and she would see it done.

Sergeant Torgan was climbing the Haloed Stair deep within the hive's astropathic sanctum when he heard the distant thump of an explosion. He spun, bolter coming up, eyes scanning for threats. Brothers Unctor and Garom echoed his motions. Around them, the men and women of the sanctum guard jumped in alarm and fumbled for their weapons. They couldn't have heard anything from this distance, not without Adeptus Astartes senses; they had been spooked by the sudden and eerily synchronised shift in the Space Marines' demeanour.

Torgan keyed the vox in his armour's gorget.

'Brother Jashor, Brother Victus, report,' he said. At the same time, he scanned the atrium below, richly appointed and spacious with its crystal statues and chuckling fountains. Minor officials and astropathic acolytes crossed the mosaic floor on errands of their own, some of them stumbling to a halt and looking alarmed as they saw the three hulking Imperial Fists sweeping the muzzles of their guns across the chamber.

'*Sanctum doors sealed, brother-sergeant,*' came Victus' voice over the vox. '*All essential personnel are within. The astropaths are undergoing final rituals of focusing before the sending. Was that an explosion?*'

'Confirmed, situation unclear,' replied Torgan. 'Hold position and stand guard, brothers. The ritual must be completed.'

'*Understood,*' said Victus.

'Brother Garom, reinforce Jashor and Victus,' Torgan ordered.

'Brother-sergeant,' said Garom smartly, spinning and jogging up the remaining steps before vanishing through the gilded portal at their head.

'My lord, do you detect some threat?' asked the lieutenant of the sanctum guard. He clutched his lasgun tightly and managed to look both nervous and stoic. The lieutenant's vox operator pressed a hand to the earpiece of her helm, and her eyes widened.

'Hostiles in docking hangar six,' she reported, her gaze flicking between Torgan and her lieutenant as though she were unsure which to address. She settled on the huge Space Marine in his glinting yellow armour. 'They disembarked from the reserve medicae shuttle. There's dozens of them...' She paused, and Torgan thought for a moment that her eyes might pop right out of her skull with alarm. 'They're... not all human, my lord,' she gasped.

'How in Throne's name did they hijack the medicae shuttle?' demanded the lieutenant. Torgan didn't like the note of panic in his voice. 'How can they be here?'

'Irrelevant,' barked Torgan. 'What is the enemy's estimated strength?'

'My lord, the hangar sentries are reporting dozens, perhaps hundreds,' said the vox officer.

'Channel?' asked Torgan, pointing at her earpiece.

'Tarsus sigma two,' she replied, and Torgan patched his vox directly into the sanctum guards' tactical channel. He winced, finding it clogged with half-coherent shouts for aid, cries of alarm and the tinny hammering of gunfire.

'What of the automated defences?' asked the lieutenant. 'The servitor guns should be slaughtering them!'

'They deactivated them,' said Torgan, frowning as he listened to the panicked shrieks of the defenders. 'One of your officers deactivated the sentry guns, spiked the controls then shot himself.'

The lieutenant paled further.

'Vox, contact Spire command and request immediate reinforcements,' he snapped. 'Everything they have!'

His vox operator shook her head in frustration.

'Nothing but static on the external channels, and... something...' She gave a hiss of pain and ripped the earpiece from the side of her helm, casting it away as though it had burned her.

'Some kind of jamming,' she slurred, and Torgan saw the veins blackening all down one side of her face. Her eyes rolled into her head and she collapsed.

'My lord, what is–'

Torgan spoke over the horrified lieutenant, issuing orders into his vox-bead.

'Brothers, Unctor and I are moving to interdict invaders. Hold your positions. Do not attempt external vox transmission – the enemy have compromised it somehow.'

Torgan removed his helm from where it hung mag-locked to his belt and lowered it over his head, expression grim. The helm's seals hissed then clicked as it locked into place. Torgan's autosenses flickered crimson across his vision then settled.

'My lord, my warriors are yours to command,' said the lieutenant, having evidently pulled himself together and recalled his training. 'Tell us how best to aid you.'

'Rally them,' replied Torgan, his voice now harsh and vox-amplified. 'Clear civilian impediments. Protect the sanctum. Do not get in our way.'

With that, he set off at a loping run, down the stairs and across the atrium towards docking hangar six. Unctor ran with him. Gaggles of frightened scribes scattered from the Space Marines' path. Behind him, Torgan heard the lieutenant's shouts as the man attempted to enforce order on what was about to turn into a stampede.

The Imperial Fists ran along richly appointed corridors and down brass-handled stairways, past elegant portraits and crystalline windows that looked out onto the mountainous spires of Hive Angelicus. They bulled their way through chambers where the innumerable robed adepts of the astropathic sanctum fled this way and that in panic. Gunfire could now be heard ringing along the corridors over the crash of overturning furniture and the screams of terrified acolytes.

'Clear a path!' roared Torgan, vox-amplifying his voice to carry over the sounds of bedlam. Terror-stricken figures spilled aside like water, clambering over one another to get out of the Space Marines' way. A few froze dumbstruck at the sight of the massive armoured warriors bearing down on them, only to be cut down from behind as a volley of autogun rounds ripped its way through an arched doorway. Blood puffed into the air. Robed figures crumpled. Fresh screams rang around the room.

On Torgan's autosenses, targeting runes flashed into being and cogitational data scrolled through his peripheral vision.

'Contact second level, multiple hostiles, engaging,' he reported over the squad vox. Then, as bullets sparked and whined from his power armour, he switched to his helm's vox-grille and bellowed, 'For the Emperor!'

Torgan raised his bolter, sighted on the handful of mutated-looking miners dashing down the corridor towards him, and squeezed his trigger. His boltgun bucked in his hands as it spat self-propelled miniature warheads at his assailants. Each shot streaked away on a contrail of fire to connect with the bodies of the attackers. The bolt shells punched through the miners' bodysuits and, micro-cogitators detecting that they had penetrated deep within their targets' bodies, detonated.

The floor, walls and ceiling of the corridor turned dark red with an explosion of bloody matter.

'More of them,' barked Unctor, adding his fire to Torgan's. Bolts hammered down the corridor and blasted more insurgents apart at its far end. 'You were right, brother-sergeant,' he continued. 'The attack has fallen here. How did they know to strike now?'

'Someone in the conclave is not what they seem,' replied Torgan. 'Whatever this is, brother, its tendrils reach far.'

'You were right to push for the sending,' said Unctor.

Torgan grunted in response and checked his auspex. He

muttered a prayer to the device's machine-spirit and gave it a distinctly unritualistic shake in the hopes of clearing its display. 'Reports of movement in multiple corridors and chambers around us,' he said. 'Insurgents are pushing up along multiple vectors. We are the only serious resistance they've met.'

Torgan cursed. If the sanctum guards could have kept the attackers bottled up in the hangar until the Imperial Fists reached them, the situation could have been contained. Now, though, it was like trying to hold back water with his bare hands.

'We cannot hold them here,' said Unctor.

'No,' replied Torgan. 'We rally on our brothers. The sanctum guard will not stop them, but they may still slow the attackers down, if only by their deaths.'

He turned back, retracing his and Unctor's steps at a flat run. Questions whirled through Torgan's mind. How many assailants were they dealing with? Was it just cultists, or did they face other, more heretical threats? The vox operator's fate suggested the latter. How long would it be before someone detected the attack and sent reinforcements?

Torgan sped through another doorway and into the atrium he had left scant minutes earlier. He was greeted by a blizzard of fire that rebounded from his armour like storm rain. Alarm runes flashed amber in his peripheral vision as shots punched through to inflict stinging wounds, one in his left arm, another in his torso.

One band of insurgents crouched three hundred yards to his left, behind an ornamental fountain of prodigious size. A smaller group was halfway up the Haloed Stair, hidden amidst bullet-riddled sanctum guard bodies.

'Stairs,' Torgan voxed Unctor before stepping from cover

and striding towards the fountain. Behind him, Brother Unctor surged through the doorway and rained fire into the cultists on the Haloed Stair. Meanwhile, Torgan levelled his bolter, thumbed his shot selector to auto and let rip. Bolts hammered out, streaking across the chamber and blitzing fountain and cultists alike. Marble exploded into clouds of whizzing shrapnel. Water and blood ran in torrents. Claw-limbed freaks were tossed through the air, their bodies blasted open or torn to shreds. Several more shots hit Torgan, one ringing his helmet like a bell, and then the last surviving insurgent broke from cover and ran, not away but straight towards the sergeant.

Torgan had a moment to note the creature's inhuman features, its hunched body and extra arm. His autosenses flashed a crimson alert rune as they detected the primed mining charges the creature was brandishing. He heard its inhuman shriek, appealing to some deity or cult leader, Torgan knew not who.

'In Father's name!'

Torgan put a single bolt into the cultist's right fist, triggering the mining charges it clutched. The explosion was fierce enough to drive him back a step and momentarily white-out his autosenses. Hot blood spattered his armour and smoke billowed around him.

As his autosenses cleared, Torgan turned away from the blazing crater that was all that remained of his assailants. He was in time to see the crimson beam of a mining laser reach out from the top of the Haloed Stair and spear clean through Unctor's helm. The Imperial Fist stiffened, his last few bolt shells flying wide to blow apart a statue of Governor Kallistus, then collapsed, all but decapitated.

'Throne,' snarled Torgan, and snapped off a volley at the

handful of cultists at the top of the stair. One shot took the laser-wielder in the gut and blew him to pieces, but his comrades vanished through the doorway and out of sight.

Torgan didn't waste time checking on Unctor; his brother was dead, and the time for mourning and the extraction of gene-seed would come later. For now, the atrium's flickering lumen and the building sense of pressure behind Torgan's eyes suggested that the sending had begun. He had to eliminate the insurgent attackers and ensure that the ritual could be completed.

Torgan ran across the atrium and took the Haloed Stair two steps at a time, reloading his bolter as he went.

'Brothers, report,' he spat into the vox.

'Contact, brother-sergeant,' replied Brother Victus. *'Insurgents pushing in from three directions. I am covering the south entrance to the sanctum annex, Garom the east, and a complement of sanctum guard have the west.'*

'Brother Jashor?' asked Torgan, pounding down another richly appointed corridor scattered with the corpses of sanctum guard and insurgents.

'Incapacitated – insurgent with an industrial saw disembowelled him, brother-sergeant.'

Torgan cursed silently.

'Hold them, brother. I am thirty seconds out,' he said.

'In Dorn's name, brother-sergeant,' replied Victus, and cut the link.

Torgan burst into the next chamber, a shrine to the Imperial faith illuminated by hundreds of flickering candles. He almost ploughed headlong into a pair of insurgents who were manhandling a heavy metal case stamped with a serpentine spiral design. The first fell to Torgan's clenched gauntlet, the punch snapping the heretic's neck. As the carved chest clanged to the flagstones, the second insurgent drew an auto-pistol and unloaded it point-blank into Torgan's faceplate.

White-hot pain flooded the sergeant's skull as a lucky shot found his eye lens and punched into his skull. Pain blockers flooded his system. Runes flashed madly. Torgan staggered, snarling, registering that he could now see only through his right eye. Blood drizzled inside his faceplate. He tasted it on his lips.

The insurgent's features twisted in a triumphant leer.

'Meet your doom, oppressors!' he screamed.

'I shall leave that to you,' spat Torgan, and shot the cultist through the head. More blood sprayed, dousing the nearby candles.

Torgan spared the carved chest a glance. A fresh surge of alarm pierced his haze of pain and disorientation.

'That is a demolition charge, big enough to bring down a spire,' he breathed. There was no time to render its machine-spirits inactive. He would have to hope that slaying the weapon's operators had been enough for now.

Torgan pressed on, feeling the tight pain of his hyper-efficient blood clotting around his grievous head wound. The bullet was lodged somewhere behind what remained of his left eye, and had no doubt inflicted damage to his cortex, but his post-human anatomy was compensating as best it could. He was an Imperial Fist, he reminded himself, as waves of nausea and dizziness flitted through his body. He was built to endure when all else failed. It would take more than some heretic's bullet lodged in his skull to slow Larrus Torgan.

Another corridor. Another chamber, this one a ritual medi-tation space meant for the astropaths to ready themselves in. Its calm serenity was spoiled by the bloody bodies strewn across its broken furnishings, the bullet holes and las-burns in its walls and the cacophony of gunfire that rang from the half-open brass doors on its far side.

The lumen flickered again. Torgan tasted bitter iron, then something so sweet as to be rotten. He smelled fresh-cut grass mingled with promethium fumes and heard snatches of something that might have been laughter but might also have been hysterical screaming.

Brain damage? Psychic phenomena? Something of both?

He did not have time to decipher. Instead, Torgan shouldered open the door to the sanctum annex and plunged into the war zone beyond. The annex was, in truth, a corridor of substantial width and ornate decoration that encircled the astropathic sanctum at ground level. Several doorways led into it from different directions, and it seemed likely that the enemy had flanked the annex and attacked through all three. However, they would all be converging on the single doorway to the sanctum proper, a thirty-foot-high slab of bronze-chased adamantine currently out of sight to Torgan around the curve of the annex.

The corridor was a ruin. Its rich crimson carpets were blood-drenched and, in places, ablaze. Its thick, armoured inner walls were marred by las-burns and spattered with more blood. Several of the stained-glass windows set near the ceiling had been cracked by gunfire, and a mixture of freezing air and diamond-hard light spilled through.

As Torgan emerged he saw insurgents to his left, their backs to him as they pressed the attack on the sanctum door.

'For the Emperor!' he bellowed, and unloaded his bolter into them. With his maimed vision, Torgan's accuracy was not what it should have been, and several of his bolts flew wide. Several more found their mark, however, and cultists exploded in puffs of gore.

'*Brother-sergeant, make haste,*' voxed Brother Victus. '*There is a psyker with them. I–*' Victus' transmission cut out, and Torgan's face drew down into a scowl of fury.

To unleash witchery here while the sending was in progress was recklessness of the worst sort. Even he knew that much.

Torgan stormed forward, his armoured feet pounding against the carpeted flagstones, his bolter barking its wrath. An insurgent came at him with a howling industrial saw and he shot the mutant down, leaping over the spinning blades of the weapon as it spilled from nerveless fingers. Landing, he put bolts into two more insurgents then swept past several wounded members of the sanctum guard, who stared at him with wild eyes.

A door to Torgan's left burst open and more cultists poured through it, autoguns blazing. He took the shots on his shoulder guard and flung a frag grenade into his enemies' midst. It detonated with a loud bang and flung shredded bodies through the air.

The sanctum's door came into view. The air was heavy with the thunderstorm tension of the sending beyond, everything crawling with a kind of greasy electric tingle. Torgan took in Brother Jashor slumped against the sanctum's door, holding his guts in with one hand and firing a bolt pistol with his other. He saw Brother Victus standing over his comrade, bolter hammering. Brother Garom lay nearby, his plasma gun inches from his open gauntlet, his armour riddled with dozens of bullet holes. A handful of sanctum guards were kneeling around them, firing their lasguns desperately. They were using their own dead for cover.

Beyond them, a statue had been toppled to form a makeshift barricade. A couple of dozen insurgents crouched behind it, filling the air with gunfire. Torgan saw her in their midst, the psyker that Victus had warned of. Her dark eyes gleamed like pools. Her stave was raised, and unnatural forces were shimmering from it to further shield her comrades from the loyalists' fire.

Torgan didn't slow. He levelled his bolter at the psyker and let fly. His bolts tore through the air and detonated against her shield, hard enough to blast her off her feet.

The cultists let out an enraged howl and surged over their barricade in a seething mass.

'Fight!' roared Torgan. 'Do not let them through! Fight for the Emperor! Fight for Dorn!'

Autoguns and lasguns flashed. The corridor was lit by the mad strobe of muzzle flare and flames. An improvised fire bomb shattered amidst a knot of sanctum guards, and they staggered back screaming and burning before being picked off by gunshots. Brother Victus waded into the charging cultists, swinging the butt of his gun in brutal arcs. A savage brawl broke out between cultists armed with picks and clubs and the last few sanctum guards with their lasrifles and bayonets. Torgan threw himself into the fight, gun butt swinging and feet lashing out, breaking another insurgent with every blow.

He would not let the sending be disrupted. He would not let these heretics win. There could be no defeat, no surrender, only victory at any cost.

Magus Jai rose to her feet, heart hammering. She was shaking with shock, adrenaline and outrage. She had almost *perished*. The filthy Imperial oppressor had almost slain her, and in defending herself she had been forced to stop protecting her brothers and sisters. Now they were dying. Worse, she still couldn't raise Haxis and J'Gath; without their demolition charge the sanctum could not be destroyed, as it surely must be. Her finely attuned psychic senses left her in no doubt as to what was happening beyond that doorway. Even now, she was failing Father in this most vital of tasks.

'I will not allow them to prevail, Father, I promise you,' she hissed. 'Victory, at any cost.'

It could not be allowed.

It would not.

Jai was not a military strategist, but even she could see that the arrival of yet another cursed Space Marine had turned the tables in her enemies' favour. They were veritable monsters, towering armoured behemoths who simply would not die. Her brothers and sisters were spending their lives dearly, but it was the armoured might and firepower of the Space Marines that would prevail here.

Then she had it.

Jai focused on the newcomer, the warrior with the shattered faceplate. She raised her stave double-handed and pointed it at him, then called upon every ounce of the power that the Star Children had given her. She sent the full force of their will questing out like a tendril, winding and coiling through the air before it punched deep into the Space Marine's wounded mind. Jai felt resistance like nothing she had ever known. She gritted her teeth and growled deep in her throat as she felt blood spill from her nostrils. It was like trying to force her bare hands through a solid fortress wall, every moment of pressure more agonising and unyielding than the one before, every second promising the terrible snap as she crushed herself against her enemy's mental defences. He staggered, his helm turning slowly in her direction. His limbs shuddered as he brought his boltgun up. Its muzzle yawned dark and cavernous amidst the mayhem of the battle. Jai cursed and redoubled her efforts, feeling agony race through her mind as she pushed herself past every sane limit.

'I will not fail you…' she gritted out between clenched and blood-flecked teeth. 'I *will not.*'

The Space Marine's mental defences collapsed so suddenly that Jai physically staggered forward and thumped into the fallen statue. The sense of release was blessed relief, and she felt a smile twist her mouth as she drove her will deep into the undefended meat of the oppressor's mind. For a moment he staggered as she fumbled, unfamiliar with the psycho-indoctrinated architecture of his thoughts. Then she had him. With a twitch of her mind Jai swung the barrel of the Space Marine's boltgun around. With another she squeezed his trigger. Bolts roared out and splattered the last of the sanctum guard across the carpeted floor.

'Feel Father's wrath, filth of the oppressor!' cried Jai, and her surviving followers gave victorious shouts.

The other two Space Marines spun in shock, but they did not fire, still struggling to comprehend just what had happened.

Too slow, she thought, and squeezed her puppet's trigger again. The bolts flew wide, one clipping the still-standing Space Marine, two more punching into the sanctum's door and blasting craters in its surface.

He was still fighting her, she realised. It felt as though she were wrestling with a giant, physically and mentally straining to bend him to her will, terrified that at any moment he would break free with bone-shattering force. It was precipitous, painful, yet somehow exhilarating.

The pause had been enough for her surviving brothers and sisters to rally. One unloaded her autogun into the exposed innards of the wounded Space Marine, finishing him off in a gory spray. Three more flung themselves at the last unharmed giant; an energised mining pick hit him in the side of the knee. Autogun rounds stitched his chest-plate. A curved blade swept up under his chin.

All three of her comrades met a violent demise seconds later as their blows clanged from the Space Marine's armour. He picked Kolv up by the throat and snapped his neck, before putting bolts into Sherva and Gixnis and blowing them apart.

Phoenicia Jai screamed, wrenching at her puppet's strings. He hurled his gun end over end through the air. It struck his brother's helm and staggered the warrior long enough for Jai to achieve her true aim. Her puppet bent down, straightened up and unleashed the howling fury of his fallen brother's plasma gun.

'You will all pay a thousand times over for the blood you have spilled,' said Jai, and clenched her mind again.

The shot lit the corridor white. A crackling orb of plasma slammed into the last loyal Space Marine and burned through his chest-plate. White fire burst from his helm's eye lenses. Smoke boiled from the grievous wound in his chest and he crashed back against the sanctum doors. Jai sent another thought-spike and her puppet pulled the trigger again. Another blast erased his brother's helmed head and sent the remains of his corpse sliding to the floor, the slagged metal of his power armour glowing.

'Damn. Y-you. Heretic...' grated the puppet, and she felt fresh pain within her mind as he fought to swing the weapon to bear upon her.

'*You* are the heretics, you and your monstrous Imperium. The Star Children spit on your corpse Emperor,' she snarled, and sent one more thought-barb into her enemy's mind. Jai felt exultation and satisfaction as he unwillingly brought the plasma gun up and pressed its white-hot muzzle against the underside of his helm. Smoke rose. Metal melted and drooled. She caught a whiff of cooking flesh and realised that she was holding her victim on the brink, enjoying his searing agony. And why not? How much pain had these monsters inflicted upon her people over hundreds and hundreds of years?

Yet she was wasting time, she realised. Every second that passed was longer for the enemy to send out their distress call. Disgusted with herself, Jai twitched her victim's trigger finger. His helmed head vanished in a howl of white light and his armoured body crashed down onto its back with a last spasm.

Magus Jai felt the exhilaration of her powers drain away and suddenly found herself leaning on her stave in exhaustion. Her limbs shook. They were so heavy she could barely lift them. She looked around at her last few warriors, at the handful of late arrivals led by Shenn, even now spilling into the annex. She wiped blood from her lips with one robed arm and gestured down the corridor.

'Find out what happened to Haxis and J'Gath,' she croaked. 'Bring the charges and get them set, now! We demolish the sanctum with the astropaths still inside and then we retreat.'

As her followers rushed to do her bidding, Jai allowed herself to sink down against the statue as exhaustion and frustration washed over her. She felt a knot in the pit of her stomach that was little eased even when her comrades voxed to let her know they had found the charges and were deploying them.

This attack had not gone as it should. She knew that; the Space Marines should have been watching over the governor, not standing between her and her objective. Father would understand – he would not be angry with her. She was more than a little surprised that she had defeated them at all. Surely they must have grown complacent during their long cycles of inaction. She realised that Father had chosen well his moment to strike.

Yet none of that changed the fact that she had been too slow. Perhaps she would still stop the Imperials from forcing their message through. Perhaps it would not get through at all – perhaps the Star Children's miraculous aid would prevent it.

The risk could not be taken. Jai knew that, as would Father, and Lhor, and all the rest of them.

The Day of Ascension could no longer be delayed. For good or ill, it began here, now.

Pride welled within Phoenicia Jai. For she had started the last war that Ghyre would ever know.

III
ONE YEAR, TWENTY-SIX CYCLES SIDEREAL LATER...

Primaris Epistolary Aster Lydorran felt the Thunderhawk shudder as it punched down through Ghyre's atmosphere. It was not a violent motion, for the powerful gunship was built to endure far worse traumas, but Lydorran was a practitioner of geokinesis; every slight shudder of force or pressure was revealed to his hyper-attuned psyker's senses.

'We have broken atmosphere,' he said over the vox, addressing Captain Tor and Chaplain Storn, who sat opposite him. All three were lashed into restraint thrones, helmed and in full armour, as were their honour guard, who took up much of the rest of the Thunderhawk's troop bay. Past the assembled veterans, past the warriors of Tor's command squad, Dreadnought Brother Ghesmund completed the formidable assemblage of Imperial Fists packed into the gunship's hold. This was only one craft amongst the entire strike force, thought Lydorran with a stirring of pride. It was a magnificent gathering of military might, and he was glad to be a part of it.

'Soon the guns of the Fifth Company shall speak their fury

again,' intoned Chaplain Storn. 'I confess, my brothers, that with all that has transpired I find my choler surging to the fore with every such opportunity for redress.'

'You speak for us all, Brother-Chaplain, but what foe do we fight here?' asked Captain Tor.

'We all heard the report from the Ghyrish high marshal, did we not?' Lydorran said. 'Insurgent cells, mutant militias and massed cultist armies, heretic turncoats amongst the Ghyrish Airborne regiments… It is a litany of rebellion that bears all the hallmarks of the Dark Gods' servants, no?'

'Indeed. And yet I wonder,' replied Tor. 'You were with me on Shondarch, Brother-Librarian, and on Osmal II. You saw how the Great Rift has gifted that heretic filth the chance to conjure malefic entities more easily, how swollen is the power of their warpcraft. You have seen how brazen the fallen traitors have become, marching openly against the Imperium even here within the very Segmentum Solar. Yet I see nothing of these phenomena in the message that Sergeant Torgan sent us, nor in the words of High Marshal Kallistus.'

Lydorran considered. His captain made a keen observation. Since his emergence from deep beneath the sands of Mars during the Ultima Founding, the Librarian had fought in only two combat actions alongside his brother Imperial Fists. Both had been bloody conflicts that saw the Fifth Company evicting heretic forces from entrenched positions on oppressed loyalist worlds.

'I have been guilty of assuming that this engagement would take much the same form as the previous,' he confessed. 'I will shrive myself with the pain gauntlet at the first opportunity, brother-captain, and endeavour to correct my failing. We must know the nature of our enemies if we are to aid the people of this world.'

'It is understandable, Lydorran,' said Chaplain Storn. 'This latest chapter of the Long War is all that you have known since you… joined our ranks. Things have no doubt changed since you were taken by Cawl in the thirty-sixth millennium. We are Imperial Fists. We must strive always to see past the obvious to the truth beyond. Precision is one of our many virtues. One cannot bring low the enemy's fortress if one does not properly perceive its strengths and assess its weaknesses.'

'Just so, Brother-Chaplain,' replied Lydorran.

'Whoever we face, they have certainly caused both mayhem and destruction,' said Captain Tor, scrolling through the runic script displayed on the data-slate he held. 'The reports the high marshal transmitted to us speak volumes.'

'Even assuming he has omitted whatever details he feels would undermine the planet's defenders in our eyes,' said Lydorran.

'You believe the high marshal has lied to us?' asked Tor. 'Do your powers tell you this, brother?'

'No, brother-captain, but the high marshal is only human, with all the faults and insecurities such a condition brings. He is a loyal servant of the Emperor who has spent more than a year fighting a desperate war. He has seen duplicity within his own ranks, where he assumed none could fester. He saw our brothers in the honour guard struck down to a man on the war's first day. Now the Adeptus Astartes descend upon his world and he fears our judgement. If his own faith in his people falters, he thinks on some level that ours will also. He is desperate to prevent that. Especially if the news about Squad Torgan's death is true.'

'He fears our judgement will fall upon the innocent and the guilty in equal measure,' mused Captain Tor.

'Him, or Governor Kallistus, for whom he speaks,' said Lydorran.

'Their fears are not unjustified,' growled Storn. A few seats down, Chapter Champion Hastur grunted his agreement.

'We cannot pass judgement on every loyal Ghyrish servant of the Emperor because of the separatist lunacy of their countrymen,' said Lydorran.

'What if all were complicit, whether through deliberate activity or the sin of laxity in their watch?' challenged Storn. 'Ignorance is no defence for heresy.'

'The people of the Imperium are its lifeblood,' Lydorran replied. 'One does not exsanguinate the patient in order to purge an imbalance of humours.'

'The people of the Imperium are its garrison,' said Storn. 'All bear the burden of responsibility for its defence. It takes but a handful of traitors to open the postern gate to the foe in the light of dusk, and but a handful more to fail to see the peril until it is too late. Soon enough the entire fortress has fallen.'

'Yet what worth has an empty fortress when the garrison is dragged wholesale from their posts and put to death upon the mere fear of laxity?' asked Apothecary Lordas, joining his voice to the debate in Lydorran's support.

'The point is moot, my brothers,' said Captain Tor firmly. 'This world matters. Its output of ore matters. So say the Departmento Munitorum and the Adeptus Mechanicus, and so agrees Chapter command. We cannot simply put this world to the torch to purge the risk of heresy, even if we wished to. Its infrastructure must be secured. Its export quotas must be restored with all haste lest forge world Shallethrax and the gun-shrines of Phodrial and Amhosak Ultima fall silent.'

'We shall have to act decisively to turn the tide,' observed Lydorran. 'Even assuming he has planed off the rough edges, the reports make for bleak reading.'

Tor nodded in acknowledgement, paging through his data-slate.

'Just over a year sidereal since the heretics began their uprising in the name of this being "Father", and in that time the defenders have lost two out of three hives.'

'I imagine they would prefer us to see it as their having successfully held on to the capital city and its attendant mines,' said Lydorran.

'I am sure they would,' said Tor, his tone wry. 'The fact is, they are losing this war, would have lost it very soon had we not arrived.' He punched a series of runes on his data-slate, projecting a holomap of Ghyre into the air before him. The image flickered, a hazy green representation of the benighted world rapidly zooming in on its only landmass. Thanks perhaps to its lone nature, it had been named simply the Continent; Lydorran could not help but approve the pragmatism.

Designator runes appeared across the Continent. They marked out the trio of hive cities that formed a rough triangle. Klaratos, its northern tip, Mastracha, its south-eastern point, and Angelicus, its westernmost. Almost a dozen mining complexes were marked as well, divided between Greater and Lesser clan ownership and each reached by armoured highways that stretched from the skirts of Ghyre's hives. Those highways were lined with macro-purgation firethrowers, Lydorran knew from their inload briefings, yet those defences had been ill maintained since the war's escalation, and now the mines risked being overrun or cut off by the rapacious biofauna of Ghyre's deadly mist jungles.

Even the planet's hive cities were suspended above the jungle's grasping reach on immense stilt legs, each several miles in diameter and interlaced with complex strata of supporting struts that had become home to unofficial shanty towns and hive slums in their thousands. As Lydorran understood it, the miners themselves dwelt largely within the lower levels of each hive and used armoured funicular railways to travel up and down the cities' legs in order to reach the mist-swathed jungles below. From there, convoys of armoured transports ran the constant gauntlet of predatory fauna along the highways to reach the armoured mine-heads themselves.

'Hive Klaratos,' said Captain Tor, conjuring crimson runes into life around the vast macro-city. 'Fallen. Half-overrun by the jungle below, if reports are to be believed. The remainder is a lawless nest of heresy from which vox-proclamations of secession from the Imperium blare night and day.'

'Not to mention heretical rhetoric exhorting the worship of their Father,' spat Storn.

'Hive Mastracha, also lost. It is nothing more now than a haunted ruin,' said Tor, causing acid-green bio-threat runes to blossom around the city's icon. 'The planet's defenders possessed a stockpile of extremis-level bio-purgation munitions that were intended for purging the planet's jungles in case of a destabilising event of just this sort.'

'A weapon of last resort, no doubt,' observed Lydorran. He considered the collateral damage to the planet's populace and infrastructure that unleashing such weapons would cause, and the immense quantities of rotting biomatter that would be left to contaminate much of the Continent in their wake. The alternative would have to be apocalyptic indeed to cast such a choice in a favourable light.

'Perhaps the defenders believed it had come to that, or

perhaps the insurgents felt possession of these weapons would afford them an unassailable bargaining position,' said Tor. 'What scant information exists in the high marshal's data-inloads suggests a firefight in the storage silo in Hive Mastracha's spire. There was a containment breach, followed by a chain of detonations. Mastracha is a collapsed shell, the jungle pared back to bare bedrock for fifty miles around it in every direction.'

Storn shook his head. The skull faceplate of his helm lowered menacingly in the crimson light of the Thunderhawk's bay.

'Inexcusable foolishness,' he growled. 'Have we located the enemy's command centre yet, brother-captain? I would recommend a swift strike upon that location with our entire strength, show these curs that the Imperial Fists are a new kind of foe to be feared.'

'Lead by example, cow them then press the advantage,' agreed Ancient Tarsun, the company's banner bearer, from his position in the throne next to Champion Hastur.

'Shipmaster Gavorn has been correlating the high marshal's data psalms with auspex scans from the *Wrathful*'s own sensoria, but no, as yet it has been impossible to determine a centralised locale for our enemies' command headquarters,' replied Captain Tor, tilting his head upwards as though to indicate the Imperial Fists strike cruiser that hung far above them in geosynchronous orbit. 'Again, the point is moot at this juncture. I do not intend to launch such a pre-emptive strike.'

'Oh?' Storn's voice sounded carefully neutral to Lydorran's ear. Not for the first time, the Librarian wished that he possessed some modicum of the subtler powers many of his brothers exhibited. He could sense the tremor of an increased heartbeat that indicated excitement or anxiety, could read subtle vibrations in the air when a person spoke that gave him some indication of whether they might be weaving false-hoods, but he had longed more than once for the ability to truly read minds. It was why he devoted what time and study he could to understanding the way those around him thought and acted, both the Adeptus Astartes and the unaugmented humans who made up the majority of the Emperor's servants. Lydorran clove firmly to the belief that insight was as great a weapon as any blade or bolt rifle, and he did his best to hone this addition to his arsenal whenever he could.

'The foe hides behind the planet's populace,' replied Captain Tor. 'I am not above making martyrs of those who cannot be cleared from the crossfire, but it is our duty to shield the worlds of the Imperium, not set them thought-lessly ablaze. Leave such ill-disciplined displays to the Flesh Tearers and their ilk. No, I will fight this war like a true son of Dorn, and that means first securing a stronghold from which to operate. We must be thorough, methodical, and above all we must remember our duty to preserve the infra-structure of this world for the wider Imperial war effort. The strike force will put down at the Mercurio Gate space port atop Hive Angelicus. We will coordinate with the planet's defenders and begin by rooting out any insurgent presence within the hive itself.'

'You suspect foes lurk amongst the loyalists?' asked Lydorran.

'In a war like this, Brother-Librarian, I suspect everyone and everything besides ourselves,' said Tor gravely.

'We secure the upper districts of Hive Angelicus and then work outwards from there?' asked Chaplain Storn.

'Just so,' replied the captain. 'Every street, every highway and maglev and hab-block is to be considered another trench or redoubt in the enemy's defensive network. We will proceed relentlessly, leave no stone unturned, and work outwards and downwards until we are certain that any insurgent presence within the hive has been expunged. I would have naught but loyal servants of the Emperor at my back and a solid fortress to launch my strikes from before I risk committing to actions within the planet's jungles.'

'Brother-captain, with respect, is this strategy not overcautious?' asked Lydorran. 'We could split the strike force, hit half a dozen mine complexes simultaneously and purge the mutant militias within hours of planetfall. *Wrathful* could turn its guns upon what remains of Hive Klaratos and annihilate it from orbit, and all of the heretics it harbours along with it.'

Storn grunted his approval of Lydorran's suggestion.

'For all your nigh-supernatural empathy, you are a man of direct means, brother,' chuckled Captain Tor. 'In the first instance, we cannot be sure of the enemy presence within those mining complexes. I would have substantially more reconnaissance data collected before I plan assaults against the very sites that make this planet so valuable to the Imperium. Between the onslaught of the jungle and our own blindness to the enemy's strength, I assess the risk of collateral damage and excessive losses to be too great. Travel through the empyrean was always risky, but we have seen for ourselves the hellish dangers of warp travel in this new age of nightmares. How long would it take, do you think, to successfully divert enough civilian labourers, craftsmen, adepts and the like to repopulate this planet should we slaughter its people? Would any of them even arrive, or would Ghyre be left as a victorious but hollow shell? Gone are the days when the common herd were the Imperium's most expendable resource, if ever they should have been considered thus. As for Hive Klaratos… Brother, I have fought the Emperor's wars for almost a century and a half. In that time, I have seen good commanders and bad. I have fought alongside heroes, but also been forced to suffer the deeds of zealots and fools. Were Klaratos the fortress of some Iron Warriors tyrant or greenskin warlord then I would erase it from on high without a second's hesitation. It is not. It is an Imperial hive city, and no matter how overrun and beset it may appear now, if we do our duty there may come a day when we see that city restored to glorious Imperial service.'

'Even our own Chapter was once reduced to but a single warrior, and yet now we are the mightiest of all the Adeptus Astartes,' said Chaplain Storn, sounding thoughtful.

'Just so, Brother-Chaplain,' said Captain Tor. 'If we could be so humbled and yet arise again to might and service, so too can Klaratos Hive. When we destroy our own worlds, slaughter our own people, we do our enemies' work for them. That is something that we can ill afford in such dark days as these.'

Lydorran picked up the timbre of absolute certainty in Tor's voice. He felt a fierce loyalty to his captain in that moment.

'I offered hypotheticals only, brother-captain,' he said. 'I agree wholeheartedly.'

'You are a fine naysmith,' replied Tor. 'Yet you see men's hearts also, do you not, Brother-Librarian? I do wonder if you keep some well of telepathic talent hidden away from us within that labyrinthine mind of yours.'

Lydorran smiled slightly behind the faceplate of his helm. He held out his hands as though in admission.

'I swear on the primarch himself that it is not so. I merely observe and do my best to dig down to the deeper meanings before me, just as skilled sappers must properly undermine a curtain wall before they can bring it down. Only in this way are such insights revealed to me. But there is more to your strategy, brother-captain. I believe that you see something more at work here, some hidden influence we do not yet understand, and you are wise enough to avoid plunging headlong into the jaws of a trap.'

'Just so,' said Tor. 'Something is awry on this world beyond the obvious. I will know precisely who we fight, what deity they truly worship and what advantage their debased faith may afford them. As you said, Brother-Chaplain – precision. Let us understand our enemies, that we might weed them out from amongst the common herd they hide behind and exterminate them the swifter.'

And avoid any unpleasant surprises, thought Lydorran. He remembered little of his existence before Archmagos Cawl's laboratories, yet he retained echoes enough to know that the galaxy was a far darker place than it had been in the thirty-sixth millennium. The battle on Osmal II had very nearly spiralled into catastrophe when their foes revealed previously unguessed prophetic abilities bestowed upon them by their daemonic patrons. Captain Tor had shown a newfound caution since that bloody fight; Lydorran would not have been surprised to discover that his friend hoped to find some kind of xenos-worship or techno cult, or perhaps even honest if horribly deluded separatists at work on Ghyre instead of Chaos worshippers.

Privately, he doubted such was the case. Not with the Rift blazing across the skies. Not with half the Imperium lost behind an unassailable veil of nightmares and the remainder fighting the servants of the Archenemy on every front.

'Let it be thus, then, brother-captain,' intoned Storn. 'We shall transform Hive Angelicus into a burning beacon of

Imperial righteousness, and in its light the shadowy secrets of our enemies shall be laid bare. Then we smite them.'

'For the Emperor,' said Captain Tor by way of agreement.

'And for Dorn,' echoed Lydorran, gripping his force stave tight in his right fist.

Thirteen minutes later, a warning chime sounded through the Thunderhawk's troop bay.

'Commencing final approach upon Mercurio Gate space port,' came their pilot's voice.

'Ready yourselves, brothers,' said Captain Tor, addressing not only the warriors in his Thunderhawk but all those aboard the other transport craft and escort gunships swooping down through Ghyre's hard blue skies. His words would even reach those warriors still in orbit, Lydorran knew, inspiring them just as much as those committed to the initial landing. 'This is no normal war we go to fight. The enemy are already within our fortifications, duplicitous and well hidden. We shall be besieged from the moment we land, beset by enemies we cannot see until they strike at us from the shadows of our own bastions. Remember your duty! Do not for an instant relax your guard! Trust only your battle-brothers! Fight for Dorn and the Emperor!'

'For Dorn and the Emperor!' came the chorus of replies over the vox. Lydorran felt something hot and proud stir in his breast.

'Parade disembarkation,' ordered Tor. 'Ancient Tarsun, unfurl the company banner. We aim to remind our allies that their Imperium is mighty and put righteous fear into our foes.' Tor rose from his restraint throne as the Thunderhawk tilted and the tone of its thrusters climbed to a high roar. Bracing himself and mag-locking his boots to the deck, the captain drew his power sword, Sunderer, and adjusted the fall of his cloak so that it spilled down over his shoulder guard. As the Thunderhawk powered in towards the space port, its prow optics fed a vid-stream into the peripheral vision of every Imperial Fists' autosenses. Lydorran rose and took his place at his captain's left shoulder, Storn to his right. At the same time, he watched the vast towers and armoured spires of the hive loom ever closer from the corner of his eye. The skies were a cobalt blue, framing the hive's armoured flanks with their myriad lights, defence turrets and smokestacks. Lydorran noted with a frown that other plumes of smoke rose from the lower hab-levels, telltale signs of the damage caused no doubt by insurgent attacks. Lower still he saw the thick mists of Ghyre's hidden jungles washing up against the hive's mountainous foothills like a softly glowing ocean.

Another chime came from the gunship's voxponders, this one an elaborate choral affair. It was followed by a deep and cultured female voice that filled the troop bay with its natural authority.

'Warriors of the Adeptus Astartes, we are Governor Osmyndri Ellisentris Kallistus the twenty-first, and we bid you welcome to our world. May the Emperor's blessings be upon you for your aid in this dark hour.'

'Governor Kallistus, we bring with us the might and judgement of the Imperium,' said Captain Tor, his voice hard. 'We will begin the purge of the heretic enemies upon making planetfall. You will place your airborne regiments and Arbites at our disposal and aid us in whatever fashion we require.'

If Tor's challenging tone had ruffled the governor, thought Lydorran, her response didn't show it. Lydorran heard no tremor in her voice, neither of falsehood nor of fear. He was impressed. Such a non-reaction from a human was rare indeed.

'Of course, Brother-Captain Tor. An honour guard shall meet you at the space port. All of our military and enforcement resources are at your disposal.'

Tor did not respond, and after a moment a static pop indicated that the link had been cut. Lydorran felt a subtle shift in pressure differentials as the Thunderhawk cycled its atmosphere in preparation to open its boarding ramp. The craft shuddered as the pilots brought it in towards the forest of looming towers, las-turrets, fuel bowsers and huge landing pads that was the space port. Two more Thunderhawks, several armour transporters and multiple wings of escorts descended in formation around them. Servo-skulls and cargo-skiffs flurried like birds put to flight as they scattered from the gunships' flight paths. Ground crews and servitors swarmed towards the chevron-edged landing pad the strike force was descending upon. They jostled with human soldiery in the grey-and-blue livery of the Ghyrish Airborne, the latter forming up into guards of honour at the shouted orders of their superiors. Banners unfurled from the space port towers, Imperial aquilas flapping in the bellicose winds of the upper spire alongside the heraldic crimson spear of Ghyre.

'They are doing their best to make an impression of their own,' commented Chaplain Storn.

'They will have to dispense with the formalities and genuflection swiftly. I wish to be about this,' said Tor. 'Cross-referencing Adeptus Arbites action reports and Ghyrish defence force missives with prime strategic targets, Hive Spire schematics and data prognostication reveals three likely sites of cult activity within Hive Spire district, six more in the Level

Primus. As soon as we have debarked we begin reconnaissance in force and neutralisation of any heretical elements discovered.'

On Lydorran's autosenses, a schematic map of the hive's highest districts flashed with designator runes: an abandoned Imperial shrine huddled in the shadow of a larger and more recent cathedrum; a confluence of service tunnels two levels below the governor's palace; a derelict hangar on the edge of the space port itself, designated for a demolition order that had been rescinded without further explicatory notice.

'So close to the seat of power,' he breathed, shocked despite himself.

'Potential sites only – there may be no cult activity within a dozen levels of Hive Spire,' cautioned Captain Tor. 'We leave nothing to chance. This enemy is insidious. Temporary force designations Prime, Secundus, Tertion, you have your strike coordinates. Chaplain Storn and I shall lead the remainder of the force in securing this space port, the governor's palace, the hive's environmental control shrine and the conclave chambers. We work out and down from there.'

The Thunderhawk touched down with a heavy thump, settling onto its landing gear as debarkation lumen strobed. There came a sharp hiss of depressurisation that caused Ancient Tarsun's banner to tug and flap, then a bright line of daylight limned the ramp as it began to descend. The huge slab of adamantine and ceramite swung smoothly down on heavy hydraulics, meeting the landing pad with a bang, and Captain Tor strode forward. Noise washed over Lydorran as he followed his captain's lead: the pompous notes of a martial band striking up; the cheering of the crowds of well-heeled spire nobles, Grand Clan representatives, clergy and acolytes who thronged beyond the cordon created by the guards of honour; the howl and whine of powerful engines cycling down; and the heavy hiss and thud of servitors as they lumbered forward to attend the machine-spirits of the Space Marines' gunships.

Near the base of the ramp, a tall officer with a dark goatee and a subtly wrought bionic right eye waited. Medals festooned the breast of his brocaded uniform, and Lydorran guessed that he was enjoying his first sight in person of High Marshal Kallistus.

The high marshal kept his expression hard and professional as he stood ramrod straight and saluted Captain Tor with the sign of the aquila. Tor returned the greeting with an inclination of his head, and in that moment Lydorran's attuned senses detected a sudden rush of kinetic energy. Instinctively he grasped for the forces of the warp, his stave crackling with power as he threw up a barrier around himself and his brothers.

He was a split second too late.

Crimson splashed Lydorran's right eye lens. His post-human hearing distinguished, amidst the tumult, the distant crack of a high-powered rifle and, closer, the terrible sound of armour and bone sundering.

Before his eyes, Brother-Captain Ercuros Tor toppled backwards like a felled giant, a neat hole punched through the forehead of his helm, its rear an exploded red ruin.

IV

The mental architecture of the Adeptus Astartes is far superior to that of an unaugmented human. Space Marines' capacity for informational intake, storage and processing is many times that of even the quickest-witted man or woman of the Imperium. Epistolary Lydorran was thus able to watch High Marshal Kallistus' eyes widen and his expression contort in horror, to see the men and women around him stare in confusion, to begin calculating in his mind the angle and trajectory of the sniper's shot, to register the tactical disposition and readiness of his battle-brothers to face combat and to maintain the effort of will required to manifest and control the shield of geokinetic energy that he had raised in an attempt to confound the attacker's shot.

He was able to do all of this even as the greater part of his consciousness processed the sight of the only man he called friend die suddenly in front of him.

'Enemy contact, shots fired. Captain Tor has fallen!' he barked into the strike force vox-channel. 'Apothecary Lordas, attend the captain.'

He had been too slow. He had failed Tor. The two thoughts chased each other through Lydorran's mind even as he kept the shield shimmering around himself, around Storn and Lordas and Ancient Tarsun and Champion Hastur.

'Combat dispersal. Secure perimeter and locate sniper,' snapped Chaplain Storn. 'Escorts, dust off. Establish combat airspace perimeter.'

Engines that had been rumbling down into quiescence now howled anew. Servitors and crew serfs staggered back, some struck by wingtips or landing gear, or caught in blasts of jetwash as squadrons of Stormtalon gunships thundered back into the sky.

Squads of Imperial Fists stormed from their boarding ramps and took up firing positions with bolters and bolt rifles raised. Aggressors strode menacingly out onto the landing pad, scattering frightened citizenry before them. Dreadnoughts stomped behind them, the ancients within their sarcophagi bellowing angry oaths.

The command squad's Apothecary, Lordas, was crouched beside Captain Tor's twitching form. Lydorran already knew what he would say. Even Space Marine physiology couldn't sustain that sort of head wound and remain operational. Lordas might save the captain's body, but Tor had been neatly trepanned by the shot.

'No brain activity detected,' said Lordas, confirming Lydorran's thoughts with a sweep of his narthecium's scanners. 'His humours remain stilled. There is nothing I can do for him. He has already gone.'

Panic spread through the crowd like an epidemic as they realised what had happened. Some ducked, casting about as though the assailant might be aiming straight at them. Some fled, making for the edge of the space port and the processionals and towers of the Hive Spire beyond. Others simply stood in wide-eyed shock, screamed in horror or fell to their knees in prayer. The Ghyrish soldiery wavered, some attempting to control the crowd, some swinging their lasguns up and seeking the shooter. Some pushed forward to surround the high marshal with their bodies, even as the terrified masses surged and shoved at them. Some detached part of Lydorran noted with approval that not a woman or man amongst them attempted to run.

The din was tremendous, worsening by the moment. Lydorran looked down at his captain, dead on the boarding ramp, then around at his battle-brothers. Though all went helmed and faceless as per their late captain's orders, the Librarian thought he felt a shared moment of understanding between them all the same.

With a twist of his mind he allowed his kinetic shield to collapse. There had been no second shot. One had been enough.

He had been too slow.

Lydorran brushed the self-recrimination aside. Failure merited penance through pain, but never at the expense of combat efficacy. Instead of useless doubt, Lydorran embraced the cold fury that welled up inside him at the sight of his fallen friend.

That he could use.

'High marshal, control your soldiery. Clear these crowds and establish a perimeter around the space port,' he boomed, his vox-amplified voice cutting through the furore. Kallistus looked stunned, whether from shock or at being spoken to in such a manner Lydorran didn't know. The man hesitated, mouth gaping. 'Now!' thundered Lydorran, and High Marshal Kallistus cringed before turning to obey the Librarian's commands.

'The assassin will be making good their escape,' said Chaplain Storn.

'They will not succeed,' said Lydorran, his anger lending a bladed edge to his words. He switched to the strike force command channel. 'I am rescinding previous orders. All brothers planetside divide your strength to reinforce strike designations Primus, Secundus and Tertion. Combat advance on all sites. Rouse your auspexes, brothers, and seek out the cowardly vermin that gunned down Captain Tor. Shipmaster Gavorn, beseech the *Wrathful*'s sensor banks to aid our search. The enemy will not make us look weak at the very moment of our arrival!'

Lydorran realised Storn, Tarsun, Lordas and Hastur were all looking at him.

'Do you not concur, brothers?' he asked.

'It is Chaplain Storn's right to command, for he is most veteran,' said Champion Hastur.

'We must act with swift decision,' added Tarsun, though Lydorran could not tell whether the Ancient spoke in support of himself or Hastur.

'We must answer this insult with uncompromising wrath,' said Storn, and in his gravelly voice Lydorran heard an echo of his own outrage. 'Epistolary Lydorran, I concur. We follow your commands.'

'Brother-Chaplain?' asked Champion Hastur, his voice tinged with surprise and anger.

'Our enemy is insidious in nature, heretical in thought and deed. This much Brother-Captain Tor suspected and confided to me. To battle such a foe requires keen insight and empyric abilities of our own. Epistolary Lydorran possesses both.'

'And yet those very powers were not enough to save the

brother-captain's life,' Hastur retorted, his words swelling to a heated shout.

'An omission that I am sure Lydorran will shrive himself for, and never allow to happen again,' Storn growled. 'Meanwhile, Chapter Champion, you persist in challenging the decisions of the very officer whose operational authority you are so quick to assert. Now, shall we argue like fools in front of the people of this world at a moment when we most need to show strength, or will you still your tongue and honour your primarch through deeds?'

Hastur bristled. Lydorran felt the rapid thumping of the Champion's twin hearts as he fought to control his anger. Storn made a show of taking Hastur's silence as acquiescence and pressed on.

'Gavorn, furnish us with an Emperor's-eye view. Where are the cowards lurking?' he asked over his vox.

'Shipboard cogitators have triangulated the origin of the shot to the venting towers on the western edge of the space port,' came the voice of Shipmaster Gavorn. 'Retrotemporal auspex augury reveals a single contact moving away from the site at speed. Rappelling line or possibly a grav-chute will allow them to reach ground level, at which point they will take to a light vehicle of some sort.'

'Do you have their current location?' asked Lydorran. Around him, the warriors and war engines of Strike Force Tor were surging into motion, forming up and moving out as the surging crowds fled before them. Lydorran didn't need empathic powers to feel their outrage, their shared anger roused into a deadly storm. Their foes had no idea what terrors they had unleashed upon themselves with that single shot.

'Confirmed, Brother-Librarian. Inloading to your autosenses now,' replied the shipmaster. A flashing crimson rune appeared in

Lydorran's field of vision. With a blink-click he brought up a schematic map of Hive Spire and saw that the sniper was moving fast along the Angelicum Prime Processional.

'They are making for the towers of the spire core,' said Lordas, consulting the same data. 'Logic suggests they have a route of egress there.'

'No,' said Lydorran simply. 'Brothers, lead the assault forces to their locations and purge all cultists you find. I will deal with the sniper.'

'By yourself?' asked Apothecary Lordas.

'I am sufficient,' said Lydorran, certain that his battle-brothers would not require his perceptive abilities to hear the need for vengeance in his voice. This act of atonement fell to him alone.

'Even with your Primaris physique you will not catch them on foot,' said Storn.

'No,' said Lydorran again, and despatched a runic summons. A moment later the roar of powerful engines filled the air and an Outrider sergeant skidded his bike to a halt beside the Thunderhawk's ramp.

'Sergeant Ullas, will you permit me your steed?' asked Lydorran. The Outrider slammed one fist against his chest-plate and slid from his saddle. Mag-locking his force stave to his back, Lydorran took the sergeant's place.

'My thanks, brother,' he said, and gunned the Primaris bike's throttle. He felt the sleek vehicle surge beneath him, and then he was speeding out along the cargoway through the scattering remnants of the formerly jubilant crowds. Landing pads, fuel bowsers and towers flashed past on either side, and his brothers receded behind him.

'Catch them, Lydorran. Make an example of them, for your sake and ours,' came Chaplain Storn's voice on a private channel

as Lydorran sped towards the arched gates of the space port, the elegant towers of Hive Spire rearing high before him.

'I will, Brother-Chaplain, for Tor,' he replied, then cut the link and concentrated upon the flashing crimson rune that marked his quarry.

Lydorran raced along a broad processional, gaining upon his quarry. Magnificent spire towers rose on either side of him, aquilas and clan emblems fluttering proudly on pennants that flew from their glittering peaks. Beautifully worked lumen poles and actual living trees lined the walkways to either side of the processional, while its central reservation was dotted with marble statues that whipped past in a blur.

The first moments upon leaving the space port had been a trial of patience for Lydorran as the great and good of Hive Angelicus scattered before him in a panic. He had been forced to weave through gaggles of wailing clergy and adepts, swerve around mechanical walking-litters whose opulently clad passengers gaped at him in dumbfounded shock, and try to avoid running down dozens of minor dignitaries, mining clan nobles, bellowing Arbites and assorted others.

Even upon reaching the processionals, where foot and vehicular traffic was blessedly segregated by shimmering energy barriers, Lydorran was forced to jink left and right to avoid expensive-looking groundcars, crawler-barques and the armoured transports of the hive Arbites. Then air raid hymnals had begun to blare from gilded laud hailers, and in response the herds of Hive Angelicus had scattered for shelter.

Whoever had given *that* order, Lydorran made a mental note to commend them later. His frustration had grown as he saw the crimson rune pulling away from him and into the fringes of the spire core. Now, with the processionals clearing by the moment, he was able to open his armoured steed up and streak along his enemy's trail like a bullet.

Lydorran leaned forward over the bike's handlebars, minimising his bulky silhouette as much as he could to lessen drag. He passed through a tunnel that took the processional beneath a towering cathedrum, arc-lumen strobing overhead as he sped down its length. Frescoes of Imperial heroes and mighty victories covered the tunnel's walls, but their artistry was lost to him in the blur of his speed. Lydorran burst from the tunnel between a pair of towering statues of Saint Calipus, wove his bike between several ornate groundcars whose occupants stared at him as he shot past, and then followed the rune down a sweeping ramp and onto a lower processional. The blinking rune was dead ahead now, beyond the next intersection and back up a sweeping spiral onto a higher carriageway. He should see his quarry in moments.

'Assault Force Primus, contact with insurgent cell,' came Chaplain Storn's voice over the command channel. The hard bang of bolters and the rattle of autoguns could be heard behind his transmission.

'Assault Force Tertion, contact at abandoned hangar also,' reported Champion Hastur. *'Caution, brothers. The foe here were few, but entry to the structure triggered multiple traps. Several battle-brothers compromised. Seventeen Ghyrish dead or wounded. Cowardly heretic filth.'*

Two of the three sites confirmed, thought Lydorran, not to mention the audacious strike at Captain Tor. Just how far had the rot of this cult spread?

His bike left the ground as he reached the crest of the spiral ramp, its armoured tyres slamming back down on ferrocrete and propelling him forward again.

'Visual contact with sniper at these coordinates,' he reported over the command channel, then thumbed the arming runes of his bike's twin bolt rifles in readiness.

The sniper vanished for a moment as they wove around a racing mass transporter. As they emerged again into his field of vision, the Librarian had unobstructed view of his prey at last. She rode a lightweight model of motorbike with bulky suspension and what appeared to be custom modifications to its engine; a fragment of the information Lydorran had inloaded about Ghyre told him that these vehicles were predominately used by the lesser mining clans as a swift if not especially safe method of traversing the jungle roadways. The garb she wore also resembled a miner's utility suit, vulcanised and hung with clip harnesses and webbing. However, he noted that a number of flak plates had been attached to it in order to transform worker's clothing into something altogether more resistant to weapon-spirits' wrath.

Strapped across her back was a long-snouted sniper rifle of a configuration that Lydorran didn't recognise.

The weapon that took Captain Tor's life.

The sight of it sent a fresh wave of loathing rolling through him, though at himself or the assassin he couldn't tell.

Lips curling back into a snarl, Lydorran squeezed the bike's throttle and goaded more speed out of his steed. He bent his geokinetic powers to aid him, fashioning a sweeping prow of kinetic force before the bike to part the air and allow it to leap forward all the swifter. The sniper's goggles flashed with reflected sunlight as she shot a glance back at him, then she hunched over her handlebars and concentrated on the processional ahead.

Muttering a benediction to the weapons' machine-spirits, Lydorran pressed the triggers built into his bike's handlebars and sent a volley of bolt shells whipping towards the sniper. She swerved past a silvery groundcar, her reactions remarkable in an unaugmented human, and the bolts rocketed over her shoulder harmlessly. The manoeuvre had cost her speed, though, and Lydorran found himself drawing closer still. He marshalled a portion of his powers, intending to tear up a section of the ferrocrete roadway before his quarry and cause her to collide with it at killing speed. Yet Lydorran felt a tingle in the back of his mind, the telltale whisper of silk across his senses that warned him of another psyker's mind at work. He snarled. The sniper glanced back again as though forewarned of his plans. Taking one hand from the handlebars, she grabbed something bulky from a satchel at her side, thumbed a switch and then deftly let the object fall in her wake.

Lydorran registered the flashing warning runes and las-sealed canister cells of the mining charge as it bounced towards him. He threw his bike into a hard swerve and poured the empyric energies he had marshalled into throwing up a kinetic barrier between himself and the explosion. The charge detonated with ferocious force. Fire licked at Lydorran's armour and the flank of his bike. Whickering ferrocrete shrapnel pinged from his shoulder guard while the battering ram shockwave of the explosion threatened to pitch him from the saddle. If he hadn't raised his shield when he had…

The Librarian hung on to the handlebars and kept his steed level. Behind him he heard the howl of brakes and the terrible impacts as drivers of haulers and groundcars failed to evade the blast.

Ahead, the sniper had pulled away again, though she had to know her lead was only temporary. The processional curved lazily to the left, and Lydorran leaned into the bend, flashing past another lumbering hauler and gaining on his prey. They were climbing steadily now, curving around the flanks of the immense Administratum offices that rose like a mountain of stone and plasteel to loom over the spire core.

'Brother-Librarian, be warned – the processional fractures ahead,' came Shipmaster Gavorn's voice over the vox. 'There is a transit-shrine with several dozen interlinked roadways, many proceeding downhive into Level Primus and the Commercias District.'

If his quarry was able to lose herself amidst the tangle ahead, it was possible she could shake the shipmaster's orbital surveillance and Lydorran's pursuit at a stroke. The Librarian thought fast.

'Gavorn, contact the Arbites precinct fortress and command them to shut down the transit-shrine,' he ordered. 'Have them rouse all servitor guns and forbid passage to all.'

'At once, Brother-Librarian,' replied the shipmaster. There would be resistance to the command, Lydorran knew. Even in the midst of a war of insurgency, even at the command of the Emperor's own Adeptus Astartes, the lawmakers of this world would hesitate at the notion of curtailing movement into and out of the prestigious Hive Spire. There would be outrage, and quite possibly civilian casualties as the servo-guns activated. At that moment he did not care, so long as the Arbites followed his order and prevented Tor's killer from slipping away.

The processional swept over a gilded bridge beneath which a man-made chasm of structures dropped away into hazy gloom. The map in Lydorran's autosenses told him that the roadway would drop down between the Cathedrum Sanctificat and the shrine to Saint Meticula in less than a mile, and thence feed into the gaping throat of the transit-shrine. He was gaining on his prey again, the two of them weaving in and out of slower-moving vehicles so closely that the collision warning chimes in Lydorran's autosenses had become a constant drone. The mass of vehicles made it near impossible for him to employ his powers, at least not without triggering mayhem that might as easily work in his prey's favour as his. Lydorran wasn't closing quickly enough, though. If the local authorities were going to obey his command, it had to be now.

The Librarian felt a stab of triumph as warning runes lit up on holoboards flanking the processional. Skeletal servitors built into the bridge's superstructure unfolded mechanical limbs, their ocular lumen flashing red as their stubber-arrays armed. A blaring voice echoed from cherubim and the voxponders of hovering servo-skulls.

'CITIZENRY, BY COMMAND OF THE ADEPTUS ARBITES AND IN THE EMPEROR'S HOLY NAME, PROHIBUM IMMEDIATE. RENDER YOUR VEHICULAR MACHINE-SPIRITS QUIESCENT AND AWAIT FURTHER ILLUMINATION.'

The booming message repeated again and again. Cowed by the threat of the servitor guns and a lifetime of indoctrinated obedience, the drivers of the groundcars and cargo haulers slowed, and as they did so, the flow of vehicular traffic thickened like blood clotting in an artery. Lydorran pushed his bike between two groundcars, its armoured cowling striking sparks from the vehicles as it shouldered them aside. He gave the two vehicles a nudge with his powers, causing them to skid sideways away from him and thump heavily into the transports to either side. Ahead he saw his quarry skid as a macro transporter rumbled to a halt directly in her path. She managed to slide into the vehicle's rear side-on, but still the sudden impact was violent enough to spill her from her saddle. The sniper vanished as the groundcar behind her skidded to a halt, and for a moment Lydorran feared his quarry had met an unsatisfying end beneath the vehicle's wheels.

Unable to force his bike further through the press of traffic, the Librarian muttered a swift benediction to render his steed's machine-spirit quiescent then brought it to a halt and jumped from the saddle onto the groundcar before him. His booted feet left deep indents in the vehicle's roof as he crossed it in a stride and leapt to the machine ahead of it. He bounded again with servo-assisted strength and caught hold of the crawl handles on the side of a promethium tanker. Lydorran pulled himself up onto the hulking vehicle's spine and ran along its length. He kept part of his attention on the roused servitor guns, whose barrels were tracking his motion as though unsure whether he was a threat to be fired upon.

There, he thought as he saw movement to his left. She was still on the move, scrambling out from beneath another groundcar like an arachnid, spinning and–

The crack of the sniper's rifle sounded loud even over the rumble of dozens of engines. The shot was rushed, but still it hit Lydorran in his midriff, hard enough that it felt as though someone had swung a thunder hammer into his gut. The Librarian grunted in pain and, grasping for the energies of the immaterium, hurled a blast of raw geokinetic force back at her.

Groundcar windows shattered and exploded. Cracks raced through the ferrocrete and the sniper flung herself desperately aside as the patch of roadway where she knelt erupted like a geyser of stone. There came a cacophony of binharic shrieks and the servitor guns opened fire. Some directed hails of bullets towards the cultist. Some chose Lydorran as their target, and impacts rang from his Mark X armour. Shots punched into stationary vehicles as they flew wide of their targets. Viewscreens crazed with cracks and were misted red by sudden sprays of gore as the occupants were hit.

Lydorran dropped from the flank of the promethium tanker

lest the mindless gun-servitors trigger an explosive fireball. To his amazement he saw that the sniper was still up, running hard for the edge of the bridge. Puffs of ferrocrete dust chased her heels as the gun-servitors followed her motion. Amidst the cacophony of gunfire and screams, Lydorran breathed a word of denial and amazement.

'No...'

The sniper reached the edge of the bridge and, without so much as breaking stride, launched herself into space. Lydorran followed her, pounding across the intervening gap, bullets whining from his armour. He threw himself from the brink and saw his prey below him, her descent slowed by a crude grav-chute module that sparked and glowed at her belt, her sniper rifle still clutched awkwardly in one hand as she attempted to lean in the direction of the lip of the artificial canyon. Soaring like a wounded pterasquirrel, the sniper cleared the brink and crashed down amidst the ornamented tangle of a balcony garden.

Lydorran fell like a stone. His leap had carried him out across the void, but he could already see that he would fall short of the edge by several feet.

'Throne,' he gasped as the bottom of his stomach dropped out and the metalwork tangle of the chasm wall rushed past his face.

He hit hard and managed to grab hold of a nest of pipes that wound up the flank of a generatorum shrine. Snarling with frustration, Lydorran scaled the mechanical cliff hand over hand, ripping jutting metal handholds from bare plasteel with his mind where they were lacking. The cultist would not escape him, even if he had to chase her through the entire Throne-damned hive city.

The fingers of one gauntlet curled over the brink of the

chasm, then the other. Lydorran hauled himself upwards, then dropped again as a bullet sparked from the chasm's lip barely an inch from his helm.

'Throne *almighty*!' he snapped. The quarry was persistent. He might have admired her, had she not been a murdering heretic insurgent. Instead, Lydorran conjured a kinetic barrier about himself and hauled upwards again. Another shot whipped in and sparked from his psychic shield instead of punching through his helm and into his brain.

'Heretic, cease your fruitless flight!' he roared. 'Face righteous vengeance with some honour!'

The cultist ripped off her goggles and cast them aside. Her eyes glinted yellow and black in the hard daylight. Her auburn hair flew in the winds that rushed up from the hive chasm, and her features were subtly altered from the human norm, clearly mutated in some fashion. Her expression twisted in angry defiance. The blood that ran from savage tears in her utility suit was a deep mauve, almost black.

'You are the ones without honour, Imperial oppressor!' she spat, and in that moment Lydorran felt, both through his powers and the sheer raw emotion in her voice, that she truly believed in the righteousness of her cause. 'You are the heretics!' With that, she grabbed a second blasting charge from her satchel and flung it at him, limping across the roof garden towards a nearby doorway as she did.

Lydorran twisted his mind and his kinetic field swept up and outwards. He struck the charge aside with the force of his will and sent it spinning away to detonate harmlessly in mid-air. Three swift strides brought him up behind the wounded sniper, who, realising she wasn't going to make the doorway, spun awkwardly and tried to raise her rifle. The Librarian backhanded the weapon aside and sent it spinning away into the bushes. His other hand pistoned out, catching the sniper around the throat. He hoisted her effortlessly into the air, her hands scrabbling for purchase on his ceramite gauntlet to no avail.

'Brothers,' Lydorran voxed across the strike force's command channel. As he did so, he fed the visuals from his autosenses to every other Imperial Fist on Ghyre. 'Vengeance.' Then, with a twist of his fingers, he snapped the sniper's neck.

He let the corpse thump to the ground and slowed his breathing. Lydorran looked down upon the sniper as she lay upon the old pathway through the garden, one arm thrown out into an overgrown tumble of flowers, her inhuman eyes glassy. She was no threat to anyone now. Still, he felt a complex spill of emotions as he stood over the corpse and listened to the cacophonous bells of the Cathedrum Sanctificat pealing out the hour. She had fought hard, exhibiting a determination and stubbornness that he was forced to respect. She had looked at him with the hatred and revulsion that one reserves for the truly monstrous, and he had sensed the certainty of righteousness in her. Yet she was a mutant, a cultist and an insurgent, whether the product of unholy worship or some foul alien influence Lydorran did not know.

'Perhaps the Apothecaries will be able to determine more,' he mused, and reached down to sweep up the corpse of his enemy and sling it easily over one shoulder. Then, deeply troubled by all that had transpired, Lydorran sent out a runic summons for a gunship to attend him at his location. As he waited he listened to the action reports of his battle-brothers flashing through the vox-net, and his disquiet grew.

There was much to be done here, Lydorran thought, and so much they didn't know.

V

'One hundred and sixteen dead. Three hundred and fifty-two injured. Clerks, adepts, merchants, artisans, clan nobles... The list goes on.' The voice of High Administrator Lunst was sharp as a whip-crack. Her every syllable dripped disapproval. 'Disruption to processional transit routes and the flow of goods and service throughout Commercias, Level Primus and Hive Spire has been and continues to be disastrous. The fiscal impact alone of this... campaign of terror cannot be swiftly calculated. I must object to the conclave in the strongest possible terms!'

'Additional – primary routes of transfer for refined ore from Aquisitorius to the Orbitas Industrial Docks have been severely disrupted,' chimed in Magos Gathabosis. 'Though the Imperial Fists have been present upon Ghyre for less than three days sidereal, I have cogitated that their ongoing martial operations have already led to a forty-two per cent drop in enderrium ore export per rotation standard.'

'My arbitrators have been reduced to little more than servitors, attempting to keep pace with the *whims* of these Space

Marines,' barked First Arbitrator Verol. 'How can we maintain an effective grip upon law and order within Hive Angelicus if our authority is ignored and overruled at every turn?'

Lydorran stood in the lower chamber of the Ghyrish conclave and listened to the furore above. The voices echoed down to him, each speaker more eager than the last to make clear the dreadful nature of their grievances, to highlight the outrageous disruption caused by the arrival of the Adeptus Astartes. *Would they be so forthright if they realised that we stood below, listening?* he wondered.

'Pampered fools,' growled Chaplain Storn. He and Apothecary Lordas had accompanied Lydorran to the conclave chambers, leaving a squad of Intercessor battle-brothers to secure the structure's entrances and approaches against possible assault. He supposed the building's defences had seemed adequate to the Ghyrish, but then perhaps that explained why they were losing this war so badly.

'They stand aloof, isolated from the people they profess to rule and more concerned with maintaining the illusion of control, of normalcy, than with doing what must be done,' replied Lydorran, subvocalising to avoid being overheard by those in the chamber above. 'They are frightened. They are only human.'

'They will not act to cut out the canker that is claiming their world, but instead rail against those with the strength to do so,' muttered Storn. 'It is an insult to the noble sons of Dorn. Do these fools not understand who we are, what we have come here to do?' He made to stride forward, but Lydorran placed a firm hand on his arm to hold him back.

'Doubtful,' replied the Librarian. 'Most of them have only known Space Marines as an oath-sworn honour guard, a handful of battle-brothers bound by an ancient pledge to aid and protect the ruler of this world. They have not seen us free to act as we should.'

'They are in for a most unpleasant surprise,' said Storn, his white brows drawing down in a frown that tightened every scar on his face. Still, he allowed himself to be held back from storming straight into the upper chamber.

'Not yet, though, Brother-Chaplain,' said Lydorran, releasing Storn with a grateful nod. 'There is a reason I commanded the chamber adepts not to herald our arrival. Let them speak a while longer. We know of these people, recognise their voices and titles, only from strategic inload – I would hear them speak unguarded. I would learn a little more of them.'

'Let us not lurk too long, then,' said Storn, sounding unconvinced. 'Tarsun's latest report confirms we've secured Mercurio Gate as our base of operations, neutralised four nests of insurgents already and commenced the late captain's projected pattern of expanding sweep-and-clear patrols. If all goes as the primarch wills, we'll have Hive Spire secured within two days. We should be out there leading and coordinating our brothers' efforts, not dallying here with fops and politicians.'

'Peace, Brother-Chaplain. I understand,' said Lydorran.

'Do you?' asked Storn. 'I wonder… You are Primaris, which sets you apart in the eyes of the more conservative warriors you now command, and you are a psyker, which separates you from all of us. Our brothers loved their captain. Many of them do not even know you. You will earn their respect on the battle-lines, not here. And mark my words, Lydorran, you will *need* their respect if we are to win this, and we *need* you to win it. This is not a normal war – Tor saw that, and so do I. Do not make me regret supporting you in this.'

Lydorran shot a hard look at Storn.

'I know of their battles. I have fought alongside them. If

you believe me such an unfit candidate, Brother-Chaplain, why did you follow my lead at the space port on the day we landed? Hastur is not the only one who thinks it should be you, not I, issuing the orders. I do not wholly disagree with him myself.'

'I did not say I believed you unfit, Aster,' replied Storn, his expression unreadable.

'Brothers, for men attempting to listen you speak a great deal,' commented Apothecary Lordas. 'Perhaps you both need another tour of service with the Tenth?'

Lydorran scowled, wanting to press Storn further about his words but knowing Lordas was correct. He had already been aware of the prejudices that even his brother Space Marines were not above, both towards witches and towards the comparative newcomers amongst their ranks. Dorn's sons were traditionalists, stiff-necked and slow to change; all that, he could accept about his comrades, even respect them for. But Storn, of all people, knew the mood and temperament of the battle-brothers he served alongside. That was his role. And by all conventions of tradition and Codex, the Chaplain should have shouldered the mantle of command. So why, instead, had he pushed Lydorran to take up the reins only to hint darkly to him of his apparent unsuitability?

Frustrated, Lydorran took his concerns about Chaplain Storn and thrust them aside into the same dark space in which his grief for Tor festered. Both would have to be addressed soon enough, but for now he needed to focus.

'...ordered me around like a common soldier!' High Marshal Kallistus was saying, clearly shocked. 'I mean, I understand the authority they command... the power of them...' His voice trailed off for a moment, and Lydorran thought that at least here was one who understood the nature of Dorn's sons a little better.

'Did you have a point to make to the conclave, high marshal?' asked Administrator Lunst, her voice arch. 'Perhaps you were going to explain why our own Ghyrish soldiery are still malingering in their barracks and fortifications while what appears to be open warfare erupts in the city's most valuable districts?'

'If these Adeptus Astartes intend to rampage thusly when they reach our mine complexes, I might question whether their help is really *help* at all!' came a shrill voice that Lydorran identified as belonging to Clan Lord Torphin Lo VanSappen. 'I for one might feel safer were they never to set foot within a hundred miles of VanSappenmine.'

Again, Storn tensed, made to move. Again, Lydorran shook his head, and the Chaplain glowered at him.

'Much as you yourself have singularly failed to do since the fall of Mastracha Hive!' barked Lady Alamica of Clan Tectos. 'You should look to your own affairs before casting aspersions upon the Angels of the Emperor!'

'You know very well, Lady Tectos, that the catastrophe at Mastracha has cut VanSappenmine off from Hive Angelicus altogether!' exclaimed Lord VanSappen. 'One cannot approach within fifty miles of the hive's ruins without being exposed to the biopurge contaminant, and the secondary routes–'

'You're too damned cowardly to–' interrupted Lord Dostos of Clan Delve, but VanSappen overrode him, his voice climbing another octave or so in the process.

'*The secondary routes*, while suitable to maintain at least a token contribution to the ore tithe from my clan, are altogether unsafe and predated by both jungle and insurgents

alike! I would be little use to my great clan were I to be
strung up by separatists… or… or swallowed by a dripfrond!'

There came the visceral sound of someone spitting, a couple of soft intakes of breath at the vulgar display, then Lord
Delve spoke again.

'If it pleases the conclave, Lord VanSappen might be a
coward, but sometimes it takes a fearful man to speak the
truth. I have seen vid-capture of these Space Marines at
work, and I submit to the conclave that they are less saviours
than they are–'

'I would not finish that sentence, were I you,' came a
new voice, this one soft and calm yet with sufficient steel
to stop Lord Delve in his tracks. Lydorran searched his
eidetic memory and came up with the man's name and
vocal imprint – Bishop Lotimer Renwyck, the voice of the
Emperor's faith upon Ghyre.

Lord Delve began to bluster something, but Renwyck
cut him off, still speaking at little more than a murmur
but managing to fill the conclave chambers with his words
nonetheless.

'Were one to speak so ill of the Imperial Fists Space Marine
Chapter, they who are liken unto the Angels of the Emperor
himself, that soul might imperil themselves with accusations of the most grievous heresy both of thought and of
word. You would not wish to run such a risk, would you,
Lord Delve?'

'I… Of course I would not. I am no heretic!' replied Lord
Delve, his reply sounding a little strangled. 'But… I mean
only to say that the method by which they have conducted
themselves since their arrival–'

'Has been only the beginning,' finished Lydorran, striding
up the ramp and allowing the voxponder in his armour's

gorget to amplify his words to a solemn boom. He sensed heartbeats quicken in alarm, tasted the tang of adrenaline and fear sweat spiking in the air as the dignitaries' entourages quailed and huddled close to one another. Lydorran came to a halt at the centre of the upper chamber's wide circular floorspace. He tilted his head back and looked up at the regal figure of Governor Kallistus XXI where she sat enthroned high above the gathering. She looked back with steely grey eyes, her gaze unwavering even as her elderly seneschal goggled at him in alarm.

'Ghyre has failed in the eyes of the Imperium. In the eyes of the Emperor himself,' barked Lydorran. 'Two of your three hive cities are lost. Many of your planet's mines have become hotbeds of insurrection. Those that remain are overrun, by the jungle or your own rebellious subjects. The worship of false deities, the rot of rebellion and heresy, spreads its tendrils through your people. Your Arbites and planetary defence regiments between them could not even secure our landing zone such that we could debark and begin operations without losing a valued hero of the Chapter to one of *your* people wielding a weapon made on *your* world.' Lydorran let a flash of real anger show through at this last point, his voice rising to batter the gathered delegates.

Let them understand who we are, what we are, he thought. *Let them realise that we represent a power that stands above their petty squabbles.*

'By all rights, we could have bombed your world into naught but smouldering glass,' added Chaplain Storn, glowering around at the assembled conclave. 'Understand that we did not discard this option because we are merciful.'

'We are the living weapons of the Emperor,' continued Lydorran, speaking into the conclave's shocked silence. 'We answer the distress call our battle-brothers died to send. Our mission is to reclaim the infrastructure of this world, to eradicate all traces of false faith and to restore the planet's proper function. Understand me. It is less than nothing to us whether you approve of our methods, or whether handfuls of alleged innocents are caught amidst the crossfire of a war that *you* have permitted to spread within your walls. We do not care about your short-term quotas. We do not care about your sense of authority. We do not care about your politics. We do not care about you. This world is one bulwark within the Bastion Imperialis. We care only that its defences are shored, that its garrison is cleansed and that it is restored in its capacity to serve and protect the wider Imperium and ultimately the Throneworld itself. Do I make myself clear, Governor Kallistus?'

Silence reigned in the conclave chambers for a full three double-beats of Lydorran's twin hearts. Governor Kallistus continued to look imperiously down upon him, the picture of regal composure. He imagined how he must look to her, small from such a height yet still a giant, his bald and tattooed pate threaded with the wires of his psychic hood, his massive armour thrumming with quiet power. He supposed people normally looked cowed when they stood where he did now, and he wondered whether privately the governor revelled in her position of power over such supplicants or whether, like the Adeptus Astartes themselves, she merely accepted it as a facet of her function within the wider Imperium.

Slowly, Governor Kallistus struck her stave and pick together with a resounding clang. The sound echoed down to stillness before she spoke.

'We understand your position...'

'Epistolary Lydorran, governor,' Lydorran supplied, his voice still stern.

'We understand your position, Epistolary Lydorran. Indeed, you have made it quite inescapably clear. We would have you understand ours. Ghyre is a loyal world that has spent years uncounted offering up its tithe without fail. Prime Clan Kallistus has ruled over this world for more than ten centuries, and we have in person overseen the governorship of Ghyre for the last one hundred and sixteen of those years. Since despatching our distress call, we have fought a most shocking and impossible war against a tenacious and unnatural foe that has turned our loyal subjects into unrecognisable heretics. It is a war that has cost us much, and yet you speak to us as though we have malingered in incompetence for the entire duration of the conflict. We have lost much.' She glanced down at the empty thrones of her fellow spire lords, Agnathio Trost and Renshi Hal. 'We would have you understand the worth, strength and piety of this world and its people, Epistolary Lydorran. We would have the Adeptus Astartes approach us as allies and fight alongside us from a position of mutual respect.'

'We do not require the respect of the Ghyrish, governor,' answered Lydorran. 'We require them only to understand that we will do what we must to save this world, and that any who oppose or hinder us are our enemies. Is this clear?'

'It is,' replied Kallistus, her tone cold. He caught, then, the telltale tremor in her voice that revealed the tightly reined anger of one unused to being spoken to in such a fashion. Yet something else lay beneath it, another substrata he could barely feel – the slowly blossoming fear of realisation.

'Then we have an understanding,' said Lydorran. He turned sharply and marched from the chamber, Storn and Lordas at his heels. Behind him, for the first time in many years at the Ghyrish conclave, utter silence reigned.

Within an hour of departing the conclave chambers, Lydorran was aboard a gunship amidst his battle-brothers, en route to the next purge site. The armoured craft thundered through the arc-lit night, passing between glittering cathedrum spires and swooping past the mountainous flanks of clan palaces that glimmered with thousands of lumen.

Apothecary Lordas sat on the restraint throne opposite Lydorran, poring over a data-slate. Lydorran himself had used a portion of the journey to refocus his mind through meditation, resting his mental faculties and regathering the strength he needed to wield and control his powers. The burden of command was exhausting, he reflected. He had not truly appreciated Captain Tor's logistical abilities before now.

'Appraise me,' he said to Lordas. A fellow Primaris battle-brother, Lordas had blocky features and close-cropped blond hair, and already boasted several scars that bespoke his commitment to tending the wounded, even under intense enemy fire. Now he looked at Lydorran over the top of the data-slate and quirked an eyebrow.

'Am I to be your seneschal now, Brother-Librarian?' he asked. Lydorran heard the note of wry humour in his brother's voice but was in no mood for it. He replied with a flat stare and held out one hand for the data-slate. Instead of passing it to him, Lordas chuckled and shook his head.

'Fortification of Mercurio Gate is now concluded. The Techmarines have overseen the raising of fifteen prefabricated bastion towers around the space port circumference, with a full spread of walls, and stab lumen and artillery trenches to their rear. They have sequestered a number of adjoining structures for subsidiary support. Squad Hathlor have taken garrison duties and have co-opted a demi-regiment of Ghyrish soldiery to fill the gaps.'

'What of the conclave chambers, the governor's palace and the hive's environmental shrine?' asked Lydorran, referring to the other sites that Captain Tor's plan had designated as priority strongpoints.

'Work proceeds apace,' replied Lordas, quickly scanning the data-slate. 'In addition, Techmarine Asphor has surveyed the defences around the spire core transit hub and primary turbolift sanctums connecting Hive Spire to Level Primus, Commercias and Orbitas districts.'

Lydorran snorted mirthlessly.

'He'll have found them all sorely wanting, no doubt,' he said. 'I almost feel sorry for whatever Ghyrish officers are in charge there.'

'He has indeed. He has ordered servitor crews and hive labour gangs in to begin bolstering the defences to his satisfaction.'

'Hive Spire first, then Level Primus,' said Lydorran, repeating the mantra he had made of Captain Tor's plan of campaign. 'Orbitas and Commercias follow. Then Militarus and Aquisitorius.' Those would both be troublesome hive districts to properly secure, he knew, the former being the macro-barracks of the Ghyrish Airborne and the latter the personal domain of the spider-like Magos Gathabosis. Yet neither would present as much difficulty as the hive's last, lowest, largest and most lawless district.

'Then Laboritas,' said Lordas, his voice grim. 'Sprawling miner-habs, gang territories, half-collapsed sump-slums... delightful.'

'Once that last district is declared sacrosanct, we will have our fortress,' said Lydorran, his tone inviting no dispute. He would not waver from Captain Tor's plan. On that he had been firm, and Chaplain Storn had seemed to approve.

Lordas grunted in what might have been assent. He scrolled through the pages of the data-slate.

'Shipmaster Gavorn continues orbital surveillance and air-interdiction operations,' he said. 'Continuing signs of unrest and guerrilla conflict around nearly every mine complex on the Continent. Unclear at this time who fights on which side, or which mine complexes truly remain loyal. A squadron of Stormhawks intercepted a hijacked ore barque four hours ago and shot it down before it could enter Angelicus airspace.'

'They know we're here now, whoever they are,' mused Lydorran. 'We can expect resistance to become rapidly more aggressive.'

'Something of an update on that front, brother,' said Lordas, consulting a separate data-psalm on his slate. 'Full dissection of captured enemies reveals a uniformity to the patterns of biological deviance not concurrent with the effects of Chaos worship. The local Officio Medicae have offered up their own findings – somewhat unwillingly, I might note – and they tally. This looks like a xenoform taint, Brother-Librarian, concurrent with genestealer infestation. Pict-capture of insurgent graffiti supports the theory. We're finding their so-called wyrm-form glyphs daubed and sprayed within the walls of their hideouts, alongside all manner of profane pseudo-religious literature pertaining to their idolatrous deity and this three-armed gunman known as Shenn.'

'Father...' said Lydorran, gripping a stanchion absently as the gunship shuddered around him. The timbre of the engines changed. They would be coming in to land soon. Lydorran knew a little of the genestealer menace, just what his psycho-indoctrination had taught him; it suggested that

Father might well be the xenos bioform at the heart of the cult, though the possibility remained that he was but a construct of mutated minds and twisted faith. Now was not the time to seek enlightenment. He clamped his helm over his head, muttering benedictions to the spirit of his psychic hood as he manually attached its clamps and feeds.

'Give me the rest, Lordas, and keep it brief.'

Lordas, his own helm secure and eye lenses glowing faintly, reeled off the remainder of the strategic update.

'Captain Tor's remains have been interred in a stasis crypt aboard the *Wrathful* until we can return him for proper entombment aboard the *Phalanx*,' he reported. 'On the ground the servo-skull swarms and Vanguard spearheads are pushing out through the last sectors of Hive Spire now, reporting back any suggestion of cultist holdouts. Everything points to this nest being the last major toe-hold they possess this high up, but we must be thorough. If Sergeant Torgan had cultivated any agents amongst the populace, none have come forward since our arrival, so we're relying on ours and the Ghyrish sweep data.'

'And the Ghyrish themselves?' asked Lydorran, running last checks over his heavy bolt pistol and communing with the machine-spirit of his force stave.

'They are obeying our orders readily enough, though beyond that they have held stubbornly to their own patrol routes, garrison duties and combat operations. The high marshal has made a point of despatching additional Ghyrish Airborne regiments to Tectosmine and Delvemine in the last day sidereal, citing a need to "suppress rebellion upon the hive's very doorstep". This despite our strong suggestion that he curtail such operations so as to have manpower ready for the next stage of our own operation.'

'He will be brought in line,' said Lydorran, feeling the gunship accelerate into a dive. The lumen flicked to a deep crimson and a ready chime tolled through the troop bay. Around him, battle-brothers came to full combat readiness, chanting last oaths to Emperor and primarch. 'We will need the majority of the high marshal's soldiery, and the Adeptus Arbites too, if we are to successfully sweep the lower districts.'

'Indeed, Brother-Librarian, but for now battle lies before us,' replied Lordas. 'One fight at a time, if you please?'

Lydorran barked a laugh.

'Just so,' he said, then switched to his assault force's command channel. 'Brothers, once again the heretic foe is revealed to us. They believe themselves safe in their fortress. Let us show them what the Imperial Fists make of such false hope.'

His battle-brothers cheered, though not, he thought, as they would have done for one of Captain Tor's rousing pre-battle speeches. *So be it*, he thought, feeling empyric power crackle through his stave on his command. *For that is not where my talents lie.*

The gunship's landing gear hit the ground. The craft's guns were already hammering, their report swelling suddenly from dull thumps to harsh thunder as the assault ramp slammed down and the Imperial Fists deployed.

They had come down on a broad platform, maybe five hundred feet across, that jutted shelf-like from the flank of a high-profile shipwrights' tower. The platform was one of several that extended from the huge structure, each serving as construction cradle and dry-dock for the beautifully appointed artisan shuttles that the business produced.

Servo-skull auspex sweeps had detected anomalous movement and energy signatures on the sixty-fourth level of the tower. A brief discourse with the local Arbites precinct revealed that this floor, along with the four floors above and below, had supposedly been quarantined due to a shardroach infestation brought in aboard a shipment of materials from downhive. There should have been nothing moving here, but when the Arbites communed with the building's enshrined machine-spirits they found all vid feeds from the quarantined levels severed.

Even now, Enforcers were tracking down the master shipwrights and as many of their artisans, serfs and clerks as could be found. Meanwhile, the Imperial Fists struck hard at the suspected insurgent stronghold.

Gunfire was already raining down from the arched windows of the tower when Lydorran's boots hit the decking of the dry-dock. Bullets and las-blasts filled the air like storm rain, lashing the Space Marines' yellow armour and rattling from the gunship's hull. Ahead of Lydorran and Lordas, the Intercessors of Squad Furian loped through the firestorm and took positions amidst the intricate mechanisms of a hull-wright's servo-cradle. Their stalker bolt rifles boomed as they returned fire, their shells punching through stained glass and plate steel with equal efficacy to detonate the cultists sheltering in the tower.

Heavy footfalls heralded Brothers Victarian and Holun, each piloting an Invictor warsuit into battle. Behind them came the Terminators of Veteran Squad Lesordus, the First Company veterans thumping down the assault ramp with deliberate strides before unleashing a fusillade of fire into the tower's flank.

Engines screamed and the gunship dusted off, ramp closing like a beast's maw as its prow swung up and away from the tower. Lydorran saw a rocket, fired no doubt from some crude shoulder-launcher, race from a window two floors up and slam straight into the armaglass of the cockpit. A fiery explosion blossomed, but as the gunship continued to climb the smoke cleared to show little more than scorching and a few small cracks marring the aircraft's canopy. Heavy bolters swung to bear, and a storm of return fire blitzed from the craft's muzzle. Shredded metal, shattered glass and gory remnants rained down, all that remained of the shooter and their firing position both.

'Go with honour, Brother-Librarian,' voxed the pilot serf. 'We'll fly interdiction in case of reinforcements.' With that, the gunship dropped away and left Lydorran and his warriors to break open the enemy fortress. Behind his helm's faceplate, the Librarian wore a hard smile. This was the part of his duties that he lived for.

'Squad Furian, maintain cover fire,' Lydorran ordered. 'Invictors, flank out and enfilade targets of opportunity. Watch for any enemy surprises.' It had not taken the Imperial Fists long to realise that, within the endless maze of conduits, vents, crawlways and tunnels that threaded the hive's structure like an insect mound, their enemies might come at them from almost any direction. The knowledge hadn't altered their plans; the battlefield would bend to accommodate the sons of Dorn, not the other way around. It had, however, made them wary.

'What of us, Brother-Librarian?' asked Lordas.

'We will advance with Squad Lesordus and force the breach,' replied Lydorran, highlighting a tall and ornately carved hangar door set into the tower's wall. 'With your agreement, veteran sergeant?'

'We'll lead the way, Brother-Librarian,' voxed Sergeant Lesordus, he and his hulking battle-brothers already advancing towards the designated doorway. Lydorran and Lordas fell in behind them, allowing the Terminators' massively thick Tactical Dreadnought armour to soak up the insurgents' fire.

From a floor above there came a rising scream and a sudden stream of shots that clanged viciously against the Terminators' armour. One of the mighty battle-brothers stumbled as a lucky round broke through, but the indomitable warriors maintained their advance. Turning slightly, one of them triggered his shoulder-mounted cyclone missile launcher and sent a cluster of fragmentation warheads streaking away in answer to the cannon's fire. The detonation lit the night and the cannon fell silent.

Even as the Terminators raked their fire across the tower's flank, Lydorran sensed a build-up of energy behind a window to the right of the doorway. He gripped his staff and focused his mind. In answer to his bidding, the deck plates of the platform shuddered then ripped upwards, rising into a formidable barricade in the moment before a searing laser beam pulsed from the window towards Sergeant Lesordus. The blast hit Lydorran's bulwark and melted the metal to slag in a blinding blast of energy. Lydorran let the molten metal spatter back to the ground and levelled his force stave, snarling a wordless command as he channelled geokinetic energies through it. A force blast leapt across the intervening space and hit the tower's flank like a battering ram. The ores within the steel skin of the tower yielded to his fury and collapsed with an implosive bang, caving in the chamber behind and crushing the unseen assailant as though in a huge mailed fist.

'My thanks, Brother-Librarian,' voxed Lesordus stiffly. 'Though doubtless my Terminator plate would have sufficed. So it has done for many long millennia.'

'The breach, if you please, veteran sergeant,' replied Lydorran, fighting to keep the irritation from his voice. Better the veteran's pride be wounded than his body.

Squad Lesordus had nearly reached the hangar doors, Lydorran and Lordas cleaving close in their shadows. Brothers Victarian and Holun were pacing their warsuits back and forth upon the flanks, blazing away with heavy stubbers and heavy bolters to suppress the enemy's snipers while Squad Furian added their own precision marksmanship. The tower's flank was a ragged mess of blast craters and broken glass. Several corpses, or what remained of them, hung from shattered windows, clad in more of those flak-enhanced miners' suits that Lydorran had seen on the sniper.

Veteran Sergeant Lesordus stepped up, swung back his crackling power fist and struck the hangar door. The blow landed with a concussive boom, the molecular disruption field that wreathed his fist sending a rippling shockwave through the door. It caved in as though it had been made of parchment, its hinges bursting in showers of sparks and flying rivets. The entire sheet of plasteel, a good twenty feet high and at least as wide, leapt backwards from the blow and then keeled over with a resounding crash.

For a breath, nothing moved within the darkness beyond the door except sparks and swirling smoke. Then there came a wild howling, and from the gloom burst a ragged mass of cultists who fired pistols, flamers and autoguns as they advanced. The sheer ferocity of the counter-attack staggered Squad Lesordus, and another of the veterans cursed as a shot punched through his elbow joint to draw blood.

'What force drives these fanatics?' exclaimed Lordas over the vox to Lydorran.

'Nothing natural, that could see our brethren given pause

by mere mortals such as these,' replied the Librarian, sensing the latent psychic charge crackling on the air around the cultists.

'Brother-Librarian, beware the rear!' came Brother Holun's voice. Lydorran shot a glance back and his eyes widened as he saw more cultists swarming up over the lip of the dry-dock platform brandishing guns, blades and bombs. They wore a motley assortment of clip harnesses and hive workers' servo-rigs.

'Dorn's fist, they scaled the underside of the platform!' Lydorran cried. 'Squad Furian, Invictors, repel assault to our rear.'

The trap had been well timed and well executed, he thought with grudging respect. Against the Ghyrish it would no doubt have proved a deadly end to their assault.

But he and his brothers were not the Ghyrish.

'Brothers, eradicate them,' he spat, before levelling his heavy bolt pistol and blasting a cultist's head apart.

The enemy broke against the Terminators like a wave against rocks and made almost as little impression. Improvised blades, cudgels and pry-bars rang against the Imperial Fists' armour to no avail. Crudely machined pistols barked, discharging hails of fire that might as well have been unleashed upon the uncaring face of a cliff. In return, the Terminators swung their power fists in unstoppable arcs, every blow not merely breaking its victim but detonating them in showers of meat, blood and shredded flak armour. Sergeant Lesordus and his brothers fired their storm bolters point-blank, the shells hitting their victims so hard that many punched clean through the first rank of cultists, leaving fist-sized holes torn through them before detonating in the skulls and torsos of the next rank back. It looked, thought Lydorran, as though the enemy had been fed into an industrial grinder.

Then came the rising whine of electrical engines. Loping from the darkness of the hangar came another wave of cultists, but these were like nothing the Librarian had seen before. Where their fellows might at least have passed for human at a cursory glance, the mutations of these newcomers were far more severe. They were bloated and hunched, their heads elongated and hairless with bulbous yellow eyes and armoured ridges cresting their skulls. Though the creatures still wore rubberised utility suits, they had been heavily modified to accommodate the chitinous limbs that depended from their bulky bodies; in several cases, Lydorran noted with disgust that there were three, or even four, of these arms to a single cultist, each ending in vicious claws that clutched heavy mining tools. He saw double-bladed cutting saws whose teeth whined with blurring speed, and massive rock drills whose whirring heads were surrounded by fine mists of jetting coolant.

Even Terminator plate might struggle to turn aside weapons like those, he thought, and stepped forward with his force stave crackling.

'Veteran sergeant, despatch the last of the chaff then aid me,' he barked. But then the mutants were upon him once more, and there was no further time for talk.

Lydorran dived aside from the downward swing of a power saw larger than his torso, its wielder hissing in rage as his weapon's blades bit into the decking instead of Lydorran's flesh. The Librarian answered by swinging the head of his force stave sideways into his attacker's head. Geo-kinetic force boomed, and the cultist's cranium detonated in a purple-black spray of ichor.

Even as the first creature fell away, another two came at him, one stabbing with a screaming drill while the other hacked at him with a pair of curved metal swords. Judging the drill the more threatening weapon, Lydorran turned, catching the downswing of the blades on his right shoulder guard while slamming the head of his force stave down atop the drill as it came at him. Another plosive bang of force sundered the weapon and smashed its wreckage into the decking, along with the severed ends of its wielder's arms. The cultist fell back with an insectile shriek, vital fluids pumping from its hideous wounds, and Lydorran spun, sweeping his staff around in time to parry one of his other attacker's blades. The other slipped past his guard, an unexpected low lunge, and slid through the seal above his left knee pad.

Pain lanced through Lydorran's leg as the blade sank deep, and he responded by summoning a surge of kinetic force and then driving his helmed forehead into his attacker's face. The cultist's leer of triumph was transformed into a bloody smear as the Librarian's charged headbutt caved in his skull and threw it back.

He ripped the blade from his knee with his free hand then threw it, increasing its velocity with another shunt of force. The blade whipped through the air and sank deep into the throat of a fourth cultist, who clutched at the weapon and toppled backwards even as Lydorran drew his bolt pistol and shot a fifth attacker thrice in the torso. The mutant exploded with a ripple of wet detonations, his innards painting the last of his comrades.

Still the mutants came on. Lydorran felt the psychocircuitry of his hood begin to heat as he strained his powers to throw up a force field that stopped a swinging saw. The weapon came around again, even as another cultist lunged at him with some sort of short-ranged lascutter. Lydorran realised an instant too late that he could not halt both attacks, and then Sergeant Lesordus' power fist was there, slamming headlong into the blade saw and causing it to shred apart in a hail of razor-sharp shrapnel. Its wielder was hurled back by the resultant explosion, while Lydorran parried the lascutter with the end of his stave and then shot the mutant carrying it through his face.

He spared Lesordus a sidelong glance as the last handful of mutants turned tail and fled for the shadows.

'My thanks, veteran sergeant,' he said.

'Your armour would not have sufficed,' replied the Terminator, his expression and body language rendered unreadable within the massive bulk of his wargear.

Lydorran shook his head and looked behind him. Two of Squad Furian were down, Lordas kneeling next to one with his reductor deployed. Yet in return the cultists had been driven back, the surprise of their attack counting for little against the stubborn indomitability of the Imperial Fists. Even as he watched, Lydorran saw several of the foe swing themselves wildly off the platform's edge, relying on their harnesses to catch them and help them swarm away to safety.

That he would not allow.

Wincing slightly at the pain in his knee, Lydorran opened his force's reserve vox-channel.

'Sergeant Ordus, Sergeant Thade, we are pushing into the structure. Enemy resistance broken. Expect runners, numbers unknown.'

'*Understood, Brother-Librarian,*' came Reiver Sergeant Ordus' reply. '*None shall escape our blades.*'

'*Nor ours,*' added Reiver Sergeant Thade. As though to emphasise their words, Lydorran heard the vox-amplified screams and thunderous report of heavy bolt pistols as the two squads of vanguard troopers went to work. One was concealed above the infested floors, one below; none would escape the vengeance of the Imperial Fists.

'What of those traversing the exterior of the tower?' asked Sergeant Lesordus as he prepared to stomp into the darkness of the enemy stronghold and sweep for survivors.

'They will not get far,' said Lydorran, and opened a vox-channel to his force's gunship.

Magus Jai sat cross-legged in the middle of a circle of flickering candles. They had been laid out to follow the jagged curves of the wyrmform glyph that took up much of the floor of her meditation chamber, and they lit the brushed-metal walls with dancing tableaux of light and shadow. More glyphs seemed to distort and dance upon the walls, interspersing the jagged writings that Jai had scribed when the hand of Father was upon her mind.

Firelight sparked like stars amidst the gemstones and gewgaws that her fellow rebels had offered her and had piled in shrine-like offering heaps in the alcoves of the chamber. A superstition had arisen, ever since the attack upon the astropathic sanctum a year before, that if one offered a token to the magus, her blessing would shield the giver from harm. If Jai possessed any such power, she didn't know about it, but she hadn't seen fit to discourage a practice that seemed harmless while offering her people hope.

Besides, some small part of her admired the way that the riches of the earth made her chambers look more sacred, more mystical. More in keeping with her role in Father's favour.

None of this concerned Jai now, however. Her eyes were closed upon the outer world. She turned her gaze instead to the void within, to the inky and somehow viscous blackness that flowed through her mind and allowed her to employ Father's gifts in the Star Children's service. It was not a pleasant experience, communing in this way; she preferred to externalise her powers, to inflict them upon her enemies or use them to steady her allies' nerves as she had done a hundred times and more since this war began. Jai was no stranger to peril, not anymore, yet still it unsettled her to slip into the cold and clinging blackness of the power that lurked within her own mind. It felt as though ice-cold oil coated her skin, as though a shadowy substance roiled within her skull and threatened to drown her in its depths.

Focus, Jai told herself. *Do Father's bidding as only you can.*

Slowly, the darkness all around her shimmered and swirled as she focused her powers and reached with them, *out* into the aching spaces beyond. Shadow flowed about her, and for an instant she heard a tumultuous whispering fill the blackness, pressing in upon her from all sides and filling her with animal terror. Phoenicia Jai ignored the sensation, as she had done many times before, and forced her consciousness on through the void to issue the summons.

I must speak with him.

It must be now.

Jai felt resistance at first, a reluctance and a hint of something else – irritation, she thought, perhaps arrogance. Who was she to give orders to him?

Now, she urged again, making no effort to conceal her anger or contempt.

The inky shadows around her stirred again. A current of void-cold whirled around her, so frigid that it burned her skin with its passing before coiling into a faintly glowing shape somewhere between a humanoid figure and a writhing wyrmform.

It is dangerous for me to speak now.

The thought hit her like a jab in the ribs. Back in reality, she felt herself bare her teeth and furrow her brow in anger.

I am Father's voice. I am His magus. You address me with respect.

She added a vicious twist to the words, enough to send tendrils of viscid gloom needling into the writhing figure and cause it to stiffen in pain.

Magus, how may I serve Father? came the pained response, and though she sensed the simmering anger behind the words, Jai was satisfied that they had been spoken with proper reverence.

Father wishes to know how you mean to work his will against these invaders from beyond the stars, she said with her mind. *You used the Star Children's warning well, and their leader has fallen, to the great joy of the cult. Yet the fists of the Great Oppressor close about our cells one after another in Hive Spire, and our efforts to fight back come to naught.*

Their numbers are few, he replied. *Though it may cost us ten thousand brothers and sisters to do it, we can wear them down.*

No, the Ascension must progress, she shot back, angry at the callous disregard for their comrades' lives that she heard in his voice. *This cannot become a war of attrition. The gods draw nigh, and we must prepare the way for their coming.*

They have angered Ghyre's rulers with their arrival, came his reply after a lengthy pause. *There is discord amongst the oppressors where there is only unity amongst our ranks. The newcomers are not beloved of the people, but rather they herd them aside like cattle and spread fear and resentment with their every deed. If we cannot fight them directly then we must bleed them slowly, attack them with cunning and mislead them at every turn. And all the while, we show the oppressed the true nature of their so-called saviours.*

Yes, they will flock to us when they see what their corpse-god offers in his supposed mercy, she thought-spoke, the last word causing ripples of disgust and bitterness to quiver through the darkness. *Do what you can to turn the oppressors against one another from within, brother. Primus Lhor and I will work Father's will, as you have suggested, from without. Between us we will break them. Star's Blessings upon you.*

She ended the communion without waiting for a response and opened her eyes. She gasped in a shuddering breath and felt goosebumps rise across her skin as the sensation of cold, oily immersion clung to her for a few heartbeats more. Slowly, breathing deeply, Magus Jai rose and rearranged her robes, before taking up her stave of office and smiling a small, vicious smile.

'We *will* break them,' she breathed to herself. 'And then, Ascension.'

VI

Chapter Champion Elrich Hastur paced across the square like a predator stalking prey. He held Lamentation easily in one hand, the artificer blade's ornate grip as familiar to him as the feel of his own limbs. His helm's superior autosenses swept his surrounds, flicking through visual and spiritual spectra as they sought enemy targets. His cloak billowed behind him in the blood-warm winds that flowed down from exchanger vents above the square. His footfalls rang against the metal ground and echoed from the shop fronts that clustered on all sides.

Five yellow-armoured Assault Marines followed in Hastur's wake. They carried chainswords, bolt pistols and, in the case of Sergeant Threnn, a thrumming plasma pistol. In the many-levelled urban tangle of the upper Commercias they went without jump packs; opportunities for rocket-propelled leaps were few, but tight spaces were many.

Especially where their enemies liked to hide.

Sudden thunder filled the air as a maglev train whipped overhead, running upon a raised track. It, and the scattering of wide-eyed faces that stared through windows on teetering upper stories, were the only evidence of civilians that Hastur could see.

'I expected greater civilian presence,' said Sergeant Threnn. 'Did the Arbites place this sector under curfew?'

'No, I forbade them,' replied Hastur, his deep voice distant as his mind worked swiftly.

'And yet somehow word flows ahead of our coming,' glowered Threnn.

'And yet...' echoed Hastur. The sergeant's frustration mirrored his own. The hive had a billion voices, it seemed. Wherever the Imperial Fists went, those voices heralded their coming in surreptitious whispers.

Butted up against the square's edge, the warehouse complex waited for them. The building was blocky and belligerent, looming over the adjoining businesses as though shouldering them aside. Arc-lumen lit its towering flanks, which rose above the smaller dwellings around it, through the hanging nests of cables and pipes and vents, through the faintly lambent smog of pollutants that passed for cloud cover until it mated with this level's roof several hundred feet up.

The cog-and-pick crest of Greater Clan VanSappen was picked out by artfully arrayed sprays of light upon the building's side.

'No light in any of the windows,' noted Sergeant Threnn. 'Sanctified door seals are in place. Seems altogether quiescent.'

The intelligence they had received from the Adeptus Arbites was that since Clan VanSappen's virtual stranding beyond the Mastracha disaster zone, all but a handful of their assets within Angelicus Hive had been temporarily shut down. This much made sense, thought Hastur. Why waste energy and resources maintaining installations that were currently no use to their masters?

What made less sense were the telltale vibrations that spying servo-skulls had detected within the supposedly empty structure. Interrogation of the macro-cogitators that regulated utility flow through this level of the Commercias further revealed a continual and ongoing power drain somewhere inside the warehouse. It all pointed to the presence of the Cult of the Wrything Wyrm.

Hastur halted before the granite steps that led up to the structure's cherub-graven front doors. Wordlessly, he gestured first to his left then to his right, towards the cramped alleyways that ran down the building's flanks.

'Understood, Brother-Champion,' said Sergeant Threnn, then paused. 'I do not doubt that we are equal to this task, brother, but...'

Hastur turned a look upon the sergeant and waited.

'The enemy are elusive, Brother-Champion. We are but six. We cannot block every rat hole and crawlway exiting this structure. Should we not have the support of the arbitrators or the Ghyrish Airborne to cordon off this sector?'

The sergeant's question was not unfair, Hastur thought, and it goaded his anger back near the surface. When the intelligence had reached them of this latest potential insurgent nest, he had voxed an immediate demand to Lydorran for an assault force and Ghyrish support platoons.

He had not believed it when he was told no, and had requested clarification in case there had been some error in comprehension at the Librarian's end. Again, and more forcefully, his request had been denied. Hastur was still simmering from the censure implied in that second curt response.

A sector of Hive Spire had been compromised three hours

earlier as previously undetected insurgent cells had mobilised in a coordinated ambush on a Ghyrish arms convoy. Several assaults had been postponed, battle-brothers redeployed to ensure the sanctity of the conclave chambers and governor's palace and to drive back and eliminate the cultists. All other available assets were engaged in sweep-and-secure operations through eighteen sectors of Level Primus and Orbitas. First Arbitrator Verol had once again asserted that her precinct fortresses were stretched to breaking point maintaining law and order throughout the hive while also managing what she described as 'the fallout' from the Imperial Fists' purge-and-secure campaign.

In short, and yet again, operations were not slated to begin in the Commercias at this time.

Hastur shook his head, a short, sharp gesture tight with frustration. Nineteen days the Imperial Fists had been on Ghyre, and they had so far laid claim to little more than the tips of one damned hive city. His Chapter had concluded entire planetary campaigns in shorter spans of time. They had besieged and broken open fortresses in a matter of hours. But here they were, advancing at a crawl, caution and temerity their watchwords.

It was shameful.

If Hastur had been in charge he would have had the governor and her preening conclave dragged away in chains by now. How dare they continue their ludicrous politicking in the face of direct commands from the Adeptus Astartes? He would have left the Ghyrish to look to their own protection, gathered all the strike force's might and struck decisively to end this fiasco!

Yet where would that strike have landed? he asked himself. The enemy writhed away like smoke at every turn, and without a secure fortification to work from and sufficient intelligence to pinpoint the foe's command structure and eliminate it, how were the Imperial Fists to aim their strength decisively?

Stubbornness and pride bade him cast the thoughts aside; he would have formulated a more aggressive, decisive stratagem and brought the foe to honest battle, he was sure. But it didn't matter what Elrich Hastur would or would not have done, for he was not in command.

Aster Lydorran was. A newcomer. A *psyker*.

'Brother-Champion?' Hastur stirred himself from his thoughts with a surge of self-chastisement. He lingered on the enemy's threshold in doubt when he should forge ahead. That was what all this was about, after all.

'It is only us, sergeant. We do not have to purge every hostile from this structure. It is important only that we strike hard and break their strength. We will drive them from their strongpoint, put fear into them of our righteous retribution and then move on to the next, and the next until what remains of our enemy's strength flees before us to the very lowest levels of this benighted hive city.'

And, he admitted quietly to himself, *by doing this I may light a fire under Brother-Librarian Lydorran, or else prove that his position of command is undeserved.*

It was not that Hastur resented Lydorran for his origins or his unnatural powers, at least so he told himself. Primarch knew most of the Imperial Fists had been quick enough to accept their reinforcements from the Ultima Founding, or even to seek the crossing of the Rubicon Primaris themselves despite the risks. From what he understood, Lydorran was of Terran stock, albeit via several millennia in stasis upon Mars. As for witches, they were a necessary evil and a potent asset. Hastur was not so stiff-necked as to deny this.

It was simply that there was a correct manner for Imperial Fists to conduct themselves in battle, and to Hastur's mind, neither Aster Lydorran nor his commands to date conformed to it.

'As you say, Brother-Champion,' said Sergeant Threnn. To the man's credit, if he felt any doubts about their mission he kept them to himself. Threnn spoke quickly over his squad vox-channel, and he and one of his battle-brothers peeled off to the left while the other three Assault Marines jogged away to the right.

Hastur watched them go then turned back to the ornate doors ahead of him. Another maglev train swept overhead, its thunder rising to a cacophony before receding again into the distant sprawl of the hive. The enemy had already had ample time to see him coming by now, but then Hastur was not hiding. If the heretics had fled, he would simply hunt them to their next bolt-hole. If they waited in ambush, he would endure the worst they could hurl at him before crushing them like the insects they were. In either case, his enemies' bastion would fall, a victory in Hastur's eyes.

The Fifth Company Champion took three quick strides to the top of the steps and swung Lamentation in a double-handed strike. The energised blade clove a diagonal cut through the doors, and, glowing molten at their edges, great chunks of ornate metal fell back into the building with a clang. Hastur ducked through the gap, the bisected face of a carved cherub staring one-eyed at him from the ground.

He found himself in a high-ceilinged atrium whose marble statues were draped in dustcloth shrouds. The frescoed floor had been defaced with a huge wyrmform, spray-painted over the representation of the Emperor enthroned. The only light was that which spilled in through the sundered doors at his back. It threw his shadow out long and stretched until it touched the dusty reception-adept's desk on the far side of the room.

Hastur swept his autosenses right and left. Contacts, movement and body heat were highlighted in his field of vision by runic designators. Further in, barely in range of his helm's limited internal auspex, Hastur detected a substantial power signature.

'Breach, contacts ahead, advancing,' he voxed.

'Squad Threnn moving to support,' replied the sergeant. *'No contact. Pushing up.'*

Hastur strode across the atrium and had almost reached the next doorway when he detected a flurry of movement from above. It came from a balustraded walkway a hundred feet up and to the right. He saw a shadowy figure, the lenses of glare goggles catching the faint light. The muzzle of an autogun lit with sudden fire.

Chattering echoes rolled through the atrium as bullets raked Hastur's armour. He let them, making no attempt to evade the attack. Then, in one smooth motion, he levelled his bolt pistol and put a round through his assailant's face.

One shell. One gory detonation. The ragged remains of the cultist's body crumpled.

As though that first death was their signal, more heretics came at him. Double doors banged open beyond the desk, beneath a bronze plaque that read 'CLERICUM'. Figures spilled through it, guns raised and spitting fire. At the same time another two contacts registered, these above and to his left. More bullets swarmed towards him.

Hastur dove to his right, landing in a roll and coming back up in a fighting crouch. Gunfire blitzed the frescoed floor where he had stood. As he came to his feet, the Champion's pistol spoke again. A cultist with a ridged forehead and mauve skin jerked as a bolt shell punched into her torso, then detonated in a shower of blood. A second heretic was erased above the collar bone as a shell exploded in his skull. A third lost a leg and crashed to the floor screaming, her gun spilling from her hands to skitter to a stop at Hastur's feet. The Champion trod on the weapon, slow and deliberate, and crushed it beneath his boot.

His autosenses chimed a warning and Hastur spun, swinging his sword in an arc that brought the flat of the blade into contact with the krak grenade spinning down towards him. With a deft twitch of his thumb, Hastur killed Lamentation's disruption field for a split second, allowing him to strike the explosive without triggering it prematurely. It whipped back along its own trajectory and detonated with an implosive bang against the underside of the left-hand walkway. Masonry and rebar tore and fell. Two howling cultists fell with it. Their bodies broke upon impact with the hard stone floor, and Hastur paid them no further mind.

'Oppressor! Monster! Father take you all!' The scream of hatred came from a tall man in an armoured utility suit who charged Hastur with a mining pick. The cultist's eyes were wide with fury. They flashed tainted yellow in the light from the broken doorway.

'There is only one monster here, deviant,' Hastur responded, easily parrying the man's wild swings with his blade.

'Get him clear!' shouted the man, sounding desperate. 'Get Father clear! I'll hold–'

Hastur disarmed his enemy with a flick of Lamentation's tip then swept the weapon around and lopped off the cultist's head. His twin hearts beat faster.

Father! Was the xenocult's deity here, in this warehouse?

The man had certainly sounded desperate enough, but would they really be so brazen as to house their false prophet, or idol, or whatever Father was, in a structure under the very noses of their enemies? *If they were certain of victory before our arrival*, he thought. *Who can know the minds of heretics? Who would wish to?*

He set off at once, striding deeper into the structure, auspex alive for signs of the foe. He saw movement ahead, swift and frantic, several hundred feet further into the structure and making for the thrumming power signature near the warehouse's heart.

Hastur quickened his pace.

'Sergeant, be advised enemy has made vocal reference to Father being in situ,' he voxed.

'Understood, Brother-Champion. Here? It seems unlikely, does it not?'

Hastur shouldered open a heavy wood-panelled door. A cultist came at him, and he ran the man through before kicking him off his blade.

'Few guards, poor security, uncomfortable proximity to Hive Spire,' he said by way of agreement. 'And yet our enemies do not fight a conventional war. Perhaps they move Father from one site to another and rely upon the very unsuitability of their strongholds to keep him from our notice. Or perhaps their deity is represented or embodied by more than one individual, more than one idolatrous relic?'

'Do we vox this in?' asked Threnn, and over the link Hastur heard his plasma pistol howl.

'Not yet,' he replied. 'Not until we know what "this" is. Converge on the power signature. Purge all hostiles, and if they attempt a breakout, contain them.'

'Understood,' said Threnn.

Hastur strode through cloistered administration chambers, past cramped work spaces each with its own devotional shrine to clan and Emperor. Here and there he saw more wyrm glyphs. Crude vat-tallow candles were clustered on desks and in corners, some flickering with weak light, others dark and wisping smoke where they had been hurriedly extinguished.

In the next corridor his blade made short work of two cultists who came at him with knives and pistols. He barely registered them, instead looking beyond them to where a larger figure with three arms and a hunched spine vanished through another door. The power source burned bright beyond it.

'Brother-Champion, we are nearing the power source. Enemy resistance increasing,' reported Threnn.

'Understood. Breaching containment storage chamber,' replied Hastur. 'It's here, brother-sergeant. Rally on me.'

Blade and pistol ready, Hastur surged through the doorway. Was Father truly here? If so, he would cut down whatever xenos abomination he discovered and end this war at a blade-stroke. Perhaps a captaincy would be his reward?

Hastur was met by the glare of massive banks of arc-lumen arrayed all around the chamber and beaming out light until it seemed to bleach the very air. Industrial units, made for deep-delve mining, far more than any labour could require but enough to draw an anomalous amount of motive force from the level's grid. He had an instant to register rows of ornate containment bays intended for unstable or highly valuable goods. He saw gantries around the chamber's edge, radiating from a vast central column, up and down whose length forests of cabling and pipework ran, spliced cables flowing like serpents to feed the lumen rigs.

In a split second he took in the ragged handful of cultists kneeling in prayer around the column, the hunchbacked mutant standing before them like a Chaplain before his oathing brothers. In that same second Hastur saw the blasting charges, clamped around the base of the column in such profusion that it seemed as though the structure suckled a swarm of parasites. Arming runes flashed baleful red upon dozens of explosive charges. In that instant Hastur understood.

Anger, shock and most of all shame flooded through him. To have been so easily led by these heretics!

'Freedom for Ghyre!' shrieked the mutant in a mangled voice as it squeezed the detonators clutched in its talons.

'Threnn, retreat! Get–'

The rest of Hastur's words were lost in the thunderous roar of the explosion.

The cultists watched from the windows of a mercantile hab-tower a quarter mile from the warehouse. The oppressors had come, as had been foretold. Disappointingly few, but that hardly mattered. From the balcony of a hab-unit offered up by an indoctrinated merchant, the cultists had watched through magnoculars as the oppressors entered the VanSappen warehouse. Minutes later a ferocious explosion rocked the hab-tower – Acolyte Jesiah and his brood martyring themselves that the prophecy might be fulfilled. The cultists had known envy then, for by their selfless sacrifice Jesiah and his people ascended to join the Star Children. They would see them again, when the Ascension was complete, and on that day all would know unity and bliss.

'Stars' blessings,' they murmured, shaping the wyrmform with their clawed fingers.

The cultists watched with avid eyes as the VanSappen

warehouse buckled from within. Fire and dust geysered from ornate windows. Glass whickered out in a glittering storm to lacerate the businesses all around. A maglev train, passing with timing so fortuitous it could only have been ordained by Father, was struck by the expanding shockwave of the blast and torn from its track. The carriages tumbled through the air, the vehicle buckling and twisting like an agonised worm, to smash down amongst the structures of the Commercias amidst blossoms of flame. The cultists were silent, awed by the destruction unleashed, sobered by the sudden cascade of ruin. There were no innocents, they reminded themselves. There were only those who cowered beneath the oppressors' boot and those with the righteousness to give all for the cause. Father would know who was who, even beyond death's veil, and he would ensure that all who deserved their eternal reward received it.

Still they watched as the warehouse crumpled, a gouged-out shell that could no longer support its own weight. Slow and painful the collapse began, but it gathered pace rapidly until the roar of the avalanche echoed across the Commercias. Like a drowning man whose last clutch for life drags others down with him, so the collapsing structure wrenched away the supports from the level above. Massive cross-beams, sparking cables, rent pipes and thousands of tonnes of ferrocrete thundered down from overhead. Water and promethium mingled in cascading profusion.

Ground cars and cargo haulers and Arbites armoured transports fell amongst the debris, plunging into the cavernous maw that had yawned suddenly in the Commercias level above.

Sparking shop-front signs fell, great slabs of the buildings they had adorned coming with them.

Buckled lumen poles toppled into the billowing smoke and rising firestorm.

Broken statuary plunged down and was dashed to ruin.

People. So many people.

The hive-quake rolled outwards, shattering windows, triggering alarm hymnals, sending groundcars skidding into one another and hurling Ghyrish citizens from their feet. For a long moment the cultists feared that Jesiah had struck too dolorous a blow as the hab-tower quivered around them and the balcony they crouched upon creaked alarmingly.

At last the thunder of the catastrophe subsided, yielding to the roar of flames, the crack and rumble of settling masonry, the screams and sobs of countless shocked and wounded. Wordless, efficient, the cultists rendered their vid-captors quiescent. They packed the recording equipment away. Swathed in the pilfered robes of minor mercantile clerks, they swept like ghosts down the hab-tower's stairs.

They had what they wanted.

Father would do the rest.

VII

Gunfire echoed through the cathedrum. The rattle of auto-guns and the sporadic shriek of a modified mining laser competed with the thudding booms of bolt weaponry. Lyd-orran moved up from one pillar to the next, pressing towards the altar where the cultists had taken shelter.

There were only a handful of heretics left from the band that had ambushed the Ghyrish arms transports as they rolled through sector eighteen. Lydorran wasn't blind to the damage their running gun battle had wrought between the ambush site and this luckless cathedrum, nor the Ghyrish lives lost in the crossfire, but the heretics' corruption must be purged, and so he had pressed the attack.

The Intercessors of Squad Ordasis pushed up through the pews to either side of him, threading between the brushed-metal prayer benches and snapping off bolt rounds at their beleaguered enemies. Marching behind them came Dreadnought Brother Ghesmund, his footfalls cracking the flagstoned floor, his war cries ringing to the cathedrum's arched ceiling.

The mining laser whooped again, an orange beam of energy spearing out from behind the altar to punch through Brother Thurian's chest. The Intercessor stumbled several more steps, managing to fire off another bolt round that blasted shrapnel from the altar and threw the laser-wielder from his feet. Then Thurian collapsed and did not rise.

'Enough of this,' snarled Lydorran, his patience running out. 'Ghesmund, eradicate their position.'

'As you will it, Brother-Librarian,' boomed the Dreadnought. Ghesmund halted his advance, bracing his massive feet with a crunch of stone. The barrels of his assault cannon began to spin, a shriek rising as they whirled faster and then lit with strobing flame. A stream of massive-calibre rounds tore into the altar and eroded it in seconds. Fire blitzed the glazed triptych that stood behind the altar and annihilated the images of Emperor, Sororitas and High Lords that loomed there, the finely wrought electrocandles that had bathed the altar in their warm light exploding. Blood flew up in sheets as the last few cultists met a grisly end, their defiant screams drowned by the cacophony of gunfire.

Fyceline smoke wafted like incense fumes as Ghesmund's cannon ceased fire and its barrels rattled to a halt. Smoke and dust cleared to reveal nothing but butchered meat and smashed wreckage where the altar had stood.

Lydorran took a breath, sent out a runic hail for an Apothecary and blink-marked the cathedrum with a golden rune – another cultist cell eliminated. The battle of attrition was gruelling, the collateral damage regrettable, but they were bringing Captain Tor's vision to fruition one sector at a time. The enemy hadn't prevailed in a single stand-up engagement, and while it couldn't be denied that they were still finding their way through the cordon here and there,

Lydorran was satisfied that the entire upper hive would be a secure fortress of Imperial loyalty within days.

'Damnably slow progress, captain,' he whispered apologetically. 'I do not doubt you would have done it quicker. But the siege takes as long as the siege takes, does it not?'

Lydorran turned away from the annihilated altar and strode back towards the shattered doors of the cathedrum. A wide-eyed priest separated himself from the shadows of a devotional shrine and staggered into Lydorran's path. His motions made him look drunk, though the Librarian recognised the symptoms of shock easily enough. The priest stumbled, and Lydorran caught him as gently as he was able, restoring him to his feet and brushing stone dust from the man's raiment.

'It is all right now, frater,' he said, attempting to soften his voice. 'We could not prevent the heretics from invading your sanctum, but we have purged them.'

'The damage...' said the man, faltering, his eyes roving the cratered interior of his cathedrum. 'What have you...'

'The Emperor will forgive a few bolt-holes more easily than he would the defilement of xenos heretics, frater,' said Lydorran sternly.

The priest just blinked at him, and Lydorran eased the elderly clergyman into a pew before proceeding on his way. He did not have the luxury of time to coddle the priest further. The man's faith would have to do the rest.

Lydorran passed Primaris Apothecary Justen beneath the arch of the cathedrum's door, and the two warriors shared a nod. He stepped back out into the artificial light of the Commercias and surveyed the trail of bodies and battle damage that marked where they had driven their ambushers from their positions and hounded them to their final refuge. Groundcars smouldered where they had skidded and crashed, their plastiglass canopies cracked with bullet holes. A toppled statue of a local saint lay with its head crushed to powder where Ghesmund had trodden upon it during his advance. Arbites and medicae transports were bulling their way through the crowded civilian onlookers, who stared with mute shock at the aftermath of the conflict.

This was no place to fight a war, thought Lydorran, not for the first time. The sooner they could declare up-hive secure and drive down into the Laboritas, the better. In fact, he thought vehemently, the sooner they could declare Hive Angelicus itself secure and push outwards into full and proper battle, the happier he would be. The hive's shadows swirled with entirely too many shades of grey for his liking.

Lydorran turned towards the waiting form of his Repulsor transport, the blocky tank hovering on a thrumming grav-cushion nearby. His auspex chimed, a priority hail from Chaplain Storn, and he answered it while slotting a fresh clip into his pistol and peripherally consulting his assault force's next designated coordinates.

Lydorran came to a halt, hearts thudding.

'Repeat that,' he voxed.

Less than an hour later, Lydorran stood, helm under one arm, in an elegant antechamber. Located high up in the governor's palace, the room was richly appointed with art and statuary. It was high-ceilinged and cold for all its ornamentation, a space intended to bring home Clan Kallistus' power and cow those who sought personal audience with Ghyre's planetary governor. A quartet of elite guards stood before the door to her audience chamber, their gene-bulked bodies clad in ornate carapace armour styled after the utility suits of the

miner clans. The aesthetic reminded Lydorran uncomforta-
bly of the cultists he had been fighting these last eleven days.

Twelve, he corrected himself, checking the ornate digital
chron that hung high on one wall of the chamber. It had just
passed midnight. The Imperial Fists' twelfth day on Ghyre
had begun.

In his mind's eye, Lydorran envisioned the thundering avalanche of stone and metal and living bodies as one hive level
collapsed into another. He pictured Apothecary Lordas and
his brothers, picking over the wrack and ruin with their reduc-
tors ready but almost certainly redundant. Lordas had voxed
through to Lydorran just minutes earlier; by some miracle
they had dragged Hastur from the rubble, crushed and locked
into a healing coma by his sus-an membrane, but they had
so far found no sign of those the Champion had led. *If he
lives, he will face such censure and dishonour that he may wish
he had not*, thought Lydorran with a grim shake of his head.

A chime sounded, clear as the ringing of pick against stone,
and behind the guards the gem-studded doors of Governor
Kallistus' audience chamber swung open. A faint scent of
incense reached out to Lydorran, accompanying the sound
of soft and sombre choral singing. The guards moved aside
without a word, and Lydorran stepped through the doors.

The audience chamber continued the theme of hammering
home Clan Kallistus' power and station on Ghyre. In shape
it was a wide corridor, gem-encrusted columns holding its
ceiling aloft. Hololithic installations depicted the greatest
moments of Clan Kallistus' reign, rich seams located, accords
signed, monuments raised, tithes fulfilled and inhuman enemies driven off. Trophies and tapestries decorated the walls;
the head of an ork warlord hung next to the shattered blade
of an Aeldari Corsair; tithe certificates hung in suspensor

fields, each stamped by the Administratum and adorned with purity seals; the tailfin of a Lightning fighter craft, hovering in a column of golden light and richly decorated with Governor Kallistus' personal heraldry.

At the chamber's end, a gilded dais rose from the black-veined marble of the floor. Built into it was a throne rendered in industrial ironwork and wreathed with pipes and cabling, a halo of arc-lumen shining from above it; this was a miner's throne, thought Lydorran, an unsubtle reminder of where Ghyre's wealth and power came from, and by extension those of its governor.

Osmyndri Ellisentris Kallistus XXI sat her throne with straight-backed dignity. Her ochre skin was sheened almost gold in the light that spilled from the lumen, and the intensity of her gaze pierced Lydorran even from the opposite end of the audience chamber. She still wore the uniform of a flight officer of the Ghyrish Airborne, and her medals glinted on her chest. Lydorran had not met many planetary governors since the Ultima Founding, and he didn't doubt that some wore the trappings of martial accomplishment simply for effect. He didn't believe for a moment that Governor Kallistus' medals were just for show.

'Approach, Brother-Librarian,' she commanded, and Lydorran did so. As he came closer, he registered other figures lurking behind the glare of the lumen halo. The governor's aged seneschal huddled so close to her throne that Lydorran had initially taken the man to be a humped segment of machinery worked into the seat of power. High Marshal Kallistus, the governor's younger brother, stood ramrod straight upon the other side of the throne, his face an impassive mask, his appearance every bit as neatly managed as it had been the day Lydorran had first seen him waiting at the bottom of the ramp at Mercurio Gate. Further back, lingering in the throne's shadow as though he wished to remain unobserved, was Bishop Lotimer Renwyck.

More gene-bulked guards stood in alcoves that ran along the chamber's flanks. From the electrical thrum of the power blades they held at the ready, Lydorran marked that their weapon-spirits were roused and ready to strike.

Not for the first time since his arrival on Ghyre, Lydorran wondered about the loyalties of the planet's rulers. How far did the cult's influence go? Who worshipped the Emperor upon this world and who the vile Father? Surely the governor herself could not be compromised, or else why would she have called for aid? But then, he reminded himself, that call had gone out only because of Sergeant Torgan's sacrifice. Besides, the foe had had more than a year to spread their tendrils through this world, not to mention however long they had lurked beneath the surface before revealing themselves. But if the foe *had* inveigled themselves into the upper echelons of Ghyrish society, how would Lydorran know? He was no inquisitor, nor was he blessed with the gifts of a telepath or empath. He, his brothers, they were all weapons of open war, and here they found themselves besieging a fortress of smoke and shadows.

Besieging? he asked himself. *Or besieged?*

Lydorran halted ten paces before the governor's throne. He rapped the butt of his stave against the marble floor and bowed his head in a carefully calculated gesture of respect. Deep enough for equals, too shallow for abasement. He saw the high marshal's posture stiffen, but the governor merely returned the gesture with a somewhat less pronounced nod.

'My lady governor, a tragedy has occurred. I come before you to account for the actions of my battle-brother Elrich

Hastur. He acted against my orders, and in doing so he has dishonoured us all. I bring you an apology, and my oath that such a thing will not happen again while my hearts beat.'

Within, Lydorran's anger was a raging, thrashing thing that he had to push down again and again. He had seen Hastur's resentment of him – it didn't take Lydorran's keen insight to recognise that. But he had trusted the Champion all the same, had faith in him as one of Dorn's chosen scions. He had chosen to believe that Elrich Hastur would comport himself with the discipline and loyalty demanded of an Imperial Fist, and in betraying that belief, Hastur had compromised not only himself but his entire Chapter in the eyes of the Ghyrish people.

'An *apology*?' the high marshal spat, voice strained, eyes flashing. 'Your *assurance*? What good is that to the hundreds of thousands killed? Words are not nearly enough to account for this bloody disaster!'

'If you knew anything of the Adeptus Astartes, high marshal, you would know that my apology is near unprecedented and my oath is adamantine,' said Lydorran, his voice dangerously low. The high marshal bristled, but he took a step back as though he had just remembered to whom he spoke.

'Brother-Librarian, I thank you for your presence and for your words,' said Governor Kallistus, her expression unreadable. 'Understand, however, that the tragedy your brothers set in motion by their disobedience is worse than any single act of destruction yet instigated by the Cult of the Wrything Wyrm within this city.'

'It *is* the worst act of destruction instigated by the cult, my lady,' asserted Lydorran. 'My Techmarines have assessed the site and deemed the collapse to be the result of massive explosive trauma delivered to key supporting structures. My battle-brothers may have walked into a trap, but they were not the authors of this devastation. If you wish to lay blame, your finger should point to the arbitrators that noted discrepancies around the VanSappen warehouse yet still allowed such a concentration of explosive materiel to be smuggled in and deployed. For that matter, turn your gaze to Great Clan VanSappen, whose facility was so easily abused.'

'All involved shall be called to account,' said the governor, her voice hard as bedrock. 'The failings of others do not excuse the failings of your own.'

Lydorran's eyes flashed, and his next words shattered that bedrock to rubble.

'I am not here to beg your forgiveness, governor,' he barked. 'We fight a war for the survival of this world, and if that war had been kept without your city's walls prior to our arrival then your streets would not have become our battleground. Look to your own failings before presuming to lecture the Adeptus Astartes on matters of war.'

All about him quailed, even Governor Kallistus. Lydorran pressed on, feeling the vibrations upon the air, sensing thumping hearts and barely perceptible tremors of fear from the unaugmented humans in the room. 'I come before you in light of this latest atrocity to ask again that the conclave of Ghyre set aside your politicking and your divisions. Throw your weight wholeheartedly behind my strategy. Accept that there will be damage, and casualties and sorrow, before victory can be won. Do not put me in a position where I must take their authority from them. Or yours from you.'

He saw the guards adjust their postures, blades lowering a little towards him. High Marshal Kallistus had gone white as bone and looked upon the verge of apoplexy or panic. Carefully, Lydorran teased strands of empyric energy through his staff, readying himself in case someone did something truly foolish. Still, the governor maintained her dignified composure. *It's as though she were discussing trade tithes*, he mused, and could not prevent a sliver of admiration colouring his thoughts.

'You are not going to do that, though, are you, Brother-Librarian?' she said, a statement phrased as a question.

'No, my lady, I am not. Not at this juncture. Instead I am going to remind you that you called for our aid, and that while division remains between us our enemies flourish.'

Lydorran sensed his misstep the moment he saw angry triumph flash across the high marshal's features, though he didn't understand what opening he had left in his defences. He was not kept waiting long.

'I fear that they may flourish all the better in the light of this,' barked Anthonius Kallistus, producing an ornate vid-caster wand from his belt. Brandishing it, he thumbed the activation rune and projected grainy footage into the air before Lydorran.

With a jolt, the Librarian realised he was watching grainy footage of Hastur and Squad Threnn approaching the VanSappen warehouse. Static crackled as though a vox signal had been intercepted, and then a voice he knew did not belong to any Space Marine spoke.

'Bring it down. Crush the traitors in their lair. The Emperor demands absolute submission.'

The footage jumped with static. Lydorran watched Hastur hack down the doors of the structure and duck inside. Moments later, there came a devastating explosion and the warehouse began to collapse. The footage shook then cut out, replaced by a flickering wyrmform.

'Witness the true nature of your liberators,' came a woman's deep voice, thick with anger and scorn. 'Witness the true nature of your Emperor. Only Father offers freedom from their oppression. Only the Star Children offer the hope of Ascension. Join us.'

With that, the recording cut out and then began to repeat.

'Enough,' snapped Lydorran, shocked and aghast at what he had seen. 'That was not the voice of Champion Hastur. This is a heretical fabrication.'

The high marshal hastily stowed his wand, but he could not keep a hint of vicious satisfaction from his face.

'A fabrication it may be, Brother-Librarian, but that transmission has found its way throughout the hive by now, of that you can be sure,' said the governor. 'And this is not the only example of cult propaganda to reach our people. Your battle on the bridge on the day of your arrival, the bombardment of the Augustian Hall of Artifice, the deaths of all those trapped in the turbolift when your gunships fired upon Thassius Tower… The list goes on. Our subjects suffer, seemingly to them as badly as the cult you claim to be protecting them from.'

'We make no such claim,' said Lydorran, his mind whirling.

'It does not matter, Brother-Librarian,' said the governor. 'You are perceived by our people as the Angels of the Emperor, here to save them from the dangers of a dark and terrible galaxy. Instead you appear to treat them with, at best, disdain. They do not understand why. Throne, before you came before us this night had you not been doing battle inside a sacred cathedrum, one that was virtually reduced to ruins? Our people are beloved to us, Brother Lydorran, and we believe that their faith is strong, but can you not see why they might begin to believe the lies of these heretics when faced with such terrifying and indiscriminate destruction?'

This time Lydorran's voice rose to a shout. Such fragility and foolishness beggared belief.

'What do you not understand, governor? Your world stands upon the brink. If your people are being lied to, then it is *your* duty to stifle those lies.'

'I am sure–' began the high marshal, but Lydorran over-rode him effortlessly.

'The entire Imperium faces a war for survival. There is no time for compassion or understanding. The Adeptus Astartes are weapons of last resort. We are the arbiters of the Emperor's will. We cannot waste time here when a hundred other beleaguered worlds cry out for our aid. Do you understand what I am telling you?'

'I do,' said Kallistus, and Lydorran could feel from the thump of her heartbeat, the tightness of her breathing and the way she gripped the arm of her throne that she truly did. Still, he did not relent, could not for the sake of this world and its people. He had to make them all see.

'Our strategy thus far, our approach to this conflict, is as cautious and as diplomatic as we can afford to be, and then only because our orders are to preserve your world's infra-structure. If we fail here, we will declare this strongpoint of the Bastion Imperialis beyond redemption. Your next *reinforcements* will come to bombard the planet with viral munitions until nothing living remains. This will not be my doing, but it *will* happen. Governor, the enderrium ore will still be there when the viral payloads disperse.'

Silence settled over the audience chamber like a shroud. Nobody moved. Governor Kallistus held Lydorran's gaze.

At last the high marshal drew breath, his eyes bulging with outrage, spots of colour burning on his cheeks. Before he could speak, Bishop Renwyck stepped forward and placed a hand upon his arm.

'The Brother-Librarian is correct, Anthonius. He speaks

the truth. Do not damn yourself with unwise words simply because you do not wish to hear what he has to say. There is greater sin in refusing to admit your failures than in facing them and seeking atonement. If we had handled matters ourselves, the Emperor's Angels would not be here at all.'

'Brother Lydorran, our people are loyal,' said the governor. 'They are as faithful to the Emperor's cause as we and our conclave. We all will pay whatever cost must be paid to avoid such final sanction.'

'Loyal. Faithful. I wonder,' said Lydorran, his tone still hard. 'Do you truly know how far the rot of heresy has spread, Governor Kallistus? I heard more than one strident voice of dissent amongst your conclave, more than one utterance that skated perilously close to heresy. Can you be sure that none of the clan lords, none of your advisers, are compromised?'

'This is *outrageous!*' barked the high marshal, shaking off Renwyck's hand. 'You make accusations against those you have no right to impugn! Ghyre is vital to the Imperium. *Vital!* We will not be questioned in this manner!'

'I can assure you that it is not, and that you will,' said Lydorran grimly. 'As I understand it, high marshal, entire platoons of Ghyrish Airborne have vanished throughout this conflict along with all their materiel, while others have been reported locked in vicious internecine warfare or openly declaring themselves for Father. If you find this method of questioning inefficient, my Apothecaries know other ways to ask.'

'Brother Lydorran, enough,' snapped the governor as the high marshal's mouth worked soundlessly. 'You address our brother, and you overstep.'

'With respect, my lady, I do *not*,' boomed Lydorran. 'I *cannot*. I am of the Adeptus Astartes, the Imperial Fists no less.

I speak with the Emperor's voice and act with His implicit sanction, and I will not hesitate to do either.'

'He speaks the truth,' said Renwyck, quiet and sober. 'If the Angels of the Emperor cannot deliver us, none will.'

'Thank you for your counsel, bishop,' said the governor, and Lydorran detected no trace of irony or anger in her voice. 'Brother Lydorran, we begin to truly understand your position and your purpose here. We wish that this had been made clearer when first you arrived.'

'I assumed that it was implicit to you and your subjects,' said Lydorran. 'See that you misstep no further in this regard.'

'We shall extend to you whatever aid we can, as will *all* of our subjects,' said the governor, pinning her brother with a steady look before turning her attention back to Lydorran. 'We ask that in return you and your warriors do what you can to garner the goodwill of our people. Understand, we ask not out of any hope that you will go against your essential natures in this, but only that, from a strategic point of view, the worse you alienate and terrify them, the harder a task our arbitrators will have in keeping them from heeding the call of the cult.'

'I can promise little, my lady, but we will do what we can to avoid furnishing the enemy with needless reinforcement,' replied Lydorran. 'And with this I must depart. There are battles that demand my attention, and I wish to review the findings of my intelligence gatherers. We are doing what we can to out-think and outmanoeuvre the heretics, lest another tragedy occur.'

'Our thanks, Brother-Librarian,' said the governor. 'Go with the Emperor's grace.'

Lydorran made the sign of the aquila and departed the chamber.

* * *

He had crossed the antechamber and made his way down a flight of marble stairs before he heard soft footsteps following. Lydorran slowed his pace as he crossed a softly lit intersection and popped open the holster of his heavy bolt pistol. However, the figure that hastened up behind him was little more than a child. Clad in the vestments of a bishopal novitiate, the boy stumbled to a halt at the sight of Lydorran towering above him.

'Speak,' Lydorran ordered, in no mood for further delays. He could already hear Storn lecturing him on the evils of being away from the battlefront for too long, how it was just such behaviour that had driven Hastur to behave as he had. Self-doubt was needling the Librarian, and he felt the need for the clarity that the pain gauntlet would bring.

'My… master… requests audience, my lord,' squeaked the boy, barely able to get the words out. 'He bids you… follow me.'

'My time and patience both are worn thin,' replied Lydorran, beginning to turn away. 'Tell your master that if he wishes to summon one of the Adeptus Astartes, he would be better to do so in person.'

The boy looked at the floor for a moment, expression stricken. Just as Lydorran began to walk away, however, the child managed to speak again, in a breathless rush.

'He said that you would say this, my lord, and he begs your indulgence in a matter of the utmost urgency. He said to tell you that some on the council speak with a crooked tongue, and that he knows where dwells the father of their lies.'

It was a clumsy enough code, but it was enough to halt Lydorran in his tracks. His mind worked swiftly, and with an impatient grunt he turned back.

'Hurry then, but if your master is wasting my time, he will wish he had not.'

ANDY CLARK

The boy swallowed, then turned and hurried away down a side corridor. The child moved at a nervous trot, but one that Lydorran soon found himself outpacing.

'Run, for I have neither time nor patience left to waste,' he commanded, and after a frightened glance in his direction, the boy increased his pace. They passed several shadowy chambers and looming statues before climbing another flight of stairs and emerging into a darkened corridor. Lydorran saw glass cases and plinths and realised that he was in a display gallery of some sort, perhaps a museum or weapons hall.

The boy looked around anxiously, his eyes less able to pierce the shadows than Lydorran's, and the Librarian felt a moment's disquiet as he heard the subtle heartbeat and breathing of another concealed somewhere in the chamber's shadowed reaches. Surely even the most resourceful of enemies would not have contrived to assail him here? All the same, the Librarian summoned his empyric energies to him again, feeling his psychic hood heat as ripples of disturbance ran through the weft of the warp.

A shape detached itself from a pool of darkness near the chamber's far end and resolved itself into the slight form of Lotimer Renwyck. The bishop glided softly towards Lydorran across the carpeted floor, brushing his hand out in a shooing gesture to the boy as he came.

'Leave.'

With a grateful nod, the child turned and fled, though not before snatching a last, wide-eyed look at Lydorran.

'Bishop Renwyck, why am I here when I should be returning to battle?' asked Lydorran.

'I do not seek to waste your time, Brother-Librarian,' said the bishop, eyes glinting beneath his cowl. 'I sense shadows gathering all around us and would tell you something that I learned from one of my preachers this day just past.'

'Speak then,' said Lydorran, his intrigue warring with his wariness.

'Just hours ago, one of my preachers was walking the streets of the Commercias but a level from where the catastrophe occurred at the VanSappen warehouse,' said Renwyck. 'My man was approached by what he described as a shadowy character who wore miner's garb and glare goggles. He said this individual looked somehow wrong to him, though he could not place why.'

'Brevity, bishop,' said Lydorran.

'Just so,' replied Renwyck, looking chastened. 'The mysterious figure attempted to convince my preacher to abandon his faith, and to give his worship instead to Father! Of course, my man reacted with all the piety and wrath one might hope, but though he decried the cultist as the heretic he was, he was unable to stop the figure from escaping before the Arbites arrived.'

'Brazen, but I fail to see how this is useful to me,' said Lydorran.

'My preacher reported the figure's words to me verbatim, Brother-Librarian, and I believe that in this exchange our enemy may have made a crucial slip. Reportedly, the figure uttered the words "Come with me to Father's side, for in the darkness of the deependelve shalt thou find the light."'

Lydorran looked at Renwyck uncomprehendingly.

'My apologies, Brother-Librarian. You are not a man of local parlance. Why would you be?'

'Enlighten me,' said Lydorran through gritted teeth, his patience worn by the bishop's rambling manner.

'Of course, of course,' said Renwyck, leaning closer as though to confide some great secret. He shot a glance around him before speaking again.

'The deependelve, Brother-Librarian, is local slang. It refers to the Delvemine. The holdings of Great Clan Delve.'

'You are telling me that this mysterious figure may accidentally have revealed that Father lurks within the Delvemine, and that by extension Lord Dostos Delve and his people may be of the cult?' asked Lydorran. Renwyck answered with a nervy nod, looking about him again.

Lydorran became very still. The bishop's heartbeat was steady, and there was no tremor of nervousness or mistruth in his voice. If he was providing genuine intelligence, then he might just have handed Lydorran the key to unlocking this entire sorry puzzle. Yet there had been so much trickery and veiled corruption already, so many baited traps. Lydorran was not about to take Renwyck at his word without first pushing hard to see if some hidden redoubt of falsehoods cracked. He teased his powers into being and subtly increased the weight of his presence, summoning an oppressive weight that literally pressed down upon the bishop's slight form. Lydorran glowered down at him.

'You understand the consequences if I find that you have lied to me?' he asked, his voice deep and menacing.

'Of course, my lord, but I am a faithful servant of the Emperor!' exclaimed Renwyck, looking genuinely alarmed. Lydorran smelled the man's fear sweat prickling his skin.

'And you understand that they will be no less severe if it transpires that you are being used as an unwitting bearer of falsehoods and trickery?' Lydorran leaned a little heavier on the bishop, and added a slight background kinetic tremor that made the shadowy exhibits shudder and rattle.

The man's eyes were wide now, and Lydorran could see

he was shaking with alarm. He looked honestly bewildered that his information had received such a hostile reception.

'I swear to you upon my faith, Brother-Librarian! The man that brought this to me is as loyal and true as I am myself. There is no falsehood here, no trickery! If I have angered you in some way, then please, tell me how I might make amends for such a sin.'

Renwyck was cracking, Lydorran saw, but not through any concealment of guilt. It was just good, honest fear, and that he understood. If Renwyck's tip-off was a trick, Lydorran believed it must be one that even the bishop himself was unaware of. That possibility still played upon the Librarian's mind, but as Storn himself had said more than once, victory to the bold, and only death left for the timid.

'We will investigate this information,' said Lydorran, already keying runic commands into his vambrace. Servo-skulls, Vanguard Infiltrators and orbital surveillance augurs would turn their gaze upon Delvemine with all haste, and if there was anything to be seen there, the Imperial Fists would see it. Meanwhile, he reined in his powers and released the quaking bishop from their grasp. The man uttered a little gasp of relief. The exhibits stopped their earthquake quiver and fell silent again.

'Thank you, Brother-Librarian. That is all that I can ask,' said Renwyck, his words drenched in pitiful relief. As Lydorran turned away, the small man caught hold of his arm with a feverish grip. 'Please, Brother-Librarian, this is a good world, a faithful world, and we do not deserve a heretic's fate. Deliver us.'

Lydorran nodded once, then strode away.

'I will,' he answered over his shoulder.

VIII

Lydorran had returned to Mercurio Gate only a handful of times in the fifteen days since the Imperial Fists had made planetfall. In part, the constant demands of the campaign had kept him moving from one engagement to the next, leading assault groups, sweeping and purging one sector after another and snatching moments of rest and meditation where he could. If he was honest with himself, though, the Librarian had also avoided the space port for the memories it held.

He had enough to manage commanding this tangled conflict, keeping a tight grip upon the reins of not only his own warriors but of the Ghyrish conclave as well, and trying not to overtax his mind and powers to the point where something disastrous occurred. Lydorran had felt more than once the greasy squirm and slither of malefic warp entities circling his soul, stalking him from beyond the veil, awaiting the slightest opening. Driven to his limits and staving off mental exhaustion through willpower alone, he didn't think reminders of Tor's death would help him retain control.

This day, however, Mercurio Gate could not be avoided.

This day, they mustered for the attack.

Lydorran strode through the bustle of the space port, past pre-fab ramparts and strongpoints stamped with the Chapter badge of the Imperial Fists, past arming servitors lumbering beneath heavy loads, between squads of battle-brothers swearing their oaths and platoons of Ghyrish soldiery quick-marching towards whatever duties they had been assigned. At Storn's suggestion, the strike force had co-opted Mercurio Gate as their base of operations, refusing the governor's offer of 'more fitting quarters' in favour of being ever ready to mobilise from within a defensible position of their own fortification.

It was a good plan with only one drawback – during the darkness of night, even the combined illumination from all the Hive Spire's structures could not entirely wash out the twisted stars. The Imperial Fists had the spiritual fortitude to ignore the many-coloured stains that curled and twisted through the void like mutant aurorae. The same was not true of the Chapter serfs who had accompanied them to the planet's surface, nor their Ghyrish allies. More than one had begun gibbering or become senselessly violent after too long labouring beneath the poisoned stars.

Initially those losses had simply been replaced, the Space Marines judging a few mortal derangements a small price to pay for increased speed of refuelling and rearming. However, since his conversation a few nights earlier with the governor and her closest aides, Lydorran had instated a new rule – the Imperial Fists alone would walk in the open during the hours of darkness, the Ghyrish emerging from sleep shelters as dawn's first light spilled over the horizon and washed out the monstrous stellar phenomena. Such was the case now, serf crewmen and Ghyrish soldiery venturing into the pale daylight to aid the Imperial Fists in any way they could.

The arrangement was just one facet of the improved relations between the Ghyrish and their liberators, both pleased that progress had been made but also frustrated that it had taken so long to achieve.

Ahead of Lydorran loomed the Thunderhawk *Vengeful*, its assault ramp lowered to allow boarding. The same assault ramp upon which Captain Tor had died, thought Lydorran. Before he could stop himself, he had shot a cold glance in the direction of the cooling towers from which the shot had come.

'What is done is done, Brother-Librarian,' came Storn's grating voice, floating out in greeting from within the Thunderhawk's bay. 'If you want to glare, aim that wrath at the future, not the past. That one your anger can still affect.'

Storn thumped down the ramp to clasp gauntlets with Lydorran in a warrior's greeting.

'There is a lot to glare back at,' said Lydorran with a slight grimace, thinking of Hastur, of the death or wounding of more than a score of battle-brothers in ambushes, gunfights, bomb blasts and frantic pursuits. Storn grunted in what might have been agreement.

'Same is true in any campaign, Aster. This one has just been more drawn out and complicated than most.'

'Give me a good, honest siege any day,' said the Librarian as the two of them turned and walked back up the ramp into the gunship's belly.

'Spoken like a true son of Dorn,' replied Storn with a crooked grin. 'Truth is, Tor's plan was a good one, but even he didn't predict how deep-rooted the heresy on this world would prove. The Adeptus Astartes are weapons of open war, not all this hunting and policing and snatching at shadows. If we had our time again, I wonder if we would not simply have come down bolters blazing and deciphered who was friend or foe after the shooting ceased.'

Lydorran shook his head, staring back out of the Thunderhawk at Ghyrish and Space Marines moving industriously around one another in the dawn light.

'I do not believe that,' he said. 'I do not believe that would have been worthy of us, nor would it have met our objectives. Where would we have struck?'

'Klaratos Hive, perhaps,' said Storn. 'There are few shades of grey about that place.'

'And yet this foe is cunning – they have shown us that much. While we vented our fury upon a half-ruined and wholly hostile city, the enemy would have made their move to seize the last loyal Ghyrish bastion from us and likely slain the governor and all her advisers into the bargain. It might have been a swifter and more clean-cut battle, brother, but ultimately that decision would have forced us to destroy all that we came here to save and seen the entire world turned against us.'

'Hah, Tor would be proud,' said the Chaplain. 'But now, look. Here I am counselling you to focus upon what lies ahead, yet it is you that has to turn my gaze from the past.' Storn shook his head as though in self-chastisement, but Lydorran couldn't escape the feeling that he had just been tested on some level.

'I had thought that we were building a bond these past days,' he said, his voice becoming hard. 'Still you push and probe as though seeking weaknesses in a green novitiate rather than a valued comrade. I know my worth, and that of my powers, Brother-Chaplain. It is time you recognised them also.'

Storn became still, his granite features unreadable. Then he nodded, and for a moment only, Lydorran thought the Chaplain looked tired and old.

'Vigilance is a habit hard broken, judgement a duty the Chapter demands from me always,' he said. 'But you are right, Brother-Librarian. We are comrades in this, commanding officer and valued counsellor, not neophyte and pedagogue. My apologies.'

Lydorran grunted an acknowledgement, though in truth he felt a stirring of pride at Storn's words. If there was one warrior upon this world whose approval he desired, Lydorran could admit to himself that it was Storn. Such validation firmly bolstered his confidence as the strike force's leader.

'The Ghyrish are finally upholding their end of the campaign as we would hope,' he said, changing the subject to more practical matters. 'Purgation of Commercias was declared complete as of nineteen hundred hours yesterday, and I received word on my way here that Orbitas has been declared secure this morning.'

'With Militarus purged and secure now too, that only leaves Aquisitorius and the Laboritas,' said Storn. Lydorran nodded, thinking of the reports they had received of sudden and explosive violence in the Militarus district when the high marshal's new edicts came down. Imperial Fists and Adeptus Arbites alike had worked with Ghyrish Commissariat officers and even priests to vet and sanction each garrison tower in turn. Lockdown curfews had held each platoon of soldiery in place until their faith and purity could be ascertained and their fitness to serve be assured. The measures must have wounded the high marshal's pride immeasurably, not to mention his reputation amongst his soldiery, but sure enough they had yielded immediate results. Like insects scuttling out from beneath upturned rocks, the traitors amidst the ranks had been revealed.

'Casualties were lighter than I expected,' Lydorran mused. 'There were fewer heretic infiltrators than we predicted.'

'Any more than none is too damned many,' growled Storn. 'Needs must while the warp waxes, but once this world is secured there'll be some hard questions for everyone in charge. The type asked by the Ordo Xenos.'

'For now, though, their cleansing coupled with the high marshal pulling back more platoons from the mines means we have the manpower to at last push down into the Laboritas,' said Lydorran.

'If we need to, after today,' noted Storn. 'You've reviewed the reports?'

'Inloaded them fully,' replied Lydorran. 'Delvemine is corrupt, that much is clear. But to suggest the cult are hiding Father there? I'm not so sure this deity of theirs is even a physical being so much as a figurehead woven from lies and rhetoric.'

'Sounds like great efforts have been made to conceal it from the airborne regiments and the magi who maintain the macro-purgation firethrowers,' said Storn. 'Scratch a little deeper, though, and there's every indication of a veritable cult fortress lurking under the conclave's collective noses. Coordinated, organised and heavily defended. It's as likely a site as we've seen yet for their leaders to lurk, even if one of them isn't the false god himself.'

'Even if we succeed in executing their leaders, there is no guarantee the cult will just collapse,' warned Lydorran.

'True, brother, but in my experience few mortals have the drive or rhetoric to whip the masses into sedition and heresy. Shorn of their agitators, this cult may lose cohesion and purpose to the point where we can depart safe in the knowledge that local forces can conclude the purge.'

'Or, if there is truly some deeper xenoform taint behind the Wrything Wyrm, then new leaders may simply emerge elsewhere on Ghyre,' countered Lydorran. 'Their god may be a more complex concept or being than we have so far envisaged. Their cohesive purpose may stem from some collective consciousness or parasitic drive that renders the concept of individual leaders meaningless.'

'Dorn's blood, brother, you analyse every action you take down to the last grains of detail,' said Storn, slapping one armoured palm against Lydorran's shoulder guard. 'It must be exhausting.'

'I am merely explaining why we are striking with a limited force, rather than committing everything to this offensive,' said Lydorran with a frown. 'If the assault is ineffectual, or if this proves to be another of the enemy's snares, we need strength enough within Angelicus Hive to proceed with the push into the Laboritas.'

'Or to counter anything the enemy may try while we have forces committed to the attack upon Delvemine,' said Storn. 'Wise, my brother. Very wise. You have doubts about Renwyck's claims, then?'

'Though I will fight to protect this world and its people, the sights we have seen since coming here have left me with doubts about every citizen of Ghyre,' replied Lydorran. 'Even the planet's leading bishop is not exempt.'

'Again, wise,' said Storn, and Lydorran heard unalloyed respect in the Chaplain's tone. It shored up his convictions.

'Come, it is time,' said Lydorran with a grim smile. 'Gather the breaching force and let us mobilise. For all this wise talk, it will feel good to fight a clear-cut battle at last.'

A trio of gunships lifted off from Mercurio Gate, two carrying Imperial Fists Space Marines and supporting walkers, the third a transporter whose adamantine grapples cradled a Vindicator siege tank named *Hammerblow* and a Destructor-pattern Predator whose flank bore the name *Blade Indomitable* and whose first combat action was said to have occurred over four thousand years before. As the gunships burned thrusters and punched through the dawn sky towards the edge of Hive Spire, a squadron of Stormtalon gunships swept in to take up escort positions.

It was a substantial force, a good half of all the materiel that Captain Tor had led down upon Ghyre. Lydorran knew that to commit so many of his warriors to this endeavour was a risk, but he believed it to be a calculated one, well worthwhile. At best, a force of this size would fall like the Emperor's own sword upon the enemy's fastness, shatter their defences with a speed that only the siege masters of the Imperial Fists could achieve, trap the cult's leadership cadre behind their own defences and see them butchered before full daylight touched the spiretops.

At worst, so formidable a force of the Adeptus Astartes would be the equal of any trap the enemy sprang. Either way, by the close of the day the Imperial Fists would have reminded everyone on Ghyre, even themselves, of the speed, ferocity and strength with which they could strike down the enemies of the Imperium. It would make for a potent statement to counter the propaganda of the cult and put the fear of Imperial vengeance into them and their sympathisers both.

Lydorran beseeched the spirits of *Vengeful's* external sensors and patched their vid feed directly into his autosenses. He watched the last towers of Hive Spire race up towards him, framed against the vastness of Ghyre's skies. They swept past, and he felt the Thunderhawk angle steeply down, his view tilting as it aimed its prow for the ground far, far below.

The mountainous flanks of Hive Angelicus shot past, cargo lighters and grav skiffs scattering from the Space Marines' flight path as their craft arrowed downwards. Exchanger towers, vox beacons, strobing lumen and smog-belching stacks flashed to either side, jutting from the hive's metal skin in a riotous profusion that reminded Lydorran of a cactus' spines. They streaked past stained-armaglass windows a hundred feet high, past the jutting tongues of mercantile air-jetties and the menacing barrels of defence turrets by the hundred.

Despite their speed, minutes passed as the aircraft continued their journey down the hive's cyclopean slopes. Lydorran meditated, shutting out the vox-chatter of pilot helots, the chanted oaths of his battle-brothers and the steady rumble of the gunship's engines. He focused inward and gathered his mental strength for the fight to come.

Tor, brother, let me be right about this. And if we are deceived, let them fear our wrath.

'*Hive base approaching. Twenty seconds to mist-belt,*' came the pilot's voice. Lydorran opened his eyes in time to see the immense legs of the hive city racing past. They were an incredible feat of engineering, like the structures that held promethium derricks and electro-pylons up but infinitely sturdier and braced by hundreds of massive support struts and cross-beams. Lydorran could see the tracks of the funicular railway that ran down this nearest leg, industrial in its scale, to carry the miners from the stations throughout

Laboritas and down through the mists to the mines below. He saw also the purgation shrines that clung to the legs like crustaceans, the muzzles of their firethrowers pointed unwaveringly down into the mist. In their lee, strung perilously between metal beams and dangling from elaborate webworks of cable and rope, were the structures of the underslums.

Foreleg, Widdershin, Railtown, Canopies, his eidetic memory supplied. Names given by the destitute but unbowed to furnish their desperate dwellings with the veneer of hope.

The mist raced up to meet *Vengeful* and the gunship plunged beneath its surface. Suddenly they were surrounded by a soft, lambently glowing haze. It pressed in around the gunship, veiling its sister craft from sight, concealing everything more than a few feet distant. Lydorran felt the cold of the mists as though their clammy caress were slithering across his skin rather than the armoured hull of his transport.

The gunship pulled up hard and sharp, and Lydorran had a split-second glimpse of the jungle canopy as it swept close below. Bioluminescent pods and glowing stems pulsed with purples, greens, blues and pinks. Many-hued tendrils coiled and writhed. Ink-black spines burst from neon-blue succulents to clang against the hull like bullets.

'Approach vector locked, data psalms spooling,' voxed the pilot. *'Formation holding twenty feet below effective auspex coverage.'*

'Good work, helot. You honour your Chapter, as do your comrades,' replied Lydorran.

'Thank you, my lord,' replied the helot, sounding pleased despite the strain of intense concentration in his voice. They were flying no more than a few feet above the turbulent canopy of Ghyre's jungle, Lydorran knew, ensuring that their enemies would not have a chance to detect their approach until the Space Marines were all but upon them.

'Brothers, gird your souls for battle,' Lydorran said, switching to force-wide vox. 'Beneath this veil of mists our enemies have fortified their lair. Hidden from the Emperor's gaze, they have multiplied like insects spawning beneath a stone. Now we shall rip that stone away, and in the cold light of vengeance they will wither and die. The time for mercy is past. All targets are to be considered hostile within the Clan Delve compound. Some may be innocent of heresy, untainted by the touch of whatever xenos madness has taken their kin. Yet they are complicit all the same. Ignorance, fear, laxity, these are none of them excuses for allowing this rot to spread around them. All are judged guilty. All must know the vengeance of the Imperium. For Dorn and for Terra!'

'For Dorn and for Terra!' they shouted in response, and Lydorran heard steel in every voice. They were as ready to strike a real blow as he, he thought. Whatever awaited them in Delvemine, he pitied it.

'Enemy compound on long-range auspex,' reported their pilot.

'Interrogating machine-spirits, triangulating defences,' added his gunner.

'Commence the attack,' Lydorran commanded. 'For the Emperor!'

The high walls of the compound appeared so suddenly out of the murk that Lydorran almost missed them as *Vengeful* flashed overhead. He had a fleeting impression of towering ferrocrete cliffs a good hundred feet high, looming over the encroaching jungle and studded with firethrowers and watch towers.

Even now the flame turrets were in operation, spitting tongues of burning promethium at the glowing bioflora and withering it back on every front.

Missiles and las-blasts leapt from the wings and muzzles of

Space Marine gunships as the craft shot overhead. Switching for a moment to *Vengeful*'s rear imagers, Lydorran saw flame turrets detonate in roaring columns of fire, saw armoured watch towers explode and rubble crashing and tumbling down the lee faces of the walls.

He had a moment to register that the mists were thinner within the compound, and to realise that this was the work of massive fan units that sucked in the vapours and funnelled them through thick pipes to spill back out beyond the walls. Then *Vengeful* was slowing, rotating on its axis and spitting shells, bolts and blasts into the figures scattering in all directions below it.

Lydorran saw ferrocrete roads splitting and branching in a complex network between bare and muddy ground. More flame turrets loomed over the approaches to deep quarry pits, the blackened earth around them testament to the jungle's ongoing efforts to push its seeds, spores and roots beyond the walls. Clusters of shanty-like lean-tos, prefab administration structures, machine hangars, tool sheds, guard towers, ecclesiarchal shrines and metal-roofed refectorums were scattered everywhere. Just to the east of their position, Lydorran noted the towering mechanical structures of the primary mine-head, overlooked by defensive towers and troglodytic structures dug half into the bedrock itself.

'Ready, brothers!' he barked, rising from his restraint throne and brandishing his stave as the Thunderhawk descended on howling engines. The craft hit the mud with a bang and its ramp slammed down. Again, a forceful reminder of Tor's demise flashed through Lydorran's mind. Again, he thrust the thoughts away and stormed down the ramp at the head of his warriors. Chaplain Storn and Apothecary Lordas followed him, one at each shoulder, and behind them came the

Intercessors of Squad Furian, the Terminators of Squad Lesordus and the mighty form of Dreadnought Brother Ghesmund.

A glance showed Lydorran that the other gunship had put down to disgorge more yellow-armoured warriors into the landing zone, while *Hammerblow* and *Blade Indomitable* were even now gunning their engines and roaring into position as their lander dusted off again. Figures scattered away from them in all directions through the mist, fleeing for their lives. The hammering guns of the Space Marine aircraft cut them down without mercy and the Stormtalons shot back and forth overhead, herding the fleeing miners away from the Space Marine landing zone.

'Lydorran to Shipmaster Gavorn. We have made uncontested landing, brother,' voxed the Librarian.

'Understood, Brother-Librarian. Be advise–'

Gavorn's words were drowned in a sudden tidal wave of interference. Static roared and crackled like an inferno. Within it, Lydorran heard vicious hissing and what sounded like whispering voices, spilling over and around one another in a dreadful susurrus. Around him he saw his brothers pause, some shaking their heads or pressing their hands to the sides of their helms. The interference was deafening, its volume swelling by the moment until with a curse Lydorran blink-clicked the rune that would shut his vox off altogether.

Nothing happened. Still the babbling din washed over him, now laced through with a thrumming basso note that reverberated through his skull with violent intensity. His alarm grew as the psychocircuitry of his hood began to heat.

Lydorran disengaged his helm's seals and wrenched it from his head with a curse. He spun around, gesturing at his brothers to do the same. Some had already followed suit, and the others hastily took their lead. He saw that black veins marred the flesh of the worst affected, who stumbled and blinked and grubbed away bloody tears that leaked from their eyes.

'Primarch's fist! Gaaah! Damnation!' The vox-amplified shout had come from behind Lydorran, and he turned to see Veteran Sergeant Lesordus and his warriors staggering and cursing under the psychic assault. So bulky was their armour that they could not remove their own helms without the aid of arming helots, Lydorran realised, and now they were as good as trapped.

'Brothers, aid them!' commanded Lydorran, sending several of Squad Furian running to the veterans' sides. At the same moment a hail of fire whipped out of the mists. Bullets rang from the Space Marines' armour. A keening beam of las energy took off Sergeant Furian's leg at the knee, and he fell with a roar of pain.

'Sight targets and return fire!' barked Chaplain Storn. Volleys of bolts whipped through the mist and knocked half-seen shapes from their feet.

Lydorran swore again as he saw *Hammerblow* slew to the right then grind to a halt. Its hatch clanged open and its commander, Sergeant Vastian, emerged, unhelmed, a trail of blood leaking from one ear and thin wisps of smoke curling up around him.

'I shot out the internal vox,' he called to Lydorran. 'We shall beg the machine-spirits' forgiveness later.'

'Good thinking, brother,' replied the Librarian, breaking off as a stooped figure sprinted out of the murk straight at him. He registered a hulking mutant, blasting charges clutched in its clawed fists, a scream of hatred twisting its features. Focusing his powers, Lydorran thrust the tip of his staff towards the cultist and sent a shockwave of force surging outwards. The mist peeled back as though before the blastwave of an explosion, and the cultist was lifted from his feet and hurled backwards with a hiss of pain. The charges he clutched detonated a moment later, the fiery flash illuminating the last moments of a handful of luckless cultists.

Lydorran's mind raced as he factored the sudden penetration of their vox-network into his battle plan. The Terminators were all unhelmed now, crimson streaks on their skin showing where ears, nostrils and even eyes had bled under the sustained psychoauditory bombardment. Their expressions were stony and furious, tainted by webs of black lines like worms beneath their flesh.

'I think we can safely say the enemy are here in force,' called Apothecary Lordas as he ran to Sergeant Furian's aid.

'But is this their idea of an ambush or simply some defensive measure triggered by our arrival?' asked Storn.

'If it is a trap, it is a poor one,' replied Lydorran, hurling another blast of force into the mist and scattering a charging mob of cultists. Bolt shells took the ones who staggered back to their feet. 'We are inconvenienced, but nothing more. We push on to the mine-head at once.'

He looked back, gesturing at the armaglass canopy of *Vengeful* for the pilot to lift off. He saw the man wave a hand in reply, noted that the gunner was slumped unmoving over his station at the pilot's back, and winced. The jamming signal would have been hard on the unaugmented crew helots, and he thanked the primarch that at least one of them had been able to withstand it long enough to shoot out the vox-unit.

The gunship's engines howled and it dusted off. As it took to the air, a thick column of laser energy stabbed from the murk and scored a deep gash in the Thunderhawk's fuselage. Lydorran heard the roar of engines the instant before a ragged column of enemy vehicles surged into view. He saw mining trucks pressed into cult service, cultists leaning over the heavy lasers with their goggles flashing. Around them raced lighter prospecting vehicles and a swarm of bikes of a similar model to that he had pursued through Hive Spire weeks earlier.

Lydorran gave no command; none was needed. As one the Imperial Fists opened fire upon the attacking vehicles, venting their pent-up fury upon them. Las-blasts tore through rugged frontal armour. Bolt shells punched into the skulls and bodies of drivers, riders and crewmen and blew them apart in bloody sprays. Lydorran roared with effort and anger as he drove his mind deep into the ground beneath a speeding truck and wrenched the earth upwards with a mighty heave that flipped the vehicle into the air. It came down with a sickening crash, skidding through the mud before exploding in a bright fireball. *Hammerblow* fired a shell almost point-blank into another racing vehicle and blew it apart in a spectacular shower of shrapnel. Brother Ghesmund and *Blade Indomitable* focused their fire into a storm that ripped through the enemy bikers to devastating effect.

There were casualties, of course. A mining laser punched through the chest of one of the Aggressors of Squad Justus, and the warrior crumpled without a sound. Heavy-calibre fire hammered Squad Furian, felling one of their number and leaving another with a bloody stump where his right forearm had been. A lucky shot from another mining laser stretched out to sweep a passing Stormtalon from the air, skewering the gunship and sending it spiralling down into a quarry pit to explode out of sight.

Still, thought Lydorran as he rolled aside from the churning drill-prow of one of the trucks, the assault had the feel of desperation more than a planned attack. This sort of armoured thrust might have shattered a Ghyrish platoon had they come to purge the perfidy lurking in Delvemine, but against the Imperial Fists it was little more than a forlorn hope.

He came back to his feet and swung his stave hard, hammering a cultist from the saddle of her bike. The vehicle sped on into the murk, wobbling off its wheels just as it vanished. The rider was thrown into the mud, dead before she hit the ground.

Hammerblow fired again, the mist jumping at the shockwave generated by its mighty demolisher cannon. Dirt, fire, sundered ferrocrete and twisted metal fountained as two of the light prospector buggies were blasted apart as one, and suddenly the last of the cult armour was in retreat. The vehicles heeled around as though at some unheard command and raced back towards the mine-head looming a few hundred yards distant.

'Full advance!' bellowed Lydorran, ensuring he was heard even over the continuous hammer of gunfire. Cultists poured in towards them from every side. Bullets and blasts raked the strike force, causing a Terminator to stagger and curse and taking a Hellblaster's head off with a lucky shot. Yet the enemy's assault had failed utterly to break the Space Marine lines.

Like a vast juggernaut gaining momentum, the Imperial Fists advanced. Their tanks flanked out to either side, rumbling through the mist and keeping pace with the loping gait of the Space Marines themselves. One of the strike force's Techmarines had disembarked from the second gunship, and now he compelled his thunderfire cannon to advance, the tracked artillery piece cycling its barrels with loud thumps as it lobbed munitions into the onrushing foe. Lydorran and Lordas led one spearhead of brothers and Storn the other, two prongs of yellow-armoured warriors driving inexorably towards the enemy's fortress.

Sawing fire whipped down from the defensive towers that flanked the mine-head, throwing up puffs of dust and mud as they stitched through the Space Marine lines. The access shafts of the mine itself were protected by a heavy plasteel blast door, almost as high as the walls that ringed the compound and stamped with the crossed-laser symbol of Clan Delve. The entire armoured mass was sunken into a rocky cliff face that itself showed extensive signs of excavation and fortification. Much of it looked recent to Lydorran's eye, additional bolstering in case of besiegement. Gun turrets nestled in flak-boarded holes in the rockface, barrels tracking right and left as they sprayed fire at the oncoming Space Marines.

'Push up! Neutralise their defences!' shouted Lydorran.

'With the greatest pleasure, Brother-Librarian!' boomed Ghesmund, and he lumbered along to Lydorran's right. The Dreadnought didn't slow, but carefully lined up his assault cannon and then triggered the weapon. The barrels howled up to speed and detonations ripped along the cliff face around the blast doors. Ghesmund annihilated one turret then tracked his fire into the next one, and the next. At the same time the exceptional strategic capabilities and rigorous Codex learnings of the Imperial Fists came into play; even without direct orders, the gunship crews knew exactly how to aid their comrades' advance.

Arrayed in a V formation, four Stormtalons and two Thunderhawks roared overhead and let fly as one against the mine-head gate. Rockets streaked down in swarms. Las-fire and explosive bolts fell like rain. Explosions blossomed across the blast doors. Metal melted into glowing slag in heartbeats and peeled apart, collapsing upon itself. Cultists threw themselves flat with wails of terror as the rain of ordnance came down, and the Imperial Fists' sharpshooters ensured they didn't get the chance to rise again.

Lydorran felt a surge of fierce satisfaction as a massive breach was blasted in the gates, the turrets around them burned and one of the defence towers toppled, trailing flame like a comet's tail. The last handful of cult armour had turned at bay before the gates and was firing madly, heretics in utility suits and sullied Ghyrish uniforms kneeling in the mud as they shot desperately at the Imperial Fists with autoguns and crew-served stubbers.

'Breach!' bellowed Chaplain Storn. 'We have a breach!'

'Crush the defenders and purge the mine. Leave none alive. Father is your priority,' commanded Lydorran, running up the slope with one hand extended and a geokinetic shield swirling before him. Bullets and grenades whined from it, and he felt his face stretch into a cold and mirthless smile at the ineffectual attacks of his foes.

Now they would see what it meant to stand against the might of the Emperor's Angels.

Then he felt it, his empyric senses picking up a mighty surge below. Energy. Fury. Tectonic force channelled and unleashed in a ruinous shockwave that was even now racing up from the depths with the ferocity of an avalanche. Lydorran's eyes widened in horror and he slowed, turning and drawing breath to cry a warning.

The ground leapt beneath his feet. It erupted. Rock and soil and fallen bodies transformed into a shredded blizzard, and he felt himself lifted bodily from the disintegrating ground. Then he was falling, falling amidst tumbling rock and wreckage and flashes of yellow armour.

* * *

Lydorran unclenched his teeth as the furious buffeting finally stopped, his disorientation and pain overwhelming. Dust flowed into his lungs, and he choked for a moment before his superior physiology filtered the invasive particles and stilled the muscle convulsions in his chest. Lydorran blinked. He was lying on his front atop a mound of rubble. He couldn't feel his left arm below the elbow. Steeling himself, he looked and saw that a massive lump of yellow-painted metal had crushed the limb. It was the front-right faring of *Blade Indomitable*, he realised with a sick lurch. Where the rest of the Predator was, Lydorran had no idea, but half of one of his arms was lost beneath this torn fragment of the vehicle, and his pistol with it.

Dust thickened the air, turning already watery daylight into a turgid murk.

Lydorran took a deep breath then pulled, once, hard. Sinew stretched and tore. Mangled flesh parted. Shattered bone crackled as it gave entirely, its jagged edges gouging at flesh now stretched taut and tearing it further. Blood squirted hot and red, swiftly turning to gory paste amidst the drifting dust. Pain shot through him, bad enough to set black starbursts speckling his vision.

The arm still wasn't free.

He cursed, shooting a glance about him to see if the foes were near. He had a dim impression of shadowy solidity not far away through the haze, of light filtering down from somewhere above, but he saw no sign of movement.

'Dorn help me endure this and do what needs must,' Lydorran muttered, and prepared to pull again. Rubble crunched. Something big moved. Adrenaline surged through the Librarian and he reached for his powers, though he knew that he was too woozy and disoriented to use them well. Then he relaxed as Apothecary Lordas knelt next to him.

'Brother-Librarian, let me,' he said, the thin beam of a las-cutter extending from his vambrace-mounted narthecium. Lydorran saw that Lordas had a vicious scalp wound, his skull visibly dented and cracked where something had struck him. Swift-congealing blood caked one side of Lordas' face, vivid crimson beneath a clinging layer of dust. The Apothecary's eye on that side was a burst sack, its fluids tracking viscous tears down his cheek, yet Lordas proceeded with his duty as though he had suffered no more than a bruise.

'Brother...' breathed Lydorran.

'Bionics exist for a reason, Aster,' said Lordas, his clipped tones revealing nothing of the agony he must be in. 'We will both need them after this.'

A quick slice of the lascutter parted ceramite, flesh and bone. White fire shot down Lydorran's nerve endings, redoubling as Lordas applied a cauterising unguent to the stump of his elbow and the flesh sizzled and seared. Then Lydorran was on his feet, staff in hand, shaking the last of the shock from his mind and helping his comrade to rise.

'They sapped us,' he said. 'They must have set the charges through works extending directly below the mine-head approach. Throne alive, we walked right into it.' His shock and shame were physical weights dragging at his limbs. Lydorran had been as sure as he could possibly be that Renwyck believed what he was saying was true. His Vanguard spies and servo-skull reconnaissance flights had revealed nothing of the covert preparations that must have been made to fashion this deadly trap. How could he have allowed himself to be deceived again, despite his every effort to the contrary? Lydorran's self-loathing knew no bounds, threatening to drown him in black misery far worse than any amount of physical pain. He had failed himself, his Chapter, Brother-Captain Tor, even the primarch and the Emperor both.

'To trigger so deep a blast, though, so widespread… they must have destroyed half the damned mine complex!' exclaimed Lordas. 'I wouldn't be surprised if they've caved the central shaft in, triggering a shockwave that close to the mine-head. Clan Delve's holdings will be in ruins. Thousands of miners buried alive…'

'I doubt the cult cares,' said Lydorran, unable to keep the bitterness and fury from his voice. 'I swear on the primarch's hand, brother, that is the last time I will underestimate the lunacy of those we face. They deceived me, and I failed you all. They have destroyed themselves in their fervour to destroy us, and our battle-brothers have paid the price.'

'We are not beaten yet, Brother-Librarian,' said Lordas. 'We need to get out of this damned pit, rally our brothers and finish this.'

Lydorran felt shame at his momentary weakness, but he crushed it down alongside all the anger and pain and resentment of this gruelling campaign.

'You are correct, brother,' he said. Lydorran braced his staff in the crook of his one complete arm, unlocked his helm from his belt and lifted it towards his ear hopefully. He winced at the continued howl of static that issued from within and mag-locked it back at his hip. 'We will have to rally our brothers without vox.'

'First thing is to get out of here then,' said Lordas, swiping caked blood from his face and discharging a mist of greenish fluid across the wound in his skull. Lydorran paused, questing out with his psychic powers. He sensed vibrations approaching through the bedrock.

'Something is working its way towards us,' he said, casting about through the swirling murk. 'That way.'

As he pointed with the stump of his arm there came a grinding rumble, followed by the crack and tumble of falling stone. Something roared amidst the murk, and Lydorran shared a look with Lordas. No human throat had made that sound. The Librarian hefted his stave one-handed. Beside him, the Apothecary checked the load on his pistol and extended the blade of his lascutter to almost a foot in length. Dust sparked and vanished as it touched the searing surgical blade.

The first mutant came at them in a rush. It was huge, twisted out of true by grotesque masses of muscle and chitin that bloated its frame. Lydorran recognised the telltale chitinous plates of tyranid bioforms and knew that his Apothecaries' suspicions had been correct. Its face was misshapen, a thick purple tongue lolling from crooked jaws, yellow eyes staring with idiot hatred. It swung a massive pick-hammer at them, a bastardised mining tool too large for any normal human to wield, and Lydorran barely caught the blow on his stave. He cursed and staggered, off balance without his missing arm.

The thing swung again, the head of its hammer sending up a shower of pulverised rubble as it struck the ground. It roared, spittle flying from its jaws, and Lordas took his chance to drive his lascutter's blade through the thing's mouth and up into its skull. Flesh cooked and spat. Teeth shattered. Lordas wrenched his fist free of the thing's maw and it staggered, black ichor pumping over its jaws and pattering to the floor. It collapsed backwards with a groan, but three more of the hulking abominations trampled it into the floor as they came at the Space Marines.

'Get *back*,' roared Lydorran, lashing out with his mind.

Rock and stone flew up in a shower that lacerated one of the monsters while the force of the shockwave hit so hard that the next one was flung from its feet amidst the sounds of rupturing flesh and shattering bone. Lordas shot the last creature through the chest, the bolt round sending a spray of gore and bone fountaining from its back. Still the thing came on, swinging a huge length of rebar. It struck Lordas a glancing blow and sent him staggering back even as the lacerated mutant surged to its feet again, black fluids flowing from its flesh in rivulets.

'Damned things are tough!' gasped Lordas, grabbing the rebar in his free palm as it swung at him again. He wrenched the crude weapon from his assailant's grasp, spun it around and rammed it through the mutant's throat. It crashed backwards, ichor jetting, limbs spasming.

'Not *that* tough,' spat Lydorran. With a vicious twist of his powers, he gathered the dust particles into the air and smashed them back together as a solid lump of rock that encased the lacerated mutant's head. The thing went wild, staggering and flailing, pounding at the stone with its lumpen fists as it began to suffocate. The stone cracked, but Lydorran wasn't finished. Another psychic *wrench*, this one hard enough to make his vision waver and whispers shiver through the back of his mind, and he twisted the new-made boulder through one hundred and eighty degrees, taking his enemy's head with it. The thing's spine snapped with an audible pop, and it collapsed to the floor like a puppet with its strings cut.

More shapes moved in the murk. More lumpen mutants lumbered towards them.

'Can we escape through the tunnel they are coming in from?' asked Lordas, gunning one of the beasts down with a trio of shells.

Lydorran quested out with his over-taxed powers and grunted in frustration.

'No, that bore goes down deep, and I'm not sure it ends anywhere but caved-in stone. They must have concealed these things in hardened shelters before they detonated their charges, hoping that some of them would survive and dig their way out.'

'Straight on top of anyone who survived the collapse,' said Lordas, cursing as his pistol clicked dry. Another mutant swung for him, and Lydorran blocked its attack with a groan of psychic effort. The circuitry of his hood was glowing hot again, and warning chimes were ringing from its emitters.

'This was no desperate defence,' he said. '*This* was their trap. The entire damned mine complex. Renwyck sent us straight into its jaws.'

'Or he was tricked into doing so,' said Lordas, stepping back from the wild swing of a huge mattock.

Lydorran lunged with his stave and cracked a mutant's skull. 'Come now, brother. We will have to scale our way out.'

He and Lordas turned from the mutants and ran. Part of Lydorran raged against it, retreat in the face of the enemy, the admission of defeat. It wasn't the way of the Imperial Fists. The other, wiser part of him remembered that their proud martial history boasted more than its share of valiant but doomed last stands. He would be damned if he and his surviving brothers were going to be added to that list.

'Here, the rubble slopes – I think we can make it,' he shouted, surging up the tumbled rockfall and digging his toes into the debris.

'Right behind you, brother. I–'

The rest of Lordas' words were driven from him in a plosive breath as a mutant smashed his legs from under him with a sidelong swipe and the Apothecary hit the rubble chest-first. Lydorran spun and hurled a blast of psychic force, only for lancing pain to race through his mind. For an instant, reality turned crimson and green at the edges and dark veins crept across his vision.

Too much, he thought. *Too much, too quickly.* He couldn't risk using his powers again, could feel the warp predators circling the light of his soul. They were almost upon him.

Lydorran's blast had thrown one mutant back and given Lordas a chance to scramble to his feet. The Apothecary took two more steps before a massive boulder, easily as large as a grown man, slammed into his skull from behind.

Blood splattered Lydorran.

Lordas' body hit the ground, sliding a little downwards, and fetched up on a rock. Horror surged through Lydorran, and then, with a cold stab, he took in the precious gene-seed canisters locked to his comrade's belt.

Nothing else mattered. Not pride, not honour, not vengeance for his battle-brother. Those canisters were his Chapter's future, and he would not abandon them to these mutant scum. Lydorran swung his staff furiously and smashed the nearest brute under the chin, throwing it back. He spun his staff then threw the weapon like a javelin. It crashed into the face of the next mutant and drove it back, long enough for Lydorran to lunge forward and snatch the belt of precious capsules from Lordas' hip.

'I am sorry, brother,' he gasped. 'Let this be the first deed of my penance.'

He awkwardly mag-locked his precious cargo to his belt, snatched up his fallen staff and locked it in turn to his back. Then he was away, pounding up the rubble, climbing one-handed up the jagged cliff face. Lydorran drove upwards, snagging a handhold then pushing up with his feet and snatching the next. The stump of his left arm hung uselessly at his side. Mutants howled and bellowed behind him, their claws digging into the rock as they pursued him.

Still Lydorran climbed, fury and sheer stubbornness propelling his wounded body to the very limit. With every lunge the glow of daylight grew closer and his hearts thumped as he heard the crash of gunfire from up ahead. The hard boom of bolters firing told him that his brothers still held out, some of them at least.

He wouldn't fail. He wouldn't fall. Not now.

Lydorran was almost torn from the rockface as a huge hand closed around his foot and pulled hard. He felt tendons strain and snap in his leg. His back gave a shout of pain as muscles strained against the full weight of the massive mutant that had him in its grip. Lydorran's hold slipped.

The lip of the pit was so close.

He had to risk it.

He snatched out a mental feeler, grasped the merest wisp of warp energy and sent it surging down through the rockface. Beyond the veil he felt metaphysical fangs snap shut, grazing his mental defences and sending white fire through his mind.

Below him he heard a crunch, and the weight abruptly vanished from his foot. He glanced down to see the mutant falling away, a foot-long spar of rock jutting from its eyesocket where Lydorran's manifestation had dragged it out from the cliff face. Three more mutants were swarming up to take their fallen fellow's place, though. They were almost upon him.

One last push, he thought, and lunged upwards, reaching for the edge.

His yellow-armoured gauntlet was suddenly clasped in one of black. Lydorran felt himself hauled upwards out of the pit to slam down on its edge. He looked up with amazement and saw a black-armoured warrior towering over him in an unfamiliar mark of power armour. One shoulder pad bore the heraldry of the Space Wolves, and the Fenrisian's features were rugged, scarred and hairy. He wore a bloodthirsty smile that bared his canine fangs in the half-light.

Something swept overhead, a dark shape with assault cannons chattering in its nose-mount. *Gunship*, thought Lydorran, warp-shock making his thoughts slow and viscid. *Not one of ours.* He looked about and saw Imperial Fists and black-armoured Space Marines fighting shoulder to shoulder, storming through the half-collapsed entrance to the mine-head, executing cultists on every side.

'Watch Captain Lothar Redfang, Deathwatch,' growled the Space Wolf by way of introduction. 'We heard you had an infestation.' Then he leaned out over the lip of the pit, aimed his boltgun straight down into the faces of the mutants below, and let fly.

ACT TWO

IX

Magus Jai stood upon a metal walkway, the fingers of one hand curled around its brushed-steel railing as she looked down upon the industrious scene below. Jai felt a brooding disquiet as she watched cult neophytes hurrying to and fro across what had once been an ore-storage silo. Now it served as an arming chamber for the cult. The neophytes came in through a hatch in the chamber's south side, each bearing on amber-hued cloth some weapon or piece of wargear that they believed the Blessed would wish to wield. These they deposited upon the broad steel benches that had been erected and decorated with wyrmforms and candles, transforming them into arming shrines touched by the divinity of the Star Children. The cultists then left in solemn procession, flowing out of an adjoining doorway and back around towards the weapons cache by other corridors.

They look like insects, worker drones bringing offerings to a hive, Jai thought. The image gave her a frisson of real horror, though she could not have placed quite why. Perhaps it was the presence of the Blessed themselves, standing silent in the chamber's centre, watching with inhuman eyes as the offerings piled up before them.

Metamorphs. The Blessed of the Star Children. They who wore Father's gifts upon their flesh and stood highest in his regard next only to his own purebred children. Feeder tendrils sprouted in twitching nests where mouths and nostrils should be, tasting the air below glittering nests of night-black eyes. Chitinous mouthparts worked, more thick plates of chitin rasping together as the metamorphs shifted restively. Some had crustacean-like claws where their hands should have been, or bladed limbs edged with serrated bone like those of some huge and horrible insect. All were hunched and powerful in build, their adapted utility suits straining to contain their divine mutations. Jai knew that the thought was traitorous, but she couldn't stand proximity to the Blessed, not even this close. She knew that they were noble, devoted in thought and deed to the cult, utterly incorruptible, bearing the stigmata of even the most gruesome blessings without complaint. And she had seen them fight, whip-fast, utterly lethal, employing the gifts they had been born to with deadly effect. Yet they smelled wrong to Jai, *felt* subtly wrong despite the beatific haloes she saw shimmering around their bulbous heads. The feeling was made worse by the compulsion to adore and love the creatures, which grew in strength the closer to them she drew only to sour as she discovered her discomfort growing too. Somehow the warring sensations felt to her like biting into some warm and comforting foodstuff only to discover cold, wet rot at its heart.

Jai shook off the traitorous thoughts as the catwalk creaked, heralding Lhor's approach. She glanced up and saw the primus striding towards her, tall, noble, his face that of an honest labourer touched by Father's blessings, his gimlet eyes those of a merciless and insightful general. Lhor's greatcoat flowed behind him as he walked. His heavy miner's boots clanged against metal with every step.

'Broodsister,' he said by way of greeting, halting beside her and staring down at the preparations below.

'Broodbrother, Stars' blessings,' she responded, and the smile she offered him was genuine both in the warmth of its welcome and the twist of its disquiet.

'Preparations near completion,' he said.

'They do.'

'You do not approve of this,' he said, a statement more than a question.

'I understand its necessity,' she said carefully.

'But you do not approve,' he repeated. She heard no reprimand in her broodbrother's voice. He understood her mind, just as she understood his, their empathy near-telepathic.

'This was to be our weapon of last resort,' she said.

'A day and a night they fought in the Delvemine,' he replied, voice grim. 'By the battle's end not a brother or sister of the cause remained alive. That ambush would have put paid to half the Ghyrish regiments at a stroke. We did not even destroy half of one Space Marine army. Now, it seems, we face a second.'

'And their strategy succeeds in Hive Angelicus despite all our best efforts,' she said, unable to keep the bitterness from her voice. 'We were so *close*, Sharvik. Our hands were around their throats, our shackles straining fit to shatter. And then the hounds of the oppressor came.'

'And they crush us, drive us back at every turn,' said Lhor, his heavy brows drawing down in a scowl. 'Despite our every effort to show our people the truth, the populace waver. They are cowed, terrified, lost.'

'And without their hearts and souls, we shall not see Ascension,' said Jai, something clenching in her chest at the mere thought of defeat. How did one face the idea that they might fail an entire world's worth of people?

'We cannot let the torch be extinguished, broodsister,' said Lhor, placing one taloned hand on her forearm where she held on to the railing.

'It must be done. The weapon must be unleashed,' she said. To her it sounded as though she intoned some terrible death sentence. In a way she supposed that was true.

'Faithful and heretics will fall together,' he said. 'Our voice upon the conclave will not survive this.' She heard regret in his voice, but strength also. Resolve.

'Had the ambush succeeded...' She let the sentence trail away, aware of its futility. They served the will of the Star Children. Fate raced towards them like an avalanche. There was no time for might-have-been. 'If our voice on the conclave is not dead already, they soon will be. The weapon may prove a mercy to them.'

'And yet,' he said, his grip tightening for a moment and then falling away. She felt the separation in that moment, the finality of the gesture, and it threatened to break her. Something welled up within her instead, fierce conviction that made her feel as though her heart beat in time with Father's own. Instead of sorrow, Phoenicia Jai felt pride.

'Weep not for they who go early into Ascension's light, for they are the Blessed forerunners,' she quoted from Father's scripture. 'For them all toil and pain is done, and when we too ascend to join the Star Children, there shall they await to welcome us with open arms and to show us the path to eternal freedom.'

'Just so,' said Lhor, offering her a fierce smile.

'Shenn will be here soon,' she said, sensing the telltale mind spoor of the cult's heroic Kelermorph drawing nigh.

'Then it is time to be about Father's work,' said Lhor briskly. He locked eyes with Jai for a moment, and she saw her own faith and determination mirrored there in his gaze.

'How will you gain entry to their fortress, broodbrother?' she asked, all practicality now. 'Reports suggest that the hounds of the oppressor guard every entrance, their servo-skulls scouring the back alleys and tunnels.'

'They know only the routes of which those in power know,' said Lhor with grim satisfaction. 'Amongst our number are tunneljacks and vent-scrubbers whose labours have gone unnoticed by their so-called *betters* for many years.'

'Their own ignorance of the people they claim to rule, the people they failed, will be their undoing,' said Jai.

'As Father wills.'

'Lead them well, then, and go with his blessing,' she said warmly.

'I bid you this also, broodsister,' said Lhor, then turned abruptly and marched away. Jai looked down again upon the Blessed, now picking over the weapon offerings upon the shrine.

Like beetles on sump carrion, she thought, and again chastised herself. They were the Blessed of Father, and with her broodbrother to lead them and Shenn to inspire them, they would deliver the killing blow to the oppressors' war machine and free the people of Ghyre after thousands of years of slavery and exploitation.

That is worth any cost, she told herself as she watched Lhor stride out to join the Blessed, as Shenn stalked in through the southern hatch with a rune-marked metal case clutched tight to his chest. *It justifies any means.*

'There is a line that we cannot cross!' said Lydorran, his voice still hoarse from mine dust but no less powerful in its outrage for all that. 'We are servants of the Imperium, the elite of its garrison. Our duty is to protect the Emperor's realm, not tear it to pieces!'

He stood in a richly carpeted antechamber within the lower levels of the conclave building, surrounded by statuary and fine furnishings. He felt like an aberration in that civilised space, his power armour still stained with gore and smirched by fire, one arm terminating in the still-settling stump of an augmetic socket. The sensation, coupled with the loss of Lordas and so many other brave battle-brothers, was not helping his mood.

Nearby stood Chaplain Storn, his expression stony, and a glowering Ancient Tarsun. Opposite the three Imperial Fists, standing at the other side of a long klarwood meeting table, were Watch Captain Lothar Redfang and Apothecary Ohsk Sor'khal of the Deathwatch. Xenos killers, alien hunters drawn from the best of every Space Marine Chapter, trained and equipped to battle every alien foe that humanity had yet encountered. A Space Wolf and a White Scar, both bearing their heraldic Chapter markings proudly on one shoulder guard, both a feral contrast to the clipped and chiselled sons of Dorn. Apothecary Sor'khal had steely-grey hair dragged back into a horsetail from an otherwise shaved scalp. His face was leathery and scarred, his eyes watchful as a hawk's and his moustaches hanging long in the Chogorian style. Redfang was huge, of a height with Lydorran despite having yet to cross the Rubicon Primaris. His hair fell in a dark mane about a long and noble face, one eye a glowing augmetic, the other creased at its corner by laughter lines. It was a face that Lydorran should have felt moved to trust, even to like, yet there was something in the way the Space Wolf bared his canines in a mirthless grin, something in the intensity of his gaze, that instead left the Librarian feeling unsettled.

'Your duty, perhaps,' said Redfang. 'Garrisons sit behind their walls, get slow, get soft. The Deathwatch are hunters. There are no walls to protect us, Fist, and no lines. The war on the alien will not be won through mercy. We saw where your mercy got you, by the time we arrived, did we not?'

Lydorran glowered at Redfang.

'I have thanked you for your aid at Delvemine, Watch Captain Redfang, and if your ego needs the padding so desperately then I will offer you my thanks again.'

The White Scar snorted in amusement as Redfang's expression soured.

'This one has your measure quick enough, Fenris,' he muttered.

'What I do *not* thank you for is unleashing your kill teams into the Laboritas to wreak indiscriminate havoc before we were ready to move. Nor do I appreciate your sending armed battle-brothers to round up the governor and her conclave as though they were wayward grox and placing them under armed arrest in their own Court of Judgement!'

Redfang flashed Lydorran a feral grin and paced over to an arched window. He leaned one forearm against the stone frame and stared out at the spires visible without.

'There is guilt amongst them, Fist,' he said. 'How do you think you ended up down a pit?'

Lydorran fought to control his anger towards this slouching

barbarian, but the Space Wolf's arrogance and presumption needled him.

'I know that much, watch captain.' Lydorran bit out each word. 'I had intended to set matters in motion to discover the full extent of the corruption. You call yourself a hunter, but your heavy-handed methods will have sent our quarry running and closed down every avenue of investigation we might have pursued.'

'Do you hear yourself, Fist?' asked Redfang, not looking around. 'Heavy-handed. Avenues of investigation. You have no idea, do you? You do not even see the kraken as its tentacles wind around you.'

'I am the commanding Adeptus Astartes officer in this war zone,' said Lydorran, his words ringing like hammer on steel. 'The mission to relieve Ghyre was assigned to Strike Force Tor, not to the Deathwatch. *We* have bled for this world, not you. If you wish to offer your aid, then I accept it gladly. If you have information pertinent to our mission, or to battling this foe, then share it and I will listen. But you do not simply barge in and start working contra to our strategy. You do not hold a planetary governor at gunpoint. Not even the Adeptus Astartes have the authority to do this.'

Redfang barked a laugh, but there was no mirth in it. The sound was as cold and hard as a branch cracking in the grip of a killing frost.

'Allfather take every stiff-necked Imperial Fist,' he growled. 'We don't have *time* for this, for your strategy. Now are you going to stand in my way or are you going to let me do my duty?'

Still Redfang had not looked round, but Lydorran saw hostility in the set of the big Space Wolf's shoulders. There was menace there, violence running hot beneath the surface, seeking an excuse to be unleashed.

'That will depend upon your methods, and whether you deign to work with us rather than around us,' he said, refusing to be baited. Redfang turned at last, growling low in his throat. Sor'khal raised a hand in a pacifying gesture. He looked from Redfang to Lydorran, and the Librarian had a sudden thought that this was not the first time the White Scar had found himself diffusing confrontations on his watch captain's behalf.

'Brother-Librarian, Lothar is right. We simply do not have the time. And from what we have seen of your strategy, you have no idea of the true danger here. Am I correct?'

Lydorran frowned, took a breath. His emotions were still turbulent from his brush with the dangers of the warp, he thought, as he realised that he too was undoubtedly being more confrontational than was necessary.

'Brother Sor'khal, we know that the enemy take the form of a widespread and highly seditious cult, preaching anti-Imperial heresy and employing guerrilla insurgency tactics with considerable success to offset their ad hoc military structure and lack of heavy materiel.'

'But you do not know what they are, what lurks at the heart of all this?' asked the Apothecary.

'We've seen instances of mutation concurrent with archival pict-capture of xenos bioforms, so we know there's inhuman corruption amongst their ranks,' said Lydorran. 'But if there is some deeper evil at work here, then no, Brother Sor'khal, I regret to say we are ignorant of it.'

'Ignorance,' growled Redfang, frustration evident in his tone. 'It kills more of the Allfather's warriors than any gun or blade.'

'Please, enlighten us,' said Lydorran, gesturing with his one remaining hand and the ghost of the one he had lost. He bristled at the Fenrisian's disrespect for his Chapter, yet after Delvemine he could not bring himself to openly challenge it.

'We are dealing with a genestealer cult, a parasitic xenos infestation,' said Sor'khal. 'It probably started small, maybe just a single vanguard organism making it onto Ghyre through concealment and cunning. Doesn't take long for their poison to spread, though. Once they start channelling their cursed spirits into people's minds and bodies, it spreads fast.'

Lydorran nodded.

'If this is your revelation, it comes late, brothers,' he said, not troubling to keep the scorn from his voice. 'We do not need the vaunted Deathwatch to tell us what foe we face. A tyranid vanguard organism will have been the root cause, yes? It has parasitised this world, spread its poison through the people and turned them from the Emperor's light. This we had surmised.'

'You know the genestealers for what they are – that much I can respect,' said Redfang, and Lydorran caught the flicker of grudging admiration in the Space Wolf's voice. 'Yet if you understand the peril, why haven't you silenced their call?'

'Their call to what?' asked Lydorran, wrong-footed.

'Their Star Children,' spat Redfang in disgust. 'Singing out to the damned across the sea of stars.'

'Star Children? What profane heresy is this? We had understood they worshipped something they call Father,' said Storn, sounding personally affronted by such a cornucopia of heresies. Lydorran was shaking his head slowly, wishing to understand more.

'Throne, you mean the tyranids, don't you?' he said. 'One of their...' A swift consultation of his memories. 'Their splinter fleets?'

Redfang banged one fist upon the wood of the tabletop, hard enough to crack it.

'This is why we have no time,' he growled. 'They are coming, swarming like kraken on a blood-tide. The cult, Father, they're like a beacon to them, a signal fire leading them out of the darkness to feed.'

'You have seen them? You know this?' asked Lydorran, his mind racing, reprioritising strategic assets and reassessing everything about Captain Tor's plan for the pacification of Ghyre. He felt his stomach plunge vertiginously at the thought that his steady and relentless methods might have damned this world rather than be saving it.

'No, but every day the cult remains active increases the danger,' said Sor'khal. 'The tyranids need not appear in the skies above for the enemy's work to be complete here. Just drawing them into proximity, into the fringes of the Segmentum Solar, is more than victory enough. These creatures cannot be reasoned with, cannot be discouraged or their morale broken. They are a plague, a swarm that devours everything before them until every last one of them is slain.'

'We know what tyranids are, Wolf,' said Lydorran flatly. 'We know what their onset would mean.'

'And we must uproot the entire cult to extinguish this, what, this signal fire?' asked Ancient Tarsun. 'You realise how far the corruption spreads upon this world, yes?'

'No, we don't have to kill them all,' said Redfang. 'We have to hunt their patriarch to its lair and slay the beast. It is the source of beacon and cult both. We behead the beast, we behead the cult. But first we have to find the damned thing.'

'We have been trying,' said Lydorran, frustrated at the Fenrisian's apparent arrogance that he alone knew how to prosecute a hunt for such a xenos beast. 'We meet trickery and false trails at every turn.'

'We need information, we get the thing's spoor, we find its tracks and we follow,' said Redfang. 'That's what my kill teams are about even now, disrupting your precious strategy. What my strike cruiser's augurs are seeking from within the sea of stars. What we are about to get out of these aristocratic whelps. You ready to help us now then, Fist?'

Lydorran scowled.

'If what you say is true, then your mission and mine coincide. It is well that you intercepted Sergeant Torgan's message, that you followed it to its source. But I would still counsel caution, even if we do require speed. The governor is loyal. She and her conclave hold the strings to power on this world. With their cooperation we can widen our search by a vast magnitude, speed both of our strategies towards their conclusion. If you alienate them, they will become your enemies and ours as well.'

'Alienate?' said Redfang, one corner of his mouth quirking up to reveal a glinting fang. 'We only have one method for dealing with aliens in the Deathwatch.'

So saying, he turned and threw open the double doors set into the room's far wall. Lydorran exchanged a look with Storn and Tarsun, and the three of them followed Redfang and Sor'khal into the echoing courtroom beyond.

The Court of Judgement was an ornately menacing chamber with a high ceiling covered by a fresco of the Emperor and his primarchs sitting enthroned, grim expressions upon their faces. A high pulpit stood at one end of the chamber, fashioned from wood and stone to resemble piled human skulls and leering gargoyles. More grotesques stared down from the galleries that lined the other three walls of the chamber, embossed with the crests of the great clans, Kallistus chief amongst them.

For most matters of law and order upon Ghyre, trials took place within one of the many judiciary fortresses of the Adeptus Arbites. Justice in such places was swift, merciless and often final. Should a member of the Ghyrish elite, a Spire Lord or the master of a great clan commit some act of perfidy and fail to get away with it, they instead found themselves in the Court of Judgement, where their peers would consider their deeds and pass judgement upon them as only those with the rarefied perspective of fellow high-born could.

There was a deliberate irony and a none-too-subtle message in the decision to incarcerate the Ghyrish conclave here. Redfang might seem like a half-feral barbarian at first glance, but Lydorran had a sense the watch captain was far cannier than he chose to appear. After all, while the Librarian didn't know the intricacies of the Deathwatch, he doubted very much that one remained with the alien hunters and received promotion to watch captain without being a quite exceptional individual.

Still, as Lydorran saw the governor and her chief advisers clustered upon the defendants' dais beneath the gun muzzles of half a dozen Deathwatch battle-brothers, he could not help but feel frustration at Redfang's methods. The delegates looked dishevelled from rough manhandling, and their expressions ran the gamut through fear and panic to towering outrage. High Administrator Lunst was railing furiously at their treatment and brandishing a crumpled data-parchment at her captors, the material of her torn sleeve wagging as she pointed the scroll accusatorially. High Marshal Kallistus looked shell-shocked, as did Seneschal Gryft. Clan Lords

VanSappen and Tectos veered between blandishments and threats, while First Arbitrator Verol stood quiet and watchful as though recording everything for later reference. Magos Gathabosis was blaring repetitiously that it made no logical sense for him to be incarcerated in such a fashion, quoting statistical damage to his optimised quotas and attempting to scuttle off the dais; he was encouraged back into place each time by the menacing barrels of bolt guns.

Lydorran saw no sign of Lord Delve or Bishop Renwyck.

At the centre of the gathering, managing to retain her regal presence and absolute composure despite her rough treatment, stood Governor Kallistus. Despite her predicament, the governor's eyes widened as she took in Lydorran's battle-ravaged appearance. She inclined her head towards him, though whether the gesture was one of recognition or sympathy or had some other, more obscure meaning, he didn't know.

Ever I wish for the power to see into others' minds, he thought.

'Silence!' roared Redfang, and even without vox amplification the sudden thunder of his voice was deafening as it echoed around the Court of Judgement. The delegates shut up at once, most of them turning several shades paler. High Administrator Lunst bristled, and Lydorran could have sworn she was about to remonstrate with the hulking watch captain, but Governor Kallistus spoke first. She looked straight at Lydorran as she did so, as though to dismiss the presence of the Deathwatch entirely.

'Brother-Librarian, we were saddened to hear of your losses at Delvemine. We trust that your injury is not too grievous?'

Remarkable, he thought. *She might as well be still sitting upon her throne.*

'He is a Space Marine, even if he's not a Fenrisian. He is built for worse,' growled Redfang. 'Are you, governor?'

Kallistus turned her regard upon Redfang as though notic-
ing him for the first time, and with no little disdain. The
watch captain was feet away from her, a hulking presence
that radiated barely contained violence like waves of heat;
Lydorran was genuinely surprised that she managed to mask
the fear she must surely be feeling.

'You would threaten the person of an Imperial planetary
governor, watch captain?' she asked him coldly. 'You go too
far, sir.'

'If you are untainted then you have no harm to fear from
us, but understand me, governor. I am of the Deathwatch.
That means whatever I do, whatever action I take, is justi-
fied. It will be borne out. So be silent and let me act, unless
your intent is to delay me long enough for your xenos allies
to break you free.' Redfang bared his teeth. 'In which case,
keep talking and I will gun you down like an ice troll caught
plundering an agri-dome.'

Kallistus gave him a haughty look, refusing to rise to his
bait, but Lydorran could sense her heart thumping painfully
against her ribs, feel the swift and fearful pulse of blood
through her temples. He was relieved that none of the other
conclave members were fool enough to speak up, not even
Jessamine Lunst.

'No one else? Thank the Allfather for small mercies,' said
Redfang. 'You are here because some of your number are
traitors, either possessed by xenos spirits or filled with their
poison.' He drew a massive and much-notched chainsword
from its scabbard at his hip. 'You are here because our brothers
in yellow have not seen fit to cut out the cankers yet.' Lydorran scowled at this, resenting the Fenrisian's divisive derision
even as he felt the painful truth of it. Storn grunted with irritation and contempt beside him.

Redfang revved the blade's serrated teeth, drawing frightened yelps from several of the assembled delegates. 'Stormtooth and I are going to make that right. Now.'

He turned and gestured with the blade. One of his battle-brothers, a tall warrior with a Mentors shoulder guard, left the ring of sentries and crossed the room to where an ornately carved door of black iron was set into the wall. Over the doorway was a brass plaque that read 'Let No Perfidy Be Hidden From The Emperor's Sight'.

The Mentor banged a fist against the door and it swung open. Another battle-brother, this one a golden-haired Blood Angel of prodigious size, hauled Lord Dostos Delve into the room as easily as a grown man might drag a small and truculent child.

'Unhand me. *Unhand me!*' spat Lord Delve, whose rumpled robes and bruised face told a story of their own. The Blood Angel did so, lifting Delve slightly from the ground then casting him forward so that the man overbalanced with a yelp and sprawled onto the defendants' dais. Before the clan lord could rise, Redfang was standing over him, Stormtooth's point hovering in front of Delve's face.

'Lord Dostos Delve, your clan extended the strangest welcome to our battle-brothers when they landed there yesterday. What do you have to say about it?' asked Redfang.

Lord Delve looked up from the ground, raised himself slightly and spat on Redfang's armoured boot.

'You see how friendly you feel when those sent to liberate you turn up with all guns blazing,' he said, but Lydorran could hear the anger and hopelessness in the man's voice. His words could not account for the mutants the Space Marines had faced, for the deliberate murder of the Adeptus Mechanicus overseers or the explosive undermining of the Space

Marines' advance, not to mention the wyrmforms daubed upon every available surface of Delvemine. There was no defence for it that would wash, and Delve knew it.

Redfang's free hand gripped the heavy material of Lord Delve's hood. He tore it back to reveal a mop of thick, curling hair. This he gripped in turn, taking a mighty fistful. He jerked it violently upwards. Lord Delve howled, not in pain but in anger, as, with an awful ripping sound, the prosthetic he wore was torn away. Revealed beneath was a dome-like scalp hued a deep mauve, thick with pulsing veins and ridge-like plates.

The crowd gasped and shrieked in revulsion.

Delve hissed, the flesh of his face rippling and tearing as alien musculature moved beneath it. Needle fangs flashed in insectile jaws that yawned wide and tore the prosthetic mask where it adhered to his true face. Heavy shapes bulged beneath his robe, and cloth tore as clawed and chitinous limbs ripped their way into the light.

Delve gave a wholly inhuman shriek and lunged with unbelievable speed, not towards Redfang but straight at the dais. Straight, Lydorran realised, for the governor.

He reacted quicker than conscious thought, gathering his powers despite the warning flare from his psychocircuitry and throwing up a surging kinetic field between the governor and the thing that had been Lord Delve.

Redfang moved just as fast, stepping with the xenocultist's lunge and bringing Stormtooth up in a howling arc that parted Dostos Delve's head from his shoulders. Blood jetted, thick and purple-black, splattering in gobbets across Lydorran's shield before pattering to the ground like rain.

Delve's body hit the floor, its insectile limbs drumming and flailing madly as though still attempting to scramble towards

Governor Kallistus. Several of the Deathwatch turned their guns upon the abomination as one. The crash of bolt fire rolled through the chamber like an avalanche. As the echoes faded, the ruptured remains of Lord Delve twitched their last and lay still amidst a spreading pool of gore.

Panicked voices were raised amidst the conclave, and several of its members tried to back away from the foul remains, but Redfang turned his gaze upon them and they all stilled again.

'That walked amongst you, and not one of you saw it,' he said, and his voice was as cold and hard as the Fenrisian winter. 'Whatever happens to this world, that fact will not be overlooked. Even those of you who are innocent of taint will have much penance to attend to before you are judged worthy to rule again.'

That was enough to quiet them, Lydorran saw. Even the governor's mask of composure cracked a little at the watch captain's words. He kept his own expression stony, yet the voices of self-doubt clamoured ever louder within. He had not seen. How could Storn and Tor ever have believed him fit for command?

'Bring in the other one,' said Redfang, flicking gore from the teeth of his blade.

Again, a fist banged upon the black iron door. Again, a figure was brought through it, dwarfed by the Space Marine that hauled him along. Lotimer Renwyck looked small and wholly powerless, yet his face retained a look of composure, and one hand held tightly to the aquila pendant around his neck. Lydorran saw the man's eyes flick to the remains of Lord Delve and widen in horror, though whether it was honest revulsion at so shocking a sight or the terror of imminent discovery he couldn't tell.

The Blood Angel cast Bishop Renwyck down next to the bolt-riddled remains, close enough that the small man splashed into a puddle of alien gore.

Once again Redfang's blade swept out, its point hovering just below the bishop's chin, its engine idling.

'Bishop Lotimer Renwyck, you provided intelligence to Brother-Librarian Lydorran that sent him and his brothers into Clan Delve's trap, did you not?'

Renwyck looked up at Redfang, his expression troubled.

'My lord, I did not,' he said, and Lydorran heard nothing but honesty in the man's voice. Redfang clearly heard it too, as his brows drew down and he tilted his head slightly as though in question.

'You lie, bishop,' Lydorran growled.

'Bishop, there is clear vid-capture of your having done this. Moreover, my brother attests you did so. You seek to trick us,' Redfang said.

Renwyck had the good sense to look frightened now, though he was keeping it under control as best he could. Cautiously, eyeing the tip of Redfang's sword, he drew his knees up under him and straightened into a position of prayer.

'If one of the Adeptus Astartes says this, then he must surely believe that it is true, but I have no recollection of doing so.'

Redfang considered the priest for a moment. He glanced to Sor'khal without lowering his blade.

'Brother, what think you? Mind-slaving? Something parasitic? Or is he just a liar to make the Trickster proud?'

Sor'khal paced across the chamber and stood over Renwyck, frowning and tugging at one corner of his moustache.

'One way to tell for sure,' he said, and raised his narthecium vambrace.

This had been their intention all along, Lydorran realised. This little bit of theatre was for the governor's benefit, a display of the Deathwatch showing restraint and knowledge as well as violence. Again, he had that sense of Redfang's hidden cunning.

'We possess auspex technologies that even our noble brothers within the Imperial Fists do not,' explained Redfang as Sor'khal went to work, panning his instruments over Renwyck's slight form and frowning over the results that appeared on his device's display. 'Their machine-spirits are trained to detect xenos bio-spoor in ways no other Chapter's sensors can. If there is taint here, we will know soon enough.'

Lydorran watched Renwyck's face as the Apothecary completed his scan. The man looked pale and frightened, he thought, but also determined as though ready to face whatever came next. Sor'khal's narthecium gave a low chime, and he blew out a breath.

'Something parasitic,' he said matter-of-factly. 'Something inside him, no doubt Delve's doing.'

'Parasitic?' croaked Renwyck, his hands crabbing into fingers as they played over his face and body. 'Where? What heresy is this?'

'We've seen it before, psycho-reactive grubs that bore into their hosts and release bursts of neuroempathic directives before smothering the memories in a blanket of bio-chems,' said Sor'khal, sounding almost regretful.

Renwyck looked horrified, and rightly so, thought Lydorran. That some xenos *thing* could be inside his body, puppeting him on the cult's behalf, changing his memories at will… The thought was grotesque.

'Take him away, put him to question,' Redfang ordered, his

tone merciless. 'His memories are buried, but they are not gone. Let us see what we can dig up.'

Renwyck was praying fervently, clutching his aquila with both hands, tears creeping down his cheeks, but he didn't resist as one of the Deathwatch raised him to his feet and hauled him away.

'Scan them all,' the watch captain ordered, gesturing to the governor and his advisers and eliciting wails of fear. 'With luck there will be another grub or two between them. If so, we will discover where the prey makes its lair soon enough.'

X

Lydorran and Storn walked slowly down an echoing cloister. For the first time since coming to Ghyre, their battered armour was in the care of their Chapter serfs, the two warriors instead clad in monastic robes. On one side they passed a long tapestry that displayed in allegorical form the events of the Great Crusade and the fall of the Traitor Horus, depicted as a daemonic thing of shadow and ichor with curling horns and a serpent's tongue. On their other they passed tall archways that led out onto a somewhat overgrown garden quadrangle, abandoned since the priests who once tended it had fled. Winged insects flitted from plant to plant, and to Lydorran's eyes the rare patch of true greenery looked incongruous amidst the sombre stonework.

The cloister was part of a shrine to the Imperial faith that had been evacuated and subsequently abandoned due to its close proximity to the Mercurio Gate space port. Some days earlier Apothecaries Lordas and Justen had claimed the structure as a meditatorium for those Imperial Fists wounded sorely enough to require convalescence before they could return to the fight. In the wake of the assault on Delvemine and the shocking events that followed, Lydorran had retreated here to think, and to give his augmetic socket time to bed into his flesh. Now, as he and Storn walked, he flexed the fingers of his new bionic hand experimentally.

'How is it?' asked Storn.

'Strange,' confessed Lydorran. Storn remained silent for a few paces, as though inviting further comment on the Librarian's new metallic forearm and hand. Instead, Lydorran said, 'You did not come here to ask me about my arm, Brother-Chaplain.'

'I did not,' said Storn. The two of them reached a long stone bench that looked out onto the sunlit garden. They sat. Lydorran's eyes roved, following the industrious insects gathering pollen from the plants. He flexed his metal fingers, hearing minute servos whine and joints click.

'Uncomplicated,' Lydorran said, nodding to the insects. 'They work, do their duty, live their simple lives and die. You do not see them troubled by sedition or heresy.'

'They are mindless and unworthy,' replied Storn, his brows drawing down into a scowl. 'They, too, are not why I am here.'

'You are here because you wish to know why I linger when I should be out upon the front lines, driving our efforts to locate this broodnest that Redfang seeks,' said Lydorran. In that moment, he felt unutterably weary, the sensation alien and unsettling to him. Storn looked sideways at him, his craggy features unreadable.

'You are allowing your augmetic time to bed in,' said Storn, his voice oddly stoic. 'Every brother in the strike force knows this. All beseech the primarch for your swift return to battle.'

'Storn, I failed them,' Lydorran replied, and the words tasted bitter in his mouth. 'I failed them, I failed you, and the governor and her people.' He left one last name unsaid, biting it off before it could pass his lips. To his surprise, Storn's expression did not change.

'You are allowing your augmetic time to bed in,' the Chaplain repeated firmly.

'Brother-Chaplain–'

'Give me some credit, Aster,' said Storn, his voice now pitched low, his words swift. 'I've been a Chaplain for the Imperial Fists for more than a century, and a more stubborn, uncommunicative and self-flagellating brotherhood I cannot imagine. You are an open tome compared to most of us, brother – it's one of the qualities that Captain Tor saw in you – so do not for a second think that you have to explain to me why you are sitting here wallowing in self-doubt. We can't afford it. You cannot afford it, and neither can Ghyre. No, you did not see the full extent of the corruption lurking in the conclave. Neither did I, nor did Torgan before you, nor did any of his predecessors. Captain Redfang saw it because he already knew what to look for. We shall all do penance with the pain gauntlet when this campaign is done, and we will be sharper-eyed in future for it, but for now there's a war to be won, and the strike force needs its leader.'

An urge came over Lydorran then to rail against Storn's words, to insist that he should have done better, fought harder, seen more, but he knew the Chaplain was right. Instead he drew a deep breath and let it out slowly.

'Tell me this much, Thyssus. Why is that leader me? Why not you?'

Storn let out a slow breath.

'Because of what Tor and I saw in you since the day you joined us on the battle-lines, Brother-Librarian. Yes, your powers lend you an edge of perception and empyric capability vital to the prosecution of this conflict, but it is much more than that. You Primaris, I'd argue you're even further removed from humanity than the rest of us. Yet you, Lydorran, you alone of all the Imperial Fists on this world retain a connection to our species, an empathy with them that keeps you grounded. Balanced. You are better than you know, and that is a strength. Tor believed in you, so I believe in you. Sometimes, Brother Lydorran, you have to take things on faith.'

Lydorran looked hard at Storn for a long moment, then snorted and turned back to the garden and its industrious insects.

'You practised that speech,' he accused.

'It is the duty of the Chaplaincy always to have inspiring words to hand,' replied Storn, his voice carefully neutral.

'I don't imagine our Watch Captain Redfang would agree with your assessment,' said Lydorran, his brows drawing down. 'The Fenrisian seems to have little enough time for empathy or restraint.'

'If there is one thing I know of Space Wolves, Aster, it is that they long to be with their own above all,' said Storn. 'I've never had the honour of serving amidst the Deathwatch, but I can only imagine that a tour of duty that takes them so far from their packmates, from that frozen ball of ice and hate they call a homeworld, must be hard for the Space Wolves to endure.'

'You're saying he is, what, homesick?' asked Lydorran, incredulous. Now it was Storn's turn to snort dismissively.

'You sure those mutants wounded your arm and not your head, brother? I'm saying that for Redfang to have remained with the Deathwatch long enough to become a captain, he must be exceptionally good at what he does, and for him to accept such a severing from the Chapter he no doubt loves...'

'He must be more selfless and honourable by far than his conduct implies,' finished Lydorran.

'And no doubt determined that if he's going to make such a personal sacrifice, then *nothing* is going to stand in the way of his making it worthwhile. And *that*, strike force leader, is what I came here to tell you.'

'Redfang has found the broodnest,' said Lydorran. A mechanical whine sounded as his new hand clenched into a fist.

'So he believes,' said Storn as the two of them rose to their feet. Lydorran set off at once, leaving his doubts behind to haunt the fringes of the overgrown garden. Storn followed.

'How?'

'A combination of kill team raids on downhive cult hideouts, specialised bio-auguries from that thug of a ship he has lurking in orbit and the excruciation of the former bishop and his fellow unfortunates.'

Once Lydorran might have felt a slight stab of pity for Renwyck despite himself. The man might have been corrupted, irredeemably so, but it had not been by his own choice. Now though, Lydorran felt little of anything towards the man save disgust; too much had been lost on his account.

'Where?' he asked as they left the cloister.

'The Fane of the Emperor Risen, one of Ghyre's former architectural wonders,' replied Storn. 'Right in the heart of the Commercias district of Klaratos Hive.'

'I would still have expected one of the mine complexes,' said Lydorran, his siegecrafter's mind spinning over the possibilities, strengths and weaknesses of such a target.

'As would I, and were we not now racing against time, I might still argue for further inspection,' said Storn. 'But Redfang is adamant. Psyocculum data, deep-scan augury of the fane's additional fortification, massed bio-spoor, excess power drain from surrounding levels of Hive Klaratos – they all point to the broodnest being there.'

'If that is so then we need to strike swiftly,' said Lydorran, his mind whirling through strategic variables. 'The cult has eyes and ears everywhere. If Redfang has kicked the nest too hard extracting this information, then it will not be long before Father knows we are coming.'

'The watch captain agrees,' said Storn. 'He's ordered a full mobilisation. Deathwatch, our forces, the Ghyrish. Of course, I rebuffed his initial suggestion that we ought to remain behind "to guard our fortress".'

'Arrogant Fenrisian arse,' snarled Lydorran as they clattered down a flight of stone steps towards the arming chambers where their wargear awaited. Once he might have dug in his heels and refused to allow Redfang to command his forces in such a fashion. Now, after all that had transpired, it was almost a relief to allow another to dictate their course for a short time. Still, such notions only went so far; he would trust Lothar Redfang to command this war alone, no matter how informed a position he might come from.

'Indeed, but in truth I do believe that a portion of our force ought to remain here,' said Storn. 'Redfang's orders will all but empty the hive, and while I'm all for striking with overwhelming strength, I believe that leaving the security of Angelicus and its governor in the hands of the Arbites and a few governatorial guardsmen risks disaster.'

'Agreed, Brother-Chaplain,' said Lydorran. 'And I believe you should be the one to lead them. If Redfang is right, then I fear it may be a duty with scant honour in it, for the enemy will likely rally everything they have to defend their broodnest.'

'But if he is wrong, then who better to hold the line with

all the belligerence and tenacity the primarch would demand, eh?' replied Storn. His smile was grim. 'Sergeant Furian and his brothers have a few new augmetics between them and they've lost a couple of brothers. Leave me them and the Hellblasters of Squad Ostor, and we will make damned sure the governor and her people stay safe.'

Lydorran halted outside the arming chamber and placed a hand on Storn's shoulder. Hammer blows and murmured prayers floated from the chamber's doorway.

'Watch them carefully, Thyssus,' he said. 'Redfang's cause might be true, but his methods were ill advised, no matter how expedient. The governor bore his insults as well as she might, but it won't be long before her counsellors remember they have titles and reputations to protect. There is a storm of outrage likely to break when they do, one that our enemies could use as cover for their own efforts.'

'I have weathered far worse, Brother-Librarian,' said Storn. 'But thank you, your counsel is wise. I will do what I can to impress upon them the importance of unity and vigilance in this pivotal hour.'

'Just keep them alive. They can bay for blood all they want once Father is dead and we are done with this damned world,' said Lydorran, with a grim smile that Storn returned.

'Understood, Brother-Librarian,' said the Chaplain, and the two of them strode into the arming chamber side by side.

Several hours later Lydorran was airborne, strapped once again into his restraint throne within the Thunderhawk *Vengeful*. The craft had taken a hammering, like much of the Imperial Fists strike force that had assaulted Delvemine. However, just like the warriors it bore into battle, its hurts had been swiftly seen to, its wargear repaired and resanctified. The sons of

Dorn were ever indomitable, and the ambush to which they had been subjected had only cemented their determination to crush the heretics that endangered this world.

Lydorran checked the runic display in his helm's autosenses then flicked his eyes through a series of external vid feeds, confirming to himself that all was as it should be. His craft was one of five hulking yellow-armoured gunships that streaked north over the mist-shrouded jungles bearing a combined force of warriors and war engines towards the distantly looming mountain of Hive Klaratos. Lighter Imperial Fists aircraft flew around them, wings of Stormtalons and Stormhawks holding position above, below and to the flanks of the main strike force. The enemy had no air assets to speak of, as far as Lydorran was aware, but the Cult of the Wrything Wyrm had surprised him more than once already. He was not about to let them fool him again.

'Managed to keep up this far – I am surprised, Fist,' came Redfang's brash voice over the command vox.

'If all Deathwatch are as ill disciplined as you, then thank the Emperor that we have,' Lydorran responded coldly. Scrolling his field of vision, he took in the flight of Corvus Blackstars that swept over the mists off to his right. The Deathwatch gunships were menacing beasts, he had to concede. They flew with their noses tilted slightly downward and their wings outswept, racing towards Hive Klaratos like omens of death. Though more compact than the Thunderhawks by far, Lydorran didn't doubt that the Deathwatch craft carried substantial arsenals of firepower. Deadlier still were the kill teams that waited within the troop bay of each ship, honed and hardened bands of the finest battle-brothers from dozens of Space Marine Chapters, trained and armed specifically to eradicate xenos threats no matter the cost.

'Was there a matter you wished to discuss, watch captain?' prompted Lydorran into the Space Wolf's continued silence.

'*Are you certain you Fists would not rather be dug in behind your nice big walls?*' asked Redfang, and Lydorran could hear the feral grin in the big Space Wolf's voice.

'You forget, watch captain, that the Imperial Fists are as skilled in the breaking of fortresses as we are at garrisoning them.'

'*Whatever you do is slow-going, though, isn't it? Don't leave my brothers waiting around for you. We wouldn't want to claim all the glory by burning out the broodnest before you even arrive.*'

'Give us an enemy to fight, watch captain, and you will see how swift our vengeance can be.'

Redfang replied with a fierce laugh.

'*Lots of ghosts clamouring for their bloodgeld after that xenos ambush, I'll bet,*' he said, and Lydorran thought he heard a little less braggadocio in the Space Wolf's tone. '*Lots of vengeance to be had.*'

'You strike high, we strike low, and we will meet you in the middle, just as planned,' said Lydorran, not wishing to be drawn into this discussion with a warrior he neither knew nor liked.

'*We're the Allfather's blades – we'll all do our duty,*' said Redfang after a moment. '*What about the Ghyrish? They as weak as they've made themselves look?*'

Lydorran spared a glance at the runes on his auspex display that indicated where multiple Ghyrish Airborne regiments trailed the Space Marine squadrons. Hundreds of gunships filled the air, Valkyries, Vendettas, Vultures and other less common patterns, bearing squad after squad of Ghyrish soldiery towards Hive Klaratos. Squadrons of Lightning fighters held position around them, and a trio of Marauder bombers thundered along towards the heart of their armada.

'They'll serve as well as they may,' he said. 'They have much to prove after all that has happened, and their high marshal has a reputation to try to repair.'

'Sound like anyone you know, Fist?' asked Redfang, and cut the vox-link. Lydorran scowled behind the faceplate of his helm, but he shrugged the barb aside. Let the wolves of Fenris howl, he thought. The Imperial Fists spoke in deeds.

Lydorran pulled up the schematics of Hive Klaratos' lower levels and gave them a last scan over, though he had already committed them to memory some hours before. They had been updated according to every scrap of information that Imperial augurs had managed to collate, and they told a tale of degradation and ruin. The cult's uprising in Klaratos Hive looked to have inflicted substantial internal damage to both structure and utilities, and auguries suggested that much of it had been patched up in only the most rudimentary fashion. One of the hive's three primary plasma generators was dead, hopefully along with a substantial portion of its outer defences, and blast rents punctured the city's mountainous metal flanks where internal explosions had torn right through.

Redfang's plan called for his kill teams to drop in around the Hive Spire and advance through the ruins of the city's more opulent districts in a swift and deadly spearhead. The larger Imperial Fists force, meanwhile, would strike at the largest of the rents torn in the hive's lower slopes, gaining access to the upper levels of Klaratos' Laboritas district then pushing upwards to converge on the Fane of the Emperor Risen from below even as the Deathwatch fell on it from above. The Ghyrish, meanwhile, would land in force across the slopes of the hive and employ their air armada and ground troops in hammering the city's defences, launching dozens of pushes into the upper districts and drawing off as much of the cult's strength as possible.

It was aggressive and potentially costly, as plans went, and if Klaratos' defences had still stood at full strength Lydorran would never have agreed to it, nor to leaving Hive Angelicus with but a skeleton garrison while the attack went in. If Redfang had impressed one thing on Lydorran, though, it was the need for speed, and while the Librarian might not like the watch captain, he did not think Redfang would press the issue so hard without due cause. If the cult was drawing some terrible xenos threat down upon Ghyre, then it had to be dealt with swiftly, and if that meant plunging into the fires of Hive Klaratos, then so be it.

Vengeful came in at a steep angle, engines screaming and hull shuddering as flak fire burst around it.

'*Breach dead ahead,*' announced the pilot, voice tight with concentration. The Thunderhawk jolted, and in his peripheral vid feed Lydorran saw a pair of missiles streak away from under its wings and lash down to explode amidst the enemy below. The breach, a ragged hole torn in the city's flank that resembled a steel-fanged maw, loomed just a few thousand yards ahead. It, the barricades and crew-served heavy weapons that defended it, and the fume-thick half-darkness that churned behind them, all raced up to meet the Imperial Fists.

A detached part of Lydorran's mind noted creepers of spined jungle foliage stretching up to the lip of the breach, their ends blackened where they had been driven back by hand-held flamer units. The Mechanicus firethrowers on the hive's legs must have been damaged and stopped working, he thought, or else been shut down by loyal tech-magi before the cult completed their conquest of the city. He doubted

very much that any of Father's worshippers possessed sufficient arcane knowledge to reawaken the machine-spirits of
the weapons if they had been intentionally rendered inactive.

'Ready, brothers!' boomed Lydorran over the vox-link,
remembering only too well the last time he had delivered
a pre-battle speech, just days earlier. *Please*, he beseeched
Emperor and primarch both, *please don't let me be leading
them into another damned trap.*

'Vengeance for Delvemine!' he roared, and his warriors
shouted it back at him.

The Thunderhawk hit hard, a combat landing directly atop
the enemy's barricades in the very throat of the breach. The
assault ramp slammed down, and Lydorran led the way out,
throwing up a kinetic shield as he did so. Small-arms fire
washed against his psychic barrier, bullets ricocheting away
or exploding against the empyric energies. A glance showed
Lydorran the ragged edge of the breach arching overhead
and the enemy's barricades stretching away to either side,
formed from wrecked vehicles, rubble, tangles of snarlwire
and whatever other detritus could be dragged into place.
The other gunships in the strike force had slammed down
to either side of Lydorran's, their bulk and firepower making a mockery of the cult's attempts at defence. Even as he
watched, Lydorran saw bolt fire shred hanging banners bearing the crude wyrmform and heretical oaths of faith in Father
and the Star Children.

Dozens of cultists had already died as the Imperial Fists
gunships came down, either crushed beneath massive landing gear, scoured away by the defence guns of the craft or
slaughtered by the Imperial Fists who were even now pouring down the assault ramps and into the wounded flank of
Hive Klaratos. Masses more were dashing up from within the

hive's carcass, however. Autogun fire raked the Space Marines, ringing against their armour in a hellish cacophony. Crude blasting charges tumbled through the air, only to be caught and hurled back or kicked savagely away. A few shots and blasts found their mark, Space Marines dropping wounded or stumbling and spitting oaths, but as fusillade after fusillade of bolts swept the neck of the breach, the cultists were reduced to crimson mist. Soon enough the defenders were annihilated, and sudden quiet fell.

Lydorran looked back to where Ancient Tarsun had followed him down the ramp, the Fifth Company's banner held high and proud in his hands. He was the last of Tor's command squad, Lydorran thought with a pang. Champion Hastur maimed and barely clinging to life, Apothecary Lordas slain by xenos-corrupted mutants. The thought stoked his anger, and with a nod to Tarsun, Lydorran led the way into the hive's interior.

'Gunships, dust off and adopt suppressing patterns. Support the Ghyrish where possible and be ready for extraction once our mission is complete,' he voxed, receiving chimes and runes of acknowledgement moments later.

'Brothers, press forward and secure primary objectives,' he addressed his warriors, blink-clicking a rune in his peripheral vision and exloading squad objectives to their autosenses. 'Hive secondary plasma generatorum is one level up and half a mile into the city. Hive turbolifts are this level, one mile in. Vanguard, Arbites precinct fortress sector eighty-six. You all know your duty, now see it done.' Lydorran and his brothers advanced through the breach and into a tangled warren of narrow streets, winding alleyways, crawl-ducts, teetering and bullet-riddled hab-blocks, seedy store fronts, impoverished and now defaced Imperial shrines and heaps upon heaps of rubbish and rubble.

ANDY CLARK

Everywhere Lydorran saw evidence of the cult's occupation, if not the cultists themselves. Wyrmforms were daubed fifty feet high onto the flanks of habs, dangled upon streamers and banners, etched into the hull plating of wrecked Arbites armoured personnel carriers or carved into the impaled and rotting corpses of loyal Ghyrish soldiery who had presumably attempted to stop the uprising in its tracks. A miasma hung in the air, a combination of dust and smoke that mixed with the gloomy half-light of the flickering lumen to reduce visibility to a hundred yards at most. He could see the embers of dozens of fires burning amidst the rising urban tangle of the inner hivescape, each one a will-o'-the-wisp amidst the otherwise impenetrable gloom.

'Auspex and map navigation,' he voxed to his brothers as they fanned out into the surrounding streets. 'This city is a disaster zone. Be wary of ambush, collapse, exposed motive force, anything.'

Lydorran advanced up a rubble-strewn street between looming hab-structures dotted with fitful lights. The Aggressors of Squad Torvas stomped along to his right, while behind them the rumbling form of the Vindicator *Hammerblow* made the buildings shudder and the dust jump with the basso vibrations of tracks and engine.

Lydorran sensed movement before it came, spinning to his right and throwing up a shield. A whirling blasting charge rebounded from it, tumbling back to land at the feet of the wide-eyed cultist who had hurled it. The heretic gave a scream and then vanished in a sheet of white light. Rubble flew across the street, clattering from Lydorran's armour. Dust billowed in thick clouds.

As though that had been their signal, shooters in the windows above let fly. Las and autogun rounds whipped down in a storm, converging on the Imperial Fists in the street below.

'Eliminate them, armour await ground targets,' ordered Lydorran, before reaching for the powers of the warp. His rested mind seized the empyric flow with ease and twisted; a twenty-yard section of frontage exploded out from the building to his right, three floors up, where the flare of gun muzzles revealed a concentration of the foe. Flailing cultists were ripped out of the building along with the window frames on which they had been leaning and the floors on which they had stood. The whole lot came crashing down in a spray of rubble, dust and blood.

The Aggressors raised their boltstorm gauntlets and let fly, playing the resultant hurricane of bolt fire across the frontages of both buildings. Windows shattered inwards. Masonry erupted in pulverised geysers as shells punched clean through the walls to explode in the rooms behind. Crimson sprays burst from the structures as cultists were blown apart one after another. With every second the atsmophere in the street grew thicker with dust, fyceline smoke and atomised gore, until even Lydorran's autosenses could barely penetrate the murk.

Again his geokinetic senses warned him of an incoming threat, subtle vibrations in the surface of the street whispering their message up through the armoured soles of his boots.

'*Hammerblow*, enemy armour moving along the street towards our position, something heavy, fifty yards and closing.'

'Understood, Brother-Librarian,' came the voice of Sergeant Vastian from within his hulking siege tank. 'Step aside if you would, brothers.'

Lydorran stepped smartly forward, pressing himself against the wall of the nearest building. The Aggressors went the other way, boltstorm gauntlets still thundering even as they cleared *Hammerblow*'s path. The sudden glare of a stablight lit like a baleful eye amidst the murk, its light filtering weakly through to limn *Hammerblow*'s enormous siege shield. There came panicked cries, barely audible over the hammering din of the firefight, then a loud bang. Something heavy whipped through the air, leaving a whirling contrail of disturbed dust in its wake, and hit the Vindicator's shield head on. The shell exploded, denting the triple-layered ceramite and defacing the honour badges painstakingly painted there but otherwise leaving *Hammerblow* undamaged.

In reply, the thunderous report of the Vindicator's demolisher cannon was enough to shatter windows and burst cultist eardrums. The dust leapt in a sudden shockwave at the weapon's discharge, and its enormous shell whooped down the street and out of sight. Lydorran squinted against the detonation that came a moment later, followed by a cascade of crackling explosions that tumbled one atop another. A desultory hail of shots fell amongst the Space Marines, but the last of the foe were dissuaded by another volley from the Aggressors. Silence fell, other than the shift and crunch of rubble, the rumble of engines and power packs and the breathy roar of a fire burning some way down the street.

'Move on,' voxed Lydorran, stalking past the blazing remains of the stolen Ghyrish Leman Russ battle tank that had been neatly killed by *Hammerblow*'s shot. 'And move that wreck aside,' he added. 'The Ghyrish loyalists will be following up behind us, and it'll give them a lot more trouble than us.'

Lydorran and his small force pushed ever deeper into the hive sprawl, and as they did he saw ever more evidence that the deliverance these people had been promised was a lie.

The tyranids drawing closer and closer was all the reward their twisted faith would bring, and Lydorran was determined to prevent that fate from ever transpiring. Reports flashed through his vox of Redfang's Deathwatch capturing the primary access spires to the upper Commercias, of Imperial Fists squads engaging in street-by-street clearance operations against insurgent forces and of the Ghyrish Airborne performing massed landings in the face of fierce but sporadic resistance; all the while, Lydorran was confronted with images of squalor and hardship mingled with seemingly mindless zealotry that left him feeling angry and frustrated.

At an intersection where a derelict filtration shrine had been demolished to block the road, *Hammerblow* ploughed through an adjoining hab-wall to allow Lydorran's force to progress. Within, the Imperial Fists saw signs of recently abandoned cookfires, heaped and threadbare blankets and stinking piles of waste that spoke of massive overcrowding and a workforce left destitute and near starvation. The picked-over carcasses of sump vermin and other, more humanoid remains only underlined the supposition.

Further in, a ragged mob came at Lydorran and his brothers even as they rendezvoused with Ancient Tarsun and the Intercessors of Squad Ulatus. Caught in the middle of a fire-blackened plaza, the Imperial Fists backed up towards one another and formed a living fortress of ceramite and blazing bolt weaponry. To Lydorran's disgust, wave upon wave of malnourished and mad-eyed cultists simply flung themselves at the Space Marines with cries of devotion to their false deities.

'Father, lend us strength!'

'The Star Children are coming! Do you feel them? *Do you feel them?*' they cried with glee.

'Die, oppressors! May Father devour your souls!'

These were not the well-armed and determined cult warriors that he had fought up until now; they were barely more than a civilian mob, brandishing everything from stolen knives and broken bayonets to smashed bottles, lumps of masonry and flinders of broken furniture. Crude icons upon uprooted sign poles seemed to float and bob atop the screaming masses, the wyrmform wrought in scrap metal or painted onto crude wooden boards. Lydorran swiftly ordered his warriors to fight the enemy hand to hand lest they pour all their ammunition into these lost creatures; it was the right choice, strategically, but he felt his anger and disgust grow with every skull he crushed and chest he caved in with his thunderous blows. By the time the awful fight was over and the last of the mob had fled back into the umber shadows, not a single Space Marine had fallen, but they were surrounded by a rampart of rent and bludgeoned dead that lay ten deep.

'This is not war, this is slaughter,' spat Ancient Tarsun in disgust as the Imperial Fists pressed on again.

'It is the wages of heresy, brother,' replied Lydorran. 'And it is a tragedy for us all.'

At last, after a series of frantic, one-sided firefights, improvised ambushes and a battle across a waste dump that seemed to Lydorran weirdly reminiscent of trench warfare, the Imperial Fists approached their target. Already runic designators had flashed green in the peripheral of Lydorran's autosenses to tell him that the Arbites precinct fortress was secure and the secondary generatorum was in loyalist hands.

Now, as they crested the ridge of rubble that was all that remained of a demolished hab-block, the towering column of Hive Spire hove into view. The great mass of ironclad girders, trunking cables, water and air pipes and glimmering lumen reached up through the floor of this hab-level like the trunk of some colossal tree and vanished into the misty upper strata, where it met with the level's ceiling and ploughed on upwards out of sight.

Lydorran halted atop the ridge, his warriors spread out around him with their guns raised. He magnified his autosenses to see that the turbolift shafts were dead and dark, their motive force gone. A broad transit ramp wound up and around the hive spine, wide enough for several lanes of groundcar traffic to scale the heights and access the next level, had any still been operational in this destitute wasteland. Huge banners hung from the girders that held the roadway aloft. They stirred sluggishly in the weak breeze of huge air vents, and the wyrmforms upon them seemed to ripple like living serpents.

'Eerie,' commented Tarsun.

'And deserted,' replied Lydorran, feeling disquiet stir in his chest. 'This feels altogether too easy. They put up a fight when we first breached, but since then we've been wading through dregs. If the broodnest is here, where are all of its defenders?'

'Perhaps they have massed their elite fighters around the nest itself?' suggested Tarsun.

'Or perhaps Redfang is wrong, and the broodnest is not here at all, and we waste yet more time as the tyranids writhe their way towards us through the interstellar void.'

'Can you reach Shipmaster Gavorn, patch a vox-missive through to Chaplain Storn and ask him for his wisdom?' asked Tarsun.

Lydorran checked his vox and shook his head. 'I cannot, this deep into the hive. With the choral shrines inactive, there is nothing to boost the signal and transmit it into the void. No, we must press on, but be ready in case this is another deception wrought by our honourless foe.'

He led the way down the rubble slope and his warriors

followed, but as Lydorran made for the transit ramp, he found the stirrings of disquiet in his gut intensifying and thought again of Hive Angelicus, left with but a scant garrison to watch over it. He was suddenly very glad that Thyssus Storn stood watch over the governor and her conclave; without Kallistus, any chance of keeping this world from sliding into anarchy would be lost.

XI

Thyssus Storn stood beside Governor Kallistus. He maintained a respectful distance of ten human paces, the minimum range within which the governor's armoured bodyguards would allow anyone to approach. *Pointless*, he thought as he stared out of the galleria windows at the spire towers below. *I could be across that gap and snapping her neck in less time than it would take them to activate those gilded power swords they brandish so proudly.*

Not that he would, of course. Storn's task was to smooth matters over with the governor and her conclave as best he could, not threaten her life.

The galleria they stood in was high up in the conclave building, only a few levels below the chambers themselves. It was richly carpeted, its rear wall lined with skeletal statues in miner's garb and hung with stylised paintings of tall and brawny Ghyrish workers labouring tirelessly at the ore-faces for a benevolent Emperor. Its long, arcing window looked out over the grand sweep of Hive Spire; its cathedrum spires, sweeping processionals, private palaces and mountainous

Administratum towers still stood proud despite the battle scars that marred their architecture. Behind Storn and the governor stood six of her hand-picked bodyguards, clad in their gilded armour, hands on the pommels of their ceremonial swords.

Storn could feel their hard eyes fixed upon him.

'Latest reports suggest that the assault forces have moved into the main body of Hive Klaratos,' he said, breaking the brittle silence. 'I am told that your airborne forces acquit themselves well in suppression operations against the heretics, lady governor.'

'One would hope that they would, Brother-Chaplain,' said Governor Kallistus, her eyes distant, the towers of the cityscape reflected in her pupils. 'My brother and his soldiers have much to prove this day.'

'*His* soldiers, governor?' asked Storn, quirking an eyebrow and glancing pointedly at the Ghyrish Airborne uniform she wore, the fistful of medals that decorated her chest. She offered him the ghost of a smile.

'*His* soldiers, Brother Storn,' she affirmed. 'The high marshal has suffered insults enough without a needless assertion of our military authority.'

'They are the Deathwatch,' he said, feeling that this was explanation enough. 'They are not Imperial Fists. Their conduct is not for us to condone or condemn.'

'I fear our conclave do not make such distinctions, nor do they hold the Deathwatch in such high regard as yourselves,' said the governor. 'They feel frightened, threatened – they are as accustomed to power and privilege as they are to the air they breathe. Even the meekest may lash out in panic when they feel themselves asphyxiating.'

'You are saying they will respond poorly to Redfang's deeds,' said Storn, frowning. He wished briefly that he, and not Lyd-orran, had led the attack upon Klaratos Hive. The Librarian was far more talented a diplomat and reader of people. True, the foe had deceived him more than once during this campaign, but to Storn that was simply proof that something truly insidious was at work upon this world, something powerful enough to fool even the Imperial Fists psyker. He was sure that had it been him in command, not Lydorran, matters would have been much worse. Storn preferred problems he could bludgeon.

'Did you know that your Captain Redfang found those parasites on not only Bishop Renwyck but also upon the bodies of two of the high administrator's scribes, the first arbitrator's autosavant and Lady Tectos' bodyguard?' asked the governor. Storn felt a flash of irritation at her lack of a direct answer.

'He is not *my* captain,' he snapped, and cursed himself as he heard subtle creaks of movement from the bodyguards behind him. Storn took a breath, let it out slowly through his nostrils. Of course, the fools were no threat to him, even with those elaborate power blades they carried, but if anything went awry he would prefer the governor's guards to be unharmed and able to protect her, rather than crippled at his hands. 'I was aware of that, governor, yes. His purge was thorough, and we shall all do penance for our failure to register such widespread enemy infiltration, but I fail to see how that is directly relevant.'

'That is just our point, Brother-Chaplain,' said the governor, and he detected a stab of some emotion he couldn't place in her voice. 'You will do penance. I doubt that the sons of Dorn let themselves off lightly for such errors, but at least you shall have the chance to be your own judges, to weigh your own worth. By the time Captain Redfang had finished peeling worms from our people's flesh, his discoveries had not only spread horror and paranoia through the conclave, but they had further created a situation in which few if any of us can now escape suspicion and, one would imagine, the harshest judgement. Many of our people have not heard of the Inquisition, Brother-Chaplain, but we are a planetary governor and we know a little of such things. Even should the assault upon Klaratos succeed, they will not stop at penance.'

Storn scowled.

'Duty demands sacrifice, lady governor, a regrettable reality of the war we all fight. For now, your duty, and that of your conclave, is to aid in the purgation of your world's xenos infestation in whatever way you can. What comes after, comes after.'

Governor Kallistus stiffened. She cast a glance at him, eyes flashing.

'You do not need to remind us of our duty, Brother-Chaplain,' she said, voice cool.

'Then you know what you need to tell them when you take your throne in the high chamber, lady governor,' Storn replied. 'You–'

He stopped as the vox-bead in his gorget chimed. At the same moment the governor's bodyguards moved as one to place their hands against the right sides of their helms, frowns deepening as they listened to the panicked transmissions that spilled across their own vox-channel.

Storn listened as Techmarine Asphor delivered a clipped, concise report, then looked up at Governor Kallistus.

'Mercurio Gate space port is under attack,' he said, the anger of a moment before swept aside like smoke before a shell blast. 'Cult infiltrators, substantial strength, must have got in through some crawlway or pipe that we didn't see.

They are going for the coolant towers in the north quadrant of the space port. Throne, if they could knock those out, cause a generatorum meltdown within Hive Spire…'

'My lady, with respect, that is not the only attack,' said one of the governor's guards. Storn and Kallistus both turned their gazes upon the man, who bore them stoically. 'We need to get you to a safe location at once, my lady. We're getting reports of enemies within the conclave chambers.'

'Explain,' barked Storn, already cycling his vox to patch into the Ghyrish command channel.

'Reports of xenos… They used the word *monsters*, my lady,' said the guard, still determinedly addressing Kallistus, unable to meet Storn's gaze.

'Your guards are correct – you need to move to a safe location, lady governor,' said the Chaplain. 'If the enemy has assaulted the conclave building, then they can have only one true objective for such a forlorn hope. My battle-brothers and I will purge the xenos – you remove yourself from their reach.'

The governor stood still as a statue, and Storn drew breath to shout at her for freezing in such a vital moment. Then he realised that her expression was not one of panic but of intense thought. The governor was weighing the options, considering what was happening and choosing her next move with the calm of a born commander, he thought, and his respect for her grew a little.

'We deem you are correct, Brother-Chaplain,' she said. 'We have a location to retreat to. Please, we would ask that you do what you can for our conclave.'

'My honour on it, lady governor,' said Storn, turning away and preparing to issue orders to the handful of warriors garrisoning the space port; they had plenty of Ghyrish with them, but Storn knew it would be the actions of the few Imperial Fists that would decide the fate of Mercurio Gate.

'Brother-Chaplain, the timing of this attack is damnably fortunate for our enemies, is it not?' asked the governor, halting him in his tracks. 'If they could reach us thus, why would they not have struck such a blow earlier in the war? Can it be the heretics still have eyes and ears inside our fastness?'

'I don't know,' said Storn. 'Whether it is luck or cunning on the foe's part, your conclave may not be the only ones driven to desperate measures by fear.'

Kallistus nodded once, hard-eyed, then turned and swept away with her bodyguards clustered around her. Storn hefted his crozius and set off in the opposite direction, already summoning the brothers of Squad Furian to his side.

He would be damned if he would allow xenos infiltrators to destabilise this planet's infrastructure any further, or strike at the very heart of the fortress Lydorran had fought and bled to secure.

The sounds were dim at first, muffled thumping that meant nothing to him. He hung in a warm haze that nothing could penetrate, untouched and unconcerned.

The sounds came again, harsher and louder. They sparked something in him, a sense of recognition and the need to do… What? To respond in some fashion, as he had been conditioned to. His twin hearts thumped. As they did, he became painfully aware of how they laboured, how they hurt. That wasn't right. None of this was right. The sense of insulation and inactivity suddenly became cloying, an artificial smothering of his consciousness that he fought against with the stubborn determination that was his bloodright.

Bludgeoning his way back up to consciousness, Elrich

Hastur forced his eyes to open. Pain rushed in at him from every direction. The glare seared his eyes, making the pupils contract painfully and prompting his eyelids to try to squeeze shut again. He pushed the sensations aside impatiently and tried to rise.

Hastur had a brief impression of a stone cell, a space that blended monastic solemnity with the antiseptic glare of an apothecarian. Then the door banged open and a heavy form crashed backwards through it. A Space Marine, Hastur realised, clad in robes and wielding what looked like a surgical bone saw in one hand. The warrior had a heavy medical compress encasing one side of his face, and rich red blood was running from a long gash in the front of his robes. Even as Hastur watched, his sluggish thoughts racing to catch up, a hunched figure lunged through the doorway and pounced on the Space Marine, overbalancing him and bearing him to the ground. Chitinous limbs whipped up and down. Bone talons sank deep. There was the crack and whine of an auto-pistol's discharge, the cult mutant trying to shoot the fallen warrior in the face only to have his wrist forced aside at the last moment. The fallen battle-brother drove his wounded forehead into the xenos' stretched muzzle. Chitin crunched, fangs broke and the Space Marine's medical compress tore away in a spatter of unguents and blood.

Hastur managed to heave himself up onto his elbows despite his body's howl of pain, and then to roll groggily towards the side of the bed. He saw flashes of metal where there should have been none and realised that all of his right arm and a substantial portion of his left leg had been augmetically replaced. What had happened to him? He couldn't remember.

The bone saw swung through the air and crunched into

the side of the cult mutant's head, dislodging the horror. It crashed aside only for another abomination in goggles and a torn utility suit to burst through the door behind it. The hideous creature wielded a massive rock saw in three-taloned hands, and it howled triumphantly as it swung the screaming blade down towards the fallen Space Marine.

Hastur reacted without conscious thought. His metal fist lashed out, intercepting the housing of the saw as it descended. He struck hard enough to dent the sheet metal and hurl the cultist's blow sideways so that it fell not upon the Space Marine but instead carved into the wounded mutant that he had just hit with his bone saw. Hastur hissed in pain as he felt sutures split and drip-feeds tear from his flesh with his sudden, violent movement. The luckless xeno-cultist suffered far worse, its wail cut off in an explosive spray of gore and pulverised bone.

Before its killer could drag his rock saw free and take another swing, the fallen Space Marine spun the bone saw in his fists and sank its sharp teeth deep into the mutant's face. Hastur heard the distinctive crunch of a skull being broken. The cultist toppled backwards, its saw screaming for a moment as it hit flagstones before its saviour-spirit cut power to the suddenly unmanned device.

Hastur blinked, eyes still adjusting to the glare, and took stock. He was alive, which his vague memories of falling stone and billowing fire suggested was improbable, but it looked as though his body had suffered for it. Besides the augmetics, he was covered in swathes of medicae compresses, and his flesh bore a road map of scars where chirurgeons' blades had clearly cut him open time and again.

The fallen Space Marine struggled to his feet. He tried for a fruitless moment to push the compress back onto his face, then gave up with a growl of disgust and instead tore it the rest of the way off, throwing it to the floor with a wet splat. Hastur could see that the warrior's features on that side of his face had been badly burned, the eye little more than a seared socket. Without the aid of that compress, he doubted the scarring or damage would ever be properly mended.

'Brother-Champion, you live! My thanks!' said the Space Marine.

'You are… welcome,' replied Hastur. He was still groggy, but as various plastic tubes and feed-lines slipped from his skin to dangle, dribbling, from the machines they belonged to, his thoughts were reordering themselves quicker. He now recognised Brother Idoras, one of Sergeant Vlaskin's Primaris.

The tall warrior hastened around to Hastur's side, plucking the last few feeds and armatures free while shooting glances at the open door. Hastur could hear gunfire, shouts and screams echoing from without.

'Can I assist you, Brother-Champion?' asked Idoras, offering an arm to help Hastur up. The Champion brushed the aid aside and stood on his own, wincing at the storm of painful sensation that raced through him at the simple motion. Something, possibly several somethings, had broken inside him and evidently had yet to heal. In all, Hastur had a feeling that if Lordas or one of his cronies saw him, they would jab him full of needles and return him to a comatose state right there and then.

'No time for that,' he said, half to himself, and cast about for his weapons and armour. 'Where are we, Brother Idoras? What is happening?'

'A monastery complex attached to the outer structures of Mercurio Gate. The xenos launched a surprise attack now that the big assault is in full swing against Klaratos Hive,' replied

Idoras, who had taken up station guarding the door with his bent bone saw. He hadn't bothered with the xenocultists' weapons, and rightly so; even had the Space Marines been able to wield such comparatively small and fragile pieces of equipment, the weapons' machine-spirits were undoubtedly corrupt beyond redemption. Better a solid lump of metal than a blade or gun that despised you for slaying its master, thought Hastur.

That thought brought to mind his relic blade. A mental image flashed through Hastur's mind of the weapon lost beneath mountains of falling stone and metal, and his hearts beat a little faster in alarm. Again he forced himself to focus.

'What assault on Klaratos Hive?' he asked, picking up then discarding several bladed surgical tools that sat on a metal gurney near his bed of convalescence.

'The Deathwatch called for it,' replied Idoras. 'Most of our force is there, Brother-Champion. There's little but walking wounded and a skeleton garrison held back to defend the fortress.'

Hastur discarded his next questions, settling instead for wrapping one mechanical hand around a leg of his bed and ripping it free with a squeal of metal. Pain rippled through his sutured shoulders, but he was left clutching a three-foot-long metal shaft with a ragged but undoubtedly sharp tip. Hardly a gladius, he thought, but as he spun it experimentally around his fist he was pleased to find that his augmetics hadn't entirely dulled his swordsman's skills. It would do for now.

'Who is in command?' he asked.

'Chaplain Storn remained in Angelicus Hive to oversee the governor's protection, but we have not heard from him since the attack began,' replied Idoras. 'For the moment,

Brother-Champion, I'd be forced to say that *you* are in command.'

'Splendid,' replied Hastur sourly. 'In that case, brother, do you know where our weapons and wargear were stored while we were healing?'

'Armoury chambers on the next floor down, Brother-Champion.'

'Lead on then, brother,' said Hastur, casting a last glance around the chamber and breathing silent thanks to Dorn that he had woken when he had. What more ignominious death could a warrior know than to be butchered, unconscious and abed, by lesser foes? He had a grim feeling in the pit of his stomach that a bloody fate might yet wait up ahead, but at least it would not be that.

The two Space Marines hastened through corridors and chambers, Hastur limping on his mechanical leg and doing his best to keep up with Idoras. Twice more the Primaris Space Marine was forced to employ his bone saw, once to smash the autogun from a surprised cultist's hands after running into him at an intersection, and again to hack open a twisted mutant that lunged at him from a shadowed doorway. Hastur fought too, and by the time the two of them thumped down the stairs to the arming chambers, the Brother-Champion's improvised weapon was purple-black with xenos-tainted blood.

Gaining in strength and confidence as his body awoke fully, Hastur stepped up and drove a kick against the door with his augmetic foot, sending it swinging violently open and knocking a shocked cultist from his feet. Hastur lunged quick as thought, and his metal stave drove tip-first into the throat of a second cultist who stood, gaping, over the bullet-riddled bodies of several Chapter serfs. Idoras came in after him, swinging his weapon up over his head and bringing it back down on the collarbone of the third and most mutated of the cultists. There was an awful crunch of metal sinking through flesh and bone, and the twisted creature hissed its pain before lashing out with a curved blade fashioned from bone. Hastur parried the blow, knocking the tip of the weapon up and leaving his enemy's guard wide open. He spun inside it, moving far faster than so large a warrior should be able to, and drove a thunderous elbow into the cultist's face. Bone broke. Blood sprayed. The cultist went down hard and did not rise. Hastur heard a click to his right and threw without looking, instinct guiding his aim. The bloodied spar of metal he had ripped from his sick bed flew through the air like a huge dart and slammed into the chest of the first cultist, the one the door had knocked from her feet. She crashed back against the wall, three feet of jagged metal jutting from her chest, then gurgled purple blood and collapsed.

While Idoras stood guard over the door, Hastur performed a rapid search of the chamber. Everything in his body hurt. His hearts were racing, and drawing breath was a conscious effort. So brief a fight would never have had this effect upon him normally.

How badly am I hurt? Hastur wondered, then pushed the thought aside. For the moment it didn't matter. He was an Imperial Fist, and he would serve until he couldn't. What came after would not be his concern.

Half-disassembled weapons and armour lay upon work benches, scattered and upended where the cultists had rooted through them. Hastur bridled at the thought of unclean hands molesting the bared machine-spirits of such vulnerable Chapter artefacts, and his hatred for the enemy redoubled.

Helms, bolt rifles, a power axe, a plasma pistol… He took the last, checking its power cell and muttering a benediction to calm its angry machine-spirit. Then he saw it, a gilded chest with a brass fist picked out upon its lid, pushed hastily back under a workbench.

Hastur opened the chest and breathed out in relief as he saw his wargear within, Lamentation lying unblemished and ready for battle atop it all. His happiness faltered as he took in the crushed and battered condition of his armour, yet he removed each segment with what speed and efficiency he could manage and laid them out on the chamber's stone floor. Efforts had been made to repair the wargear, he saw, efforts by someone with prodigious skill. Still, he suspected his armour would be barely serviceable. At least his relic blade had endured whatever disaster he had been caught in.

'Much better than nothing,' he told himself, then glanced at Idoras, who was still guarding the door. 'Brother, aid me and then gird yourself for war. We will not win this fight clad in robes.'

Idoras shot him a fierce grin.

'We are sons of Dorn, Brother-Champion. We could win it in naught but our skins.'

'All the same,' said Hastur, already struggling to don his gear. It would be damned awkward without any helots to aid him; he and Idoras would have to assist one another as best they could, and they wouldn't have time for all the proper invocations, but it could and would be done.

As his battle-brother connected input sockets and slammed Hastur's chest-piece into place, the Champion grabbed his helm and activated its vox-bead. He cycled rapidly through the channels, his chest relaxing a little as he saw the connection runes flash green.

'Chaplain Storn, do you hear me? This is Champion Hastur. I am preparing to take command of the defence of the space port.'

There was a pause, then Storn's voice came back, his words booming over the roar of bolter fire and the monstrous shrieks of xenos.

'Hastur! Dorn's fist, brother, this is welcome news! The conclave chamber is overrun. We're trying to save as many as we can.'

'Understood, Brother-Chaplain. I will not let them take the space port,' replied Hastur.

'The coolant towers!' barked Storn. *'They are going to demolish the coolant towers.'* Then his vox-link cut out amidst predatory shrieks, leaving Hastur gripping his helm hard in both hands. The coolant towers; if the enemy blew them up, if they could overload the control shrine, they would trigger a catastrophic meltdown of Mercurio Gate's generatorums. Hastur again heard the roar of falling stone and metal, the draconic bellow of explosives detonating and fire billowing.

'No,' he said as fractured memories came back to him and shame rose in his chest, warring with cold fury. 'No, not again.'

Chaplain Storn cut his vox-link to Hastur as a four-armed xenos abomination leapt from the conclave chamber's helical ramp and straight towards him. Genestealers. These vile, chitinous killing machines Storn had faced before, and he could recall few baser or more foully heretical creatures to curse the Emperor's realm.

And these fools worship them as deities? thought a detached part of his mind in that instant. *They truly are beyond redemption.*

The xenos leapt with breathtaking speed, its movements

so lightning fast and ferociously aggressive that even Storn's post-human instincts could barely keep pace. He managed to bring his crozius up crossways, and its energised head met the ridged bio-armour of the attacking alien with a dense crunch. Ichor sprayed, but still the genestealer's elongated head lunged towards him, and its inch-long fangs snapped shut a hair's breadth from the faceplate of his helm. For an instant its unholy yellow eyes stared into his, and Storn saw a depth of animal fury and malign intellect that shook him to his core. Blade-like talons lashed faster than thought, scoring sparking lines through his armour. Then he fired his bolt pistol, and the round tore up through the alien's chest to detonate in its centre mass. The genestealer exploded, showering Storn with viscous gore. Its talons still twitched and clutched weakly at him even as its ruined remains slumped to the floor.

Storn took stock. The lower conclave chamber was a wreck. Skulls and ancient miners' relics were scattered across the ground amidst sprays of shattered armaglass that twinkled like stars. The fine wood panelling of the walls was spattered in blood, and more spread in puddles from the torn and ruined bodies of Ghyrish soldiery and utility-suited cultists. A few of the latter had still been alive when Storn and four battle-brothers from Squad Furian burst into the chamber. They weren't anymore.

But then, they were never the threat here, were they? thought Storn.

From above came crashes and screams, gunshots, xenos shrieks and the rending sound of claws upon metal.

'Up the ramp,' barked Storn to his brothers. 'Suffer not the unclean alien to live, my brothers! Purge them from this sanctuary of Imperial rule! Scour them from existence, and in doing so, know that you do the primarch's work!'

Storn led the way up the right-hand ramp with two hulking Intercessors close on his heels. The other two battle-brothers took the left-hand path, bolt rifles raised and sighting as they passed up through the mezzanine and into the conclave chamber.

It was one of those brothers that was hit first, before he had even had time to turn and address the xenos coming at him. The thing sprinted with unbelievable speed across the chamber's wide circular floor and hit the Intercessor like a thunderbolt. Talons and claws sliced and slashed. Bright red blood sprayed in fans, and the wrestling figures crashed back down the ramp and out of sight.

The upper chamber was like a scene from a nightmare. Limp bodies hung like butchered carcasses over the balustrades of the delegates' platforms, their blood soaking the walls in runnels. A fan of mangled bodies on the chamber floor showed where the Ghyrish soldiery had attempted a last stand in defence of the terrified delegates and paid with their lives. Higher up, a handful of the conclave's members and their hangers-on still cowered on their platforms, trapped in the chamber with their killers by security doors that had automatically sealed when the alarm was raised.

Those killers crawled up the walls and perched like monstrous gargoyles atop the chamber's gothic statuary before launching themselves, claws flashing, into each fresh knot of victims. Storn could count only a handful of genestealers, but they had transformed this place into an abattoir and killed dozens of luckless victims already.

He raised his bolt pistol and sent a staccato burst of shots whipping up towards a higher gallery. The bolts flew true, but his target lunged aside from them, digging its claws into the chamber's wall then barrelling into High Administrator

Lunst and her surviving scribes. Heavy cloth and flesh tore as the genestealer ripped its way into the screaming acolytes. To her credit, Storn saw Lunst herself level an autopistol at the alien with a scream more of anger than fear and unload the weapon's clip. Most of the shots flew wide or sparked off the platform's balustrade. A scythe-like talon whipped around and opened the high administrator's throat. As she crumpled, another of her acolytes was smashed bodily over the railing to plunge fifty feet to the hard floor of the mezzanine. He landed with a horribly final crunch, torn parchment stained with blood fluttering down upon him.

'In the Emperor's name, eradicate the xenos!' bellowed Storn, and his brothers' bolt rifles thundered. One genestealer was riddled with shots as it hunched over the mangled form of Magos Gathabosis, whose vox-emitter was giving off ragged blurts of binharic. Its body detonated messily, spattering acidic juices across the already maimed tech-priest. Another of the aliens lost an arm to the explosive blast of a bolt shell; without the slightest hesitation, it spun and launched itself down upon its attacker, another two shells detonating its back and spine in a trailing spume of gore that did nothing to stop the alien driving a sword-like talon clean through its victim's helm. Xenos and Space Marine fell dead together on the chamber floor in a bloody heap.

Who still lives? thought Storn, playing his autosenses swiftly around the chamber. Clanlord VanSappen was butchered meat, though Lady Tectos was still alive, crouched on her high platform with a handful of lackeys around her brandishing blades and pistols. Storn suspected they had survived mostly thanks to no genestealer having worked its way up that far yet, but he knew they would not last long if one did. Seneschal Gryft lay sprawled between a pair of butchered Ghyrish soldiery, halfway down a flight of marble stairs that connected the governor's throne to the main chamber. Lunst and Gathabosis he had seen die, while a portly and becassocked priest who had to be Renwyck's replacement dangled from the railings of his platform, his entrails hanging in ropes and his eyes glassy. Bodyguards and aides and savants were scattered everywhere in bloody heaps.

There.

He saw movement on a low platform, and a volley of shotgun blasts smashed a genestealer backwards through the railing to slam into the ground below. The thing whipsawed madly as it tried to right itself, claws gouging the floor, hissing screeches erupting from its slavering jaws. Storn lunged, crozius swinging, and crushed the creature's skull. Its body spasmed madly then lay still. Above, he saw the pale face of the first arbitrator peer down through the broken railing, two senior Enforcers at her side and all of them clutching smoking shotguns. He also saw another bio-killer crawling down the wall above them headfirst, about to pounce.

Storn mag-locked his pistol to his thigh, took several running paces and then launched himself in a servo-assisted leap. He caught hold of the ragged gap in the balustrade where the alien had smashed through it and hauled himself up. The genestealer pounced at the same moment, slamming down onto Verol and her two attendants and bearing all three to the ground. Behind Storn, bolt rifles roared. Above him, screams both human and xenos intermingled in a hideous cacophony. His twin heartbeats thundered in his ears.

The Chaplain hauled himself up one-handed with an angry roar and rolled onto the platform, coming up in a fighting crouch. He was in time to see the genestealer's blade-limbs rising and falling with maniacal speed, puncturing one of the senior Enforcers again and again. Storn drew his pistol and fired, and the shot plucked the creature from its prey and threw it against the sealed security doors that had been meant to keep the delegates safe. Xenos ichor spattered up the metal.

'First arbitrator, do you live?' asked Storn, his voice vox-amplified into a fearsome boom.

Verol heaved aside the armoured bodies of her slain comrades and staggered to her feet, one arm still clutching her shotgun, the other wreathed in blood from a deep shoulder wound.

'I do, Brother-Chaplain,' she said. 'We need to evacuate the survivors from this chamber and contain the xenos before–'

Storn did not hear the rest of the arbitrator's words, as just then a clawed hand grabbed his ankle in a grip like steel and wrenched him backwards with vicious strength. Storn's feet went out from under him. His faceplate smashed against the stone of the platform, and then he was falling to hit the mezzanine hard enough to crack it. His pistol spilled from his grip. His senses reeled. Warning runes flashed, then something heavy landed atop him and a lance of agony raced through his leg. He was rolled violently onto his back, and more hot knives of pain penetrated his chest in quick succession. He tried to swing his crozius, but something pinned his arm to the ground. Storn had a fleeting impression of spittle-soaked fangs, jaws stretching wide, and realised that he was about to die.

XII

Champion Hastur limped down a long, covered footbridge that connected the Imperial shrine in which he had awoken to the space port he had vowed to defend. It passed over an abandoned six-lane transitway, the road's surface pocked with craters and scattered with a handful of burnt-out wrecks that marked where a previous cult assault against Mercurio Gate's defences had failed utterly.

Hastur could only hope that this day would run the same course. He had a handful of battle-brothers who had rallied to him as he swept through the cloisters of the shrine with Idoras at his side. They had been armed and armoured as quickly as could be, and though all of them were sorely injured to one degree or another, not one had refused his call to war. Now he led them towards where a ferrocrete barricade blocked off this entrance to the space port.

'Demolished from the inside,' noted Idoras, who went unhelmed since his helm had been ruined by the attack that had so scarred his face.

'This must be where the cultists broke through to assault the field medicae,' replied Hastur.

'Cowardly heretic bastards,' commented one of the warriors accompanying them, a hulking Aggressor named Lastoran.

Hastur grunted and led the way through the sundered barricade, past discarded and bullet-riddled bodies of Ghyrish soldiery and down a wide flight of marble steps that led into a high-ceilinged space from which administrative offices depended. Ahead, hard daylight fell through a line of high arched windows that flanked a blackened doorway. They silhouetted the hastily erected barricade that spanned the doorway and the pair of Ghyrish soldiers crouched beside a heavy stubber there. The two were rattling off volleys of shots across the open ground beyond, one guardsman feeding ammunition into the stubber while the other played the weapon right and left.

The ammo carrier looked back at the sound of the Space Marines' footsteps, and his eyes widened. He thumped his comrade on the shoulder and she spun, laspistol coming cleanly from its holster to point straight at the Imperial Fists. She hurriedly lowered the gun, staring in amazement at the sight of Hastur and his walking wounded.

'My lords!' gasped the gunner. 'My lords, it is a blessing to see you alive! We thought the cultists...'

'They tried and they died for it,' replied Hastur. 'What is the situation?'

'My lord, the enemy are here in force,' said the gunner. 'They emerged an hour ago, came up through an old set of decommissioned ventilation tunnels that weren't on any schematics. The three-armed gunman leads them. Techmarine Passilidus began rallying the defences, but the gunman slew him and...' Her face twisted into an expression of dismay.

'And much of the Ghyrish garrison panicked and fell back from the sudden attack in their midst. We rallied here, in the commissary hall, in hangar four, but our forces are scattered and badly mauled.'

'What of the Imperial Fists?' asked Hastur impatiently. He had little enough sympathy for human frailties while every part of his body screamed at him in pain.

'There were only a handful here, my lord,' said the gunner, looking like she was barely stopping herself trembling. 'All the bigger gunships went with the assault force, so they had no transport to fall back to. They got a couple of escorts into the air, and they fought for a while, but the cultists shot them down... My lord, your brothers stood and fought when we fled. I fear they were overrun.'

Hastur squashed the urge to strike the two soldiers from his path as the cowards they were. *They are but human*, he reminded himself. *They stand here now, fighting against the foul xenos. It is better than many of their comrades' actions, no doubt.*

'Where are the enemy?' he asked.

'Unsure, my lord. Their pursuit was... slowed by your brothers' efforts. A mob of them caught up to us as Lieutenant Scrathe was rallying us here. They picked off the lieutenant, scattered us and broke through to the medicae. A few of us managed to stay clear until they'd passed then set up this gun and barricaded a few offices. We were hoping–'

'Rally whatever strength you have here and follow me,' said Hastur, cutting her off. Given the soldier's report, he didn't expect the Ghyrish to be of great help, but more guns, more bodies... Any improvement of the odds was welcome at this stage.

'My lord, we are few,' she replied.

Hastur fixed her with a fierce stare.

'If the foe is left to complete their work here, they will detonate the space port's generatorum,' he said. He saw her expression twist at the realisation of what that meant. Then, gratifyingly, new steel entered her gaze.

'My lord,' she said, then motioned for her ammo carrier to go and fetch reinforcements. Meanwhile, the gunner herself began to fold down the heavy stubber, ready to lug it forward on the advance. As she did so, a flurry of autogun rounds thumped into the sandbags behind which she crouched. One clanged from Hastur's shoulder guard. He looked pointedly at Brother Lastoran, who nodded then strode straight through the barricade and into the bright sunlight beyond the doorway. His boltstorm gauntlets roared. The autogun fire stopped abruptly.

Hastur turned to see a ragged crowd of Ghyrish soldiery gathering. He counted nearly thirty in all, emerging like vermin from bolt-holes and barricaded strongpoints and staring at him with a mixture of hope and fear. Most clutched lasguns, a couple flamers. There was one more heavy stubber team, no vox-sets and no sign of senior officers.

'What is your name?' Hastur asked the gunner, who had finished stowing her weapon to move it. She looked up at him.

'Corporal Jansys, my lord.'

'Corporal Jansys, you are now in command of these soldiers. You will support our advance upon the coolant towers in whatever way you can.'

Without waiting for a response, Hastur followed Lastoran through the gap in the barricade and out onto the ferrocrete expanse of the space port. Signs of battle were clear here, wrecked fuel tenders gouting smoke, bodies scattered across the grey ground where they had fallen. In the distance he could see one of the landing pads ablaze, and by magnifying his autosenses he picked out skirmishing bands of infantry, both Ghyrish and cultist, dotted across the space port.

The coolant towers rose a quarter mile to the north of his position, the maze of alleyways between them cast into dark shadow by their towering metal mass. The enemy must already be amongst them, might be moments from completing their sabotage even now. There wasn't time to rally every scattered band of Ghyrish soldiery, nor to hunt for any survivors of the Imperial Fists garrison, and he didn't dare employ his vox in case the foe was listening. This fight required a swift and unexpected strike to run the enemy through before they could so much as reach for their blades.

'Forward,' said Hastur, pointing his blade at the coolant towers from which had come the shot that killed Captain Tor some weeks before. 'We make haste, catch the enemy unprepared and cut our way through them.'

With that, he set off across the open ground, autosenses sweeping for snipers, needles of pain lancing through him with every step. Hastur tasted blood but ignored it. He had a duty to do, and the more he remembered of what had happened to him before, the more he felt the need to atone rising up within him to eclipse all else.

A shotgun boomed, and abruptly the killing weight atop Chaplain Storn was swept away. He wasted no time springing upright, ignoring the pain that stabbed through him as he cast about for his attacker. The genestealer had been knocked aside, but it was far from dead, already scrambling upright and coming at him again with a ferocious shriek. Storn swung his crozius, but the effort was sluggish as blood spilled from deep gashes in his forearm. He struck the alien a glancing blow, still enough to shatter its jaw thanks to the molecular disruption field of his crozius, but the thing slammed into him all the same and Storn cursed as a knife-like blade of bone sank through his armour and into his gut.

'Hold it up!' yelled a voice from above him. 'Hold it up and I'll finish it!'

Storn snarled as he smashed grasping claws aside, felt the blade ripped from his innards to plunge instead into his side. He could feel strength flowing out of him as his blood ran freely, but his spirit was utterly indomitable. Thyssus Storn would not die here, ripped apart by xenos vermin! He clamped his free hand around the alien's throat and, with a roar, hefted it into the air. It raked clawed feet at his face-plate and crazed one eye lens, but Storn was unrelenting. He heaved his attacker high. The shotgun boomed again, and xenos gore showered down on the Chaplain for a second time.

Wearily, he dropped the corpse to the floor and looked about him for the next attacker. There were none; the gene-stealers were all dead, as were the Intercessors he had led into the chamber. Above him, First Arbitrator Verol looked down upon him, ashen-faced, her shotgun still raised against imaginary foes.

'My thanks, first arbitrator,' he said, swaying slightly with pain and blood loss. Already he could feel his wounds clotting, his Space Marine physiology fighting to keep him combat-ready despite the deep wounds he had taken. He would need an Apothecary sooner rather than later, he thought, but for now he could still fight well enough.

'You are most welcome, Brother-Chaplain,' she replied, her voice shaking slightly with adrenaline and shock. 'Are there any more of those… things?'

'I do not believe so,' he replied. 'I am needed elsewhere, first arbitrator. Can you manage the evacuation of this chamber?'

The few who still live, he thought grimly.

'I can,' she said. 'I've Enforcers en route in armoured transport. We'll pull back to the precinct seven-seven-four fortress.'

'Do so,' said Storn, frowning as another priority hail rune flashed in his peripheral vision. He blink-clicked it, and a sudden wash of gunfire and screams assaulted his ear.

'*...anyone. Brothers, does anyone hear me?*'

Storn instantly recognised the voice. It was Sergeant Furian. Still recuperating from his sore wounding at Delvemine, Furian and his battle-brother Ullas had been assigned to stand watch over Hive Spire's environmental control shrine.

'Brother-sergeant, this is Storn. What is your situation?' The hard bang of a bolt rifle echoed through the vox-link, followed by the howl of powerful lasers and a whoosh of flame.

'*The heretics are here, Brother-Chaplain. They came out of the damned walls and hit us hard. Cannot hold them. Storn, they have a weapon, some sort of bio-contaminant. They–*'

The link cut out suddenly, leaving Chaplain Storn with an icy feeling worming its way up through his guts. A bio-contaminant, a weapon... The thought of Mastracha Hive leapt suddenly into his mind, every living thing annihilated by the biopurge weapon in a matter of minutes.

'Verol, forget evacuation. Reroute those transports to the conclave building's main entrance and inform the Enforcers I will be arriving to take personal command of them directly,' he barked, staunchly ignoring the blood trail he left behind as he made for the head of the helical ramp.

'What about the evacuation?' she asked. Higher up in the chamber, he heard Lady Tectos raising her voice, calling down for aid.

'There is no time. The heretics have wrong-footed us *again*,' he spat. 'If we do not reach the environmental control shrine in the next few minutes, Angelicus will go the way of Mastracha Hive.'

Behind him, he heard Verol curse roundly, and then there was a rattle and a clatter. He looked over his shoulder to see the first arbitrator lowering herself over the drop from her platform, using one of her slain comrades' gun straps as an improvised rope. Verol hissed in pain as her wounded arm was forced to bear her weight, then dropped and hit the mezzanine in a roll. She came to her feet awkwardly and jogged through the carnage, racking her shotgun slide one-handed.

'If that happens, we all die and I've failed the city and the Emperor both,' said the first arbitrator.

'If that happens, we both have,' replied Storn as the two of them hurried down the ramp to the lower chamber. The stench of blood and the wails of trapped dignitaries chased them from the room.

The moment Hastur heard the snarl of engines rise amidst the coolant towers, he knew the element of surprise had been lost. It was not so surprising, he supposed, considering he and his forces had had to approach across open ground, but was it so much to ask that the enemy had been careless and not left a rearguard?

Apparently so, he thought with a grimace as light prospector bikes sped from the darkness between the towers, cultists whooping and firing pistols from their saddles.

'Into them, for the Emperor!' roared Hastur, and broke into a charge. He felt stitches tear in his flesh as he forced his body to move faster, but what was one more note of pain amidst such a cacophony?

A cultist came at him, a crude pipe held in one hand, the other wrapped around his bike's throttle. Domed forehead, blast goggles glinting in the sunlight, wyrmform-inscribed bandana wrapped around his mouth and nose; Hastur would have dismissed the man as ganger scum if it hadn't been for the lengths he had seen these cultists go to in the name of their twisted gods. Pivoting on the ball of one foot, Hastur whipped his blade around, his timing split-second perfect. The sword slashed through the man's pipe, his shoulder and up through his neck. The bike sped on, its headless rider still gripping the throttle and jetting blood until the bike toppled then crashed and rolled to a stop.

Bolt shells and las-bolts flashed past Hastur, raking more of the bikers from their steeds. The cult outriders returned fire, knocking several of the Ghyrish off their feet. At the rear of the desperate charge came a heavier quad bike, a bulky mining laser bolted to its side. The rider whooped as she fired the weapon, her shot punching through one of Hastur's battle-brothers and dropping him to his knees with a glowing crater bored through his chest.

'For primarch and Emperor!' shouted Hastur, firing his plasma pistol and engulfing the quad bike in a searing blast of superheated energy. The cultist and her mechanical steed turned to ash in a heartbeat, and Hastur limped on through the glowing fragments.

'Easy enough,' commented Idoras as they pushed up to the dark mouths of the alleyways. The bulky coolant towers rose like metal trees, tangled with intertwining pipework and clustered together, leaving spaces bare feet across between them.

'They sought to slow us, not beat us,' replied Hastur, before turning to address his motley assemblage of Imperial Fists and Ghyrish soldiery. 'Divide up and push for the heart of the complex. You all know where the control shrine is located, yes?' When no one averred, he pressed on. 'We do not have long. It may already be too late. If they succeed here the blast will claim us all anyway, so flight is senseless. Do you understand?' He looked directly at Corporal Jansys as he said this, and she answered with a determined nod.

'Forward, then, for the Emperor. Failure is not an option.'

Hastur plunged into the darkness, Idoras and Lastoran close behind him. He kept a map visible in his peripheral vision, his autosenses marking the control shrine with a crimson rune. It was maybe five hundred yards ahead, amidst the winding maze of towers and pipes, and his limping stride ate up the distance.

Hastur turned at an intersection and received a rattling volley of autogun shots from point-blank range. The bullets ricocheted from his armour and faceplate, and the cultist who had fired them charged with a scream of hatred. He aimed a home-made bayonet at Hastur's chest, but the Champion backhanded the man from his feet before the blade could connect. His blow bounced the cultist against the flank of a tower and broke his neck, but already another assailant was coming at him, this one a bigger mutant wielding some sort of energised saw. Behind him, Hastur heard Brother Lastoran curse, and an instant later there was a furious explosion. Smoke and shrapnel billowed around Hastur, and he felt fresh pain in his hip as something jagged punched through armour and flesh to lodge in the bone there. Gunfire roared close and deafening between the towers.

With no time to turn and look, Hastur swept his blade up and smashed the energy saw aside. It carved deep into a thick pipe, and a jet of steam howled out to engulf the attacking cultist. He choked and reeled back, giving Hastur a moment in which to shoot a glance over his shoulder. Lastoran was down, torn open by the point-blank blast of a mining charge. Idoras stood over his body, bolt rifle hammering, his scarred face bleeding again. Shadowy figures dropped amidst the smoke as the Intercessor's shots found them.

Hastur spun back in time to see the scalded cultist coming at him again. The energy saw came in, and Hastur whipped his blade up to parry. Searing las-power met blessed adamantine forged upon the *Phalanx* itself, and sparks exploded. Hastur went to turn his foe's blade and cut low, but a tearing flash of pain in his chest caused him to falter. The cultist's xenos-cursed features twisted in a leer of triumph, and he swung his las-saw high for another chopping blow.

'Throne-damned amateur,' spat Hastur, twisting his blade in his grip and ramming it point-first into his enemy's throat. 'How have scum like you given us so much trouble?' He ripped the blade free in a spray of xenos gore, and his enemy staggered away, gurgling, to collapse in a heap.

'Lastoran's gone, Brother-Champion,' said Idoras, his former affable insouciance replaced with anger.

'Keep moving, brother,' replied Hastur. 'If they blow this place into the Emperor's arms, then his sacrifice will be for nothing.'

He rounded the intersection and pressed on, following his map. Ahead he saw a handful of Ghyrish charge into a cloud of roiling steam, screamed battle cries on their lips and lasguns flashing. There came a roar of heavy firepower and the Astra Militarum troopers were cut to bloody chunks. One soldier staggered back out of the steam cloud, blood pouring down her face. She had time to cast a despairing look at Hastur before a shot clipped her head and threw her onto her face.

'For the Emperor!' Hastur bellowed, breaking into a charge that made his hearts hammer and his joints scream in pain. From ahead, through the steam, he heard a muffled curse and the clatter and rattle that told a tale of frantic attempts to reload.

Hastur burst from the haze to see a makeshift barricade ahead, formed from hastily sawn-off lengths of pipe. A military-grade autocannon was mounted on a tripod behind it, two turncoat Ghyrish soldiers just slotting a fresh magazine into the smoking weapon. They looked up in panic at his pounding footsteps, and Hastur hit the barricade without slowing, one shoulder lowered. The impact jarred through him and something broke inside his chest, but the heretics fared far worse. Their cannon crashed over and was buried in heavy lengths of metal. One of the traitors was hit in the face by a flying pipe and went down without a sound, while the other let out a shrill scream as a heavy section of pipe landed on his legs and crushed them into the ground.

Hastur stepped through the wreckage and laid his blade at the point of the man's throat. According to his autosenses, the shrine was dead ahead, just around the next corner.

'What lies in wait?' he asked. 'Speak and I'll make it swift.'

Despite his obvious agony, the cultist just stared up at Hastur with hate-filled eyes.

'Slow it is, then,' said Hastur, treading very deliberately on one of the man's arms and grinding the bones beneath his armoured boot as he stepped over him. The cultist gave a scream through gritted teeth, and the Champion moved on. Mindful of the fight at the intersection, he leaned carefully around the corner to see the shrine dead ahead. It was a blocky, single-storey ferrocrete cube with a Mechanicus cog embossed on its flank and a metal door that hung open, torn half off its hinges. Figures moved within, and Hastur's superior autosenses detected pulsing power signatures.

Idoras gave a sudden grunt of pain, and Hastur spun to see the big Intercessor stagger. There was a ragged hole in his chest, the exit wound of a fragmentation round. Idoras blinked at Hastur in surprise, tried to turn, and another shot went in through his jaw and blew out the back of his skull. Hastur cursed as a spry figure prowled through the veil of steam, ragged cloak billowing around him, pistols smoking.

'Shenn,' he snarled, the rumble of his vox turning the name into a curse. The three-armed gunman tipped him a mocking nod then raised all three guns and let fly, stepping back into the steam as he did.

Hastur spun his blade, smashing bullets out of the air as he stormed forward. One shot clipped his thigh. Another punched solidly through his shoulder and erupted out of his back, staggering him and causing him to cough blood into his faceplate.

Hastur was amidst the steam, and if his enemy had hoped it would conceal him, he was to be sorely disappointed. The Champion's autosenses showed him precisely where Shenn was and allowed him to aim a vicious cut at the gunman even as more bullets pinged and whined from his armour. Shenn read the blow's trajectory and dove forward, rolling under the attack and past Hastur before coming back up in a whirl of cloak and pistol barrels.

Another shot cratered Hastur's chest-plate, and the Champion cursed as he realised Shenn was just keeping him busy, occupied as far from the shrine as possible. It was working though, he thought; duelling the three-armed gunman was like fighting a whirlwind, bullets whipping towards him in a constant stream as the cult's hero dove, rolled and ducked around Hastur's blade amidst the roiling steam. Hastur managed to rip the tip of his blade through Shenn's ribs and drew a spray of ichor, but in return a volley of shots rang his helm like a bell and tore a bloody furrow along the side of his neck.

Finesse was not going to win this battle, Hastur realised. Fresh, unwounded, he could have revelled in the strange duel before slaying his enemy gloriously in the Emperor's name. But wounded, possibly dying and very certainly running out of time, matters were sorely different.

Leaving his guard open for a few desperate seconds, Hastur whipped his blade through the pipes that stretched overhead and fresh blasts of steam filled the narrow alley. Bullets rattled from his armour and external temperature warnings chimed in his helm, but then Shenn was reeling, dragging his cloak over his face and darting back towards the shrine as the steam scalded his bare flesh. Hastur raised his plasma pistol, beseeching it to fire with the greatest possible bellicosity before pulling the trigger. A furious plasma blast ripped from its barrel, the weapon's housing heating so fast that it burned his palm right through his gauntlet.

Hastur dropped the weapon with a curse but saw in that instant that it had done its duty. The plasma blast had ripped past Shenn and hit the flank of a coolant tower. The explosion hurled molten metal and liquid coolant in all directions and, already blinded by steam, the three-armed gunman staggered back with a cry of shock as he was scalded and burned. Hastur struck, one-handed, inelegant but lethally effective. His blade plunged into Shenn's back and exploded through the gunman's chest, drenched in purple gore. Hastur ripped the weapon free, and his enemy dropped to hands and knees before slumping to the ground in a spreading pool of ichor.

Ears ringing, lips wet with his own blood, body one huge scream of pain, Elrich Hastur limped along the final alleyway and plunged into the shrine. Inside, he had a fleeting impression of shadowy figures hunched over a complex array of detonators. Then his blade flashed and xenocultists fell dead, their gore drenching the bomb they had been building. One acolyte spun and raised a pistol, but Hastur swatted it away almost contemptuously before striking the creature's head from its neck. The last cultist crumpled, neck stump jetting vital fluids, and Hastur followed it down to the floor. He clanged to his knees beside the cultists' bomb, then toppled onto his side, his blade spilling from his hand.

'Dorn forgive my errors, let this be penance enough,' he muttered again and again, feeling his lifeblood running out onto the stone floor, seeing in his mind's eye the VanSappen warehouse collapsing, his brothers torn apart by the blast, until at last darkness took him.

Primus Lhor stood over the fallen bodies of the oppressors and watched as his brothers and sisters prepared the bio-purge bomb for activation. They didn't know the proper sanctification rituals, but that hardly mattered when those were offered only to a false deity of cogs and gears. Father had explained to Lhor and his brood how the bomb's spirits could be awoken without all the technical mumbo jumbo that the Adeptus Mechanicus insisted was so holy.

Just another mechanism for keeping the people down, he thought bitterly. How sad that it took selfless acts like this to throw off the shackles of the masses. Still, he was honoured to be Father's instrument, and he would see them all again when the Ascension was complete.

The shrine was cavernous, containing dozens of substations

and ritual chambers. Sister Mechlen had laboured there as a decontamination serf, however, and she knew the route to the primary ventilation shrine. She had died at the hands of the enemy, as had all but a last handful of the Blessed, but their sacrifices had seen the hated oppressors cut down, the Ghyrish guards slain and the way to the shrine laid open.

A few Ghyrish hung on, driven back to the outer service corridor, trying their best to storm back in and stop him. Lhor knew they would fail. They would not get past the last of the Blessed, not in this divine hour. And besides, they would be too late even if they did. A broodbrother turned to him and gestured at the heavy metal case they had wired into the primary ventilation hub. He could hear air whooshing through the massive pipes, turbines turning within as they drew it down fresh from the towers of Hive Spire and funnelled it into the rest of the hive districts with incredible force and speed. It was a system of inequality, just like everything else on Ghyre, he thought with disgust. The upper districts received fresh, comparatively clean air. By the time it reached the Laboritas it was polluted, third-hand, barely oxygenated enough to sustain life and all too quick to trigger myriad respiratory diseases in young, old and infirm alike. And yet they had not risen to the cult's call, these willing dupes of Angelicus. They had faltered in fear, forsaken Father's message, thrown in their terrified, short-sighted lot with the oppressors.

Well, now all the ventilation fans were dialled up to their highest setting, and all it would take was a press of the lurid green rune in the centre of the purge-bomb's panel to send the contaminant funnelling out through every duct and airway of the city. Hive Spire, Commercias, Militarum, Laboritas… Every district would be flooded with biopurge gases within minutes. Every last living thing in the hive would die, from the lowliest sump scum to the high-and-mighty governor herself, and all would become one in the beautiful light of Ascension. He was setting them free, even those who had done nothing to deserve such a boon, and with the same blow he would reduce the last loyalist stronghold on the planet to a hollow tomb. With no armoured city to retreat within, whatever forces the enemy had left in the field would surely be hunted down and torn apart piece by piece by the masses who rose in the wake of the oppressor governor's fall. That was Father's will, thought Lhor, and he would see it done.

The door to the upper gallery blew in with a muffled bang, and a vox-amplified roar of fury rang through the shrine. Lhor's head snapped up as Enforcers stormed through the door behind the hulking figure of a skull-helmed Imperial Fist in black-and-yellow armour.

'Too late,' he breathed, and slammed his fist against the rune.

Storn saw the figures clustered around the shrine one level down, saw their three-armed leader raise one hand and depress the rune of awakening on the bomb's casing. A high-pitched whine filled the air as micro-atomisers went to work within the deadly device and a lurid green sludge began to funnel through the pipes that connected it to the hive's primary ventilator. Almost at once, thin green gases billowed from the ducts throughout the shrine, and the Enforcers staggered and choked as they were engulfed.

'In the Emperor's name, no!' roared Storn. He swept his crozius through the handrail of the walkway to clear his path, took two steps back and then leapt from the walkway with a bellow of fury. Already he could see warning runes flashing crimson in his peripheral vision as the gases ate away at the seals of his armour and filtered through rents where he had been wounded. Even as his boots hit the metal deck plates of the ventilator shrine, he heard the Enforcers behind him screaming and gurgling in terror as they died.

Throne, he thought in dismay, *it works so damned fast.* He heard Verol give a wail of pure horror, and couldn't help but shoot a glance back to see her slumped against the railing, her skin bubbling and sloughing from her bones. He felt sorrow and anger that he had led them to their deaths. Red tinged the edges of his vision, and he realised the same thing was moments away from happening to him. There was no way to live through this, Storn realised, but perhaps he could still do his duty.

Turning back, he saw that the handful of cultists around the primary shrine were doing no better than the luckless Enforcers. They staggered and collapsed, gurgling prayers to their heretical deities as their eyeballs ran to jelly in their sockets and foaming vomit spilled over their disintegrating lips.

Storn barrelled towards the shrine, feeling his gorge rise and his flesh sear as the gas ate away at him. If he could strike the bomb with his crozius, perhaps he could destroy it. He had no idea what sort of spread the contaminant would achieve if it was all released here, in its raw form, but it couldn't be as bad as the ventilation system carrying it as a gas to every living being in Hive Angelicus. Could it?

He swung back his crozius, feeling bone growing brittle and muscle separating, threatening to spill the weapon from his hand. Then something reared up before him, a ghastly apparition of bubbling flesh and stark white bone that wore a tattering greatcoat and clutched at him with three crumbling arms.

Storn reeled, his body on fire with agony, revolted at the feeling of dissolution racing through his flesh. Through a sheet of crimson, he saw the rotting thing clutch feebly at him. Surely it should already have been dead, yet with its last strength it was wrestling against him, holding him back from the bomb. Then he locked gazes with its one remaining eye, saw the fathomless hatred and cold predatory intellect there as he had seen it in the eyes of the genestealers, and he understood. Whatever this being had been, now it was but a meat puppet for Father, one last weapon to fling at him that the cult's plan might succeed.

The thought sent a last surge of anger and hatred rushing through Storn. Even as his flesh bubbled and ran like hot mud, even as his bones splintered and his eyes burst and the gruesome flesh puppet raked at him with its talons, he let that fury lend him the strength for one last swing of his crozius. The weapon's crackling head slammed into the bio-purge bomb, blowing it apart in a spray of acrid green fluids, and Chaplain Storn knew nothing more.

XIII

Shattered glass fell like bladed rain as the stained-glass ceiling of the Fane of the Emperor Risen burst apart from explosive overpressure. Shards smashed against Lydorran's armour as he strode through a hail of autogun fire, geokinetic energies crackling around him in an ionised hurricane. Raging firestorms blazed through the crypts and mourners' pews to his right and left. Sparks and rolling smoke filled the air, cut with whorls and streaks where bullets and bolts ripped back and forth. Echoing gunfire filled the world with thunder that made the Librarian's organs feel as though they were shuddering in his body.

Lydorran's boots crunched upon bones and glass as he advanced into the heart of the Crypt Sacrosanctal, directly into the teeth of the cult's last defensive position. Imperial Fists followed him in. They threaded between the crypt's thick stone columns as they directed perfectly drilled hails of fire into their desperate foes. The cultists' mutant features could be glimpsed through the smoke, bobbing up from behind a sturdy barricade of pews, statuary and smashed stonework they had thrown up across the southern entrance to the Mausoleum Eternal. The first ever governor of Ghyre, Matthias Doversal, lay in state somewhere beyond that barricade, preserved for posterity within a shimmering stasis field. At least, he had done before the fall of Hive Klaratos. Lydorran doubted they would find the patriarch of the Ghyrish nobility left unmolested by the insurgents. But then, Doversal wasn't the father Lydorran had come to find.

'Squad Kasmus, suppress them,' he voxed, and a pip of confirmation flashed back to him. Fifty yards to the rear, the Devastators of Squad Kasmus raised their weapons and sent a quartet of missiles roaring down from the crypt's steps to smash into the cultists' barricade. Four fragmentation warheads burst in perfect concert, fired by warriors well used to clearing the firesteps of enemy fortifications. Shrapnel filled the air, and wherever it bit home into mutant flesh, sprays of blood and torn meat erupted.

Lydorran drew deep upon the wellspring of the warp, feeling his psychocircuitry heat as the pressure of that power grew until he felt as though he were holding back a thundering avalanche with his mind. He roared and slammed the base of his force staff into the flagstones of the crypt, channelling and releasing the apocalyptic mass of energy in an almighty pulse. A geokinetic shockwave tore through the floor, flagstones blasting skyward as the energies raced through them. The shockwave hit the cult barricade and blew it apart as though a giant had ripped its fists up through its middle. Shattered stone and broken bodies flew upwards and met the still-falling blizzard of glass. The entire structure shuddered. Cracks spidered through walls and floor. The enemy's gunfire cut off as though a tap had been turned, and as chunks of stone, wood and metal crashed down throughout the crypt, Lydorran's warriors faltered, given pause by the sheer destructive fury their leader had unleashed.

'Fist, what in the Allfather's name was that?' came Redfang's voice over the vox. 'Thought the place was about to come down on our heads! You know you don't shell a place when you got your own men in it, yes?'

'No shelling, psychic siegecraft only,' replied Lydorran, flashing hand signals at his warriors and sending them prowling forward through the billowing dust and smoke. Redfang was silent for a beat before he replied, and Lydorran heard a note of wary respect in the Fenrisian's voice when he did.

'That was you?'

'It has been a long and frustrating war,' replied Lydorran. 'I am hastening its end.' Redfang grunted in response then cut the link. The Librarian frowned behind his faceplate. He had expected Redfang to return some arrogant rejoinder about being the one to have brought matters to a swift end, and the fact that the Space Wolf had not done so deepened Lydorran's feeling of concern. Was Father here? They had met resistance, certainly, the cult unleashing mutant monsters, triggering hidden munitions and throwing themselves into suicidal charges as the Imperial Fists pushed in through the lower crypts and the Deathwatch advanced through the shrine's high galleries to meet them at the structure's heart. Yet their numbers and munitions had proven little challenge for the might of the Adeptus Astartes, who had had to fight far harder for Delvemine than for Klaratos Hive. Even High Marshal Kallistus' regiments were making swift and certain progress, and their casualties had been moderate at most. It was hardly the furious and final defence of an insect queen in its hive, he thought. Had the Imperial Fists really been so overcautious, the enemy truly so weak once their smoke and mirrors were torn away?

Lydorran hoped that was the case, but his and Ancient Tarsun's conversation kept replaying in his mind.

Perhaps they have massed their elite fighters around the nest itself?

Or perhaps Redfang is wrong, and the broodnest is not here at all.

If that was the case then the Imperial forces had still crushed an enemy fortress, he told himself. It would still be a show of Imperial strength fit to cow the less committed of the cult's followers, and it left one less enemy stronghold for the Wrything Wyrm to operate out of. Yet still Lydorran's unease grew; if their false deity was *not* lurking in the chambers ahead, then where was it, and what heresy might it be working while their overwhelming strength was directed here?

Lydorran realised that he had fallen to the rear of the Imperial Fists' advance, standing in brooding contemplation amidst the drifting dust and smoke as his warriors filtered past. Up ahead, the sounds of gunfire echoed afresh from within the Crypt Sacrosanctal. He could hear Tarsun's voice echoing as he bellowed oaths of loyalty and courage, and more distantly a feral howling that could only be Watch Captain Redfang directing his own warriors into the fray.

'Fight now, questions later,' Lydorran told himself, and strode through the wreckage of the enemy barricade into the heart of the Fane of the Emperor Risen.

They found the remains of First Governor Doversal strung up from a crude industrial wyrmform at the heart of his mausoleum. Taken back into time's corrosive embrace, the body had rotted and now hung as the abused and spoiled centrepiece of a sprawling xenocult shrine. It was here that the enemy staged their last-ditch defence, and here they died. By the time Lydorran joined the fight, his warriors had hit the cultists from one side while Redfang and his black-armoured Deathwatch struck furiously from the other. Bolters boomed, the Deathwatch weapons loosing specially selected shells whose reserves of bio-acids sprayed the tight-packed cultists as they burst amongst them. Flamer blasts turned clusters of cultists into reeling torches. Lydorran saw figures in magisterial robes brandishing industrially fabricated wyrm icons, screaming exhortations at their deformed followers who in turn howled their heartfelt hatred as they took shots at the encircling Space Marines. Lydorran saw a tall, three-armed woman in elaborate robes charge at Redfang wielding a pair of energised picks and an autopistol. The watch captain swayed easily around one swinging pick, caught the other on the churning teeth of his chainsword then pistoned his free hand forward and crushed the cult leader's skull. Her body cartwheeled backwards from the force of the blow and ploughed into the heaped devotional offerings around the base of the wyrmform icon. Her fall was met by wails of dismay and fury from the last few cultists, but by now their anger was all but impotent. They were surrounded, denuded of cover, plan or hope, trapped within a closing ring of power-armoured warriors who quickly stamped out the last remnants of resistance.

'Keep some alive,' ordered Lydorran, and within moments several of the remaining cultists had been roughly disarmed and restrained by Imperial Fists. The captives struggled and cursed but stood little hope of escaping the Space Marines' ironclad grip.

Lydorran tore off his helmet and mag-locked it to his belt, then approached the nearest captive, who was being held in place by Intercessor Sergeant Ulatus. Lydorran loomed over the cultist, noting his yellow eyes and black-slit pupils, the mauve cast to his flesh and the bony ridges that marched up from his nose across his bulbous scalp. The man's face was daubed with smudged kohl and gold paint that Lydorran presumed marked him out as some form of senior figure. He glared up at Lydorran, shaking not with fear, the Librarian realised, but with anger and hatred.

'Murdering bastards!' spat the cultist, his voice hoarse with emotion and smoke inhalation. 'Look at what you've done! These people wanted freedom from your oppression! They wanted Ascension, that was all! And you have the nerve to call *us* monsters!' His fanged maw mangled the words, but they were recognisable enough. Lydorran felt little inclination towards subtlety; he reached out a hand, and with a gesture and a pulse of psychokinetic force he snapped the neck of another of the captives. The man's yellow eyes bulged, and he drew in a ragged breath to begin ranting again.

'Your lives are worthless to me,' said Lydorran before he could. 'I will kill your comrades just to get your attention. Do you understand?'

The cultist stared up at him, eyes burning.

'Don't tell him anything, Isaac,' urged another of the cultists, fighting against the Intercessor who held her by both arms in an inescapable grip. 'Let them kill us. You know where we're going, what awaits.'

Lydorran shot a meaningful glance towards Redfang, who was pacing from one fallen cultist to the next, using his armoured boot to crush the life from any who still twitched.

'I shall make your death quick,' the Librarian said. 'He will not. So tell me, where is Father?'

The cultist leader blinked in evident surprise. Then he began to laugh, a snarling and mangled sound.

'Look into my eyes, oppressor,' he said with a leer. 'Father is there. Father is everywhere. Father is in all of us, and he is everywhere. His whispers herald the coming of the Star Children just as–'

Lydorran grabbed the man's jaw and squeezed, cutting off his laughter amidst the crunch and grind of stressed bone.

'Spare me your heresy, scum,' he growled. 'Where is Father?'

'I… don't… know,' slurred the cultist, his eyes still bright with triumph. 'Father… awaits Ascension… in his holy sepulchre. It… isn't… here.'

Lydorran didn't need empathic powers to hear the simple truth in the man's words. The cultist's glee was too evident to ignore. The Librarian took a slow breath then nodded once. There came the crunch of bone as several necks were snapped as one, and the remains of the cultist captives slumped to the bloodied floor.

The Librarian closed his eyes, marshalling his emotions before looking up at Watch Captain Redfang. The Fenrisian was exchanging quiet words with Apothecary Sor'khal, the tall Blood Angel that had manhandled Bishop Renwyck so casually, and several other warriors from a spread of Chapters. None of Dorn's gene-sons were amongst them, Lydorran noted, and wondered if that was deliberate.

There is no clash of loyalties there, he thought.

'Watch Captain Redfang, Father is not here, and it seems he never was,' said Lydorran, the haft of his stave rapping against the stone floor as he approached the Deathwatch. He was conscious of Ancient Tarsun and a number of yellow-armoured battle-brothers massing at his back.

Redfang ignored Lydorran, though the warriors he was

speaking to glanced towards the Librarian. Lydorran saw something in Apothecary Sor'khal's eyes, perhaps warning. The White Scar gave the slightest shake of his head, but it only served to harden Lydorran's resolve.

'Watch Captain Redfang, perhaps the gunfire has rendered you temporarily deaf?' said Lydorran, placing a hand on Redfang's shoulder guard to turn him. The Space Wolf growled and shook Lydorran's hand off, turning with his lips skinned back from his canines.

'Please, keep wasting my time stating the obvious, Fist,' he growled, and his eyes flashed with anger.

'You told us you were sure,' said Lydorran. 'You brutalised and intimidated the governor's conclave, interrupted our operations in Hive Angelicus, spent lives and materiel on this fruitless assault, and for what?'

'I don't answer to the Imperial Fists,' spat Redfang, turning fully so that his chest-plate met Lydorran's with a clang. The Librarian stood firm, jaw set, refusing to be cowed by the waves of feral aggression that radiated from the Fenrisian.

'You answer to the Imperium, to Segmentum command,' he replied with implacable calm. 'This assault was wasteful, and it makes me wonder how much of your apparent certainty is nought but guesswork. Is Father real, or simply some heretical construct? Is there really such pressing need for haste, I wonder? Or did you simply say what you needed to in order to force our compliance with your reckless way of war?'

'You step too far, Brother-Librarian,' said Sor'khal with a scowl. 'The Deathwatch know much about many xenos threats. We bear the burden of greater knowledge than any sane servant of the Emperor would wish to possess, and we understand the danger better than any. Father is not here, but he *is* out there, and every day he lives brings the tyranids closer.'

'So why don't you go hide behind your fortress walls and leave the hunt to those with some instincts?' snapped Redfang.

'We would better serve the Imperium if we fought together rather than separately,' said Lydorran, the watch captain's scorn triggering nothing more in him than a weary disappointment.

'*We* would better serve the Imperium without your second-guessing, or the clans of this world dragging at our heels,' Redfang replied, then turned away. 'We'll tell you if we need a wall knocking down.'

With that, Lothar Redfang stalked out of the crypt with his battle-brothers close on his heels. Lydorran looked around the bolt-riddled chamber, took in the dangling ruin of the first governor, the blasted stonework and ruined frescoes that had once made this a place of pilgrimage from all over Ghyre and beyond. He had a momentary premonition of the entire planet reduced to such a corpse-choked tangle of ruins and shook his head. Was this what victory looked like to the Deathwatch? The xenos threat slaughtered to the last but the rest of Ghyre dragged into the flames along with them?

'Come, brothers,' he said, realising that his warriors were watching him with stoic patience, awaiting his order. 'We regroup at Hive Angelicus. I have need of Chaplain Storn's counsel before we make our next move.'

Lydorran led his warriors out of the ruins of the Fane of the Emperor Risen and upwards through the gutted hive. They passed blazing heaps of corpses, sundered cultist barricades and triumphant bands of Ghyrish soldiery laying siege to the last enemy enclaves. The Imperial Fists made for whatever remained of the hive's Orbitas district, intending to call in their gunships and lift off from one of its suborbital landing pads.

Three levels below Orbitas, external vox signals finally found them through the soup of energy discharge, atmospheric interference and swirling electrogheists thrown up by the battle. Lydorran received Shipmaster Gavorn's hail first with surprise, and then, as he listened, with dawning horror.

And then, at last, with anger.

The Orbitas had come through the battle for Klaratos remarkably unscathed; major landing and refuelling sites were so valuable upon Ghyre's jungle-choked continent that both the cult and the Ghyrish alike had sought to preserve its facilities for their own use, and so the Orbitas had remained, jutting from the hive's flank like some vast metallic plateau. Swarms of Imperial aircraft came and went from it, thousands of Ghyrish soldiery and dropped-in ground crews bustling here and there as platforms and facilities were checked for concealed booby traps, aircraft were refuelled and re-armed, cult prisoners were executed by firing squad and regimental preachers blessed those Ghyrish who had made it through the fighting as well as the neatly lined-up bodies of those who had not.

'Redfang!' roared Lydorran as he stormed through the midst of the hubbub. Ghyrish soldiers flinched at his furious shout, watching with wide eyes as he passed. Ahead, up on a ferrocrete landing platform, the watch captain and his comrades had been about to board one of their sleek Corvus dropships. The Fenrisian turned, and one look at his hard expression told Lydorran he had also heard the news from Angelicus. Sor'khal started forward, intending to intercept Lydorran and the Imperial Fists marching behind him, but Redfang raised a hand and waved his comrade back.

'I told you to leave us to our hunt, Fist,' said Redfang, and Lydorran felt fresh rage beating at his temples.

'You drew us away!' he shouted, jabbing a finger into Redfang's chest with a dull clang. Even as he did so a part of him knew that he had been complicit in that action, that he hadn't deigned to work *with* the Space Wolf and so had allowed this to happen. Yet he was too angry, all the unbending pride of his genetic heritage rushing to the fore as his choler took hold. 'You left the fortress all but undefended, and worse, you dishonoured us all by convincing us to do the same. Look at what it has cost us all!'

Lydorran knew that more and more Ghyrish were gathering, staring uneasily at this furious exchange between the Emperor's legendary angels. They couldn't know about the attack on Hive Angelicus yet, he thought, or they would not have looked so confused, so alarmed. Hearing it like this could be disastrous for the Ghyrish morale, yet he simply couldn't hold his fury and frustration in check any longer. His sorrow at the loss of yet more brothers and his shame at being outmanoeuvred by the insurgents yet again mingled with his frustration at Redfang's unwillingness to listen, to work *with* the Imperial Fists or take any note of their counsel. It all mixed together into a seething storm that he could no longer hold in.

'War costs lives,' said Redfang. 'We bleed, they bleed. There will be time for wailing and rending garments later, Fist.'

'You dare mock at this time?' spat Lydorran. 'Angelicus Hive Spire is gone, and half the upper districts are in quarantine lockdown. Hundreds of thousands are dead, and from what I hear it was very nearly millions. Eighteen loyal Imperial Fists are dead, nearly a quarter of a damned company along with one of the greatest warriors I've ever known, and the few of my battle-brothers who made it out aboard shuttles are walking wounded who may never fight again. The governor is missing, presumed dead. Her conclave, missing, presumed dead. The heads of the Ghyrish Ecclesiarchy, Administratum, Munitorum, Arbites, all missing, presumed dead. It's a Throne-cursed disaster, watch captain. And it is entirely of your making!'

Redfang bristled, his hand jerking towards the pommel of his chainsword before he stopped himself. Lydorran saw the motion and spat in disgust, ignoring the murmurs of shock and alarm that rippled out through the watching Ghyrish.

'Look at you. Half feral, ill disciplined, without even the self-control to take an accusation without reaching for your blade. I do not know how the Deathwatch select their officers, but if you are their exemplar then I am glad never to have served amongst their ranks!'

'You prate of what you know *nothing*,' snarled Redfang, placing one open palm on Lydorran's chest-plate and pushing him backwards a step as though to dismiss him. Lydorran slapped Redfang's hand away and squared up to the Fenrisian again with a flare of unthinking fury.

'I know that you have thrown away Imperial lives for *nothing*,' he said. 'And now you are too much of a coward even to give account for them! What will you do next, watch captain? Shipmaster Gavorn told me of your *order* that he ready his ship's weaponry for targeted planetary bombardment! When will it be too much, wolf?'

Redfang snarled, a low, guttural sound full of barely restrained aggression.

'What would a Primaris mind-witch know of this war or its stakes?' he growled, pushing Lydorran again, harder. 'While you were sleeping under the Martian sands, we were fighting for this galaxy, losing brothers and worlds and making bloody sacrifices we could ill afford. I've buried warriors finer than you or any of your plodding Dorn-sons will ever be, and still the Allfather demands more of us.'

'More? Will you burn the entire world to purge the xeno-cult? Slaughter all these loyal soldiers along with their planet in your mindless charge towards victory at any cost? Slaughter them as surely as you slaughtered Storn and the governor and all the rest of them?' asked Lydorran, and the anger in him suddenly guttered at the awful, haunted expression that flashed across Redfang's features, there and gone. It was replaced by cold, hard rage.

'I will kill every living thing on this world with fire from the skies if I must,' he said, and his eyes were chips of Fenrisian ice. 'To stop them before they reach the Segmentum Solar, the Throneworld… To extinguish their beacon, I would do it in a heartbeat. *That* is what the Deathwatch needs in its officers, Fist. *That* is why I will never, ever see the Fang rising proud over Fenris again.'

'My ship will not fire upon your orders, and my brothers will not permit such a cull,' said Lydorran, and his words rang like hammer on anvil. '*I* will not permit it. Transforming Ghyre into a lifeless wasteland would make us no better than the monsters you claim to hate.'

Lydorran saw the blow coming a split second too late; the Fenrisian moved with a liquid speed that belied his hulking frame, and his armoured fist crashed into Lydorran's nose hard enough to mash it across the Librarian's face in a spray of blood.

Gasps and cries of dismay rang out all around as Lydorran staggered back and was caught and held up by several of his battle-brothers. His pride burned at the insult of the blow, and the faces of his dead comrades flashed before his mind's eye as he surged back at Redfang, aiming a punch with his free hand that the Fenrisian half-dodged. It clipped Redfang's ear, and Lydorran's armoured knuckles tore away a chunk of flesh and gristle.

Redfang howled his fury and launched himself at Lydorran, grabbing the Librarian's shoulder guards in a vice-like grip. Redfang's forehead slammed into Lydorran's face, and this time the pain was such that Lydorran's vision greyed at the edges for a moment. He rocked back in the watch captain's grasp, and his force staff left his grip as his fingers momentarily loosened.

Lydorran tasted blood and realised that Redfang was rearing back for another savage headbutt. Before it could connect, he brought up an armoured knee and slammed it crosswise into Redfang's inner thigh, hard enough to dent the plate there. The Fenrisian jerked instinctively away, and as his grip loosened, Lydorran threw off Redfang's hands and hammered three swift body blows into the Space Wolf's chest. The punches rang like bells as armour struck armour and drove Redfang back far enough to give Lydorran a moment's breathing space.

'Enough!' snapped Lydorran, spitting a mouthful of blood and motioning back several of his brothers who had made to intercede.

'Not until you understand,' growled Redfang, shooting a warning glare at his own comrades and circling Lydorran. 'Not until you see how far I'm willing to go.'

With that, Redfang sprang again, but this time Lydorran was ready for him. He swung up a forearm and smacked the Fenrisian's punch aside before launching a jab of his own that connected with Redfang's chin. Bone cracked and Redfang's head snapped back. The Space Wolf gave ground but Lydorran didn't follow, hoping that he might have knocked some sense into Redfang. His own fury had boiled away the moment the argument came to blows, and he was now acutely aware of the Ghyrish watching aghast as their supposed champions brawled like animals before them.

His hopes were dashed as Redfang came in again, swinging an almighty haymaker with his right fist. Lydorran blocked again, only to realise too late that the broadly telegraphed attack had been a distraction. Redfang dropped, sweeping with one foot and savagely smashing Lydorran's feet out from under him. The Librarian yelled as he fell, hitting the ground with a crash of metal on ferrocrete. He rolled quickly aside, his eyes widening as he heard Redfang's boot stomp down where his chest had been, hitting hard enough to crack the ferrocrete.

Had his erstwhile ally lost his mind? Was this the wild beast of Fenris unleashed, the rumours and whispers about Russ' sons proved for all to see? Or worse, was this entirely calculated aggression? Was Redfang aiming to take Lydorran apart, maim him so badly that none would dare challenge his word again? Did the Fenrisian truly believe that was what he had to do in order to fulfil his duty?

Lydorran surged back to his feet and spun in time to knock aside several more swinging punches. He fought as his Chapter taught, solid as stone, unyielding, relentless, expending no more strength or energy than he had to while his foe tired himself upon his defences. Yet Redfang was big, Primaris big despite having never crossed the Rubicon, and he fought with a mixture of animal ferocity and predatory skill that soon saw Lydorran's armour dented in half a dozen places. How long could this continue, wondered the Librarian, seeing again the pale faces of shocked Ghyrish in a staring sea around the landing pad. How long did he dare *let* this continue? Until the onlookers lost all hope, and word spread of the division between the Space Marines who had let Governor Kallistus and all her conclave die? Until Redfang beat him senseless?

Redfang's fist caught him in the chest and staggered him, before a second blow hammered into his jaw. Lydorran heard something crack, spat out a shattered tooth, and before he knew what he was doing he felt himself reach for his powers. He could lend siege-hammer strength to his blows, he knew, could finish this fight with a single punch before the situation worsened any further.

Lydorran saw the trap before he stepped into it. If he beat Redfang that way he might win this fight, but in doing so he would shatter the Imperial alliance altogether. Who knew how much damage to the war effort today had done already, how much capital the surviving cultists would gain from the governor's death and the brutal massacre of Klaratos' defenders? How much worse would matters be if he underlined his fearsome 'otherness' to the Ghyrish by using his powers upon a fellow Imperial warrior? He would alienate the Imperial Fists from those they sought to protect, make them look every bit as cruel and monstrous as Redfang had made his own forces appear, and he would drive an irrevocable wedge between his brothers and those of the Deathwatch in the process.

This has to go the other way, thought Lydorran. *As far as it must.*

With that, he dropped his guard and said clearly, 'Enough, watch captain. I concede. But I will not be party to a bombardment. I will not permit a slaughter. We must find another way.'

Redfang's lips pulled back from his canines in a snarl.

'Damn your stubbornness,' he said. 'Why can't you *see*?'

He launched himself at Lydorran.

The Space Wolf delivered a thunderous blow to the Librarian's jaw and then faltered slightly in surprise as his victim did not even attempt to block the strike. Stars exploded across Lydorran's vision, and he slammed to the ground for a second time, only for Redfang's boot to smash into his midriff with battering ram force. Lydorran doubled up and felt blood spatter from his lips onto the ferrocrete. He felt himself hefted upwards, Redfang's armoured fingers curling around his gorget to drag him up off the ground, then again the armoured gauntlet slammed into his face, and the back of his head hit the ground with enough force to crack bone.

Lydorran's vision blurred then refocused. His thoughts came slowly and his movements were sluggish, but he rolled over and pushed himself up to his knees. He looked up at Redfang, who stood over him, shoulders rising and falling with his panting breath.

'I think… we *all*… see,' he said, spitting another mouthful of blood onto the ground. Redfang snarled, his eyes wild, and in that moment Lydorran was sure that if the watch captain had acted with controlled aggression before, his frustration, his desperation to find the enemy at any cost, his furious need to be obeyed had all conspired to sweep that control away. Obsession had taken Watch Captain Redfang, the need to prove he would pay any price in the name of victory, the need to justify the price he had already paid, and Lydorran was sure that Redfang was ready to kill him.

The Fenrisian drew back his fist again with a howl, and then suddenly found himself unable to move. His eyes bulged with shock and rage as he strained against the invisible bonds of geokinetic energy that now held him.

'I let you do this,' said Lydorran, driving himself to his

feet. The effort of keeping his powers focused with his head ringing like a prayer bell was tremendous, yet focus them he did. 'Do you understand that, Lothar Redfang? I *let* you do this so that all would see where this division will take us.'

Redfang struggled, and Lydorran felt the furious strength of the Fenrisian as he strained his psychic fetters almost to breaking point. The watch captain tried to spit some oath or insult, but Lydorran would not allow him even that. Not yet.

'I am going to release you now, do you understand? But if you raise your hand to me or any other Imperial servant again, then know that it will make you no better than the beasts we hunt, and all here will bear witness.'

With that, Lydorran released his psychic hold upon Redfang and dropped to one knee, breathing hard. The Space Wolf stared at him, eyes wild, shoulders rising and falling with panting breaths. He flexed his fingers like claws, but he made no move to attack.

Lydorran met his gaze, lip curled in disgust.

Suddenly, Sor'khal was there, grabbing Redfang's arm with both hands, dragging the watch captain around and staring hard into his eyes.

'Brother! Fenris! Stop this now. Have you lost your mind?'

Redfang looked for a heartbeat as though he would strike Sor'khal too, then seemed to recognise the Chogorian, and the strength went out of him. The watch captain's shoulders sagged, and he swept his gaze around the assembled onlookers as though seeing them for the first time.

'We won't win like this, Lothar,' said Sor'khal, lowering his voice so that only Redfang and Lydorran could hear his words. 'We can't. It will be Jaghorrah all over again. What use to the Imperium are a string of dead worlds? The Fist is right. How long until we *are* no better than the xenos?'

Redfang shook his head bitterly, looked at Lydorran's blood where it had stained the knuckles of his gauntlets. He took a slow, deep breath, his eyes closed, and when he opened them again it was as though a shadow had passed over his features and left them somehow clearer, lighter. To Lydorran's surprise, the Space Wolf actually flashed him a wry smile that contained entirely too many canines to be reassuring.

He reached down and grasped Lydorran's forearm in a warrior's grip, then pulled the Librarian to his feet. The Imperial Fists started forward, Tarsun reaching for his pistol, but Redfang held up a hand, palm open, and tilted his head back slightly as though baring his throat.

'Peace, Fists, peace. There has been enough violence done between us this day,' he said.

'*By* you, perhaps,' growled Tarsun, but Lydorran shook his head wearily.

'He's right, this division serves no one,' he said. 'We need to decide our next action, and do what we can to reverse the damage caused to the Ghyrish morale by this spectacle.'

'Well I hope you have a damned good idea, Fist, because if we...' Redfang trailed off, frowning as he saw commotion amongst the Ghyrish soldiery. Then came cheers, first one then more, rippling through the ranks.

'What?' asked Lydorran, wiping blood from his jaw and shaking his head. He looked to Tarsun, who had his head cocked, one hand to the side of his helm as though he were listening intently to his vox. Then the Ancient looked up, and his words reignited the spark of hope inside Lydorran's breast.

'The governor, she got out,' he said. 'She's on her way here by air, Brother-Librarian. And she says she knows where the

enemy's nest *really* is. She's sending rendezvous coordinates.
She believes she knows where we can find Father.'

XIV

'Back aboard the *Vengeful* yet again,' said Lydorran to Ancient Tarsun as their gunship swept low through the jungle mists. Wings of Imperial aircraft trailed in their wake, displaying the yellow of the Imperial Fists, the black of the Deathwatch and the burnt orange of the Ghyrish Airborne.

'We shall owe her a debt of gratitude by the time this war is done, to the machine-spirits of all our aircraft,' replied the Ancient.

'If we win this damned war, we'll owe a debt of gratitude to more than just our machines,' said Lydorran, thinking briefly of all the heroes his company had lost upon this accursed world.

'I'll be thankful just to return to conventional siegecraft, preferably against a foe that declares themselves openly and fights with some honour,' said Tarsun, shaking his head ruefully. He ran one gauntleted palm through his short-cropped stubble and down over his scarred face in a gesture of weariness.

'I don't envy the Deathwatch the nature of the battles they must fight,' said Lydorran by way of agreement.

'Small wonder Redfang is a little cracked,' grunted Tarsun.

'I don't think Watch Captain Redfang is going to be a problem again,' said Lydorran, working his jaw ruefully. His face gave off warm pulses of pain despite the attentions of the Deathwatch Apothecary, Sor'khal.

'He beat you half to death, Brother-Librarian,' said Tarsun reproachfully. 'If Hastur had seen that–'

'I allowed it, Tarsun,' replied Lydorran. 'He had to see for himself the line he was crossing, the line I wouldn't follow him over. I think the watch captain is an honourable and dedicated servant of the Imperium. He just needed to see that we cannot defend the Imperium if we become as monstrous as that which threatens it.'

'A lesson you decided to deliver at the expense of your face,' observed Tarsun dryly. 'Throne, Lydorran, I nearly shot the Fenrisian bastard.'

'I'm glad that you didn't, brother,' said Lydorran. 'Besides, a fresh scar or two can't hurt my reputation with the more traditional of our warriors.'

'Depends how they were earned.'

'They were earned well, teaching the wolf how resilient and unmoving the sons of Dorn can be,' put in Dreadnought Brother Ghesmund, who stood near their restraint thrones with his massive feet mag-locked to the deck. 'Any who dispute this are fools.'

Lydorran smiled slightly at that. Few would be brave enough to gainsay the heroic Ancient. He was about to reply when a priority hail chimed from his vox. He heard the telltale whine that told of powerful scrambler-spirits being summoned to defend the sanctity of the close-range channel.

'Governor, well met,' he said, linking to the proffered command channel.

'Brother-Librarian, we are glad to hear your voice,' replied Osmyndri Kallistus.

'Lady governor, please accept my apologies for the losses you have suffered this day.'

'If anyone has penance to do, it is me and mine,' came Red-fang's voice as he patched into the command channel. Lydorran blinked in surprise.

'Watch captain, Brother-Librarian, our enemy's attack was insidious, as honourless as they have ever been since this conflict began,' replied the governor, and Lydorran had the sense that she was reciting a speech that had been rehearsed more than once in the last few hours. 'Had your forces been present at Angelicus Hive, we doubt it would have stopped what happened, so much as greatly increased the butcher's bill of our enemy's victory. Watch Captain Redfang, if not for your offensive against Klara-tos Hive, many of our regiments, not to mention our own brother, would have been caught by the cult's suicidal attack. Instead he, and they, fly at our backs into battle even now, offered the chance to fight for the world they love. Brother-Librarian Lydorran, were it not for the heroic actions of your Chaplain Storn we might have died there ourselves, and the entire city been engulfed in the dis-aster that followed. We do not see cause for penance, but rather the hand of the Emperor at work in preserving the armed forces required to finish this war for good and all.'

There was silence over the command channel for several heart-beats as Lydorran and Redfang absorbed the governor's words.

'Your message suggested you know Father's whereabouts,' prompted Redfang.

'We couldn't risk the information to an open channel,' replied the governor. 'But yes, it seems clear to us now where the beast must lurk. The warhead that was deployed against Angelicus Hive Spire was a biopurge bomb.'

Lydorran frowned. He had heard the term weeks before, and now, with a swift dive into his eidetic memory, he had it.

'The munitions that triggered during fighting in Hive Mastracha,' he said.

'The same,' replied the governor.

'I understood that contagion had emptied Mastracha of all life, that its effects remained potent,' said Lydorran. 'Could they have entered the hive to recover the weapon? Protective suits, rebreathers – would that have been enough?'

'It would not,' replied the governor. 'Angelicus was fortunate in that the discharge of the weapon was channelled upwards by your Chaplain's efforts, rather than down into the body of our hive. The high altitude and swift winds of Hive Spire served to swiftly dissipate the weapon's fumes, and still we are given to understand that few survived above the Commercias, while Tectosmine is even now being evacuated lest the weapon's fumes fall upon them. That was one warhead. Mastracha Hive was slain from within by dozens.'

'Then the only way our enemies could have had such a weapon is if they had stolen it before the disaster,' said Lydorran.

'It is more than that, though, isn't it?' growled Redfang. 'Think, Fist. Have you even looked at Mastracha Hive since your arrival?'

'The Wrathful subjected it to scans, of course,' said Lydorran, frowning. 'We found no life signs within fifty miles of the hive, no movement, and all machine-spirit signatures were hopelessly unstable and corrupted. Mastracha is dead.'

'On the surface it is,' replied Redfang. 'Governor, you're suggesting Father is underneath the city's ruins, aren't you? It's the perfect place for a lair. Fangs of Russ, how did I miss that?'

'That is our belief, watch captain, yes,' replied the governor.

'Enough solid rock between the biopurge agent and our enemy's lair would shield them, we believe.'

Lydorran's frown deepened. Something still did not cogitate. He thought of how easily the contagion would spread down through even the most secure tunnels and bulkheads, certainly if the enemy were using the city's ruins as the hub of their war effort. He pulled up a schematic of Hive Mastracha and its surrounding region on his data-slate, expanded its radius slowly, his siegecrafter's eyes flickering over every detail of the region. Then he stopped, revelation hitting him like a thunderbolt.

'The mines,' he said. 'VanSappenmine is located sixty-two miles east of Mastracha amongst the Blistercrag range. If they extended their deep bores through the roots of the mountains and then westward, they could have excavated chambers deep beneath the piles driven in to anchor the hive's legs. But it would have been the labour of decades, and suicidally hazardous.'

'Does this uprising strike you as having been hastily prepared, Brother-Librarian?' asked the governor archly.

'I found no sign of parasitism or xenos mutation in Clanlord VanSappen,' said Redfang. *'The arbitrators' investigation after the blast in the VanSappen warehouse turned up no links whatsoever. Governor, are you sure of this?'*

'We have known... knew... Torphin Lo VanSappen since we were young, watch captain,' replied the governor wearily. *'We found him ever to be vainglorious, lazy and stupid. We can well believe that such rot could have spread beyond his self-centred notice.'*

'Governor, the situation upon Ghyre hangs by a thread,' said Lydorran after a long moment's thought. 'My warriors and Redfang's alike took losses in the assault upon Klaratos

Hive, as did your airborne regiments. The attack upon Hive Angelicus looks like a spectacular victory for the cult. Even if word of your survival can be disseminated amongst the people, there will be many now who look to what has happened and believe that the Wrything Wyrm can strike with impunity wherever they please. If we launch another false strike, it will cost us more than lives. Another mistake could cost us this world.'

'We have watched while others fought for our world, Brother-Librarian,' said the governor, and Lydorran was surprised to realise that beneath the ironclad composure of her voice he could detect an undercurrent of fierce anger threatening to break the surface. 'We have sat our throne and done our duty as figurehead and debater of policies, even as those we purport to serve have fought and died in our name. It has not been easy, but if it has offered one benefit, it has provided us with perspective. We did not have the courage to gainsay Watch Captain Redfang before the Klaratos offensive–'

'Hah! I would have scorned you if you had,' spat Redfang, and Lydorran couldn't tell who the Space Wolf sounded angrier at, the governor or himself.

'Be that as it may, our suspicions were already growing, but it took this last atrocity for us to finally open our eyes to what the Emperor was telling us,' continued the governor. 'We believe with all our heart that our enemy lies deep below the roots of Mastracha Hive, and now that we know this, we will sit and watch no longer. You fight for our world, gentlemen, and so we ask you to have faith in our belief. Our duty as governor is to defend this world. Let us do it, and let the Emperor judge whether we are worthy of his forgiveness or not.'

'Governor, do you intend to fight in person?' asked Lydorran. Before he could voice any sort of objection, Tarsun thumped him on the shoulder guard and gestured to his data-slate. The Ancient had keyed the device to display the Thunderhawk's external vid feeds, and as Lydorran watched, a squadron of hawk-like fighter craft streaked through the middle of the Imperial air armada to take up positions at its leading edge. He saw seven craft, six heavily modified Lightning interceptors in the livery of House Kallistus led by a magnificently gilded, swoop-winged fighter craft of a pattern he could not place. Batteries of laser weaponry hung from its wings and multi-barrelled cannons jutted pugnaciously below its muzzle.

'What is that, archeotech?' asked Tarsun in wonder. Seeing the heraldry displayed proudly on the fighter's tailfin, Lydorran shook his head and smiled despite himself.

'That, brother, is the governor. Looks as though she's come out of retirement.'

'Chaplain Storn sent us an encoded vox even as he was on his way to try to stop the bombing,' said the governor. 'We and our gubernatorial guards had time to reach our private hangar in the spire tip. We will not squander the chance we have been given huddling in some bunker behind the lines.'

'If we're doing this, we need a plan,' said Redfang. 'The Hive ruins are lethally contaminated, and the only route of entry we suspect exists runs along sixty miles or more of tunnels that they could surely collapse on us in extremis. The beast's lair won't be easy to reach.'

'I believe I may have a solution, though it will be dangerous in the extreme,' replied Lydorran, his mind racing. 'Permit me a moment to hail Techmarine Asphor and Shipmaster Gavorn and patch them into this channel. We will require their expertise. And governor, I should warn you, if you agree to this it may have consequences for your planet for decades to come.'

'*The consequences of defeat would doubtless be worse, Brother-Librarian,*' replied Kallistus. '*Recount your plan, please.*'

They were still almost eighty miles distant from the ruins of Hive Mastracha when Lydorran's plan was set in motion. He watched the horizon through *Vengeful*'s vid feeds, his eyes locked on the glimmering line where the pearlescent sea of jungle mist met the bruised blue of Ghyre's dawn skies. Faintly he could make out the unnatural whorls of the Cicatrix Maledictum where it polluted the heavens, but he forced himself to ignore the corrosive sight and focus instead upon the distant black silhouette that marked where the hive rose to scrape the Ghyrish atmosphere.

'If this does not work, we'll have to abort swiftly,' noted Tarsun. 'Cannot risk flying straight into the contaminated zone.'

'It will work,' replied Lydorran, flexing his augmetic hand around the grip of his stave. He hoped he sounded more convincing than he felt. He and his comrades had gone over the plan in exhaustive detail, had spent almost an hour examining alternatives, but every scenario they constructed ended in failure. They could not gain access to the broodnest via the VanSappenmine without giving their enemies too long to react, or to cave the tunnels in upon them. They had no guarantee that any other entrances or exits to the suspected nest existed, and any efforts to scout such possibilities would cost them days, days during which the planet's situation might destabilise entirely and all would spin off its axis. Nor could they land troops in the contaminated zone to search for routes down upon the surface without condemning them to swift and horrible death.

'There is only this,' he muttered to himself.

Then fire stabbed down from the skies, and it was too late

to turn back. As he watched the searingly bright lance beam split the heavens, Lydorran had a momentary sensation of vertigo, as of stepping off a high precipice and beginning to fall. He thrust the feeling aside, recognising it for the doubt that it was, and gritted his teeth.

In the distance a bright light blossomed, fire roaring up from the point where the lance beam had stabbed through Mastracha's metal hide. A second beam speared downward, then a third, then a fourth, like blades of light impaling the man-made mountain.

'Gunnery seneschals report direct hits upon hive's primary and secondary generatorums,' came the crackling voice of Shipmaster Gavorn over the vox, his words distorted as atmospheric electrogheists whirled in frenzied madness away from the impact points of the lance beams. *'Deathwatch strike cruiser reports accurate impacts and–'*

Whatever else Gavorn had to say was lost in a sudden hurricane of electrodisturbance. An instant later the horizon was illuminated by a rapidly expanding sphere of blinding light and leaping flame. The detonation raced outwards and upwards with ferocious speed, a ravenous newborn star devouring everything in its path.

'Throne of Terra…' breathed Tarsun. Lydorran could only nod in mute awe as impossible destructive fury was vented before his eyes. The shockwave reached them, racing away from the explosion as though in terror, and *Vengeful* bucked furiously as it rode out the impact. Bursts of bright light on the edges of the vid feed told Lydorran that not all the Ghyrish craft had been so well piloted or fortunate as his own, but he couldn't tear his eyes away to assess the damage. The mist rolled over them in a lambent tidal wave, and as the Thunderhawk punched through its other side it was met by a scene of apocalyptic devastation. The jungle was exposed, its mists temporarily driven back, and Lydorran saw that the predatory riot of xenoflora was in uproar. Thorned tendrils coiled madly from beneath vast klarwood trees that had toppled onto them as the shockwave tore them from their roots. Drip-gullets lumbered through the fronds and slashing blade-leaves of smaller plants, their ambulatory root balls carrying them away from the devastation as quickly as they could go. Ephemeral streaks of grey flesh and flashing golden scillia showed where the so-called mist-beasts fled for the cover of the fog banks.

Further towards the blast, Lydorran saw that the jungle was aflame, studded here and there with immense chunks of scorched metal now unrecognisable as anything other than wreckage. Further still and the jungle was vanished altogether, even the withered remnants that had been left by the biopurge now annihilated wholesale. As *Vengeful* streaked closer to their target, Lydorran saw that massive cracks had rent the scorched bedrock, radiating out from the epicentre of the blast and running between more metallic masses of debris, some of which were the size of small settlements in their own right. Perhaps the most awe-inspiring sight of all was the seemingly impossible column of fire and metallic debris that still climbed up and away from the detonation, just as Techmarine Asphor had predicted it would. The blast had blown a wound into the very atmospheric envelope of the planet, and its sheer force had been enough to hurl vast portions of the ruptured Hive Mastracha up through the resultant vortex and into the void beyond.

Lydorran muttered prayers to the machine-spirits of the Imperial vox-network, beseeching them to vanquish the electrogheists and restore communication as swiftly as they could.

The lance fire had detonated the hive's already unstable plasma generators, which in turn had triggered its central magazines and promethium reserves, and the resulting fireball had been enough to catch the enormous reserves of biological gases still trapped within the hive structure where several hundred million living beings had fallen to hyper-rapid decomposition just weeks before.

The resultant blast had been everything Lydorran had hoped for, perhaps more. But had the rest of his plan worked, or were they flying into a contaminated deathtrap?

'We will be into the contamination zone in less than a minute, Brother-Librarian,' said Tarsun, warning in his tone.

'This is Lydorran to any void-borne elements,' voxed the Librarian. 'Gavorn, anyone, did it work? Do you have auspex data? Did it work? Please confirm.'

Static roared back at him.

'Thirty seconds,' reported Tarsun. 'Brother-Librarian?'

Lydorran thought of the consequences of failure. The blast might, if they were very fortunate, have killed Father and all of his foul brood, but somehow Lydorran doubted it. If the enemy were cunning enough to site their stronghold beneath a bio-contaminated death zone, they were cunning enough to dig down deeply enough to prevent orbital bombardment from reaching them. They could keep hammering the site, but it might take hours to break through, and by that time Father could have fled to any number of bolt-holes. No, Red-fang had been fiercely insistent on this point, and Lydorran had concurred; they needed to break into the broodnest, locate Father themselves and kill the beast by their own hand before broadcasting evidence of its ruined corpse to every settlement on Ghyre. Only in this way could they break the Cult of the Wrything Wyrm once and for all.

ANDY CLARK

But for that to happen, they needed to sterilise the blast zone around Mastracha. And that, in theory, had been the job of the immense fireball that the Imperial warships had just unleashed.

'In theory,' he muttered, desperately listening for the slightest sound of verbal confirmation from the vox.

'Ten seconds, Brother-Librarian!' said Tarsun. 'Orders?'

Storn's words came back to Lydorran then, and he heard again for an instant the distant drone of insects in a cloister now scourged of all life, hundreds of miles away atop Angelicus Hive.

'Sometimes, Brother Lydorran, you have to take things on faith.'

'Proceed,' he ordered.

Every Imperial Fist in the dropship's troop bay tensed as the Thunderhawk streaked on towards the contamination zone. They would know quickly if his decision had been wrong, Lydorran thought; even the Thunderhawk's atmospheric seals might not endure the bite of the concentrated biopurge agent long enough to stage an abort, and even if they did, the Ghyrish would surely drop from the sky like flies.

They flew on.

Nothing happened.

Hive Mastracha grew closer. Lydorran blew out a relieved breath. Then came a violent shuddering and a lurch that threw him sideways in his restraints.

'Is it the contaminant?' he barked.

'–egative, my lord,' the pilot's voice crackled back through the slowly stabilising internal vox. 'Renegade airbo... cult aircraft... from the east... in force!'

'They have scrambled aircraft to intercept,' said Tarsun,

before taking his helm and locking it into place. Lydorran
followed suit.

'Impossible. They could not have taken off in response to
the blast,' he said. 'They wouldn't have got here so swiftly.
They must have known we were coming. The rot must truly
run deep. Another traitor remains.'

'They must have circled the contaminated zone, looking to
either pull us away from the broodnest or stop us before we
got there,' continued Tarsun, bashing his data-slate against
a bulkhead until its fritzing readout stabilised. 'Damnation,
there they are. The blast lent them some sensor cover, though
it looks to have thrown their formation into a dozen kinds
of disarray.'

'–rother-Librarian, do you read?' came the governor's voice as
the vox-channels fought to stabilise. 'Enemy squadrons punching into… flank from the south-east.'

'We see them, governor. Can your airborne regiments engage?'

'Confirmed, Brother-Librarian. Leave the air war to the Ghyrish.
It… where we excel,' she said, and in his vid feed Lydorran
saw the governor's fighter and its escorts peel off to the left,
their guns lighting with fury. 'Push on to the broodnest. Take
the Marauders with you – bombers may be of use to you, but they
will be nothing but a hindrance in aerial combat.'

'Confirmed,' came Redfang's response. 'Hunt well, Governor Kallistus.'

'We shall,' she replied. Lydorran watched as the Ghyrish
squadrons wheeled south and east, turning to meet the
onrushing swarm of Valkyries, Vendettas and purloined
fighter craft all adorned with wyrmforms. He saw Kallistus'
ornate fighter roll to the right to evade incoming las-fire
before straightening out and spearing an enemy gunship
with beams of ruby light. The cult craft exploded in a glaring

fireball, and Governor Kallistus dove through the blast and vanished from sight.

'All Adeptus Astartes craft, defensive fire only,' he ordered. 'Don't break formation, don't deviate, push for the blast crater and the broodnest. And someone protect those bombers.'

Their first pass filled Lydorran with dread. Of Hive Mastracha nothing remained except for scattered debris that covered a miles-wide area. The ruins of what had once been a city of millions flashed by beneath *Vengeful* before giving way to a vast, glowing crater at the catastrophe's epicentre. He had hoped to see the broodnest torn open below him, its tunnels and chambers laid bare and its defenders scattered as flaming carrion. Instead he saw only a crater of glowing bedrock, licked by flames and riven by cracks.

'Dorn forgive us if we've struck wrongly again,' he said. 'There's no sign of the damned nest whatsoever.'

'Enemy aircraft on our tail, my lord, closing quickly,' reported the pilot. *'Engaging evasive manoeuvres.'*

Lydorran all but ignored the pitch and yaw of the Thunderhawk as it jinked, dove, then spiralled back upwards in a long arc to line its guns up on the cult fighter craft assailing it. He had no eyes for the air war erupting around him as Space Marine gunships and cult interceptors duelled over the blazing crater. He could only search ever more frantically for the slightest sign that the enemy's fastness lay down below. The crater was massive and deep, he thought. How much further down could the broodnest have been dug?

If it is there at all, a traitorous voice whispered in his mind. Surely by now he should have been able to sense the psychic presence of the patriarch?

'Watch Captain Redfang, do you have visual confirmation?' he voxed.

'*No, nothing, not a felid's paw in the snow,*' replied Redfang, and Lydorran felt his hearts fall. Then the watch captain barked a laugh.

'*Fangs of Russ, there they are! Xenos augurs on our strike cruiser just got reconsecrated, Fist. The broodnest is down there. Psychonometrics and energy readouts are spiking like you wouldn't believe. Damnation, they got their own damn hive underneath this one, but augurs reckon it's another twenty feet or so of solid bedrock before we reach it.*'

Redfang broke off, and Lydorran checked the whirling soup of contacts on his auspex. He saw that several enemy aircraft had dived headlong into Redfang's squadron of Corvus gunships and that the two wings of aircraft were now engaged in a violent aerial ballet.

'Commanding officer Marauder bomber squadron, this is Epistolary Lydorran, do you read me?' he voxed. The response came back at once, a young woman's voice, clipped and determined.

'*Receiving, my lord. What can we do for you, sir?*'

'The enemy stronghold is located below the bedrock of the crater, twenty feet or more down,' said Lydorran, suppressing his frustration and sense of powerlessness as the Thunderhawk shuddered around him again. 'Can you make us an entrance?'

'*Absolutely, my lord,*' she replied at once. '*You keep them off us long enough, and we'll knock you as many holes as you could want.*'

'Understood. Do so,' ordered Lydorran, before sending a flicker of runic commands to his escort pilots. As one, half a dozen Stormhawk Interceptors broke away from ferocious

dogfights and swooped around to form up on the wings of
the trio of Marauder bombers. Lydorran watched through
vid feeds as the massive aircraft lumbered towards the crater.
Their turrets spun and chattered, hammering sawing lines of
fire into the cult aircraft that spiralled madly around them.
The Stormhawks added their own fire, las-beams leaping out
to swat turncoat Lightning fighters from the skies and dash
their wreckage across the crater below.

'*Commencing run,*' came the voice of the Ghyrish commander, and Lydorran saw the first of the huge aircraft clear
the rim of the crater. He sucked in a breath as a blazing cult
fighter spun through the crisscross web of Imperial fire and
dived headlong into the Marauder's fuselage. The huge craft
lurched, and its superstructure split as it was smashed off
course. The two craft, their wreckage fused together, fell out
of the air and slammed into the crater wall before being
consumed in a thunderous explosion as the Marauder's pay-
load went off.

'*Throne alive, keep them off us!*' yelled the Ghyrish commander. '*They're suicidal!*'

'All pilots, the bombers must make their run. Repeat, the
bombers must make their run,' voxed Lydorran to anyone
who could hear. 'Protect them at all costs!'

His own Thunderhawk streaked around and lunged
through the smoke-filled air, streams of tracer fire lashing
around it. Its guns spoke, and an enemy craft came apart in
a spray of flaming wreckage as it tried to line up an attack
run on the second bomber. More enemy craft exploded as
their pilots tried with frantic intensity to stop the bombers
and the Imperial pilots turned their every effort to intercepting them in turn.

'*Bombs away, bombs away, now, now, now!*' came the clipped

voice of the bomber commander, and as the two massive aircraft passed over the crater with bullet holes riddling them and flames belching from their damaged hulls, a twin rain of high explosives fell upon the crater below. Explosions rippled furiously across the ground, and where they struck they gouged massive craters. Lydorran thumped his throne in triumph as he saw first one hole then another crack, crumble and fall away into the hollow space below. *Now* he sensed his prey, the psychic spoor of something vast and dreadful billowing invisibly up from the opened rents like steam escaping a geyser.

'*You have your entrance, my lord!*' came the officer's voice, though he heard the strain of wounding in it. The two craft were barely in the air, the cult fighters still harrying them with lunatic intensity.

'You have done the Emperor's own work,' replied Lydorran. 'Now get yourselves clear before they bring you down.'

'*Absolutely, sir, the Emperor pro–*'

The fierce blast cut off the end of the commander's words, and the wreckage of her bomber fell out of the sky to slam into the blackened plains below. Lydorran felt his expression set in a furious scowl that the sight of the bomber's killer being shot down moments later did nothing to alter.

'Too many good Imperial lives have been claimed by this Throne-damned madness,' he growled. 'It ends now. Imperial Fists, Deathwatch, whoever is left, full combat deployment against the breach. Armour, deploy to the surface. If the enemy attempt to land reinforcements, slaughter them without mercy.'

'*You know, Fist, I think you and I could be battle-brothers after all,*' said Redfang over the command channel, and Lydorran heard entirely too much manic cheer in the Space Wolf's voice.

'Whatever it takes, watch captain, just so long as this monster dies today and its whole cult with it.'

'Together, then, let us hunt the beast.'

Moments later, *Vengeful*'s landing gear hit the crater floor, its assault ramp already slamming open. Lydorran pounded down it as he had time and again on this accursed world, pistol in one hand, force stave in the other. This time, he promised himself, would be the last.

Around him, Imperial Fists infantry stormed towards the ragged craters that marked the breach into the broodnest. Black-armoured Deathwatch kill teams ran alongside them, ignoring the enemy fighter craft that streaked down for opportunistic strafing runs through their ranks. Lydorran threw up a crackling force field as he ran, extending it as far as he could as a renegade Lightning streaked low overhead and spat las-bolts in his direction. It exploded violently barely twenty feet above him, its wreckage streaking down. The Stormhawk that had killed it swept over the Imperial Fists and back up into the vicious dogfight above, followed by the cheers of Lydorran's battle-brothers.

Then the dark crater yawned before him. He glanced right to where Redfang kept pace, the Space Wolf unhelmed and laughing like a lunatic as his mane flowed behind him. There was no time for caution now.

'Glad to see you've kept up this far, Space Wolf!' Lydorran called over the vox, then leapt into the dark rent.

XV

Phoenicia Jai was thrown from her feet by a ferocious shockwave. Her ears rang as concussive waves of sound beat against her, so loud they rapidly metamorphosed from true sensory stimuli to an unending wall of pain. The tunnel shook madly. Cracks leapt along its walls and ceiling, spitting out rock dust as they burst open. The lumen strips that hung from the ceiling flickered. Several exploded in showers of sparks as their illuminating gheists fled in terror.

Jai rolled onto her side, screaming but unable to hear herself do so. She was dimly aware of her brothers and sisters around her, sprawled and terrified. Word had been flooding into the Temple of the Star Children for hours via miners' vox-sets and concealed broadcast hubs; first had come the news that Klaratos Hive had fallen to the Imperial oppressors, then that the crushing blow had been answered as word reached them of the success of Primus Lhor's attack upon Angelicus Hive. Jai had burned with pride at the news, even as she had felt her heart break with sorrow for the loss of her broodbrother.

Then, less than an hour before, warnings had filtered in of an Imperial attack force closing on the temple by air. Jai had swallowed her sorrow at losing Lhor and begun circulating between the grim-faced bands of neophytes who garrisoned the upper levels of the Temple of the Star Children. She hadn't truly believed that the enemy could reach them here, not with the biopurge wastes above and Father's power to protect them. It was her duty to provide strength and reassurance to her people all the same, to spread the strength that came with Father's faith and ensure that if, by some freak chance, any of the Imperial attackers made it this far, they would meet suitably stern resistance.

In truth, Jai had been excited. Surely this was a catastrophic misstep by the foe? Even as the conflict for Ghyre hung in the balance, they were committing what appeared to be the vast majority of their strength to an attack that was surely doomed to fail. She had feared, when they crushed resistance in Klaratos Hive, that the fight would be beaten out of her brothers and sisters. Yet to know that the governor and all of her hated conclave were dead by Father's hand, and then to see the armies of the oppressors hurl themselves fruitlessly to their deaths attempting to answer that blow? Jai knew deep in her heart that such a potent combination would be all it would take to see the populace surge up as one and overthrow whatever remained of Imperial rule upon Ghyre.

Then, as she strode along one of the upper access tunnels and dispensed soft, calm words of benediction and encouragement to her comrades, the shockwave had hit.

A chunk of stone tore loose from the ceiling and fell with sudden violence. It landed atop a neophyte brother to Jai's right and crushed him, spraying her face with hot blood. Jai's eyes widened and, screaming inaudibly, she rolled away before a second chunk of stone could crash down after the first.

Father. She couldn't get cut off from Father, and if she wound up at the wrong end of this tunnel that was precisely what would happen. Jai hauled herself to her feet, grabbed her staff and half ran, half fell below the collapsing section of the roof. As she went, Jai sent a pulse of encouragement to her brothers and sisters to follow her lead; as one they staggered upright as best they could and tried to follow, even those at the far end of the access tunnel. Another boulder fell, and another, then with a roar that was drowned out by the wider cacophony, an entire stretch of the tunnel fell in not twenty feet behind Jai's heels.

Some of her brothers and sisters made it.

Some did not.

Jai kept moving, stumbling along the shaking corridor, using her staff to help her maintain her balance as she made for the guard chamber at its end. The roof and walls there were armoured, double reinforced to withstand any danger of bombardment or collapse. If she and her comrades could get there, they would be safe.

Jai sent a pulse of compulsion ahead of her. Though they had already sealed and bolted the chamber's door, the cultists stationed there threw it wide again at her mental urging and the magus reeled through. Cultists followed her, before another violent shockwave threw most of them from their feet afresh. More blood spurted as one of the guards smashed her head against the chamber's door before, with a supreme effort of will, Jai used her powers to seize control of the wounded woman's body and use it to heave the door closed.

Jai slumped to the ground as the savage tremors continued, exchanging looks with the shocked neophytes all around her.

At last the shaking and roaring began to subside, leaving a persistent ringing in Jai's ears that left the sounds around her muffled and dull.

She rose to her feet and began helping her brothers and sisters to do the same.

'Magus, what has happened?' cried one, blood running down her face from a cut behind her bone-ridged hairline. Jai scooped the neophyte's fallen autogun from the floor and pressed it back into her hands.

'The oppressors assail us, Clariss, but Father is stronger than they. Take up your weapon and be ready to fight for your faith.' She turned, taking in the array of frightened faces and wide eyes around her. 'You all have to be ready to fight for what you believe in! To fight for Father! To fight for freedom!' she said, her voice rising into a defiant shout. 'They come to us armed with the wicked blades of cruelty and hate. They drag behind them their oppressors' chains to bind us once again. But we have broken those shackles before! My brothers and sisters, we bear the light of hope within our breasts, and we will *never be shackled again!*'

Around her, Jai saw fearful expressions harden into something more determined. She could almost hear her brothers' and sisters' hearts beat faster, see their spines straighten with pride. They clutched guns and mining tools in white-knuckled grips.

'How many of our brothers and sisters have they slain?' she shouted, and as she did, she allowed sparks of her anger to billow from her mind and ignite the dry tinder of her comrades' own. 'How many loved ones have you lost to the oppressors? How many have they killed with their idiot brutality?'

Murmurs of agreement became shouted oaths around her.

'Will we let this evil continue? Will we roll over like whipped curs and let them take Father from us? Will they deny us our Ascension?'

'*No!*' they roared back at her, heavy picks and autoguns brandished over their heads, oaths and invective spilling from their lips. Jai felt the upswell of zealous fury fill the chamber like pressure building in an airlock, and she fed it, stoked it with subtle pulses of her own power. Her comrades would need every ounce of their anger and determination if they were to win this fight, she told herself. This was not manipulation; it was support, encouragement, inspiration such as countless generals had given their soldiers over countless millennia. So what if she was pushing them with her mind? She wasn't Lhor, didn't have his magnetic presence or natural aptitude for command, and so as the cult was robbed of its primus, she would have to do her best in his place.

That meant using every gift that Father had given her, and using them to their fullest.

'Though the enemy are at our gates, though they strike at the heart of our faith, I tell you, brothers and sisters, that we stand upon the very cusp of victory!' she shouted, reaching out with her mind until she felt the liquid darkness of Father's own consciousness and let it flow into her, through her, and on into her brothers and sisters, not just in this guard chamber but throughout the Temple of the Star Children. Distantly, Phoenicia heard explosions and the unmistakable hammer of bolt weaponry, but in that moment all she felt was a surging flow of power, the boundless exhilaration of serving as the conduit for something infinitely greater, of inspiring hundreds upon hundreds of souls to a fury of holy purpose that they would never have achieved alone.

'Today the monsters are upon us, monsters dressed in the guise of angels, and I tell you, brothers and sisters, that they have nothing in their hearts but hatred!' she roared, her voice echoing around the reinforced chamber and carrying on through the tunnels and halls of the temple. 'They will not stop until every last one of us is dead, until Father is dead! Will we allow this?'

'No!' they howled again.

'Then rise up as one, my brothers and sisters. Fight for your comrades and your distant families and all those you care about and love. Fight for the cult, fight for Father, fight with the fury of the Star Children themselves! Those who die with such purpose in their hearts will surely know Ascension! The oppressors will know only death!'

Jai basked in the howls and cries of those around her, the defiant shouts and cult oaths that echoed to her from deeper within the temple's excavated sprawl. She hefted her staff and, filled with a sense of righteous purpose stronger and more intoxicating than anything she had ever known, set off through the still-shuddering tunnels towards the sounds of gunfire. Towards Father.

The chamber that Lydorran dropped into was deeper than he had expected. He fell for a good three-count, and as he did so he conjured his geokinetic energies and channelled them down and out. Lydorran hit the stone floor like a falling comet, and as his armoured boots and the butt of his staff slammed into graven bedrock, a shockwave of psychic power roared out from him in all directions. Stone exploded upwards. Dust billowed amidst crackling golden lightning. Human shapes were plucked up and hurled away like leaves in a gale to slam into tumbling metal gurneys and cut-stone architecture. Cultists hit the walls so hard that the stone cracked and their blood exploded in fans that reached the ceiling.

Redfang slammed down beside him a moment later and rose from his crouch with a low whistle. Sor'khal and Ancient Tarsun followed suit. The chamber they had jumped into might have been a sacrificial site or some form of strange ritual surgery. Now it was a wreck, smashed so completely by Lydorran's powers that its original purpose was almost unguessable. Cultists lay like broken dolls amidst the devastation, a few still groaning and twitching weakly.

'And yet I beat you in a fist fight...' said Redfang wonderingly.

'That is not how I recall it,' replied Lydorran, his tone dry as desert sand.

'Thought you would let me have that one, Fist,' Redfang said, and shook his head.

'Expediency,' said Lydorran as more Space Marines dropped down through the rents in the ceiling.

'We go again sometime,' said Redfang with relish. 'Only this time we have a barrel of mjod each first to celebrate victory, and you don't hold back. I'd rather beat you in a fair fight, eh?'

'Let us secure that victory first, watch captain,' said Lydorran, and Redfang answered him with a wolfish grin.

'Time to slay the beast at last,' he said, and revved Stormtooth's teeth with relish.

'Just so.'

'Team Pasandrus, Team Troska, north entrance,' Redfang called to his kill teams, who were assembling amidst the whirling dust with their guns and blades at the ready. 'Team Agnathio, Team Phratos, south tunnel. Team Alessius, with me – we're taking the east route.'

The black-armoured Space Marines moved out on Redfang's orders, the colours of a dozen Chapters and more flashing in the gloom from their shoulder guards, shot selectors chambering alien-killing rounds into their bolt weapons. At the same time Lydorran issued orders of his own over the Imperial Fists' command channel, and squads of yellow-armoured Intercessors, Infiltrators and Reivers moved to support the Deathwatch as they advanced.

'What of the heavier infantry?' Redfang asked. 'It's quite a drop, but sure as a pelt in a Fenrisian blizzard, they'd be damned useful down here.'

'Move back to the chamber wall, please, watch captain, and allow us to oblige you,' said Lydorran, and he, Redfang, Tarsun and Sor'khal ducked back out of the pool of daylight that fell through the rent. There came a rippling series of detonations and a long section of the ceiling fell in. Rubble dropped with artful precision, crashing down atop a foundation of scattered wreckage. Redfang laughed as he saw that the mass of falling stone had been caved in to form a crude ramp that led down from the crater's surface above. A heavy crunch signalled the first footfall of an Imperial Fists Terminator, and Redfang shook his head in admiration as Squad Lesordus tramped down into the chamber, followed by the Aggressors of Squads Torfan and Justus.

'Will that suffice?' asked Lydorran.

'It won't hurt our chances, eh?' chuckled Redfang, then looked up as the sounds of bolt and auto-fire echoed from the adjoining tunnels. 'Time to move though. We shook 'em, but the nest's waking up.'

'Sergeant Lesordus, if you would?' said Lydorran, and the grizzled Terminator sergeant replied with a vox-pip before marching into the eastward-leading tunnel entrance with his squad. Redfang and Lydorran moved up in the Terminators' wake, their warriors massing around them while the Aggressors of Squad Justus formed a lumbering rearguard.

They advanced swiftly, stepping over the groaning figures of cultists crushed by fallen rubble and sweeping each dust-filled chamber with their guns as they progressed. Watch Sergeant Alessius, the big Blood Angel, consulted a complex hand-held auspex that Lydorran saw was giving off a constant stream of runic readouts and pinging blips.

'Connecting corridor proceeds fifty yards ahead then diverges,' reported the Blood Angel as they crossed a partly collapsed intersection. Squad Lesordus' guns roared briefly, filling the tunnel with sound and strobing light for a moment before falling silent again as whatever bewildered defenders they had encountered were swiftly butchered.

'Left-hand fork straight down, right, Alessius?' asked Redfang, nostrils flaring as he scented for prey. The Blood Angel shot a glance at his watch captain.

'Don't know why we even bother with this thing,' muttered the Blood Angel, nodding.

'Because one of these days someone's going to improve the watch captain's looks with a frag grenade or something, and then his nose won't work so well,' replied Apothecary Sor'khal. Lydorran shot a sharp glance at the White Scar, as did Tarsun, but Redfang just laughed and aimed a casual punch at Sor'khal's shoulder guard. Lydorran had the profound sense in that moment that the two warriors had fought together a very long time, had shared victories and losses far beyond the scope of his own experience, and that the mockery and insubordination hid bonds of brotherhood as strong as adamantine. He longed for that connection with his own brothers, then reminded himself that now was not the time for such concerns.

'Sergeant Lesordus, sweep right then lead left,' voxed Lydorran, and received another vox-pip as confirmation. The Terminators stomped down the left fork of the tunnel, passing a crudely worked statue that sprouted organically from the bedrock to preside over the tunnel junction. It looked to Lydorran somewhere between a saint and a gargoyle, its head bulbous, the hands of two of its four arms holding miner's tools and broken shackles clutched between the other two.

'We are in the right place and on the right trail,' said Redfang, suddenly serious.

'The statue?' asked Tarsun.

'We have seen its like before,' Sor'khal answered with a dark glower.

'Fists, matters will get worse from this point onwards,' growled Redfang. 'They will throw everything they have at us. Guard your minds and your souls – this filth will come for them both.'

'The sons of Dorn stand firm at your side, watch captain,' replied Lydorran. 'We are the fortress that no xenos artifice may unmake.'

Redfang grunted acknowledgement, and the force pressed on. As they advanced, Lydorran's ear was filled with a steady stream of reports from his battle-brothers. Even as part of his awareness scanned the flicker-lit stone tunnels for any signs of the foe, the rest assembled and reassembled a constantly flowing strategic picture. The warriors they had despatched into different tunnels of the complex had all met heavy resistance but were pushing forward, stemming enemy attempts to intercept Lydorran's own force and demolishing guard chambers and armouries one by one. Techmarine Asphor reported that the governor and her squadrons were engaging the enemy both in the air and on the ground along the jungle fringes, effectively preventing enemy reinforcements from reaching the engagement zone around the crater. There, the Imperial Fists' pilots were still duelling the finest of the cult aces in a vicious dogfight while the Space Marine armour added their own fire to the fight and formed an adamantine ring around the breach into the broodnest. As per the plan, Redfang's gunships had dusted off and streaked eastwards bearing a secondary force of elite Deathwatch warriors; even now, drop pods were plummeting from the flanks of the Deathwatch strike cruiser to slam down amidst the defences of VanSappen-mine. Black-armoured warriors were knocking out the enemy's anti-aircraft defences in short order, opening the way for the Blackstars to launch a decisive strike and prevent the tainted Clan VanSappen from flooding reinforcements down the tunnels to aid Father. The Imperial forces were spread thin, and word was already reaching Lydorran of enemy reinforcements racing pell-mell from every side as the cult attempted to protect its patriarch; they needed to find the beast and slay it quickly, before even the massed armies of the Imperium could be overrun.

Lydorran's attention was dragged back to his immediate surroundings as they passed beneath the stony gaze of more gargoyles and below a low, candle-lit arch into a huge chamber. The Librarian took in weirdly arcing support columns carved from stone to look like organic limbs, disturbing frescoes on the wall of xenos-looking creatures with the glowing haloes of saints raising up their faithful in their taloned hands, great waxy mounds of candles whose tallow was blood-dark and whose flames flickered with an oily yellow light. He saw a towering stone idol, clearly carved using mining lasers and then gaudily adorned with gems and precious metals; it towered over the brushed-steel prayer benches that filled the space, its vast alien body powerful and menacing, its face a freakish amalgam of human and xenos, its clawed arms and broad wings outstretched in benediction. Above it was painted a fresco of the darkness of space filled with glowing light, angelic figures and coiling tendrils that reached down to topple crudely rendered cities and shatter symbolic chains. Below it, between its feet, was a noisome tunnel mouth that led down into a dark, fume-wreathed pit. Slimy tendrils of organic matter had slithered up from that yawning maw to encircle the legs of the statue; they pulsed with slow, abhorrent vitality and gave off a lambent purple glow.

'Throne, this is madness,' he breathed.

'It's the worst kind of xenos heresy,' replied Redfang.

Then the gunfire began. The enemy poured in from arched doorways to either side of the grotesque statue. They appeared upon prayer balconies cut into the stone of the walls. Mutants, hybrids, screaming almost-humans all clad in the utility suits of the Cult of the Wrything Wyrm, all wielding firearms and weaponised mining gear and baying for the Space Marines' blood.

A storm of fire engulfed the Terminators of Squad Lesordus, and a deafening cacophony of metal on metal filled the heretic cathedrum.

'Sergeant Lesordus, forge a path,' ordered Lydorran. 'Squad Justus, purge those balconies.'

'Team Alessius, secure the nest,' barked Redfang, and he started forward into the firestorm. Lydorran caught his arm, and the Space Wolf turned back with a snarl.

'The pit, that is where we need to go?' asked Lydorran.

'They'll keep coming. Longer we're here, worse it'll get,' replied Redfang. 'We need to be down that troll hole, now.'

Lydorran nodded and released the watch captain.

'We will cover your advance,' he said.

Redfang revved Stormtooth and bounded forward, Sor'khal and the warriors of Team Alessius at his side.

'Allfather!' roared the Space Wolf, shrugging off a stream of autogun fire and whipping his blade's teeth through the neck of a three-armed mutant. He kicked the choking cultist from his path and spun, scything the arm from a second foe and spilling the guts of a third. Apothecary Sor'khal fired his pistol into the press of cult mutants, exploding a bulbous, eyeless head armoured with chitinous ridges. Sergeant Alessius and his brothers played their boltguns right and left, acidic shells exploding amidst the mutant throng and gouging gory craters with every blast.

At the same time, Sergeant Torfan's Aggressors played their boltstorm gauntlets along the balconies to either flank. Cultists jerked and danced as bolts struck them, then detonated in gory sprays as the explosive munitions did their work. A ruby beam of laser energy stabbed down from a balcony to the right and transfixed one of Sergeant Torfan's battle-brothers, toppling him without a sound. In return, the sergeant annihilated the balcony with a thundering hail of bolts that rained shattered stone and xenos-tainted gore down on the tide of enemies below.

'With me, Ancient,' said Lydorran, and he strode forward into the storm. Tarsun's banner rose high beside him, brandished proudly above the roiling battle for all to see. The Terminators of Squad Lesordus advanced relentlessly before it, their storm bolters hammering, their cyclone missile launcher shooting frag warheads into the press of the foe to explosive effect. Power fists swung in unstoppable arcs, pulverising screaming cultists and sending their shattered saws and drills spilling from their claws.

Lydorran saw a hulking brute wading in from the left, a deformed monster covered in purpleish muscle and wielding a hammer bigger than a grown man. The thing rose head and shoulders above even Sergeant Lesordus, and its candlewax features reminded Lydorran horribly of the beasts that had ended Apothecary Lordas' life. He fired his heavy bolt pistol at the abomination and blew bloody craters in its chest, but it only roared and forged on faster, thrusting cultists aside with its bulk.

'Veteran sergeant! To your left!' voxed Lydorran. Again that pip of acknowledgement, Lesordus pivoting ponderously at the waist to unload his storm bolter into the monster. Again the bolts exploded within its flesh, and this time the mutant staggered, but still it came on, raising its hammer high and giving an awful, groaning roar. Lydorran summoned his powers and hurled a shockwave of force through the press of cultists towards the beast, but he knew it would be too slow.

The hammer whistled down with horrible strength and collided squarely with Sergeant Lesordus' helmet in the instant before the mutant was driven sideways by Lydorran's blast. Ceramite and adamantine cracked, and though the helmet didn't break, it was driven savagely down and back. An awful sound came over the vox from Lesordus, something choked and filled with shock and pain, then the massively armoured warrior toppled over backwards with a crash and the cultists flowed over him.

'Dorn's fist!' cursed Lydorran. He swept his stave in a glowing arc that smashed a swathe of cultists high into the air then charged, roaring, at the reeling mutant. Its chest was a ragged mass of gore and torn flesh. Lydorran glimpsed pulsing, unclean organs exposed to the air, yet still somehow the thing stayed on its feet. Its revolting face leered at him, three eyes blinking stupidly, and it swung its hammer sideways through the press. Several cultists were smashed aside by the blow. One of Alessius' battle-brothers, a Lamenter whose armour was already rent and mangled down one side, was unlucky enough to be caught a glancing blow and thrown from his feet. Then the hammer met Lydorran's blocking stave, transformed into an immovable bastion by the full force of his geomantic powers. A shockwave of kinetic force exploded from the impact, driving cultists and Space Marines alike away as though a bomb had gone off in their midst. The monster's hammer shattered in its hands, spraying its rent innards and gruesome face with shrapnel even as the impact drove Lydorran back so hard that his heels dug grooves in the stone floor.

With a roar, he spun his force staff then brought it arcing down upon the monster's head with the force of a wrecking ball. Its skull shattered like an egg, its head exploding in a gory spray. The thing pawed mindlessly at the spurting stump of its ruined neck and then fell sideways onto a gaping knot of cultists.

'For the Emperor! For Dorn!' cried Lydorran, leaping atop the thing's fallen corpse and firing bolt shells into the shocked enemy around him. Imperial Fists and Deathwatch alike added their fire and opened a path to the mouth of the pit amidst welters of gore.

'Move up!' roared Redfang, spinning and carving his screaming blade through a trio of cultists at once. They fell back before his fury, and he shot another enemy in the gut before dropping his shoulder and smashing a path through the reeling foe. He hit one mutant square in the face, shattering its lamprey fangs and sending it toppling over the edge of the pit with a choked scream.

The rest of the Space Marines pushed up behind Redfang, guns booming again and again, the enemy's desultory fire still ringing from their armour. Lydorran took swift count and saw that three of the six Aggressors and four of the five Terminators still stood, along with all but two of Team Alessius. Tarsun still held his banner high despite a glowing hole gouged though one side of his chest-plate, and Apothecary Sor'khal was drenched in xenos ichor but seemed unharmed.

'They are falling back, the cowards,' spat Tarsun. 'So much for their paltry faith.'

'There'll be more on the way, lots more,' replied Redfang, glancing between the slime-slick pit and the corpse-strewn ruin of the cathedral. The towering statue had taken a direct hit to its face during the fighting, and its features were now ravaged but for one topaz eye that still glared from amidst cracked and blackened stone. 'The patriarch, Father, it can control its worshippers like puppets if it wants to. It won't let them run far.'

'All the more reason for haste then,' said Lydorran. 'Squad Lesordus, Squad Justus, you won't make it down this slope, too steep and too slick. Remain here as rearguard. Do not let the enemy's reinforcements break through.'

'Understood, Brother-Librarian,' said Sergeant Justus. 'We will build a redoubt of their bodies.'

'You too, Tarsun,' said Lydorran, placing a hand on the Ancient's chest-plate as he stepped up next to the lip of the pit.

'You would dishonour me thus? I am coming with you,' said the Ancient, his voice set and stubborn.

'You are wounded, and the company banner will not pass down this noisome hole without being laid upon the ground, which you have sworn an oath never to permit,' Lydorran reminded him. 'I give you command of this rearguard, Tarsun. There'll be foes aplenty for you to slay.'

The Ancient looked at him for a long moment, his expression hidden behind his helm's faceplate, then gave a grunt of acknowledgement and planted his standard before the mouth of the pit.

'If you're done with the tearful goodbyes, Fist?' said Redfang pointedly.

What might have struck Lydorran as disrespect just days before, he now recognised for the mocking camaraderie it was.

'I was merely giving you time to catch your breath, Fenrisian,' he replied, then gestured to the hole. Redfang stared at him for a moment and then barked a laugh.

'Let us finish this, in the Allfather's name,' said the watch captain. Then, blade and pistol in hand, he stepped over the edge into the steeply sloping gullet of the pit and began his descent into darkness.

XVI

Lydorran slithered down the tunnel's gullet directly behind Redfang. Sor'khal and the other Deathwatch followed in their wake, heads ducked low to avoid bashing their helms against the encrusted stone. The slope was so steep that it truly was little more than a pit, and Lydorran used his staff to help him avoid losing his footing altogether and sliding out of control into the darkness.

How far away are the tyranids now? he wondered as he looked upon the foul bio-architecture of the pit. *Are we already too late?*

He supposed that one not of the Adeptus Astartes would have been terrified. The precipitous slope, the tight confines and the near-total darkness were bad enough; the foul organic accretions that clung to the pit's walls in ever thicker layers were worse, pulsating as though in time to a beating heart and releasing gouts of stinking slime whenever one of the Space Marines leaned too heavily upon them. Yet the worst was the undeniable sense of dread radiating up from below. Waves of malice and menace beat against his psyche,

ANDY CLARK

and he felt a thrumming note build in the psychocircuitry of
his hood as it warded off the worst of the unnatural energies.

'There is some psychic trickery at work,' he voxed to his
comrades. 'Something is trying to get inside our minds and
inspire terror.'

Redfang shot a glance back up at Lydorran, his feral features
barely visible in the bruise-coloured half-light that pulsed
from the organic growths.

'I don't feel anything, Fist, but if you say–'

The xenos struck with shocking suddenness. It burst from
the mouth of a side tunnel concealed behind the masses of
bio-organic growths and wrapped its clawed limbs around
Redfang before ripping him backwards off his feet and into
the hole it had burst from.

At the same moment, there came a yell from above,
followed by the belching roar of a flamer discharging at
point-blank range. Hungry light filled the pit, dazzling Lydorran momentarily as he sought for the monster that had
struck at Redfang. Instead he saw another of the horrors,
a purestrain genestealer scrambling out from a side tunnel
with nightmarish speed, its gaze fixed upon him and its
fanged maw yawning wide.

Something heavy struck Lydorran from behind and pitched
him helplessly forward. His feet slid out from under him,
and he crashed down upon the scuttling alien as he fell.
Whip-fast, its clawed limbs lashed around the Librarian, and
the two of them tumbled down the pit, locked together in
a savage embrace. The genestealer's jaws snapped closed on
Lydorran's helm, and he hissed in pain as chitinous fangs
sank clean through to pierce his jaw on one side and his
ear on the other.

Talons raked at his chest-plate and ripped through flesh,

black carapace and fused cartilage. Quick, clever claws closed around his augmetic wrist and applied vice-like pressure fit to crack even Space Marine bones. A gangling limb wrapped around him, pinning his other arm to his side with pneumatic strength and jarring his grip on his staff so that the weapon clattered and slid away into darkness. Another ripped his pistol from where he had mag-locked it to his thigh and squeezed hard enough to crack the gun's casing and buckle its barrel before releasing it to go spinning away into the dark.

The tunnel rushed past in a racing, bludgeoning, slime-slick blur.

His wrist. It was the xenos' only mistake and his one chance to survive. Even as Lydorran felt his helm begin to cave in on his skull as the pressure of the thing's jaws increased, he flexed his augmetic wrist and twisted his hand at an angle that no natural joints could have managed. Artificial tendons strained and micro-motivators whined in protest, but the sudden motion was enough to shake off the genestealer's grip. Tumbling over atop the alien then rolling back as he plunged down the pit, Lydorran pistoned his suddenly free fist upwards and drove a crushing punch into his assailant's throat, enhancing it with a raw surge of psychic strength. His armoured knuckles tore through the foul bio-substance of the thing's neck and up into whatever passed for its skull. It spasmed, flailing and whipsawing with the frantic motions of a maimed insect, and then the pressure from its limbs and jaws slackened.

Lydorran tried to push the thing free, tried to grab hold of anything that might arrest his slide, but the genestealer was still locked onto him where its fangs had punched holes through his helm, and with its extra weight atop his own there was no chance of slowing his plummet.

The feeling of weightlessness came suddenly as Lydorran and his dead assailant shot out into open air and fell. It was only a short drop, a handful of seconds at most, but the impact was hard enough to momentarily drive the consciousness from his skull.

Lydorran snapped back to wakefulness to find armour integrity warnings chiming in his ear and flickering red runes flashing at him from his peripheral vision. His autosenses sputtered on and off as he turned his head, and he groaned at the pain that flashed from all over his body.

Moving as quickly as he could, the Librarian heaved the tangled corpse of the genestealer from atop him and rose, feeling analgesic blockers discharging through his bloodstream. He wrenched off his mangled helm and cast it aside, squinting into the gloom as he did so.

The pulsating purple light was brighter here, stronger, somehow unclean in its vitality. It illuminated a scene from a nightmare. Lydorran was at the heart of a huge cavern that looked to have been hewn and shaped from an existing natural fissure. Its floor was jagged and uneven, razor-sharp stalagmites jutting up like fangs in a monster's maw. Equally vicious stalactites stabbed downward to meet them, wound about with purple, glowing bio-flesh, and everywhere deep cracks vanished into stygian depths. The chamber's walls had been elaborately worked into dozens upon dozens of statues, like those that jutted from the corridors on the higher levels but fashioned with infinitely more care and skill. Their stone forms tangled together in knots of intertwining limbs, lashing tongues and bared fangs that were so lifelike they seemed to twitch and stir in the pulsing light. Dark gems flashed in hollowed eye sockets. Screaming Imperial oppressors were depicted in supine poses of defeat, many with limbs torn away or entrails spilling while the haloed xenos demigods tore them limb from limb and their worshippers scrambled over one another to offer them praise.

At the chamber's far end the ground sloped steadily away to where a monstrous throne rose from amidst a wide pool of dark and oily slime. Larger by far than even the ornate throne of Ghyre's governor, the awful seat seemed to have been carved from a single enormous stalagmite, its curves flowing in an obscenely organic fashion and sweating a luminescent fluid that trickled down into the pool.

For an instant Lydorran's senses were fooled into thinking that the huge creature that squatted atop the throne was another shockingly lifelike carving, this one depicting a chitinous, six-limbed genestealer of massive build and bloated strength. Then it shifted, its bulbous cranium pulsating slightly and its sensory pits flaring. Eyes the yellow of molten gold cracked open and fixed upon Lydorran, and the Librarian felt the invasive pressure of something vast and alien trying to thrust itself unceremoniously through his mental defences. His psychic hood glowed hot, and he gritted his teeth, pushing back with all his mental might.

The creature that could only be Father hissed and recoiled, swiping one huge taloned hand through the air as though batting something away. Then it unfolded its enormous limbs and began to move.

Lydorran cast about for his staff and felt a shock of loss run through him as he saw the weapon, cracked in two where it had come down atop one of the viciously sharp stone blades. That was when he took in the bodies that sprawled, mangled and rotting, across the cavern floor all around him. Imperial officials, corpses in the uniforms of Ghyrish officers and highly placed Administratum adepts, priests, clan overseers, arbitrators... There were dozens, some freshly slain, others so old as to be all but skeletons. All exhibited trauma wounds from their plunge down the pit, suggesting they had been cast down it during ritual ceremonies. Each one also exhibited massive cranial wounds.

As though something cracked open their skulls like ration packs and sucked out their brains, thought Lydorran. Was this what the cult offered Father? Was this how the xenos' disciples seemed always to know what the Imperial defenders were going to do next, knew where to strike them and when?

He didn't have time to work it out now; Lydorran could still dimly hear booming boltguns, xenos shrieks and furious war cries that told him at least a few of the Deathwatch still lived. But he was here, alone with the genestealer patriarch, and it was his duty to kill the monster.

Lydorran rose and channelled geokinetic power through his limbs as Father crawled talon over claw into the oily pool and slithered through it before rising, dripping and monstrous, upon its bank. The xenos demigod drew itself up to its full height, spread its taloned hands wide and hissed at the Librarian in clear challenge.

Energy crackled around Lydorran's fists. 'I will crush your filthy skull in payment for all the good Imperial lives you've cost. For Dorn, for the Emperor and for all the noble battle-brothers that have fallen upon this accursed world!'

The Librarian broke into a run, ignoring the pain in his body as he pounded across the slimey rock towards the towering alien. As he ran he conjured small, tight bolts of psychic energy and hurled them towards Father in a half-visible meteor swarm.

The patriarch's eyes flashed and Lydorran's psychic attack

winked out of existence like a smothered flame. Father lunged forward, moving every bit as swiftly as its lesser progeny, and swiped dagger-length talons at Lydorran's face. The Librarian wove under the vicious strike and attempted to drive a psychically augmented punch up into the patriarch's face. Another taloned arm intercepted the blow, smashing Lydorran's fist aside before the alien's second set of human-like hands thrust out and hit the Librarian full in the chest-plate. The impact was hard enough to crack the Imperial aquila that spread over Lydorran's breast, driving the air from his lungs and throwing him back across the chamber.

Lydorran came down hard and rolled, using spurts of geokinetic power to drive himself back to his feet with superhuman agility. He saw Father coming for him, surging across the cavern floor with horrible speed. Lydorran reached out with his powers and sheared several of the bladed stalactites away from the ceiling before hurling them like javelins at the patriarch. One drove through Father's chitinous back and deep into its body. Father threw itself away from the others and they shattered harmlessly against the cavern floor, but Lydorran had achieved his first aim; the patriarch's attack had been averted. Now it prowled around him, burning yellow eyes fixed upon his.

The Librarian saw the foul intelligence that lurked in those eyes. He saw the depths of malice, the towering immensity of a fathomless intellect that spiralled away into maddening distance, that seemed to bridge impossible gulfs and reach out to something more, something distant and vast and terrible that flowed through the cold reaches of infinity, something... something...

Lydorran realised with a sudden jolt what the patriarch was doing. He wrenched his mental defences back into place, sent frantic impulses racing along his nerves, willed his suddenly heavy limbs to move, to react.

He knew in that instant that he would be too slow. Lydorran tried to raise his arms to ward off the massive talons lashing down towards his skull, but it wouldn't be enough.

It wasn't.

The patriarch's first blow tore through Lydorran's augmetic arm in a shower of sparks and sent the limb clattering away, severed once again just below the elbow. The second ripped a long gouge down his other forearm, parting his power armour like parchment, and though he was able to duck back from the full disembowelling force of the third blow, it raked his armour open, sprayed his blood across the cavern floor and threw him through the air again. Lydorran hit the cavern wall, demolishing several unclean carvings with his armoured weight, then hit the ground hard.

Blood pumped from his wounds. His head spun and his hearts thundered. Adrenaline and stimms flooded his system to keep him conscious, to give him the speed to react. He threw up a psychic shield just in time; Father hit it like a speeding maglev train, and the geokinetic shield exploded with enough force to slam Lydorran back against the wall again and send Father reeling, foul liquid spurting from cracked chitin plates.

The patriarch fixed its golden gaze upon Lydorran, and the Librarian summoned what psychic strength he had left, determined that the monster wouldn't make an easy meal of him. Father sprang, crossing the cavern at a flat sprint, talons raised, fangs bared. There came the thumping roar of a bolt pistol and explosions burst across the patriarch's flank. The creature's unnatural reactions were such that it half twisted away from the volley of shots, but still its flesh burst like erupting blisters.

The patriarch half fell, half skittered sideways, and came up with its tail coiling and its talons flexing. Lydorran looked woozily across the chamber to see Redfang limping into view from the darkness of a side tunnel. Blood ran freely from an ugly gash in his leg and a ragged wound in his side, but the Space Wolf was drenched in xenos ichor and he still had his pistol and his chainsword in hand.

'Thought you'd go and get the glory for yourself, Fist?' he called. Lydorran didn't have the strength to offer more than a pained grunt in response.

Father hissed as the watch captain staggered into his brood chamber, three more Deathwatch battle-brothers at his back. Lydorran saw the big Blood Angel, Alessius, a Salamander he did not know, and beside him, Sor'khal of the White Scars.

'Now we've got you, monster,' snarled Redfang, and as one he and his brothers let fly.

The storm of fire whipped across the chamber and Father leapt aside, scrambling with inhuman speed and agility through the bladed stalagmites then springing up onto one of the walls. The patriarch swarmed along the rockface every bit as quickly as it could run, hissing furiously as bolts exploded all around it. Its cranium pulsed, and Lydorran cried out a warning as Father's eyes glowed gold, but for the moment he was too wounded and dazed to hold back the flood tide of the patriarch's will. Brother Alessius staggered and cried out as his eyes suddenly turned dark with burst blood vessels and crimson spurted from his nose and ears. The Blood Angel staggered backwards, spraying wild-fire towards the patriarch and clipping the xenos with one of his specialist bolt rounds. It exploded in a sudden bright flare of plasma, and Father gave an agonised shriek.

Lydorran felt the stormfront pressure of the patriarch's psychic attack blink out in an instant, but it had already done enough. Alessius dropped to one knee, weeping crimson tears, and Father pounced from the wall to the cavern floor, hitting the Blood Angel like a battering ram. Gore exploded in all directions as the patriarch ripped its talons through Alessius' body and tore the battle-brother's head from his shoulders before hurling the mangled corpse at Redfang and Sor'khal.

The two Space Marines staggered back, Redfang falling with a roar of anger and becoming entangled with the armoured body of his battle-brother. Father tensed to spring, claws flexing ready to plunge them into Redfang and tear the Space Wolf apart. With a furious howl of denial, Lydorran drove himself to his feet and flung out a hand. A shockwave of kinetic force pulsed across the chamber and slammed into Father like a battering ram, shattering chitin and throwing the monster backwards into its foul pool. Lydorran dropped back to one knee as the effort of his psychic manifestation dragged at him.

'On your feet, Fist. The Emperor has need of you yet,' said Apothecary Sor'khal, appearing at his side and reaching down. Lydorran locked his remaining hand around Sor'khal's forearm and allowed himself to be pulled to his feet. The next he knew, a trio of syringes were sliding into his neck, just behind his jaw. There was a hiss as vials in Sor'khal's narthecium discharged their contents into Lydorran's bloodstream.

'Fight now, hate me for the after-effects later,' grunted the Apothecary as Lydorran felt fresh vigour surge through his body. His vision swam and came back into focus in time to see

Redfang drive himself back to his feet and shoot the Librarian a grateful nod. Lydorran's twin hearts thundered as his Larraman implant went into overdrive to clot his ghastly wounds.

'The beast is at bay. Let us finish this!' roared Redfang, levelling his pistol and hammering shots into the patriarch as it rose again from its oily pool. Lydorran, Sor'khal and the Salamander moved to aid the watch captain, but before they could there came a scream of purest hate from the far side of the chamber. Lydorran looked up and saw a priestess of some sort striding into the chamber with a mob of cultists at her back. Her domed cranium and slightly mauve-tinged skin revealed her as one of the patriarch's brood as surely as the wyrmform atop her staff or the oily tang of psychic power that radiated from her.

'Another psyker, bring her down!' Lydorran shouted. Sor'khal raised his bolt pistol and fired, but the priestess flicked her hand and one of the cultists threw himself mindlessly into the path of the shot. The bolt blew him bloodily apart, and the priestess levelled her staff in the direction of the Space Marines.

'Protect Father, my brothers and sisters. Slay the oppressors! Fear no evil, my comrades. Victory or death! Victory or death!'

The mob screamed with one voice and surged forward. Many were wounded, Lydorran saw, some so badly that it seemed impossible they could still be alive, yet they came on all the same, driven by the psyker's sledgehammer will.

Redfang cursed as shots rattled against his armour and he was pushed back from the pool. One round split the flesh of his cheek and spattered blood into the oily slime. Another thumped into the raw flesh of his wounded leg and made the Space Wolf stagger.

'To the watch captain!' roared Sor'khal, mag-locking his pistol to his hip in favour of drawing a curved Chogorian power sword and charging headlong at the mob. Lydorran and the Salamander joined him, the latter raising his flamer and spraying liquid fire across the howling cultists. Half a dozen were engulfed at a stroke and they reeled and screamed, but Lydorran felt another savage pulse of will from the priestess and the burning cultists staggered onwards. Two of them opened fire with autoguns that rattled streams of shots at the Salamander before exploding in their users' hands. The rest took the opportunity of his momentary bewilderment to hurl themselves bodily at him. They wrestled with the Salamander, and his vox-amplified yells of fury echoed as flames licked over his armour and the cultists' grasping arms entangled his weapons.

Lydorran punched the first cultist to come at him, hitting the man so hard that his miner's respirator was driven bloodily back into his face. He backhanded another cultist away, sending her broken body tumbling into the patriarch's pool, where the oily fluids churned and bubbled madly as they engulfed her. He heard Redfang yelling furiously, still firing his bolt pistol in Father's direction even as the cultists surged around him. Sor'khal hacked and slashed, driving a path towards the psyker, whose face, Lydorran saw, was twisted in an expression of maniacal hate and madness that sent a chill through him. She had lost all control at the thought that they might harm Father, he realised. Psykers in such a reckless condition could be a danger to far more than just themselves.

He turned to swipe another cultist aside, weathering a rattling hail of shots that rebounded from his cracked chest-plate, and then suddenly he was tumbling sideways again as a concussive wave of force smashed him from his feet. Ears ringing, Lydorran looked up to see that the Salamanders battle-brother and his assailants were gone, annihilated by a sudden explosion. He cast about wildly for the source of such devastating heavy weapons fire, then realised with a sick lurch what must have happened; the flames had reached the warrior's krak grenades, or perhaps the fuel reserves for his flamer, and triggered them all at once.

Lydorran had not even had a chance to learn the warrior's name.

The explosion had shredded a swathe of the cultists, but those that had survived were already lurching back to their feet. He saw Redfang already up and charging headlong at Father, chainsword swinging in a howling arc that clove through the patriarch's outstretched talons. The priestess saw it too, and she gave a howl of near-bestial rage before swiping her staff in a savage sideways curve. Psychokinetic energy slammed into Redfang and hoisted him off his feet to sail through the air and crash down on one of the bladed stalagmites. The rock spur burst up through the Fenrisian's torso, and blood spattered between his lips as he snarled and writhed, trying to free himself before he slid further down the blade.

Lydorran focused his will and the stone spike shattered, allowing Redfang to fall sideways with a grunt of relief.

The momentary distraction had been all his enemies required. Lydorran spun back in time to take a gun butt to the face. He felt his nose break for the second time that day, and as he staggered back a handful of cultists flung themselves at him, glassy-eyed and howling. The Librarian reeled as they battered and hacked at him with bludgeons and picks; he punched one in the throat, causing them to crumple, kicked the legs out from beneath another cultist and stamped on their head, then summoned his powers and hurled a psychic battering ram towards the priestess. The rock of the cavern floor fractured and exploded as the attack surged home and the cult psyker deflected it with a desperate pulse of psychic energy.

'This is how you fight oppression? With psychic slavery?' Lydorran yelled at her over the tumult of battle.

'You *drove* us to this,' she spat back. 'There is no price we would not gladly pay to be free of your tyranny.'

'There is nothing willing about what you are doing to these puppets,' he snarled, and unleashed another pulse of geo-kinetic force at her. Again the psyker parried the blow with her mind, and Lydorran felt a sudden pressure on his senses as Father bore down upon him with a rasping hiss. A bolt shell whipped past his face, almost close enough to graze his flesh, and exploded inside the patriarch's open maw. The monster fell back, flailing and shrieking, ichor spilling over its jaws and splattering from ragged wounds that had been blasted in its gullet. The priestess screamed too, as though in sympathetic agony, and around her the cultist mob staggered and blinked in bewilderment.

Lydorran glanced right to see Redfang, bolt pistol still smoking, storming back into the fight despite the spar of rock that protruded from his chest. His face was pale, his gait limping, and his breath came in wheezing gasps. Blood spilled from the corners of his mouth, but his eyes were still wild with battle lust.

'Forget the psyker, slay the beast!' he roared. 'If Father dies, its cult dies with it. That's the only way we save this world from the damned tyranids.'

'Your freedom is a lie,' said Lydorran, locking eyes for a

moment with the priestess. Then he hurled one last bolt of geokinetic energy. The ground before her exploded, showering the psyker with shrapnel and spinning lumps of rock the size of fists. One struck her temple, and she fell, her eyes rolling back into her head. The cultists lost focus altogether; some staggered and fell, others went glassy-eyed, while others still seemed to wake from a deep slumber and began screaming in shock as they saw the slaughterhouse in which they stood.

Lydorran turned to see Sor'khal already lunging at the patriarch. The White Scar's power sword flickered with blue energy as it cut the air, parrying the vicious swing of the alien's talons then reversing to lash towards its face. Father reared back and swiped with its bony tail, knocking the Apothecary's legs out from under him. Sor'khal fell with a shout, and the patriarch stabbed down at him with one taloned fist. Before the blow could connect, Redfang was there, swinging Stormtooth in a screaming arc that took the alien's hand off at the wrist.

Father reeled back, ichor pumping from the stump. Its cranium pulsed and its eyes seared with golden light that made Redfang and Sor'khal shudder and go slack.

'Enough... trickery...' snarled Lydorran, gathering an almighty surge of psychic power until he felt his psychocircuitry burn his flesh and the stuff of the empyrean churn madly around him. He unleashed it in a single almighty wrench that tore loose a massive column of rock from the ceiling and brought it down with tremendous force atop the patriarch.

Still Father was too quick to be entirely caught by the attack, but neither was it swift enough to evade it altogether. The stone piledriver slammed down upon its shoulder, ripping away two of its arms, gouging a massive wound in its flank and pinning it to the ground like a monstrous, squirming insect.

Lydorran took three steps forward to stand over the writhing monster, raised his armoured gauntlet and drove it down in an almighty blow that smashed through Father's cranium and deep into the pulsating mind-matter within. The patriarch's body locked in a shuddering spasm, its jaws fell open in a silent shriek and its eyes blazed until Lydorran thought they must burst into flame. He set his jaw, turned his fist and wrenched it up and outwards, tearing free a quivering handful of synaptic biomatter before hurling it aside with a grunt of disgust.

Father twitched. Its tongue lolled. It clawed weakly at Lydorran's ankle, but there was no strength left in it. With a final, desperate rattle of breath, the patriarch of the Cult of the Wrything Wyrm died.

Lydorran staggered and dropped to one knee, relief and exhaustion threatening to fell him at last. He felt a hand on his shoulder guard and looked up to see Redfang staring down at him with fire in his eyes.

'That was well done, Fist. You have a place amongst the Deathwatch waiting if you want it, I think.'

Lydorran managed a hollow laugh.

'Not unless my Chapter Master himself orders it so, Fenrisian. God-Emperor give me a nice, straightforward fortress to knock down.'

Redfang threw back his head and laughed with savage delight, though the sound trailed off into a bloody cough soon enough. Sor'khal was at his side in a moment, eyeing them both with weary dismay.

'I need to get you both back to the surface. Spirits of the storm, you've taken enough wounds to put you in a damned sarcophagus.'

'Not yet,' replied Redfang, suddenly serious. 'First, we record this.'

He unhooked his helm from his belt and slotted it into place. Lydorran knew the Space Wolf would be using his autosenses to record vid footage of Father's ruptured corpse and the butchered cultists that lay all around their fallen god.

'The moment we're close enough to the surface, that footage goes out to every pict-screen and display 'lith on Ghyre,' said Redfang, before wrenching his helm free again and mag-locking it back to his belt. 'Let them see what remains of their Father.'

'Won't the cult refute it?' asked Lydorran as Sor'khal helped him painfully to his feet. He limped across the chamber, between the corpses, to where the halves of his force stave lay smashed on the ground. He picked them up with what reverence he could muster.

'They can try,' said Sor'khal as he applied a medicae compress to the wound in Redfang's chest, where they had wrenched the spar of stone out at last. 'But it won't work. The patriarch exerts a form of telepathic control through his senior cultists.'

'Those close enough to him, the really trollwrought freaks, by now they all have pretty sore skulls, if they're alive at all,' said Redfang, flashing Lydorran a savage grin. 'The fight will go out of the rest quick enough when they see that happen and we show them some nice, clear picts of what their god really was.'

'Was it enough? Did we stop the beacon in time?' asked Lydorran as he limped back to join the two Deathwatch battle-brothers. Redfang's expression became sober.

'No way to know until we can get to the surface and command some deep-space auguries,' he said with a half-shrug. 'Meantime, there's a war to be finished.'

'There must be a way back up to Tarsun and my brothers,' said Lydorran, hefting the two halves of his stave in his one good hand. 'We're little use to the war effort in this state, brothers, but if we link back up with our warriors, we can extract in good order.'

'Speak for yourself, Fist. I'm in better shape than most who fought here,' retorted Sor'khal grimly as his reductor whined and its blades extracted the fallen Alessius' gene-seed.

'And I could still...' Redfang coughed for a moment, fresh blood flecking his lips. 'Could still beat you bloody, you leathery old Chogorian bastard.'

'Of course you could, Fenris. Now cease your prattling and let us get back to the surface. You are dishonouring the spirits of the dead.' With that, Sor'khal set off towards the tunnel entrance he and Redfang had entered through. Redfang shot Lydorran an unrepentant smirk and followed the Apothecary. The Imperial Fists Librarian shook his head and took a last look around the corpse-strewn broodnest and the handful of shocked cultists still curled up whimpering upon its floor; he considered giving them the Emperor's mercy, but decided they were neither threat enough to need it nor honourable enough to deserve it. Instead, Lydorran turned and limped slowly after his comrades, back towards the surface.

Phoenicia Jai tasted blood. She felt pain race through her skull, worse than anything she had ever felt, and her eyes snapped open as a wail of agony escaped her throat. Jai rolled over and vomited, gasping breaths and staring desperately around. She absorbed the sight of Father, grotesque to her now where before he had looked like a beautiful, haloed angel. She saw the sprawled bodies of the cultists she had led to their deaths and the glassy-eyed stares of the handful who still lived. A few sat, rocking and muttering to themselves. Others were roaming the chamber as though searching for something, or sobbing over the burnt and mangled bodies of the dead.

I did this, she thought, and the idea threatened to break her sanity. She had been so sure that her cause was righteous, so determined that victory and Ascension were worth any price.

She looked again in disgust at the burst and splattered monster she had called Father.

How? she thought, and fresh horror coiled up inside her, forcing her to gag and retch again. *How did I ever believe this monster was a god?*

Fear gripped her then, and a sense of loss and confusion so profound that for a moment she considered simply rising and wading into the viscous slime of Father's pool. Its digestion fluids wouldn't take long to break her body down, she knew, and the thought of agonising self-flagellation followed by oblivion had a certain appeal. She shook her head. No, she couldn't just…

This is where it brought you, she thought, and hugged her arms tightly about herself as she felt the chill of the deep cavern penetrate her slight form. *This is where obsession and power have brought you.*

Jai didn't know what to do, but as she looked at the battered remnants of her former followers, she felt a sudden fear. Where before they had been brothers and sisters of the brood, now they were just strangers, strangers she had forced headlong into near certain death with powers she no longer had.

How long until they see me, and realise what I did? she thought with sudden panic. Jai cast around and, spotting a nearby cultist clad in a rebreather and rubberised hood, tore both from the corpse and swiftly donned them. Her head still pounding as though a dagger had been driven into her skull, Phoenicia Jai shed the high collar of her robes, set aside her staff and quietly slipped from the chamber into the darkness beyond.

It had all been a lie, a cruel xenos trick. She saw that now, and she didn't know what to do. *First, survive*, she thought, and dabbed at the blood that was beginning to weep from the corner of one eye. She took one last glance at Father's ruptured remains and wondered if the monster's death spelled her own doom. As the daggers of pain in her skull worsened, Jai could well believe it. Still, numbed by fear and remorse she could barely begin to process, possessed by the simple desire to survive if she could, Phoenicia Jai stumbled away and was soon swallowed by the shadows of the caverns.

EPILOGUE

On a cratered plain above the stronghold of the fallen foe, a warrior mystic emerges into the light of day. His wounded body burns with pain. His soul groans with fatigue. Yet he stands straighter, holds his head higher as he sees the warriors assembled there before him. Dozens, most of those that his Chapter had sent to this war-worn world. As one they drop to one knee, hold out blades and guns by way of a salute. As one they honour him. Hero victorious, leader proven, accepted and respected. The warrior mystic's war is not done, will never be done. For now, though, as aircrafts tear through the skies overhead and the last great bastion of the foe burns beneath his feet, this is victory enough.

From above him, aloft in skies aflame with the fires of her people's vengeance, a ruler looks down and smiles a thin smile. Let him be honoured, she thinks. Has he not given just as much as she in this desperate war? Familiar voices cry of victory, their fierce elation carrying through her aircraft's vox and raising her spirits aloft as even this magnificent fighter craft could not. She draws breath to address her people, for there is much to be done if they are to claim back their wounded world.

Another aircraft soars skyward, its prow aimed towards the darkling void beyond the skies. Within its hold lies a champion amongst angels. He was wounded unto death, yet still he clings to life with the stubborn determination of the sons of Dorn. Ahead lies the cold metal embrace of a Dreadnought's sarcophagus. Despite all odds, his war is not yet over either.

Deep below the surface, lost amidst dark tunnels rendered alien and terrifying by loss, a former prophet stumbles to a halt. She turns, her back to a graffiti-covered wall. The words behind her speak of deliverance from beyond the stars, but they offer her no comfort, no sanctuary. She knows now that they were a lie. It had all been a lie, in the end. A single lumen globe flickers overhead and goes out, flickers and goes out. In its sporadic illumination figures move closer. Angry eyes and sharp blades glint in each flash of light. She will not fight them. She has no right. She closes her eyes as they gather about her and raise their weapons high.

Across the interstellar gulfs the hungry gods swarm. Tendrils taste the psychic signal as it sings out from feeding grounds that draw closer by the hour. They are titanic, endless, untiring. They hear the siren song as it rings out through the icy darkness of the void, and they seek it with singular determination.

Like a star's light blinking out in death, the beacon is suddenly gone. The leviathans slow, tendrils coiling through the void in confusion.

They cast this way and that.

They taste the solar currents.

They wait, coldly, infinitely patient for their beacon to light again.

It does not. Pulses of energy surge along vast synaptic relays. Thoughts coil, dark and alien and ineffably vast, through many minds that are in fact one mind.

The feeding ground is lost, too far still to scent without its beacon. They are denied their prize. Yet their hunger remains.

Across the vast canvas of the stars shine dozens of other beacons. Sonorous notes echo through the void, flickers of light and sound projected by organisms whose only task is to guide these deities of flesh and chitin to their next feast. More spring to life all the time, some near, some far, all singing out with bright insistence, all promising rich harvests to come.

Acting upon an impulse even greater than their own, the immense leviathans turn their course and drift on, tendrils waving sinuously and trailing out behind them as they slip on through the dark of the void.

One feeding ground is lost, but the feast still lies ahead.

There are other worlds.

There will always be other worlds.

ABOUT THE AUTHOR

Andy Clark has written the Warhammer 40,000 novels *Kingsblade, Knightsblade* and *Shroud of Night*, as well as the novella *Crusade* and the short story 'Whiteout'. He has also written the novels *Gloomspite* and *Blacktalon: First Mark* for Warhammer Age of Sigmar, and the Warhammer Quest Silver Tower novella *Labyrinth of the Lost*. Andy works as a background writer for Games Workshop, crafting the worlds of Warhammer Age of Sigmar and Warhammer 40,000. He lives in Nottingham, UK.

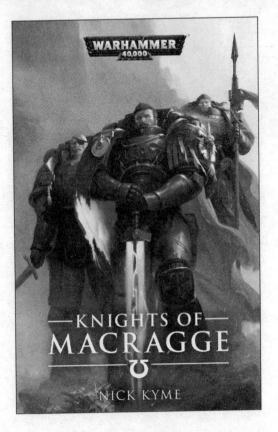